KNEE DEEP

AN ONI PRESS PUBLICATION

KNEE-

BOOK ONE

JOE FLOOD

DEEP

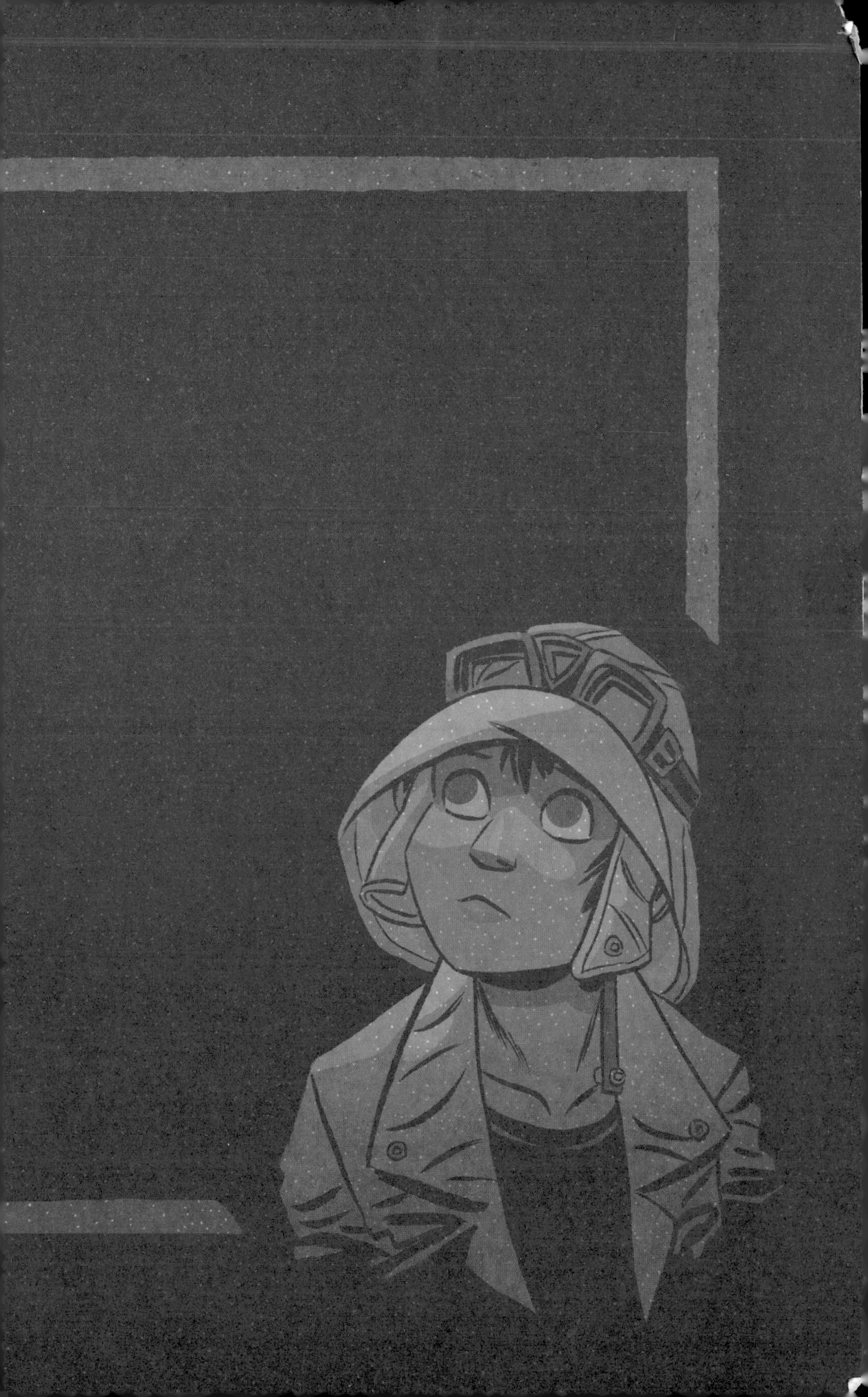

Designed by **Sarah Rockwell**

Title Logo Designed by **Kate Z. Stone**

Edited by **Andrea Colvin**, **Shawna Gore**, and **Amanda Meadows**

Coloring Flatting by **Mariane Gusmāo**

Additional Coloring Assistance by **Emily Elmer**

onipress.com 🅕 🅨 🅘 /onipress
joefloodcomics.myportfolio.com | @JoeFloodComics

PUBLISHED BY ONI-LION FORGE PUBLISHING GROUP, LLC.

Troy Look, vp of publishing services
Katie Sainz, director of marketing
Angie Knowles, director of design & production
Sarah Rockwell, senior graphic designer
Carey Soucy, senior graphic designer
Vincent Kukua, digital prepress technician
Chris Cerasi, managing editor
Bess Pallares, senior editor
Grace Scheipeter, senior editor
Gabriel Granillo, editor
Desiree Rodriguez, editor
Zack Soto, editor
Ben Eisner, game developer
Sara Harding, executive assistant
Jung Hu Lee, logistics coordinator & editorial assistant
Kuian Kellum, warehouse assistant

Joe Nozemack, publisher emeritus

First Edition: May 2023
ISBN: 978-1-62010-938-0
eISBN: 978-1-62010-951-9
Printing numbers: 1 2 3 4 5 6 7 8 9 10
Library of Congress Control Number: 2020947310

— FOR LIZ & PHOEBE —

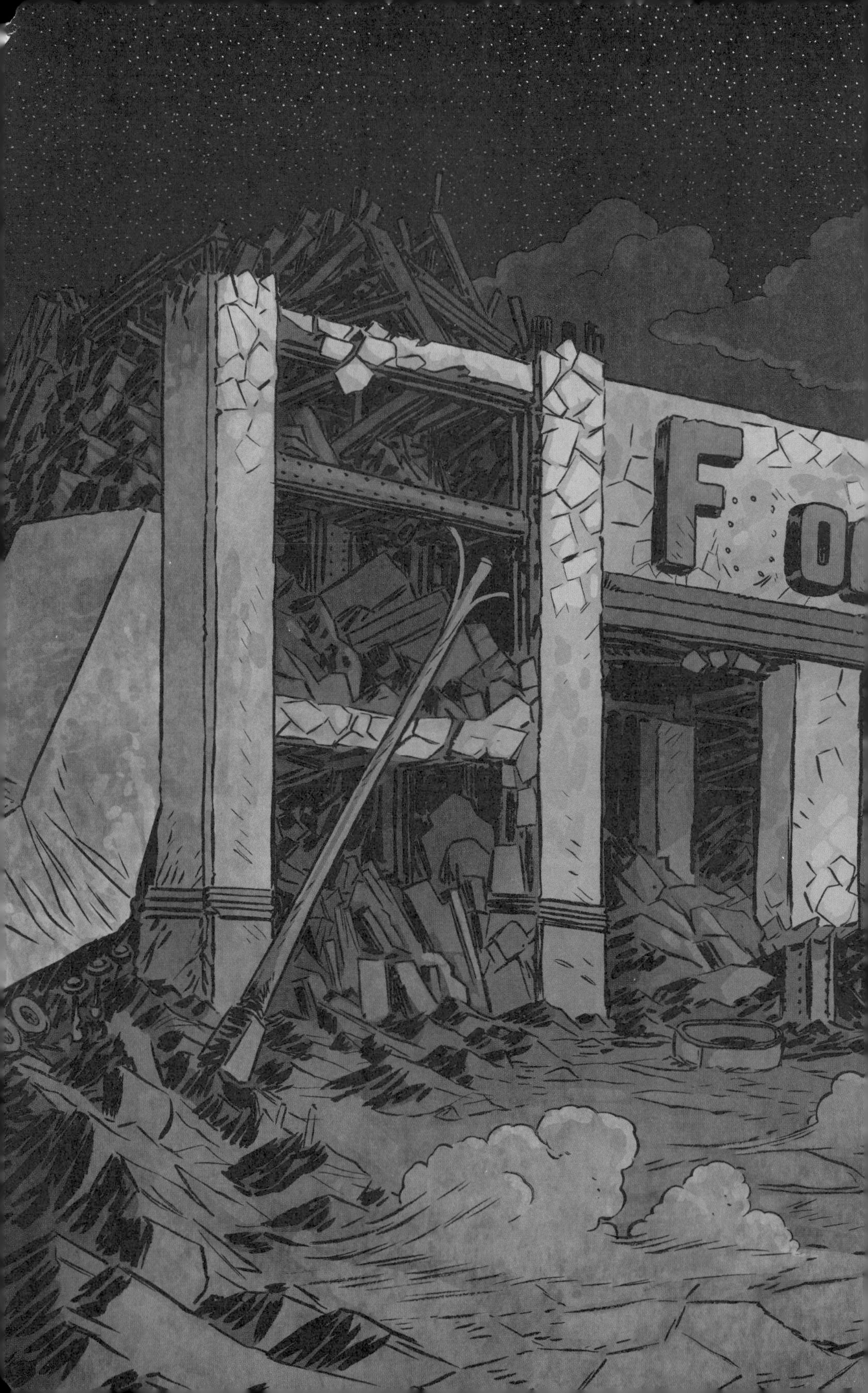

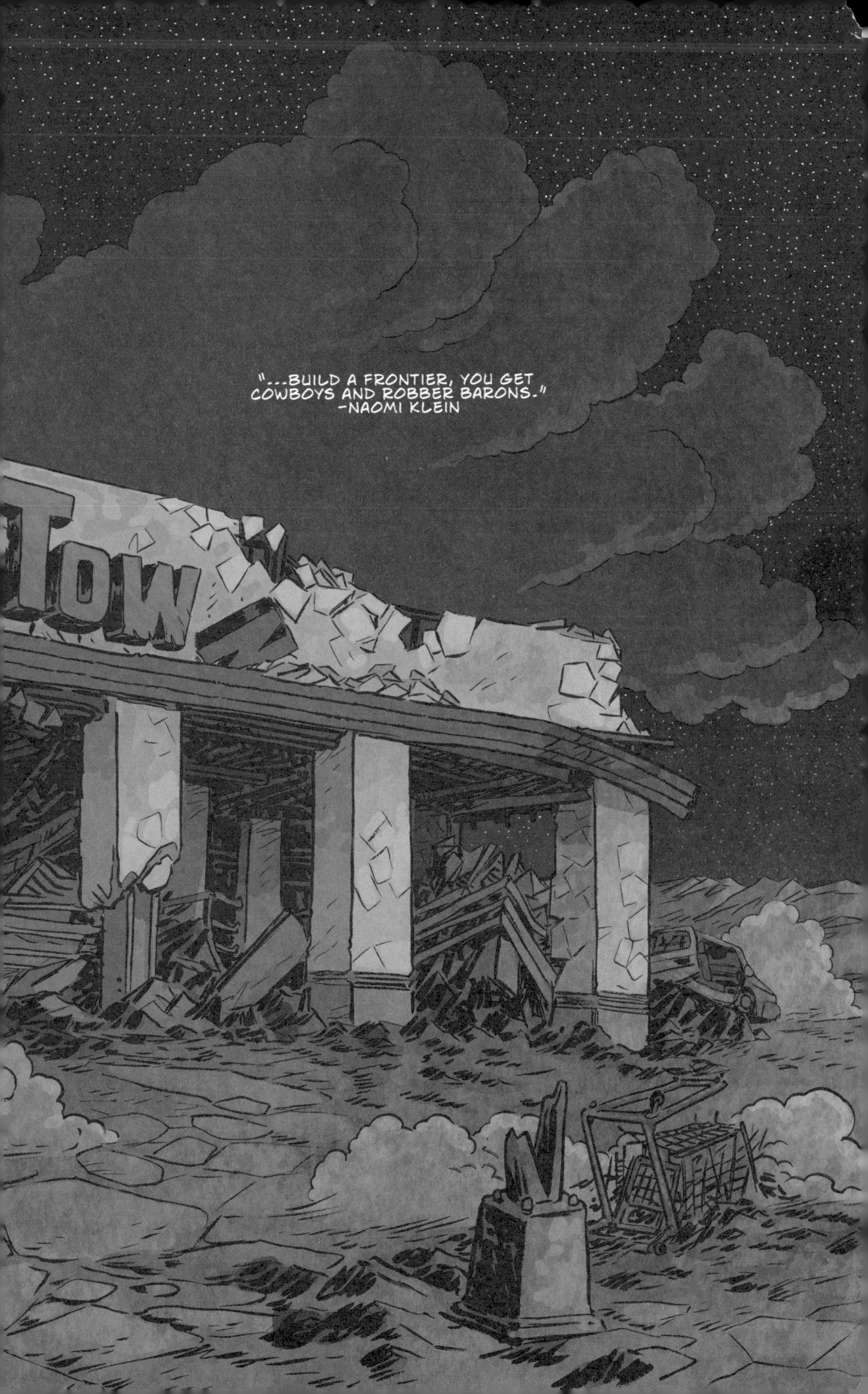
"...BUILD A FRONTIER, YOU GET COWBOYS AND ROBBER BARONS."
-NAOMI KLEIN
TOW

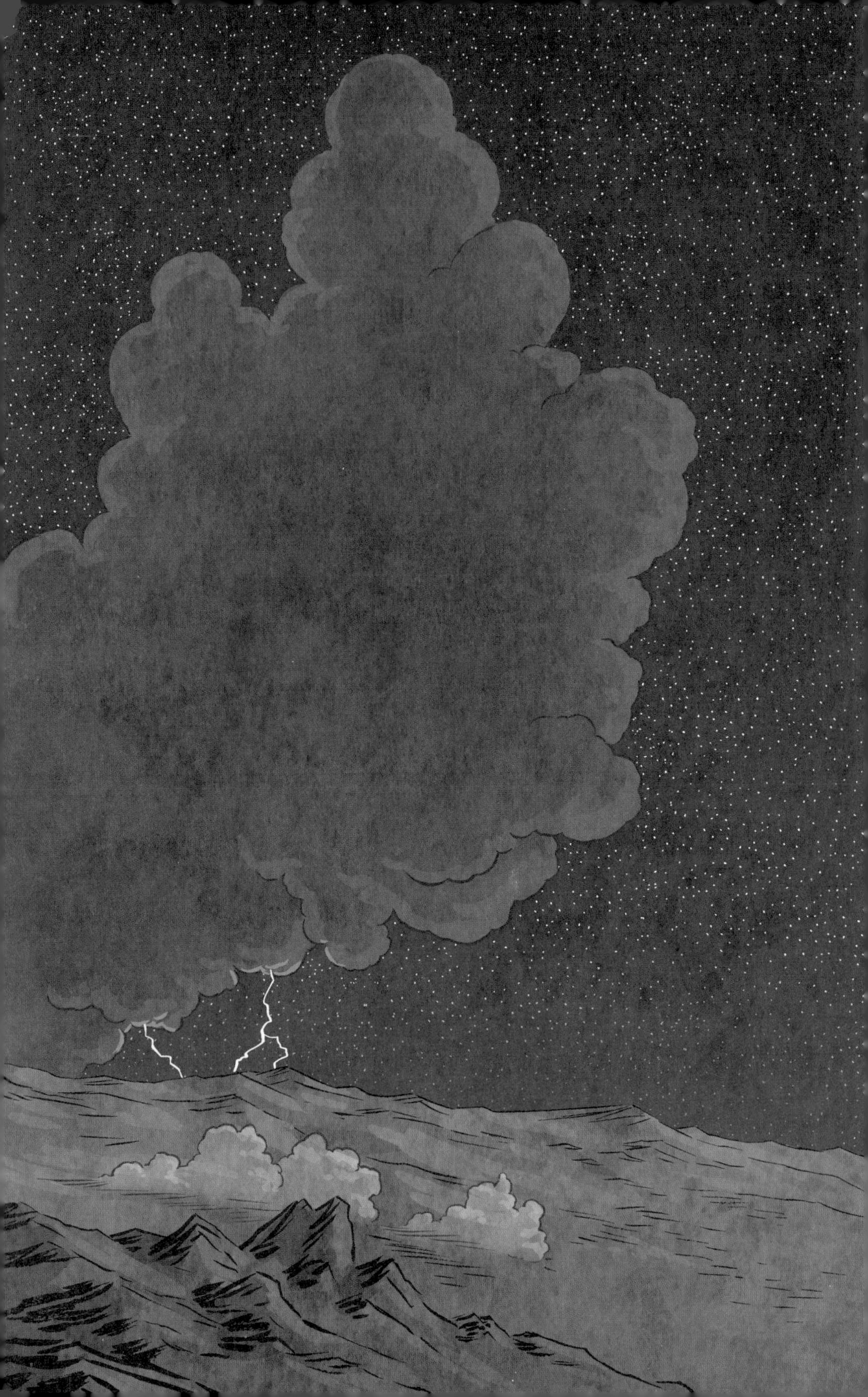

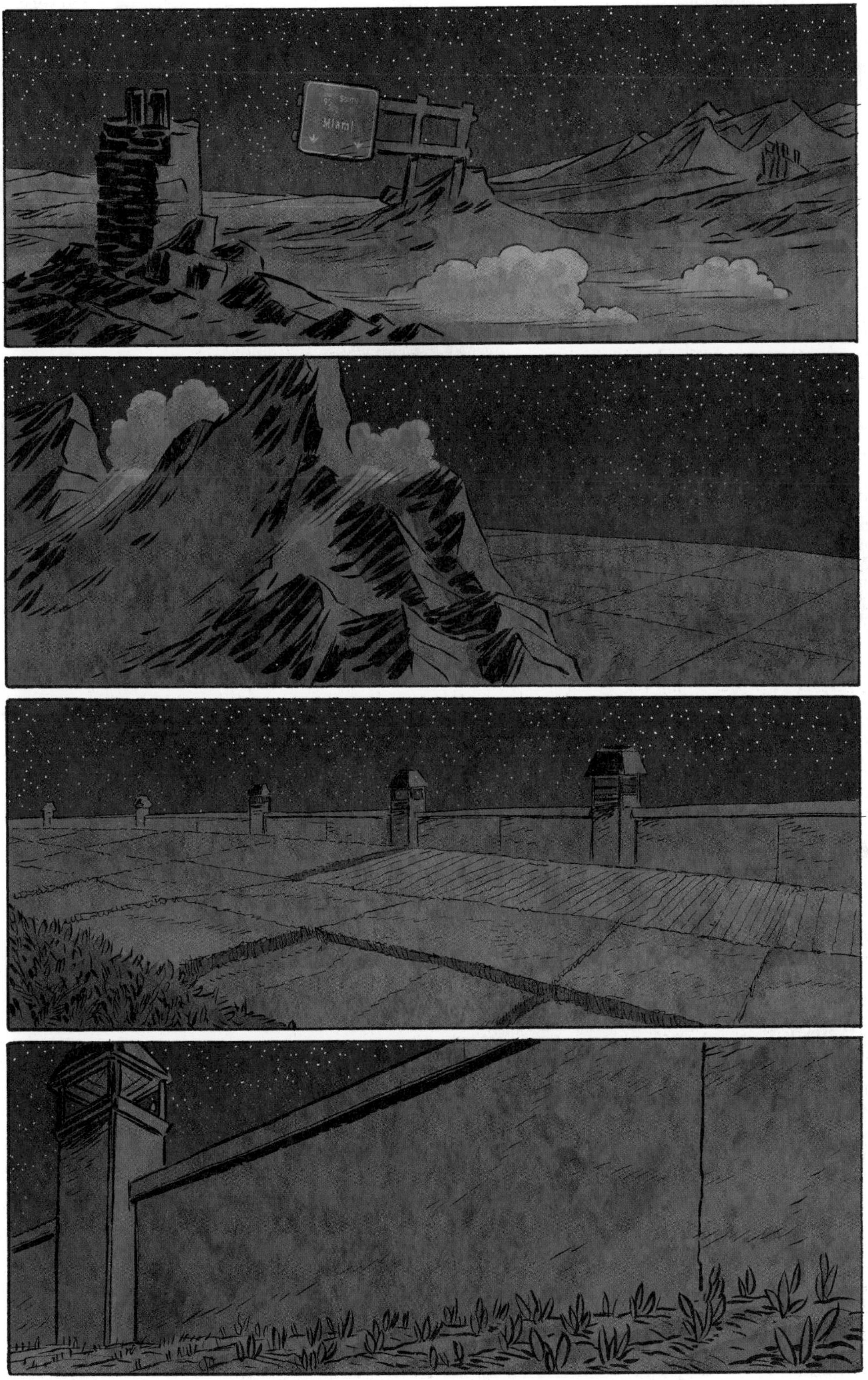

Miami

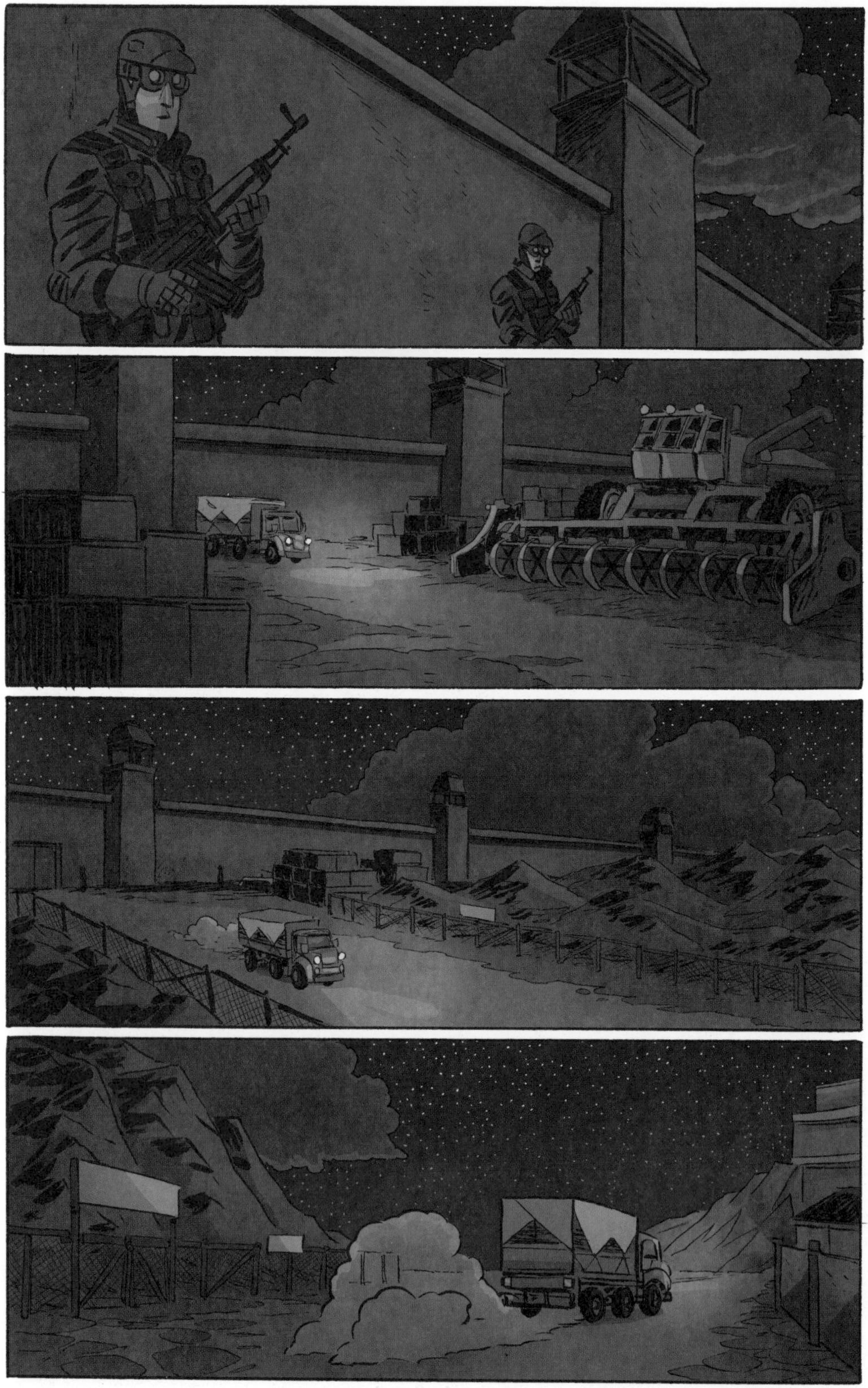

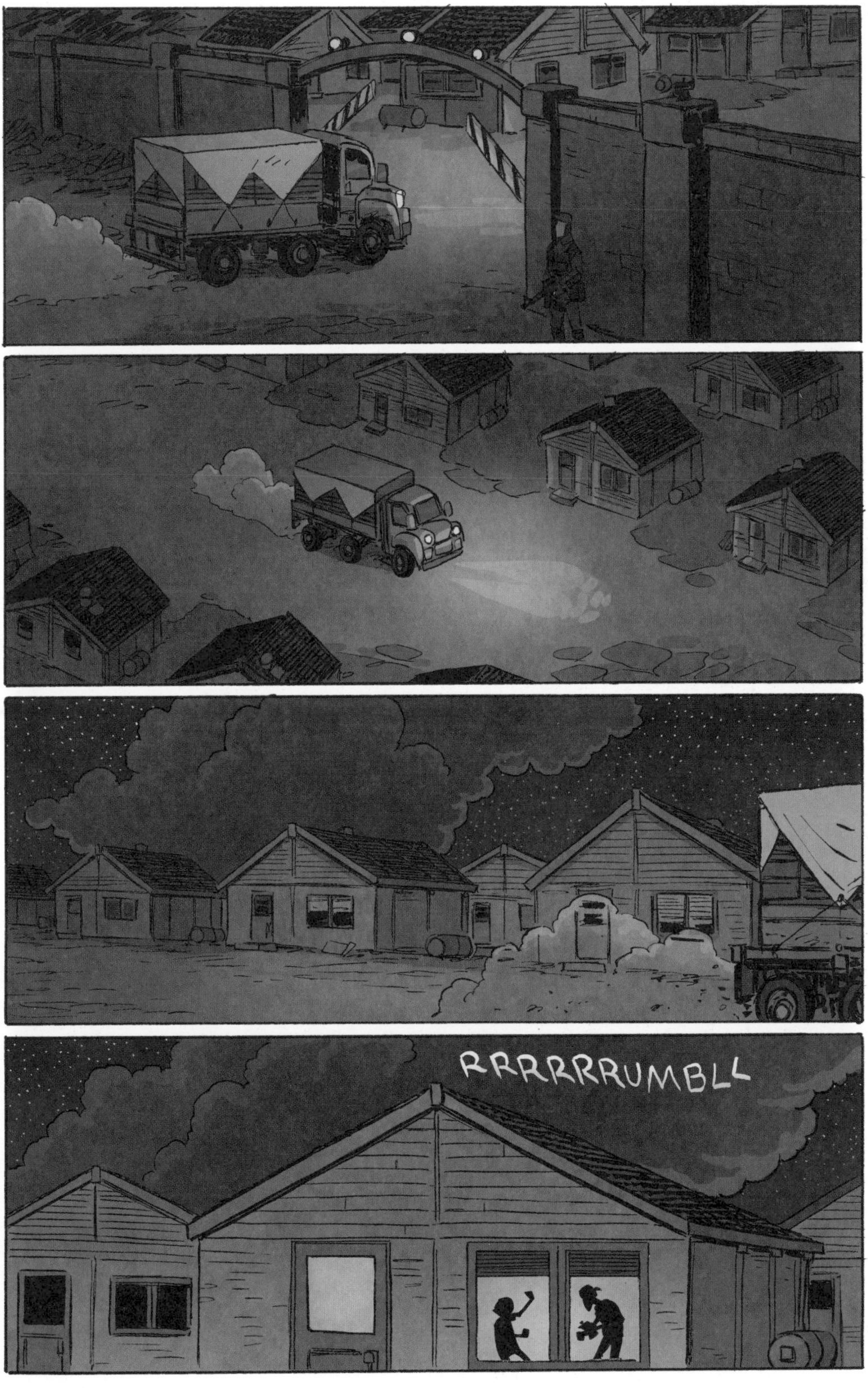
RRRRRRUMBLL

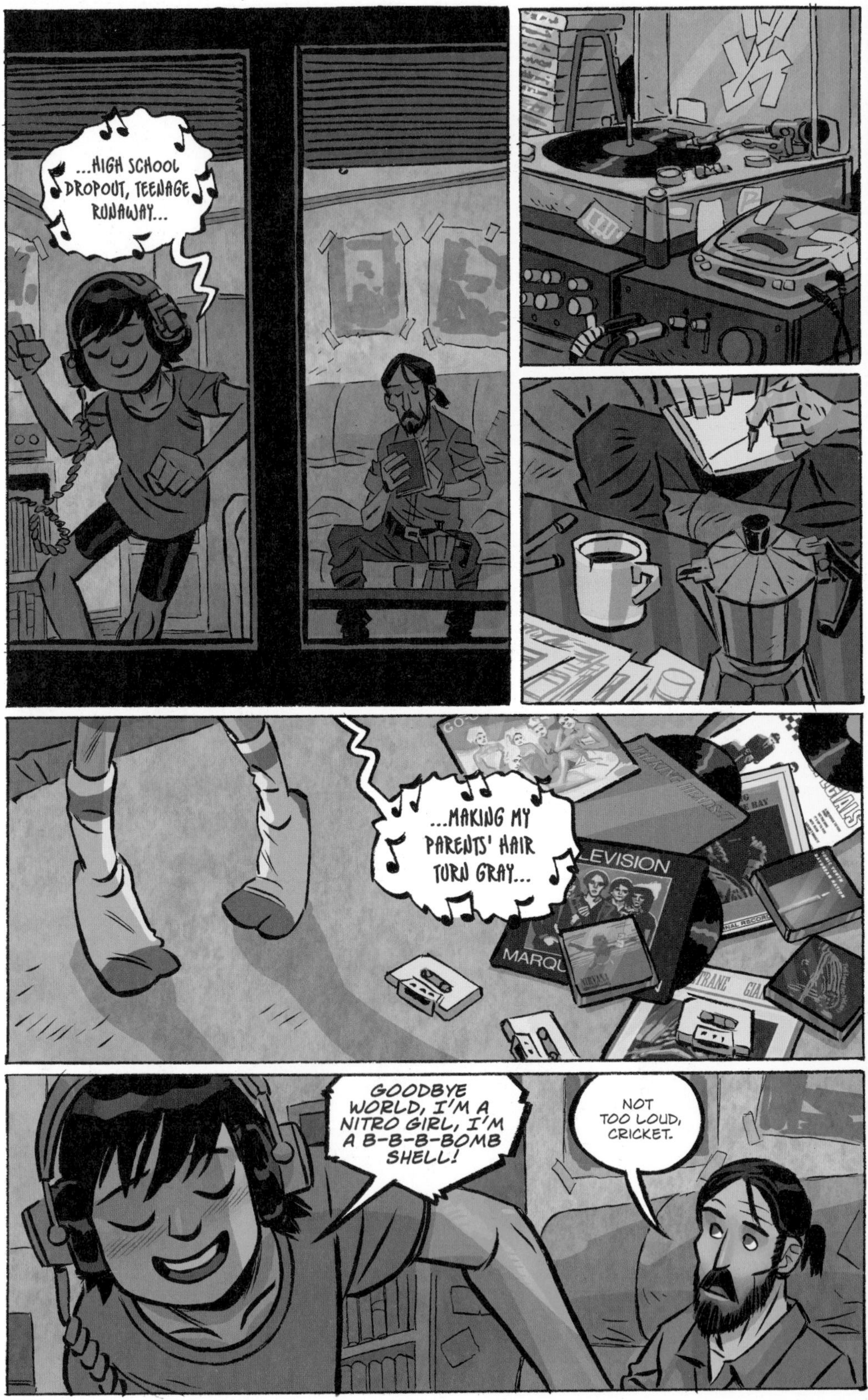
...HIGH SCHOOL DROPOUT, TEENAGE RUNAWAY...
...MAKING MY PARENTS' HAIR TURN GRAY...
GOODBYE WORLD, I'M A NITRO GIRL, I'M A B-B-B-BOMB SHELL!
NOT TOO LOUD, CRICKET.

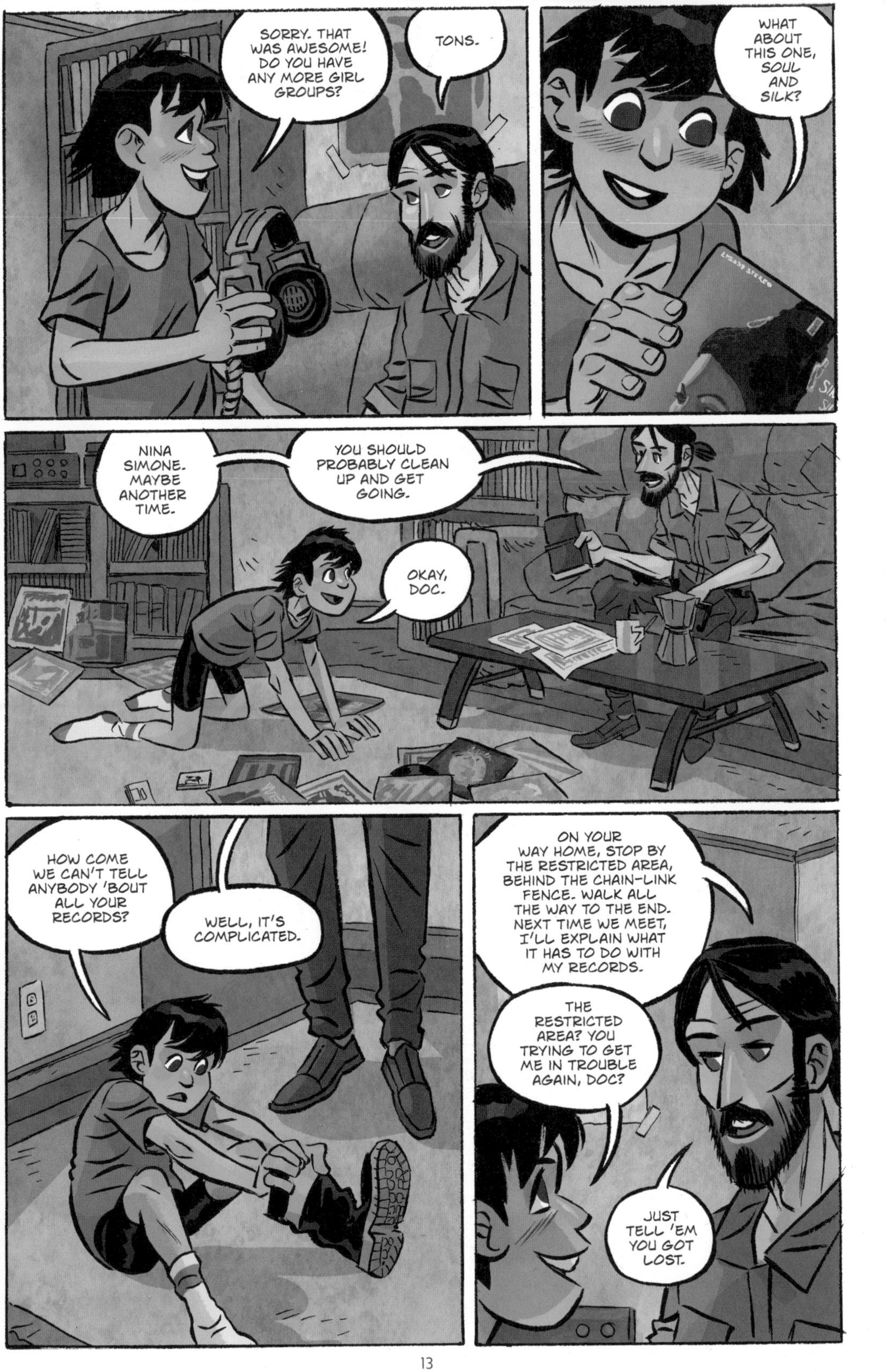
SORRY. THAT WAS AWESOME! DO YOU HAVE ANY MORE GIRL GROUPS?
TONS.
WHAT ABOUT THIS ONE, SOUL AND SILK?
NINA SIMONE. MAYBE ANOTHER TIME.
YOU SHOULD PROBABLY CLEAN UP AND GET GOING.
OKAY, DOC.
HOW COME WE CAN'T TELL ANYBODY 'BOUT ALL YOUR RECORDS?
WELL, IT'S COMPLICATED.
ON YOUR WAY HOME, STOP BY THE RESTRICTED AREA, BEHIND THE CHAIN-LINK FENCE. WALK ALL THE WAY TO THE END. NEXT TIME WE MEET, I'LL EXPLAIN WHAT IT HAS TO DO WITH MY RECORDS.
THE RESTRICTED AREA? YOU TRYING TO GET ME IN TROUBLE AGAIN, DOC?
JUST TELL 'EM YOU GOT LOST.

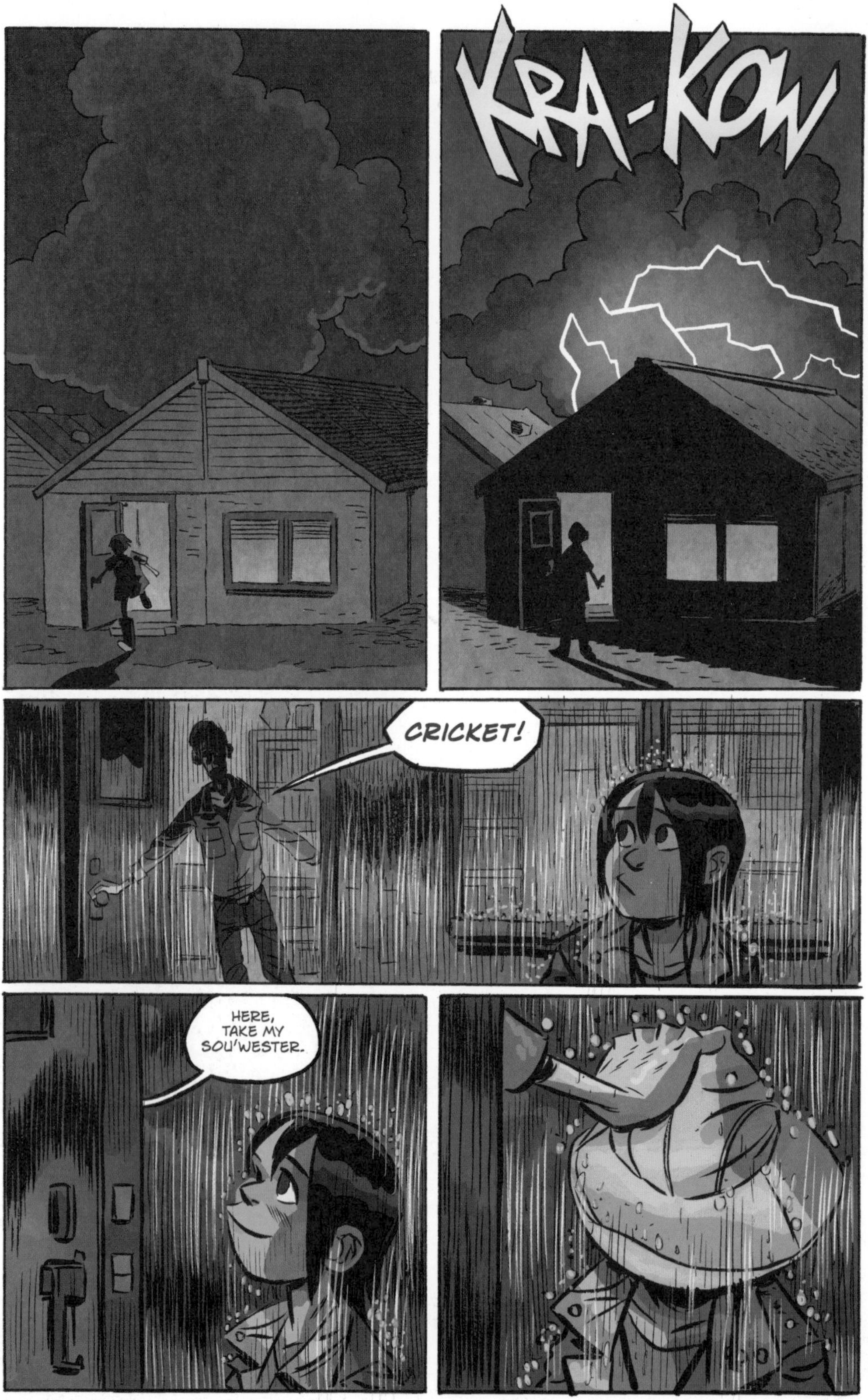
KRA-KOW
CRICKET!
HERE, TAKE MY SOU'WESTER.

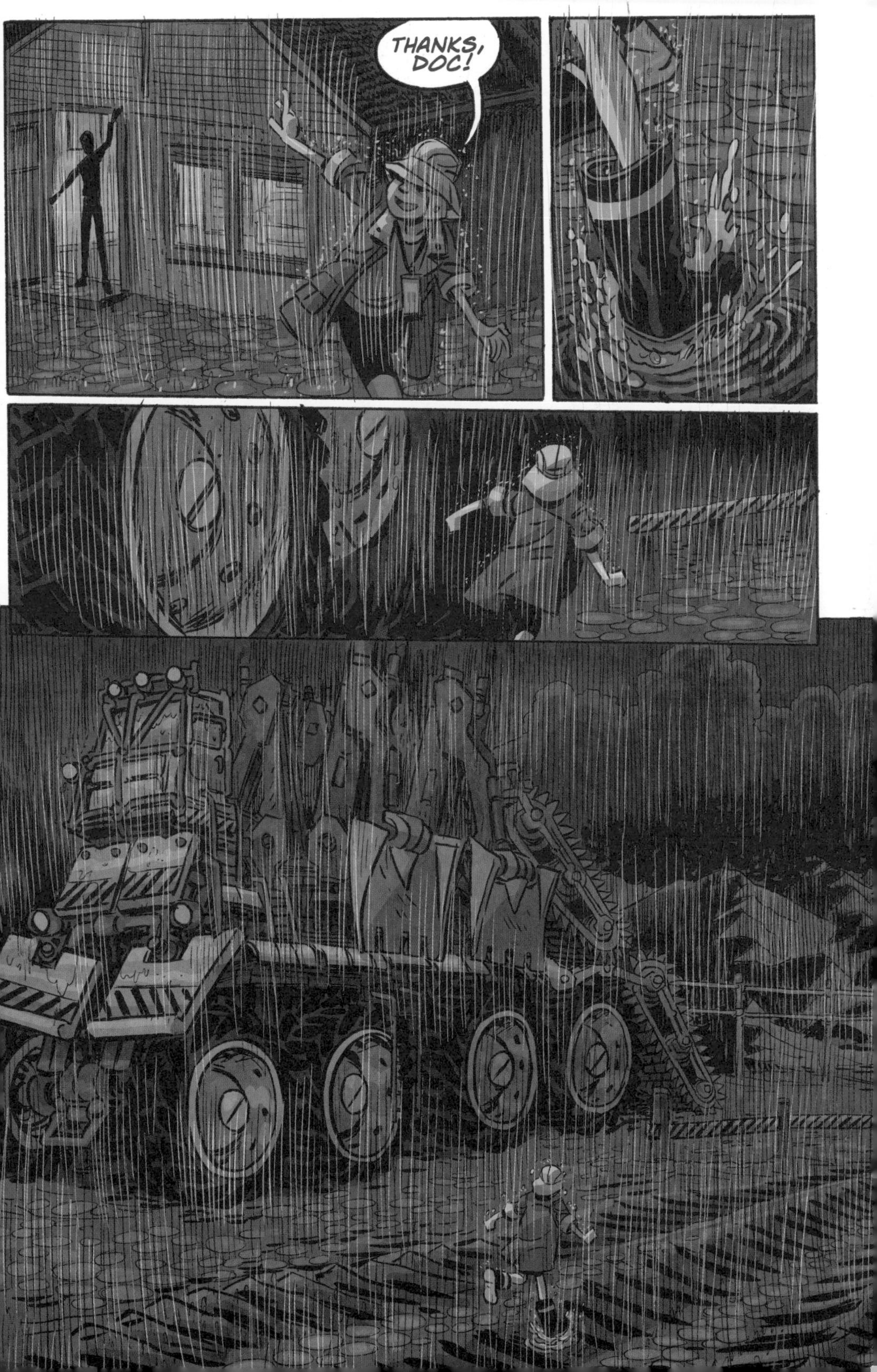
THANKS, DOC!

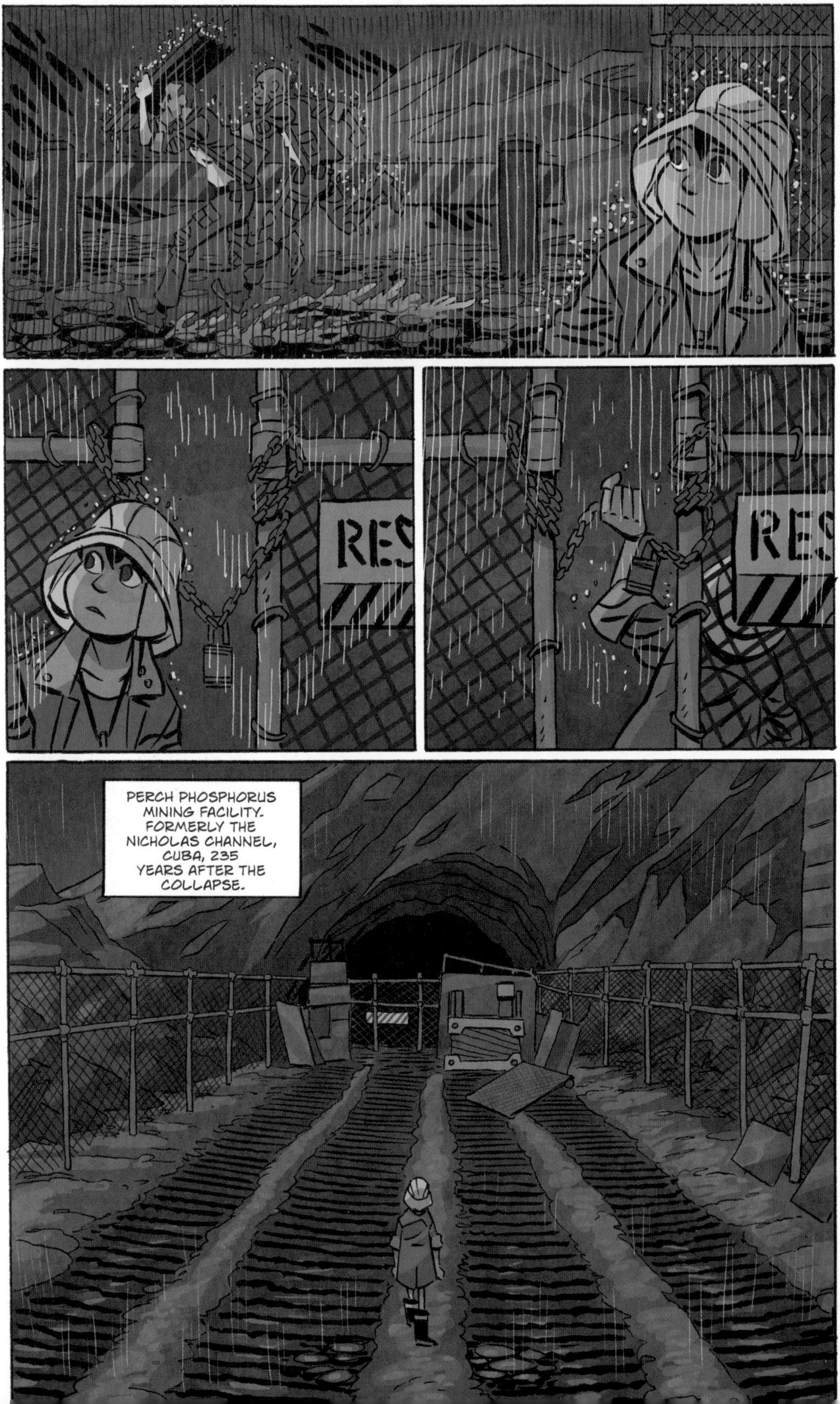
RES
RES
PERCH PHOSPHORUS MINING FACILITY. FORMERLY THE NICHOLAS CHANNEL, CUBA, 235 YEARS AFTER THE COLLAPSE.

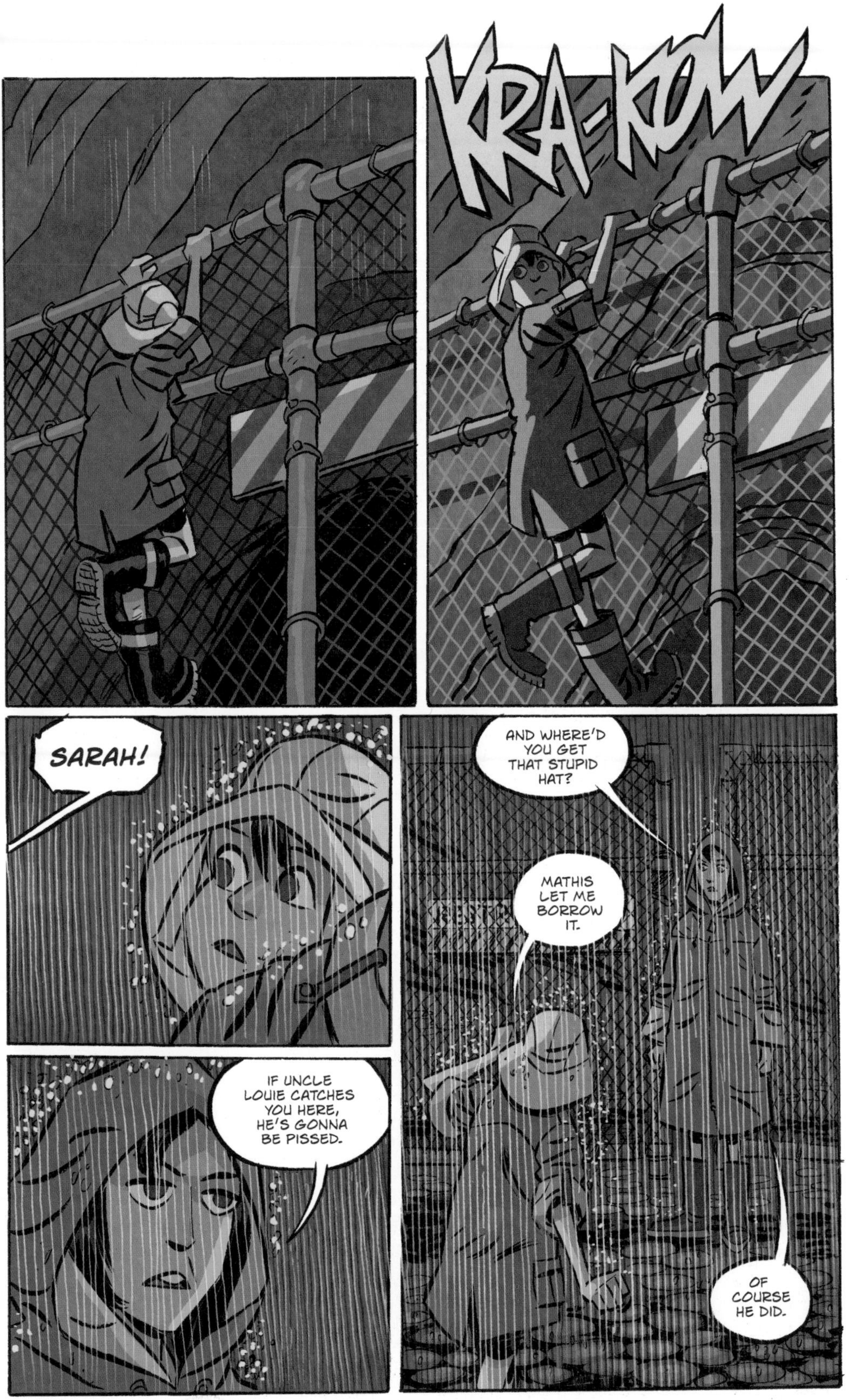
KRA-KOW
SARAH!
IF UNCLE LOUIE CATCHES YOU HERE, HE'S GONNA BE PISSED.
AND WHERE'D YOU GET THAT STUPID HAT?
MATHIS LET ME BORROW IT.
OF COURSE HE DID.

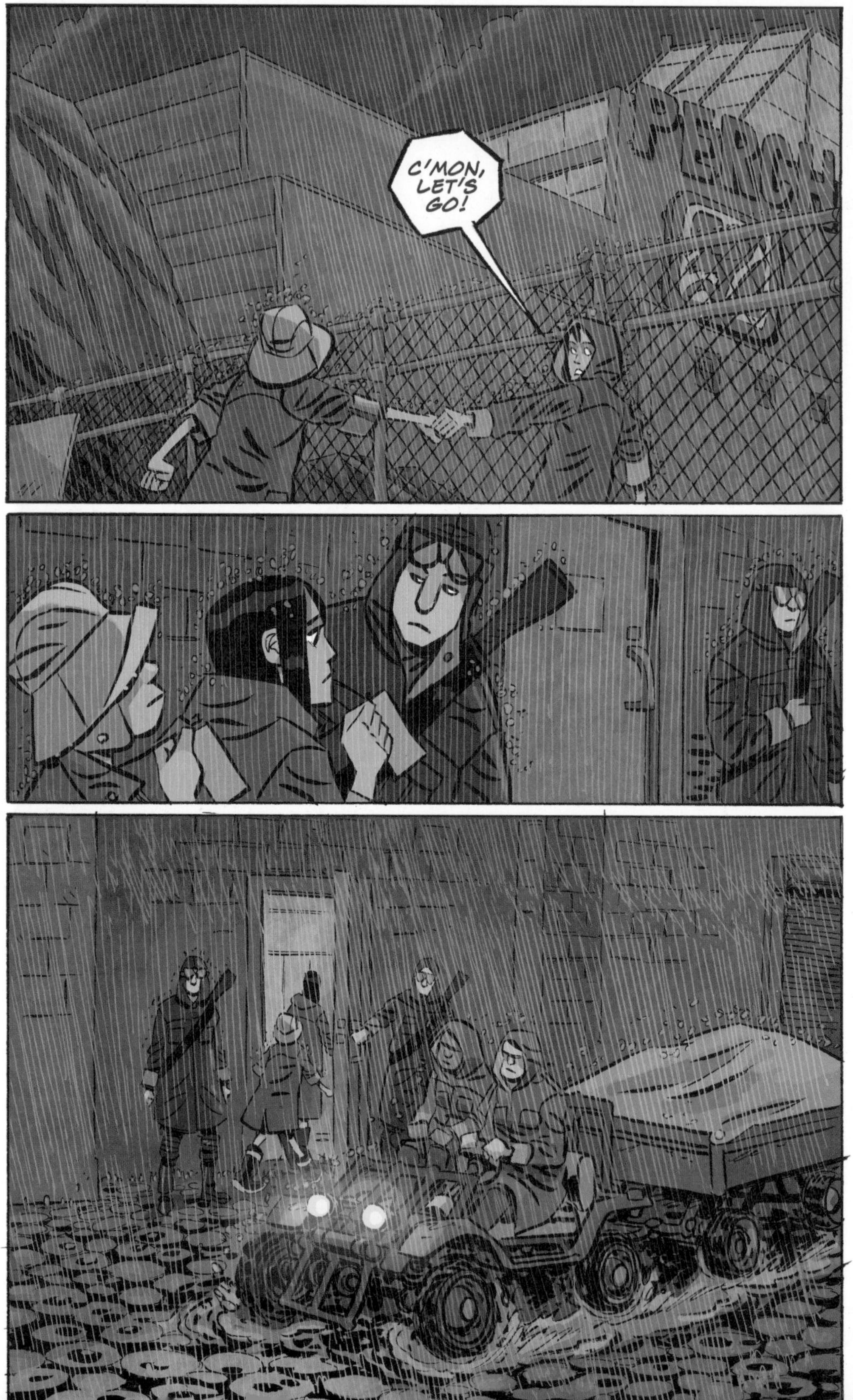
C'MON, LET'S GO!

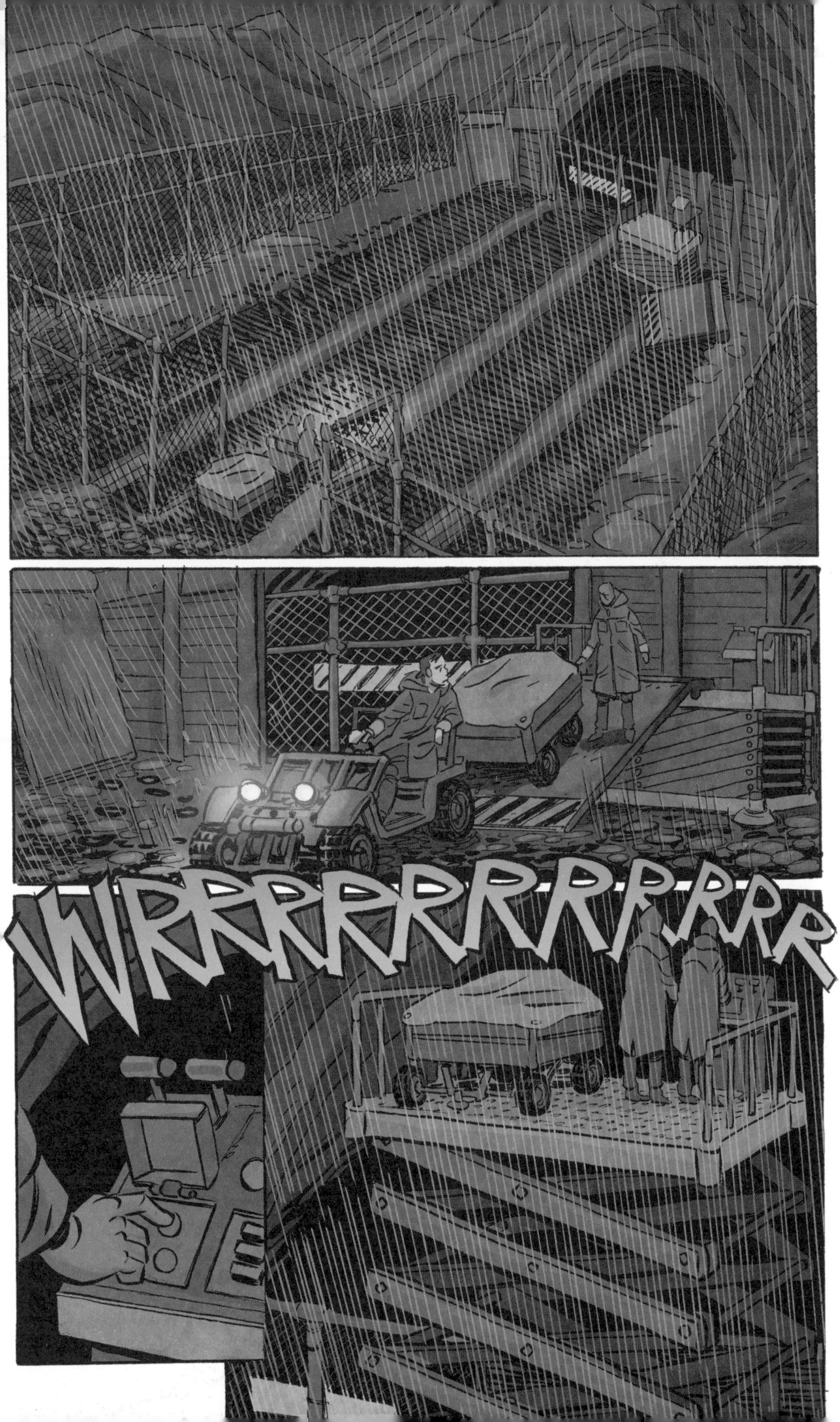
WRRRRRRRRRRR

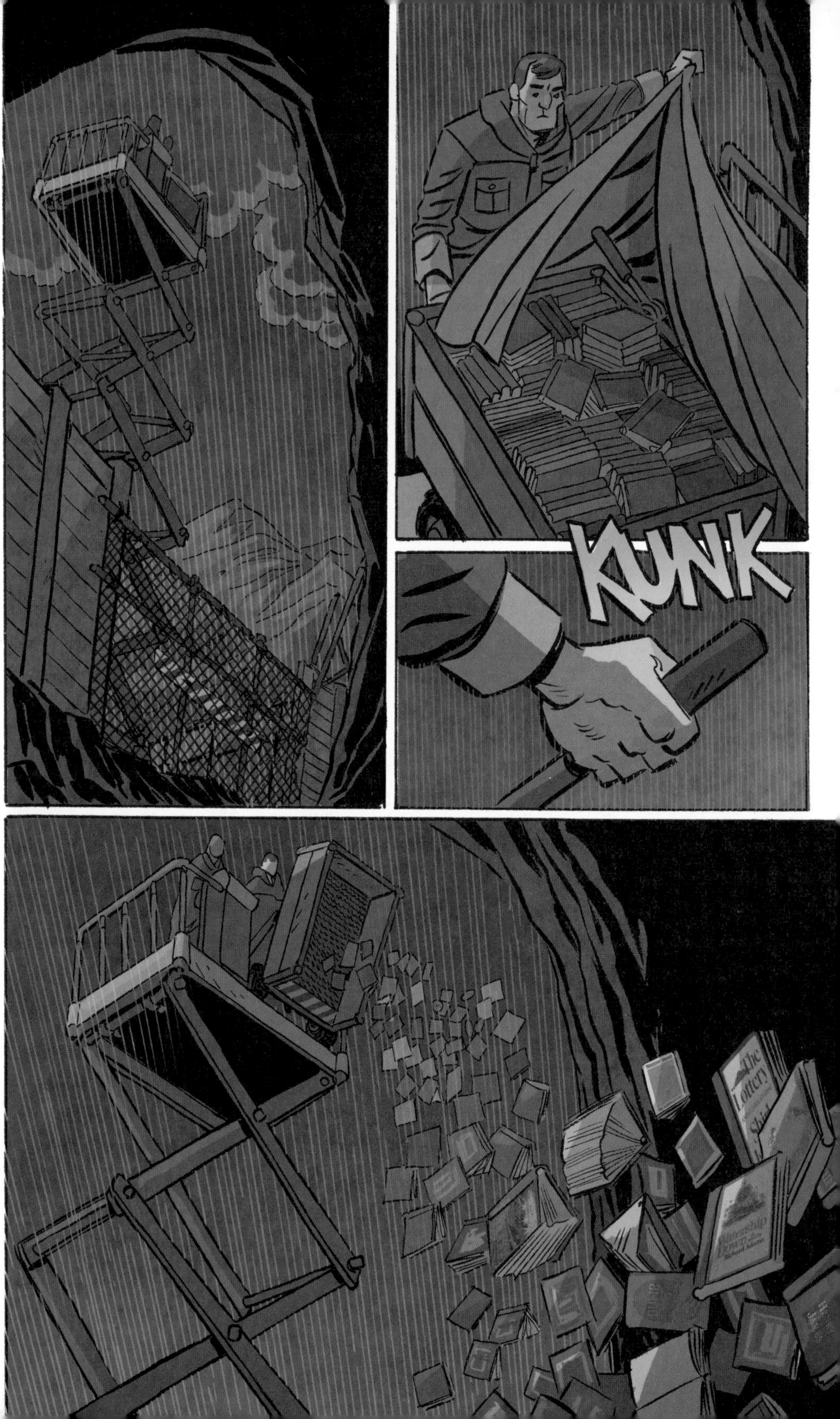
KUNK
The Lottery

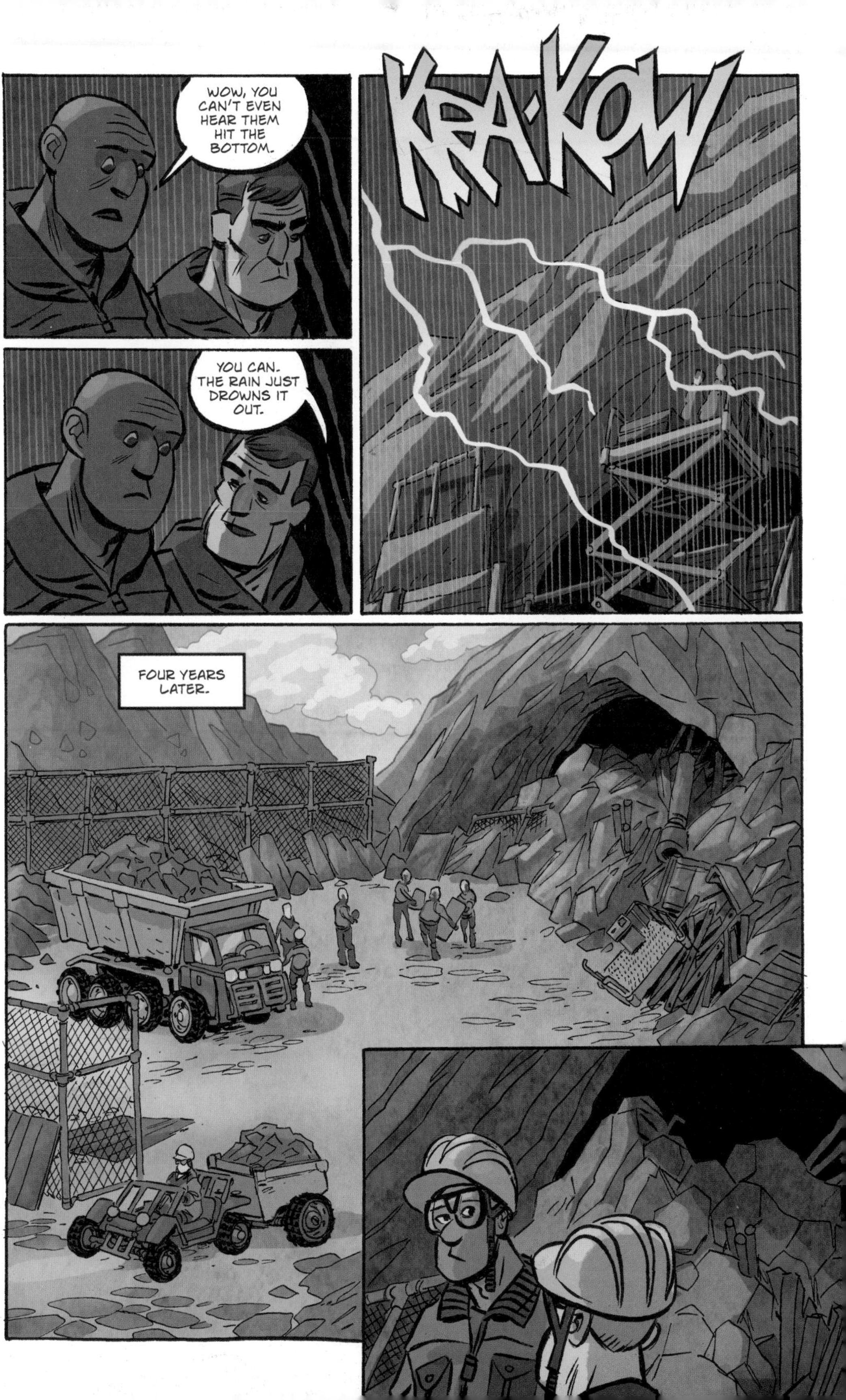
WOW, YOU CAN'T EVEN HEAR THEM HIT THE BOTTOM.
KRA-KOW
YOU CAN. THE RAIN JUST DROWNS IT OUT.
FOUR YEARS LATER.

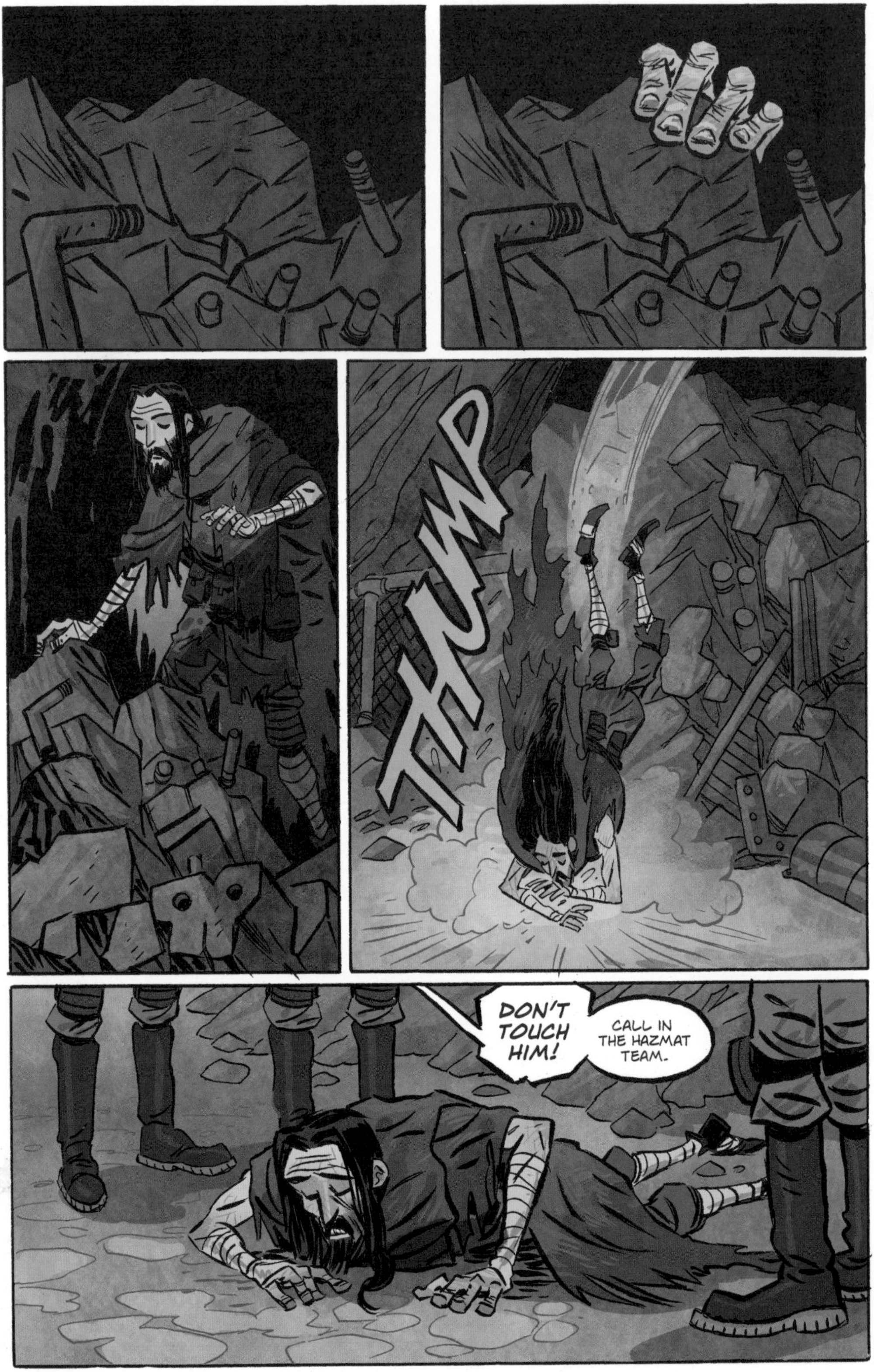
THUMP
DON'T TOUCH HIM!
CALL IN THE HAZMAT TEAM.

THE AREA IS CLEAR, SIR.
GOOD, GET THE TENT.
ZIPPPP

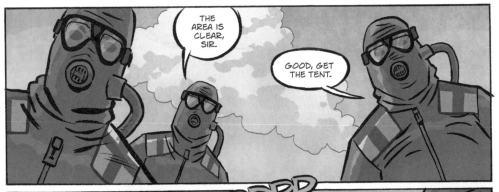

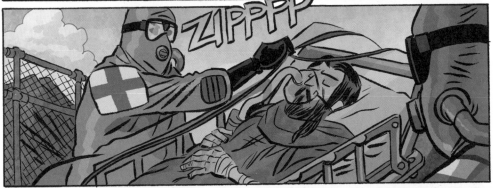

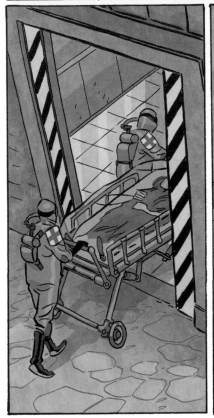

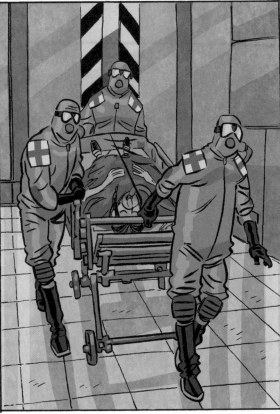

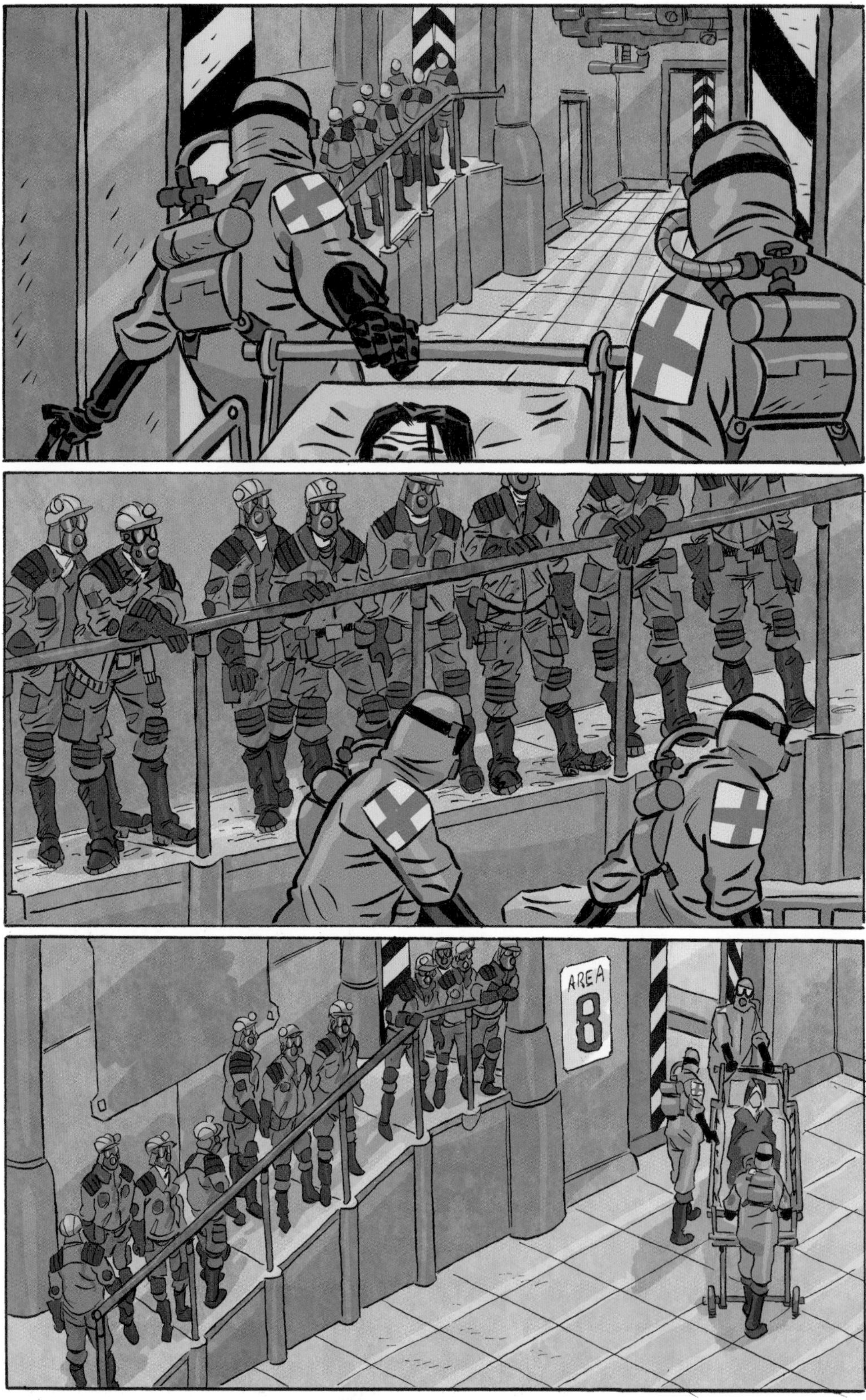
AREA
8

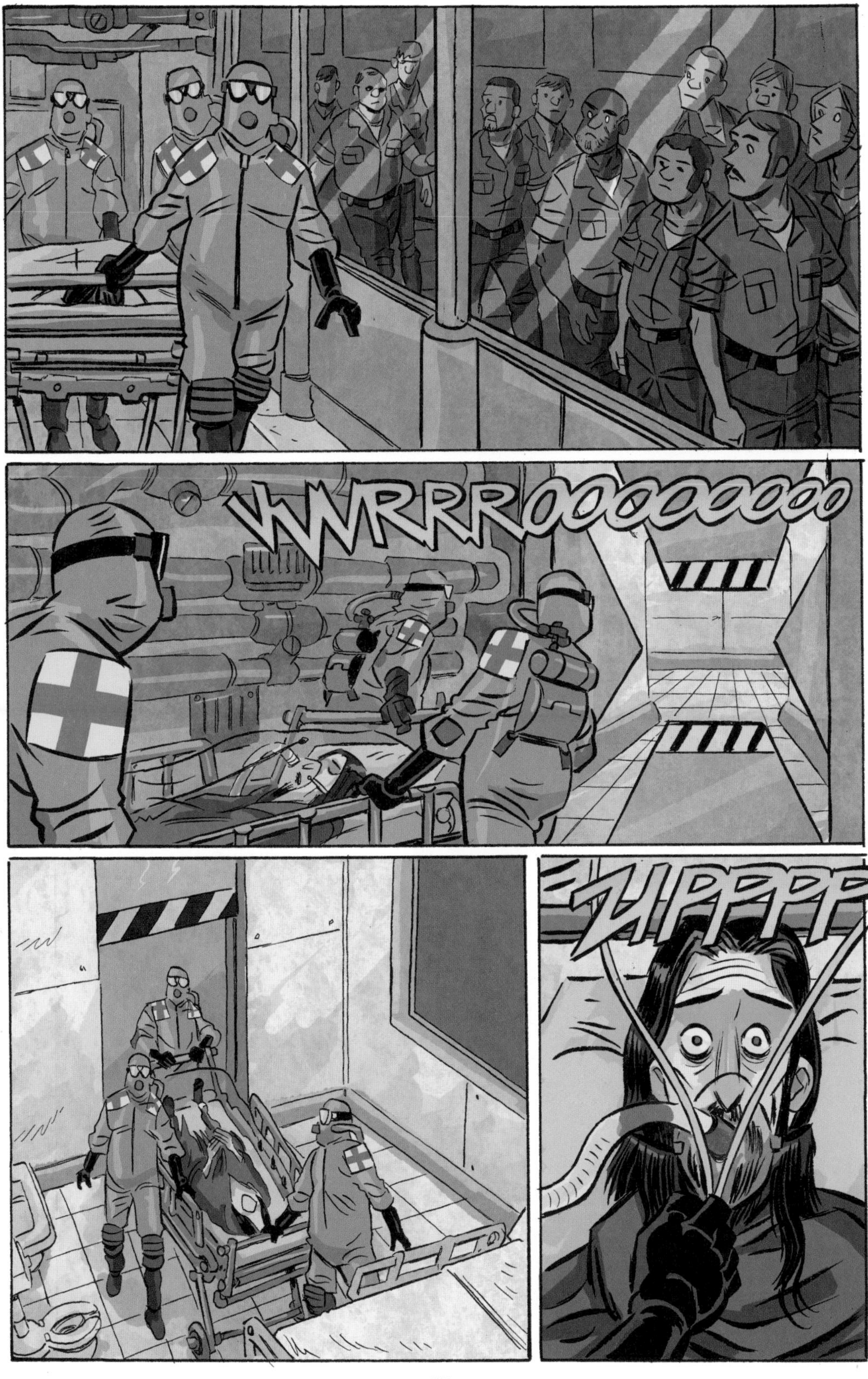
WRRROOOOOOOO
ZIPPPP

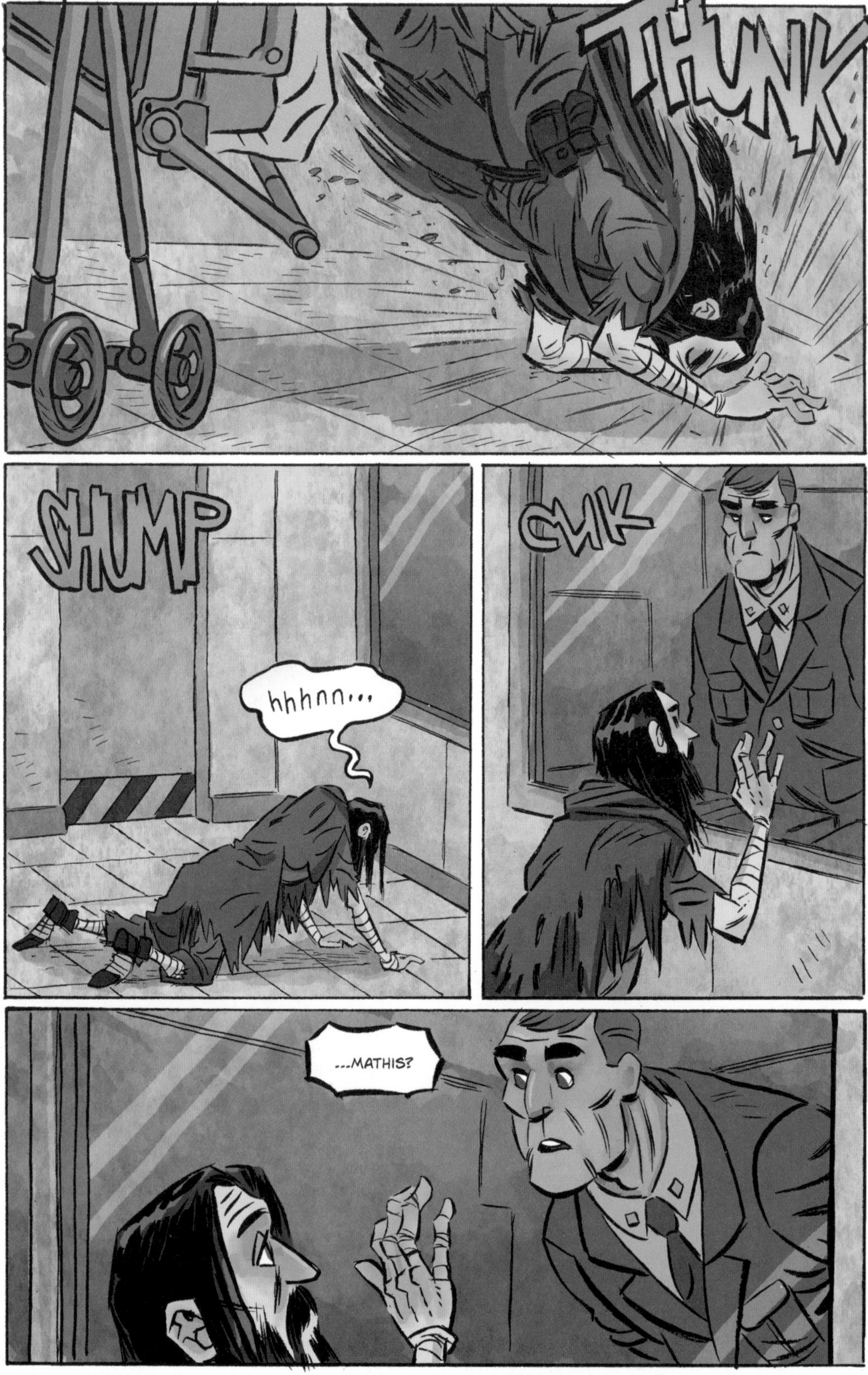
THUNK
SHUMP
hhhnn...
CLIK
...MATHIS?

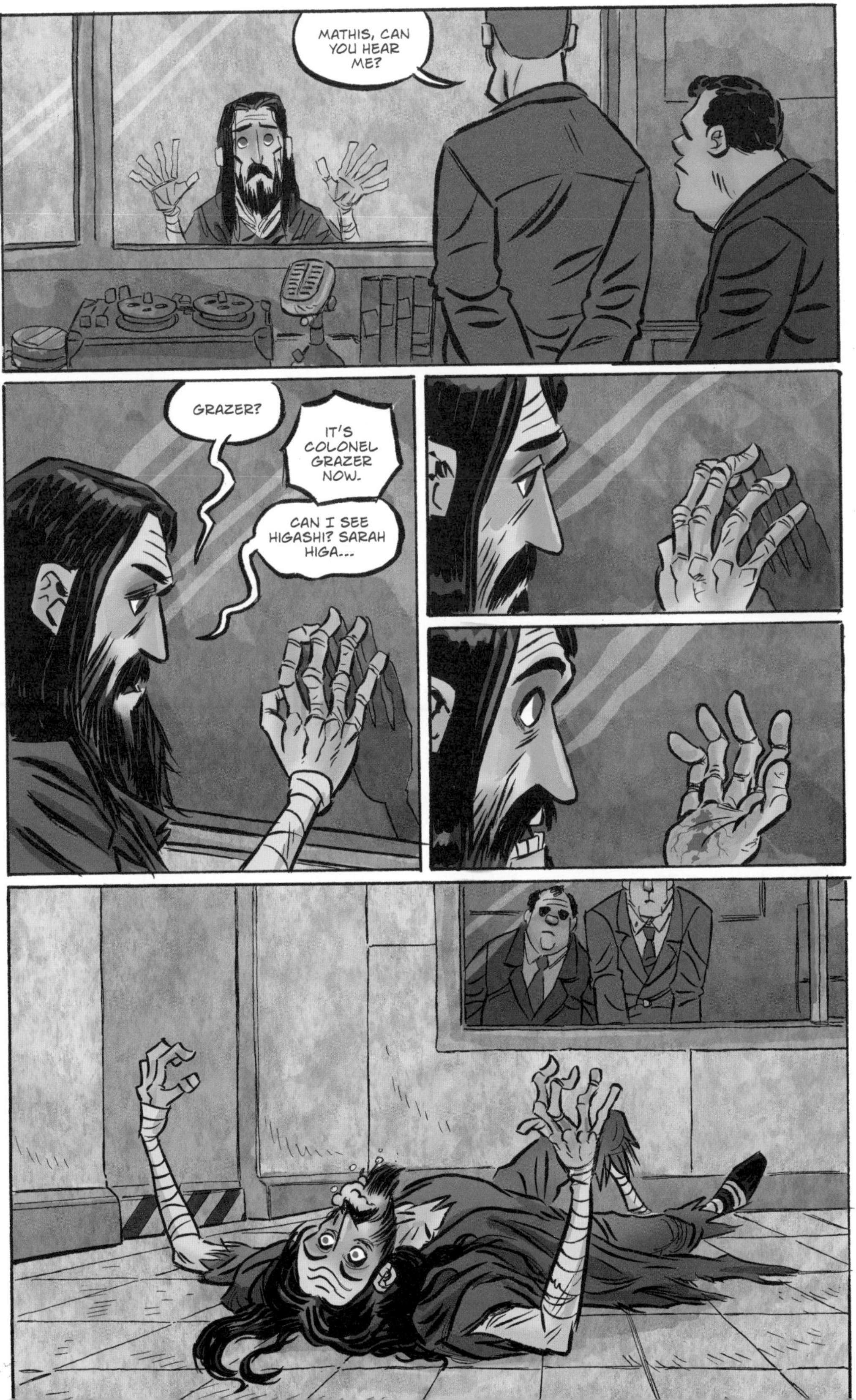
MATHIS, CAN YOU HEAR ME?
GRAZER?
IT'S COLONEL GRAZER NOW.
CAN I SEE HIGASHI? SARAH HIGA...

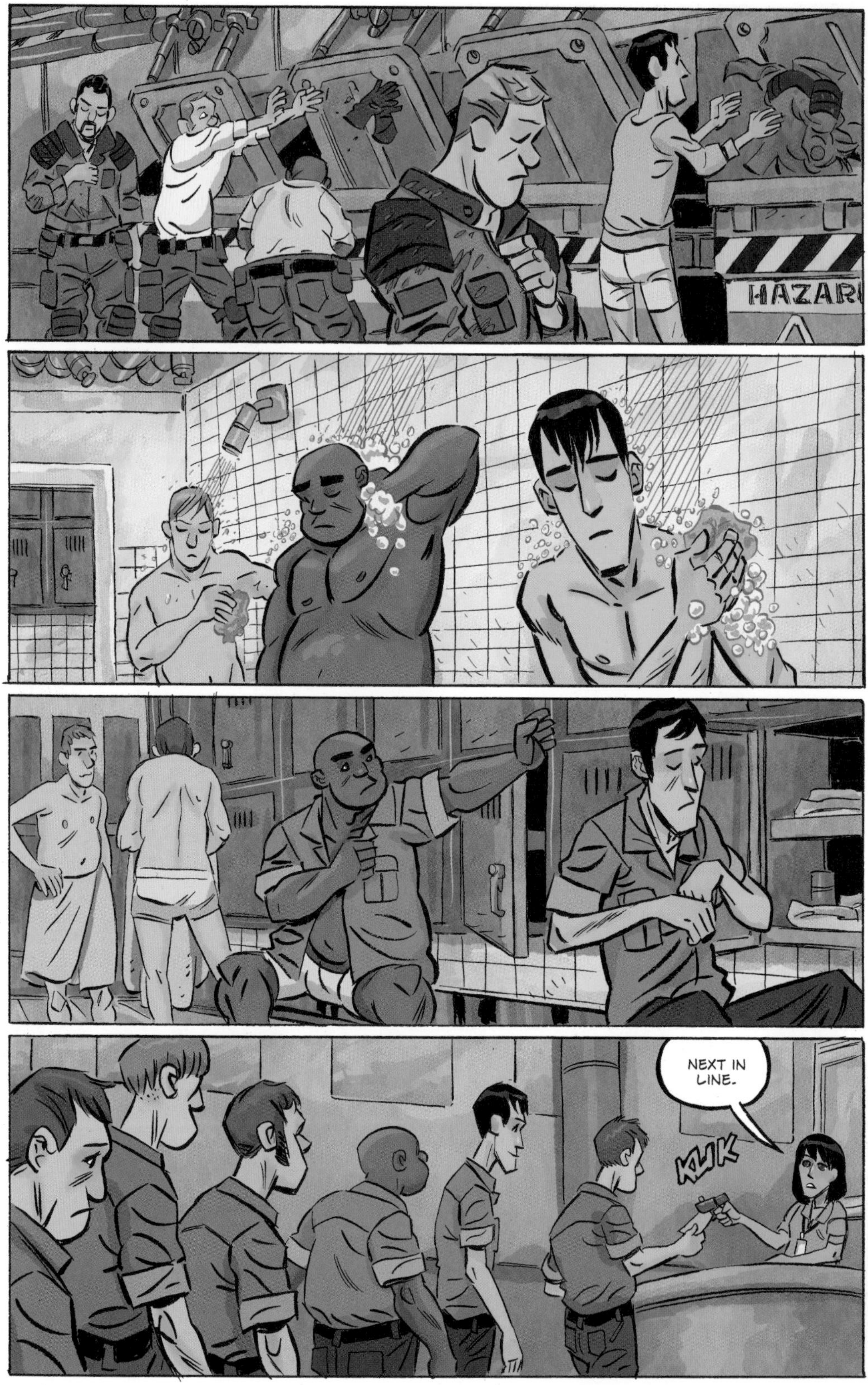
HAZAR
NEXT IN LINE.
KLIK

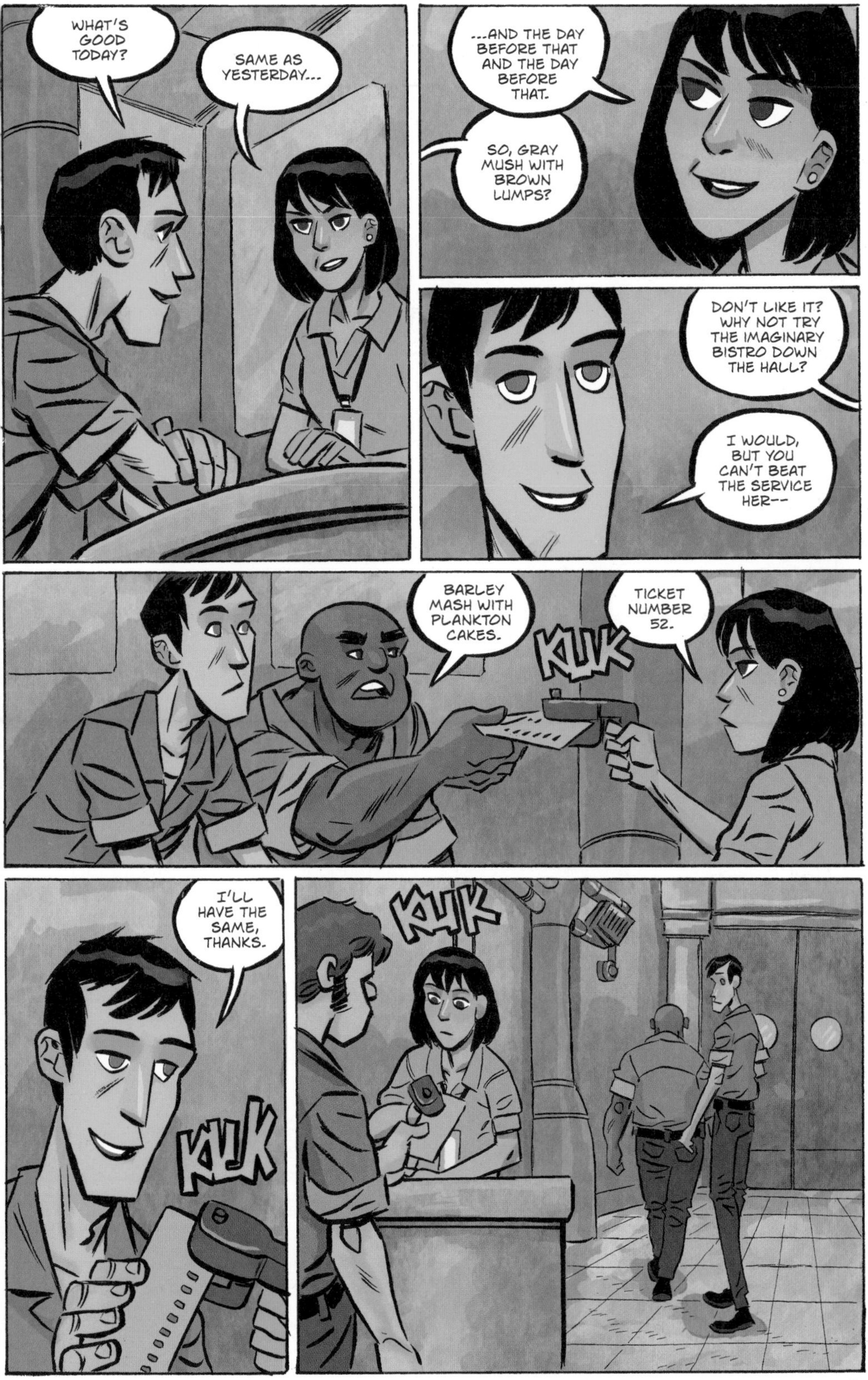
WHAT'S GOOD TODAY?
SAME AS YESTERDAY...
...AND THE DAY BEFORE THAT AND THE DAY BEFORE THAT.
SO, GRAY MUSH WITH BROWN LUMPS?
DON'T LIKE IT? WHY NOT TRY THE IMAGINARY BISTRO DOWN THE HALL?
I WOULD, BUT YOU CAN'T BEAT THE SERVICE HER--
BARLEY MASH WITH PLANKTON CAKES.
KLUK
TICKET NUMBER 52.
I'LL HAVE THE SAME, THANKS.
KLUK
KLUK

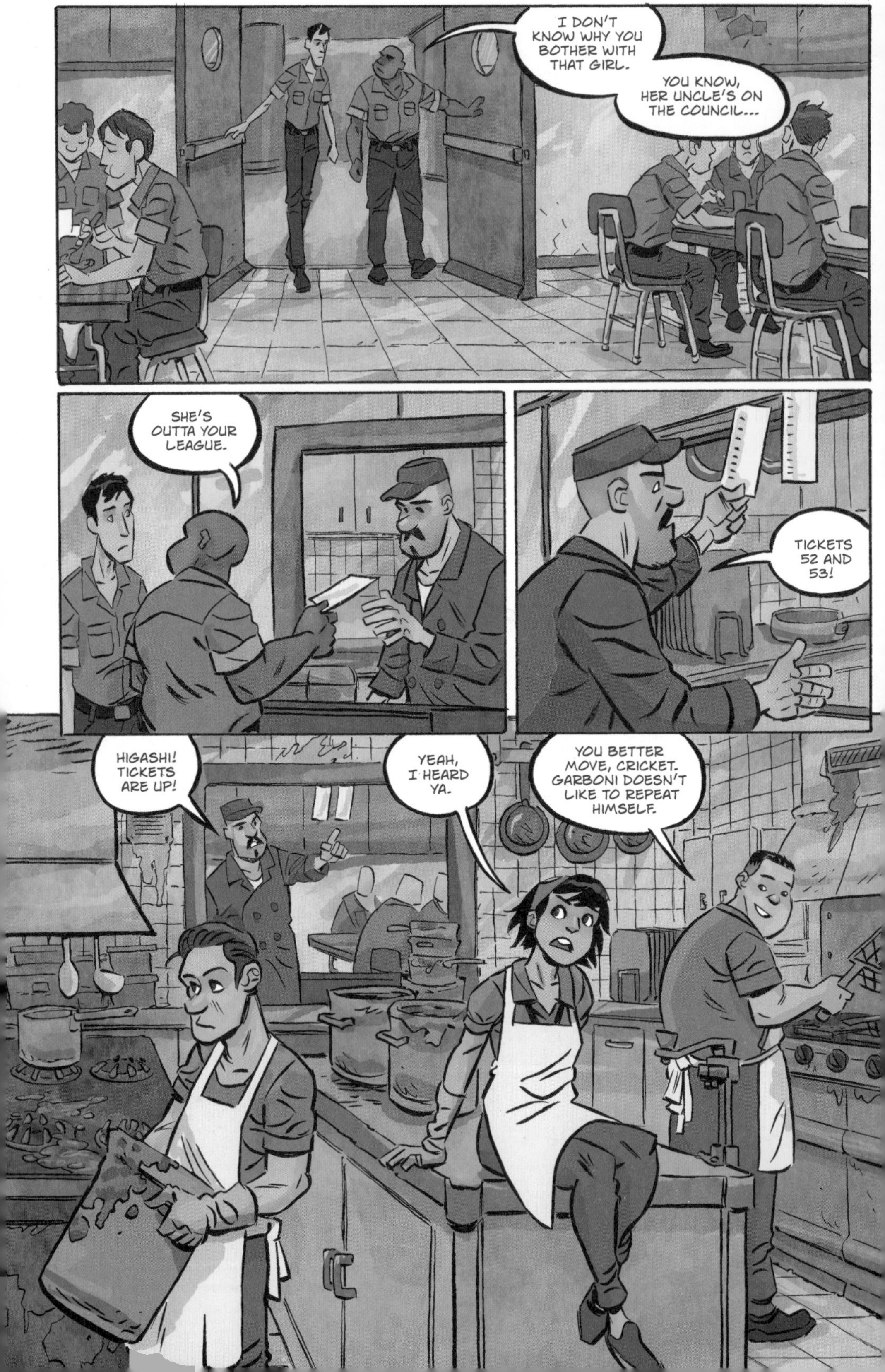
I DON'T KNOW WHY YOU BOTHER WITH THAT GIRL.
YOU KNOW, HER UNCLE'S ON THE COUNCIL...
SHE'S OUTTA YOUR LEAGUE.
TICKETS 52 AND 53!
HIGASHI! TICKETS ARE UP!
YEAH, I HEARD YA.
YOU BETTER MOVE, CRICKET. GARBONI DOESN'T LIKE TO REPEAT HIMSELF.

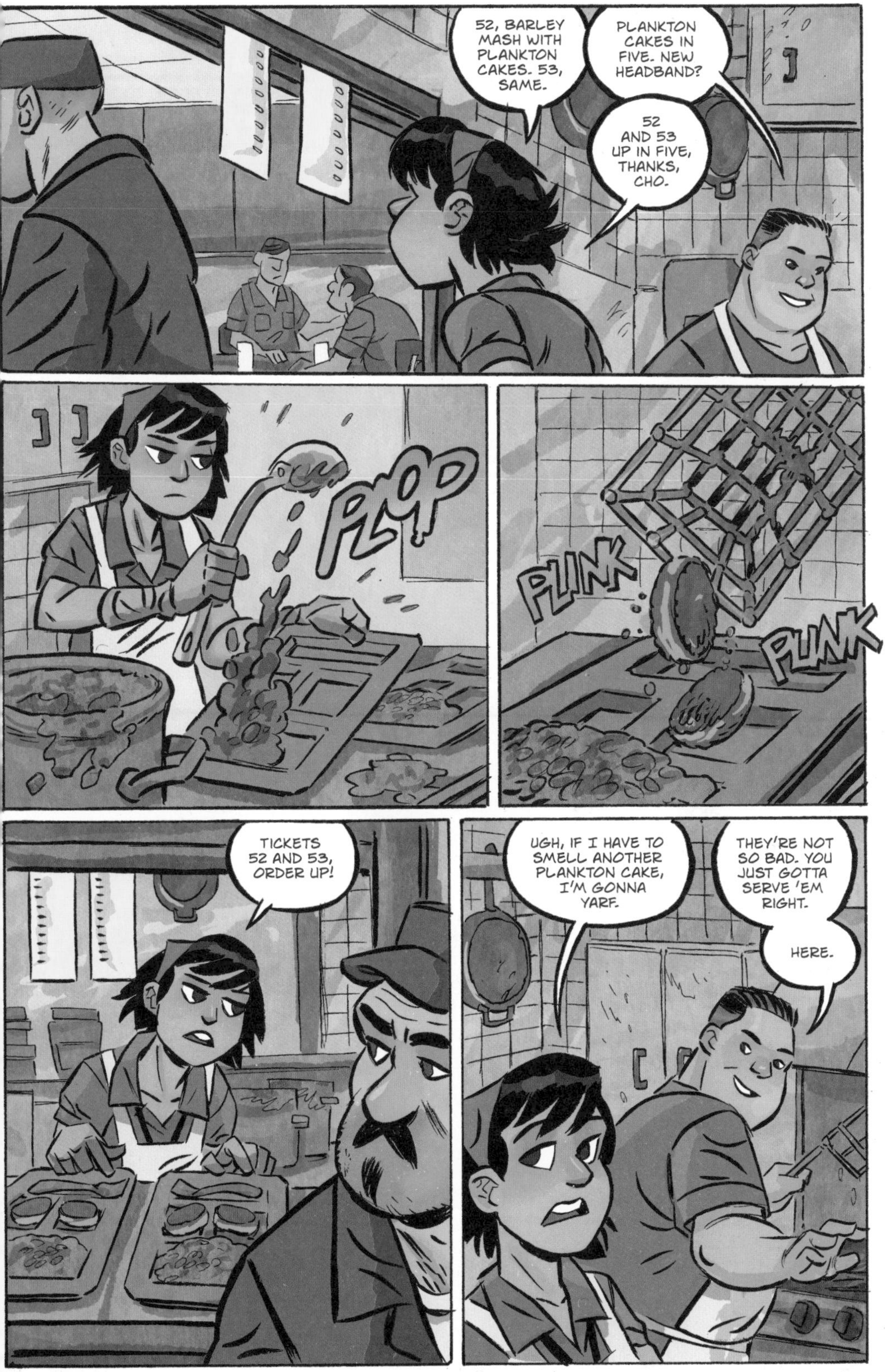
52, BARLEY MASH WITH PLANKTON CAKES. 53, SAME.
PLANKTON CAKES IN FIVE. NEW HEADBAND?
52 AND 53 UP IN FIVE, THANKS, CHO.
PLOP
PLUNK
PLUNK
TICKETS 52 AND 53, ORDER UP!
UGH, IF I HAVE TO SMELL ANOTHER PLANKTON CAKE, I'M GONNA YARF.
THEY'RE NOT SO BAD. YOU JUST GOTTA SERVE 'EM RIGHT.
HERE.

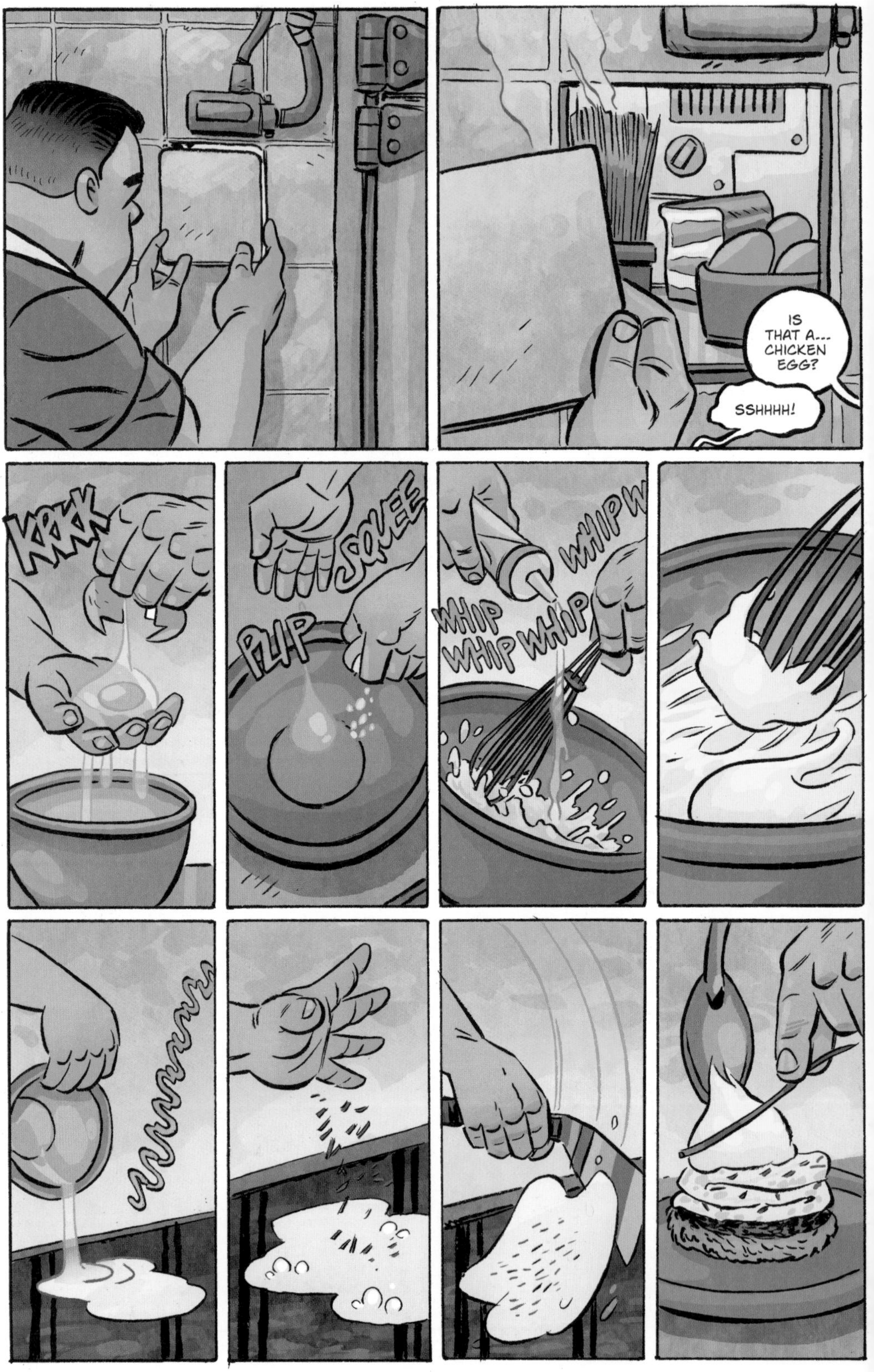
IS THAT A... CHICKEN EGG?
SSHHHH!
KRKK
SQUEE
PLIP
WHIP W
WHIP
WHIP WHIP

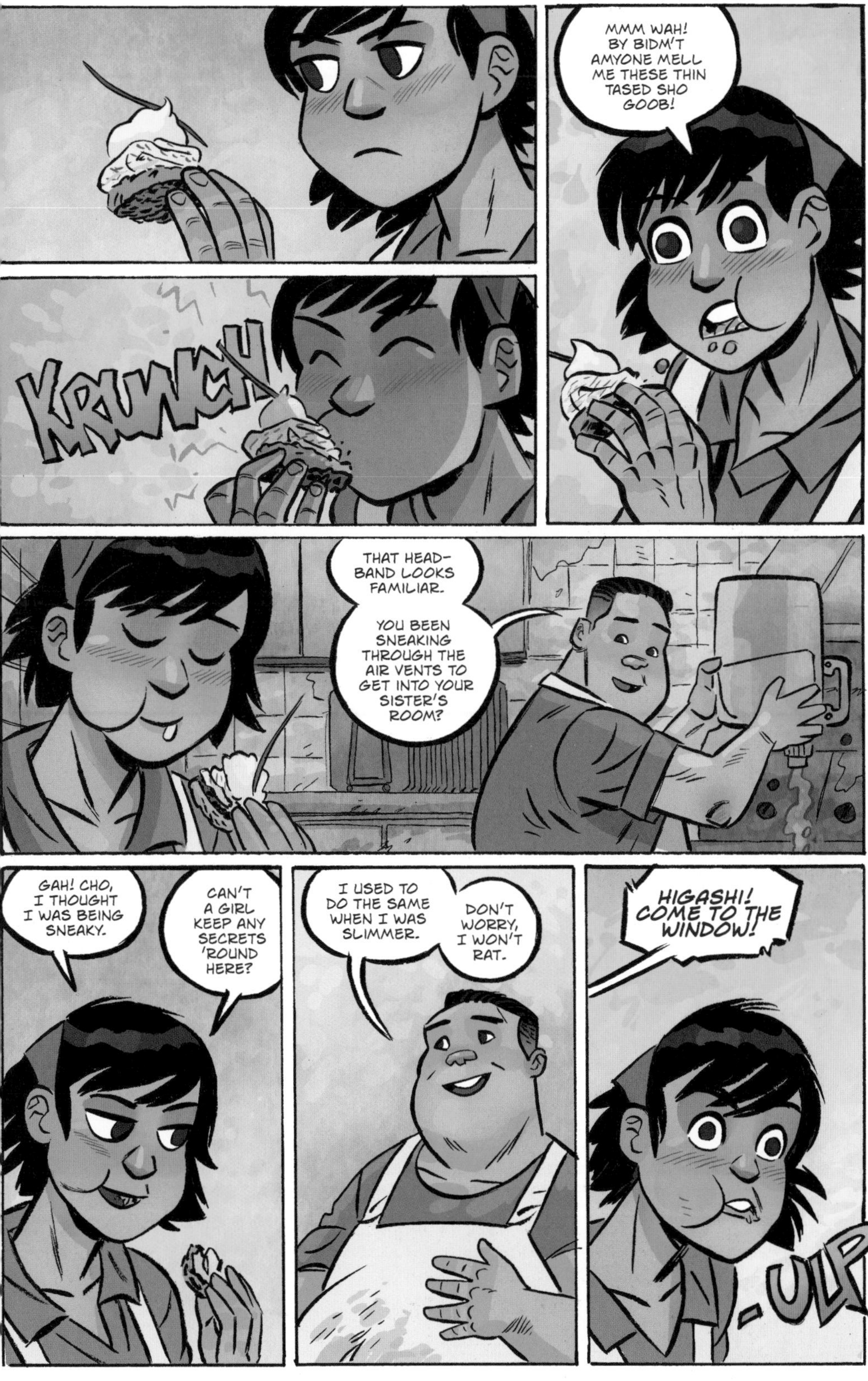
KRUNCH
MMM WAH! BY BIDM'T AMYONE MELL ME THESE THIN TASED SHO GOOB!
THAT HEAD-BAND LOOKS FAMILIAR.
YOU BEEN SNEAKING THROUGH THE AIR VENTS TO GET INTO YOUR SISTER'S ROOM?
GAH! CHO, I THOUGHT I WAS BEING SNEAKY.
CAN'T A GIRL KEEP ANY SECRETS 'ROUND HERE?
I USED TO DO THE SAME WHEN I WAS SLIMMER.
DON'T WORRY, I WON'T RAT.
HIGASHI! COME TO THE WINDOW!
-ULP

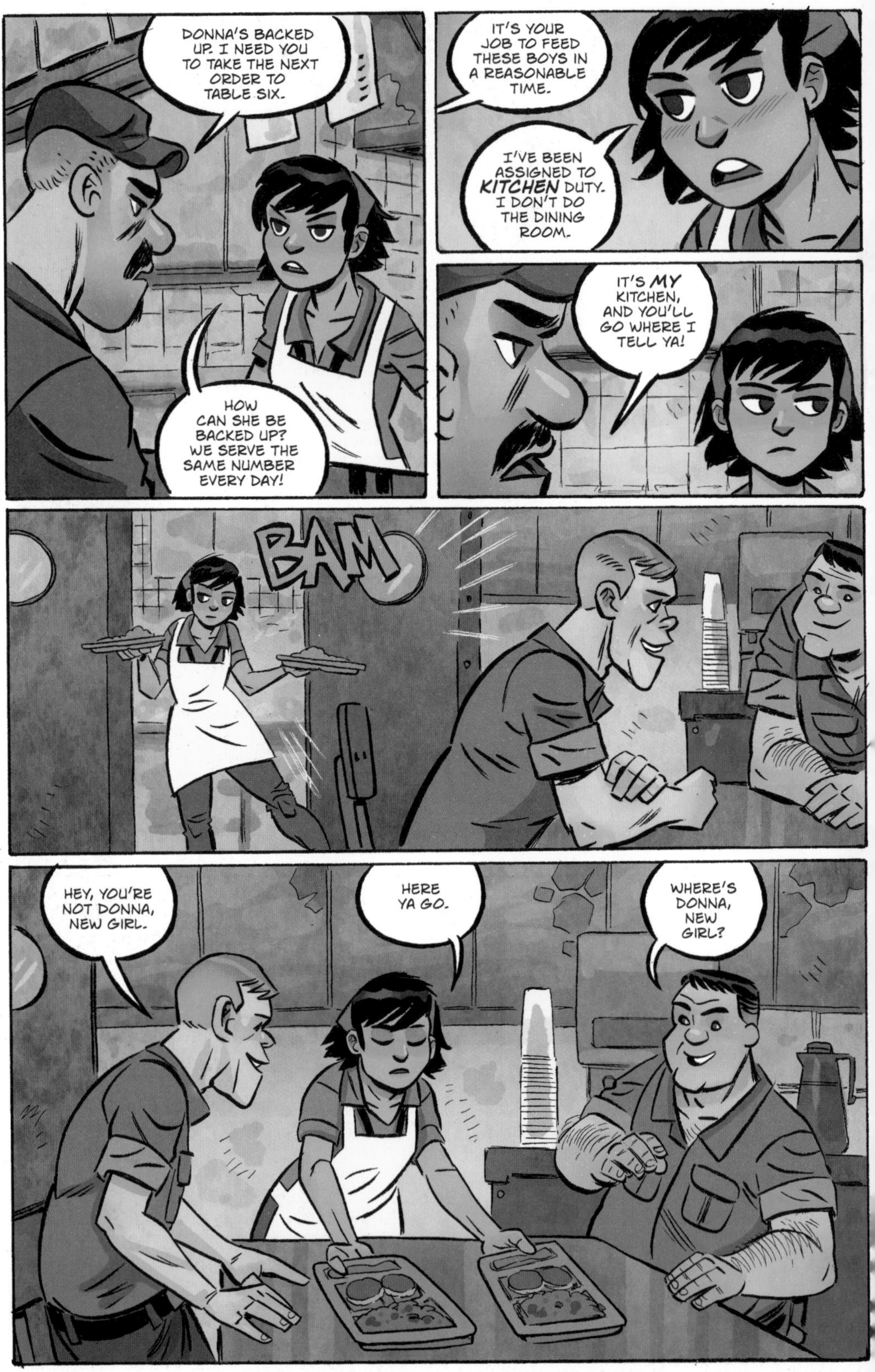
DONNA'S BACKED UP. I NEED YOU TO TAKE THE NEXT ORDER TO TABLE SIX.
HOW CAN SHE BE BACKED UP? WE SERVE THE SAME NUMBER EVERY DAY!
IT'S YOUR JOB TO FEED THESE BOYS IN A REASONABLE TIME.
I'VE BEEN ASSIGNED TO KITCHEN DUTY. I DON'T DO THE DINING ROOM.
IT'S MY KITCHEN, AND YOU'LL GO WHERE I TELL YA!
BAM
HEY, YOU'RE NOT DONNA, NEW GIRL.
HERE YA GO.
WHERE'S DONNA, NEW GIRL?

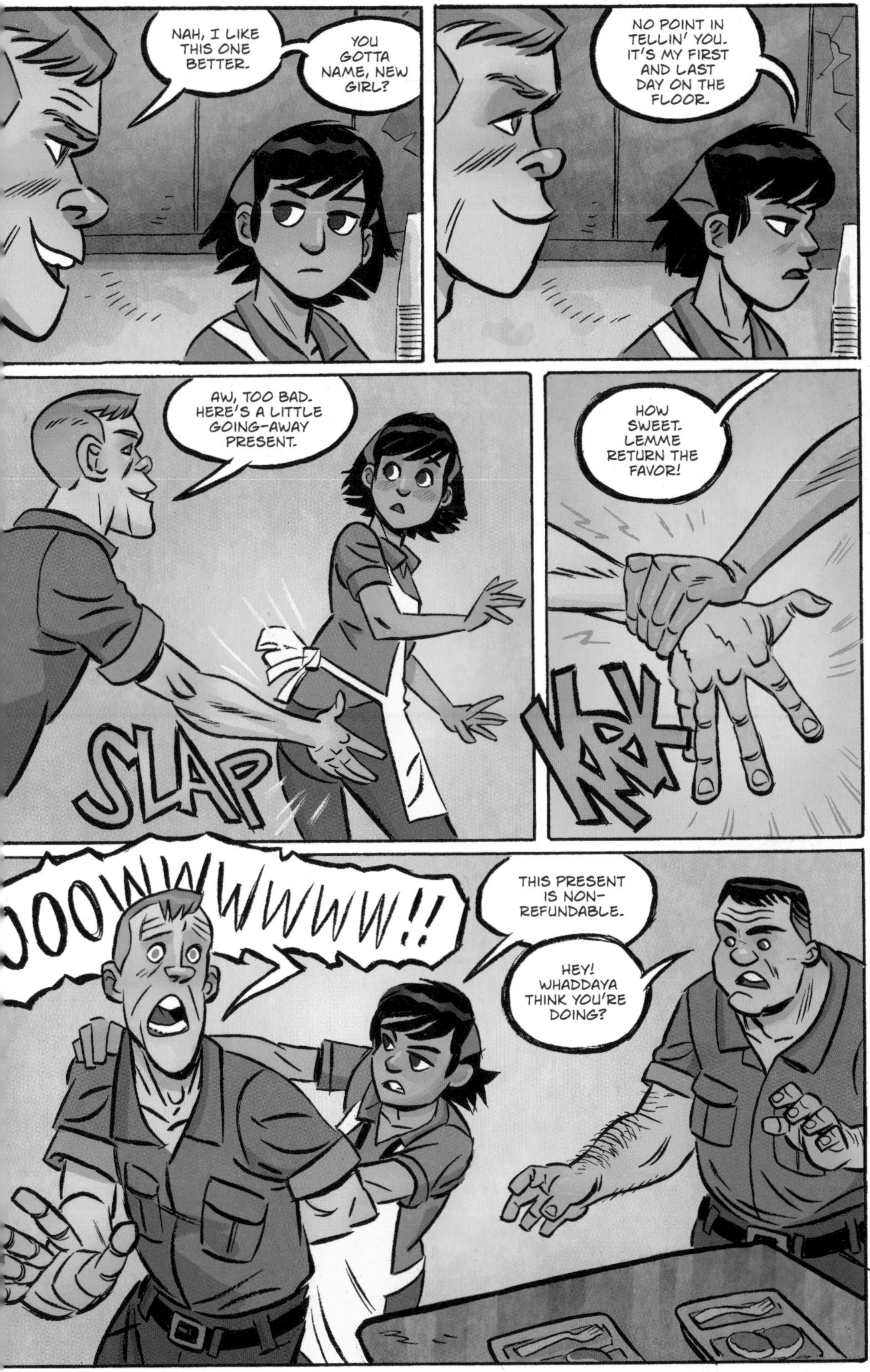
NAH, I LIKE THIS ONE BETTER.
YOU GOTTA NAME, NEW GIRL?
NO POINT IN TELLIN' YOU. IT'S MY FIRST AND LAST DAY ON THE FLOOR.
AW, TOO BAD. HERE'S A LITTLE GOING-AWAY PRESENT.
SLAP
HOW SWEET. LEMME RETURN THE FAVOR!
KRAK
OOOWWWWWW!!
THIS PRESENT IS NON-REFUNDABLE.
HEY! WHADDAYA THINK YOU'RE DOING?

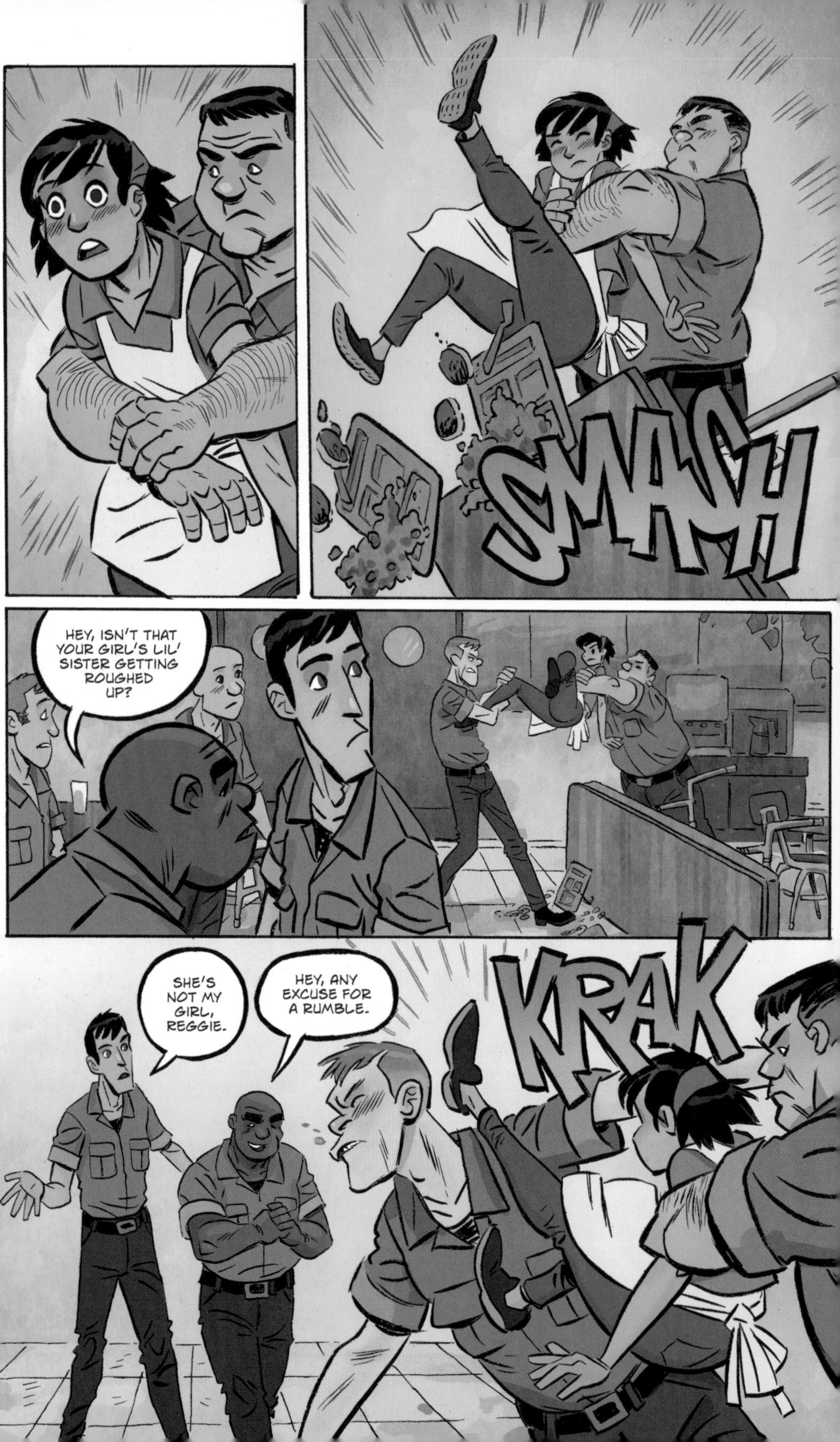
SMASH
HEY, ISN'T THAT YOUR GIRL'S LIL' SISTER GETTING ROUGHED UP?
SHE'S NOT MY GIRL, REGGIE.
HEY, ANY EXCUSE FOR A RUMBLE.
KRAK

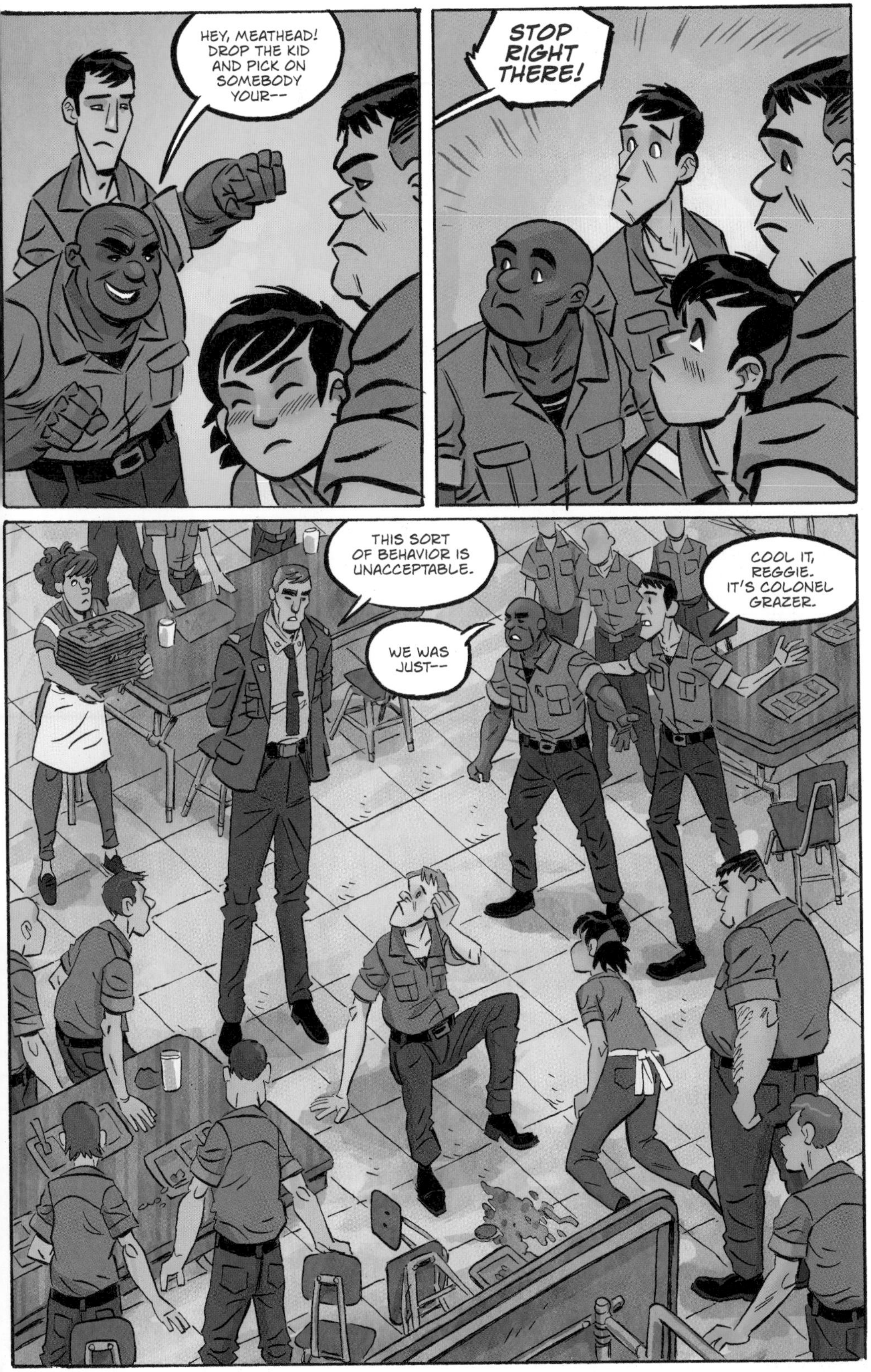
HEY, MEATHEAD! DROP THE KID AND PICK ON SOMEBODY YOUR--
STOP RIGHT THERE!
THIS SORT OF BEHAVIOR IS UNACCEPTABLE.
WE WAS JUST--
COOL IT, REGGIE. IT'S COLONEL GRAZER.

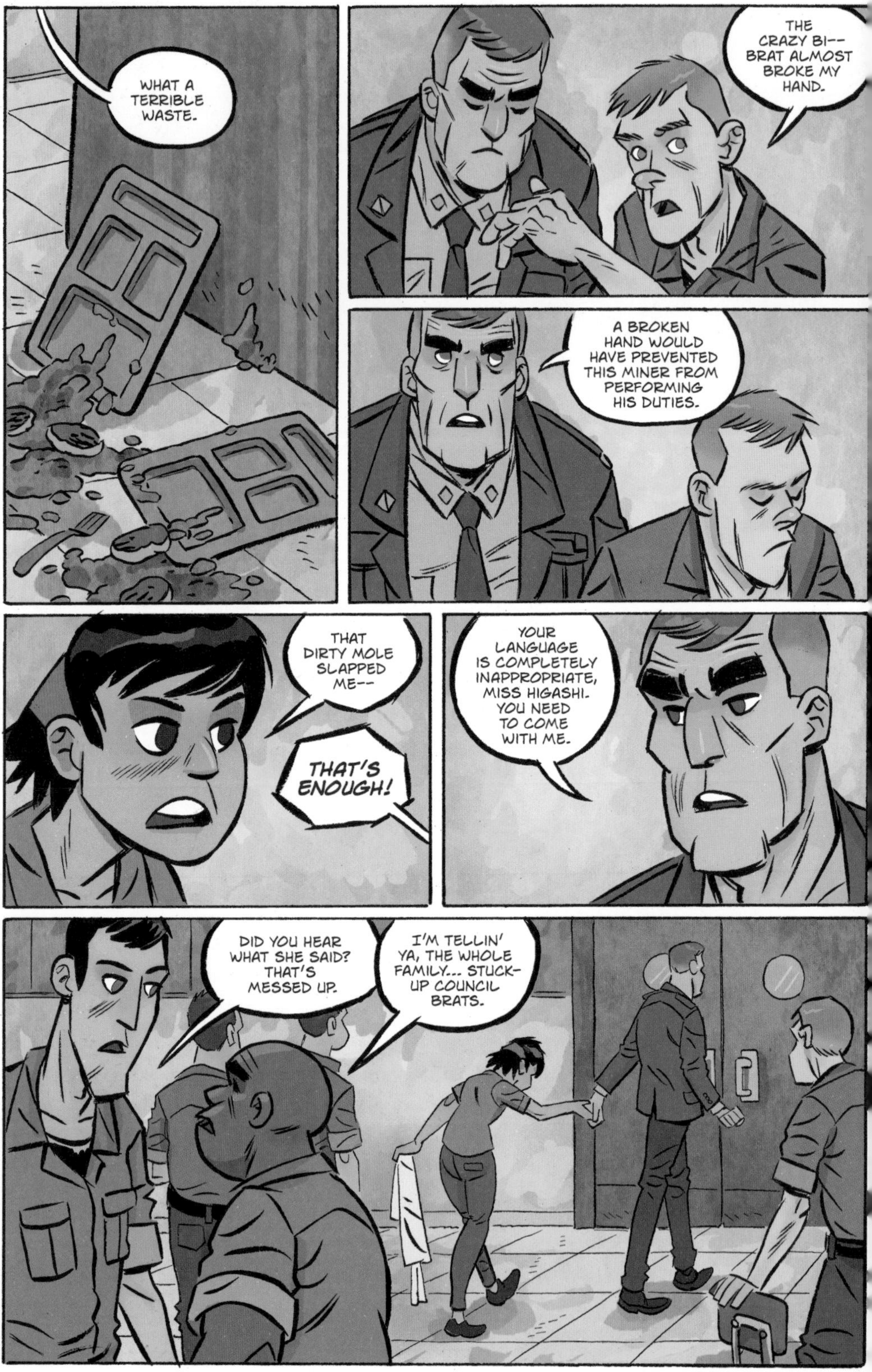
WHAT A TERRIBLE WASTE.
THE CRAZY BI-- BRAT ALMOST BROKE MY HAND.
A BROKEN HAND WOULD HAVE PREVENTED THIS MINER FROM PERFORMING HIS DUTIES.
THAT DIRTY MOLE SLAPPED ME--
THAT'S ENOUGH!
YOUR LANGUAGE IS COMPLETELY INAPPROPRIATE, MISS HIGASHI. YOU NEED TO COME WITH ME.
DID YOU HEAR WHAT SHE SAID? THAT'S MESSED UP.
I'M TELLIN' YA, THE WHOLE FAMILY... STUCK-UP COUNCIL BRATS.

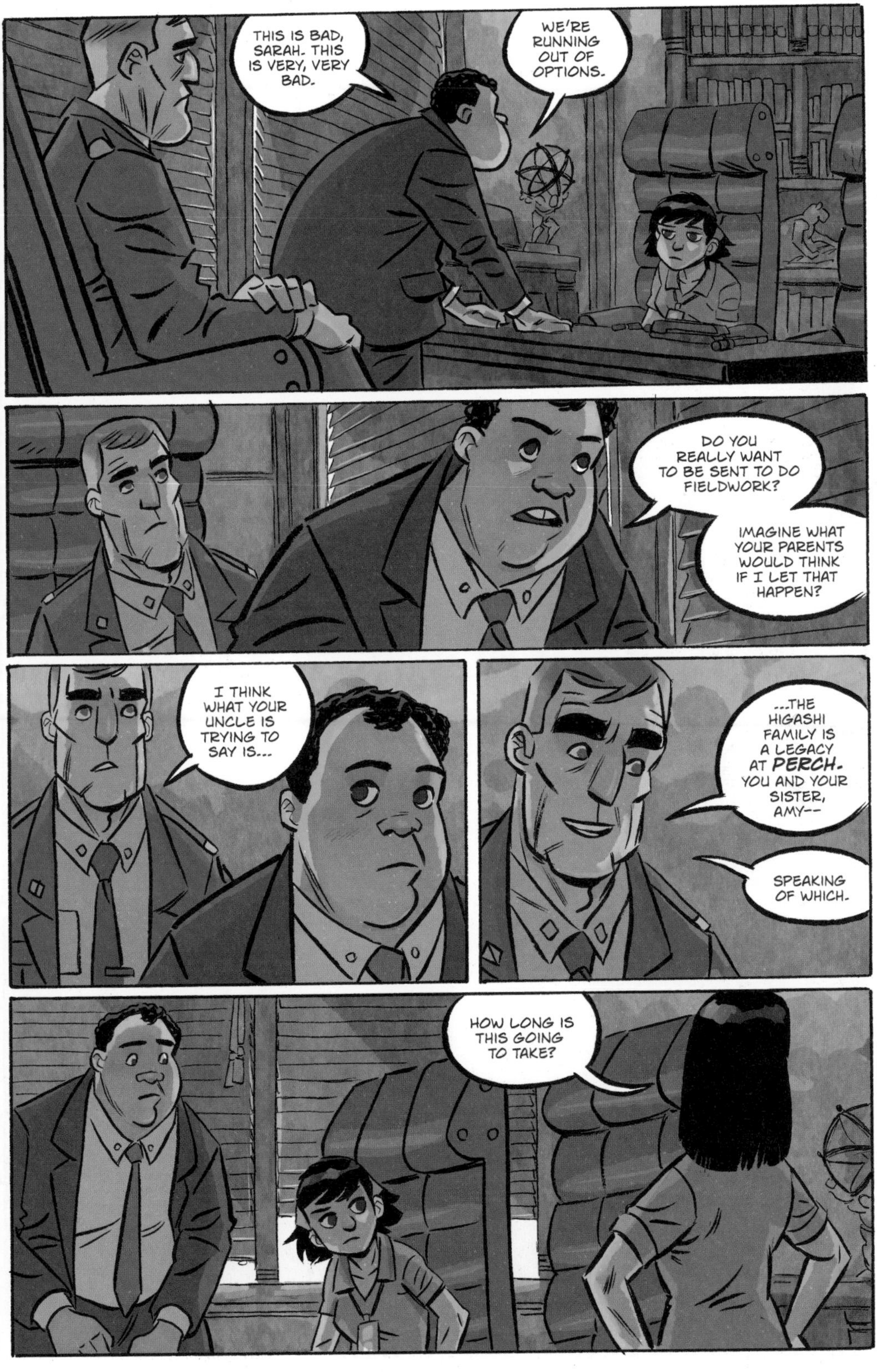
THIS IS BAD, SARAH. THIS IS VERY, VERY BAD.
WE'RE RUNNING OUT OF OPTIONS.
DO YOU REALLY WANT TO BE SENT TO DO FIELDWORK?
IMAGINE WHAT YOUR PARENTS WOULD THINK IF I LET THAT HAPPEN?
I THINK WHAT YOUR UNCLE IS TRYING TO SAY IS...
...THE HIGASHI FAMILY IS A LEGACY AT PERCH. YOU AND YOUR SISTER, AMY--
SPEAKING OF WHICH.
HOW LONG IS THIS GOING TO TAKE?

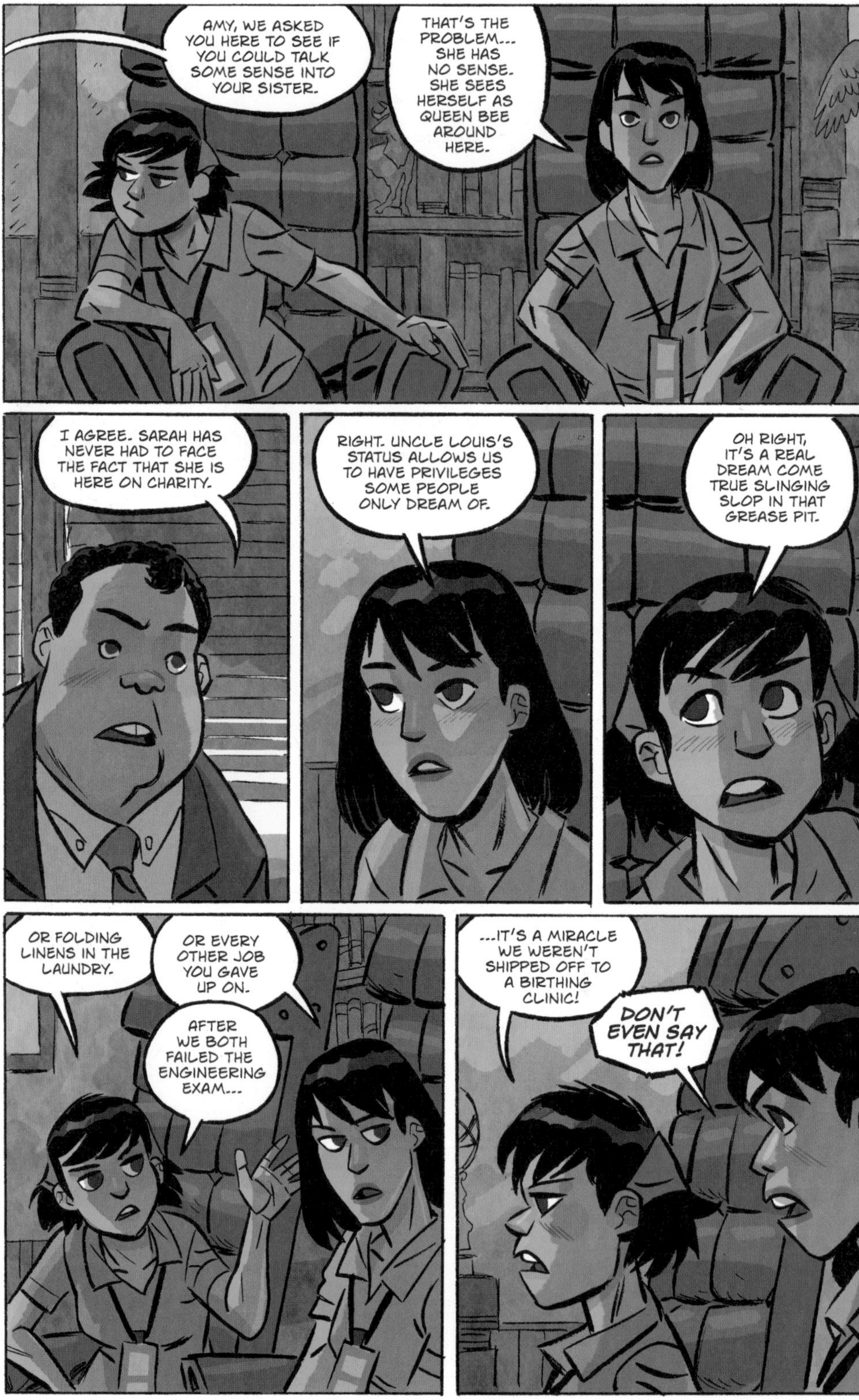
AMY, WE ASKED YOU HERE TO SEE IF YOU COULD TALK SOME SENSE INTO YOUR SISTER.
THAT'S THE PROBLEM... SHE HAS NO SENSE. SHE SEES HERSELF AS QUEEN BEE AROUND HERE.
I AGREE. SARAH HAS NEVER HAD TO FACE THE FACT THAT SHE IS HERE ON CHARITY.
RIGHT. UNCLE LOUIS'S STATUS ALLOWS US TO HAVE PRIVILEGES SOME PEOPLE ONLY DREAM OF.
OH RIGHT, IT'S A REAL DREAM COME TRUE SLINGING SLOP IN THAT GREASE PIT.
OR FOLDING LINENS IN THE LAUNDRY.
OR EVERY OTHER JOB YOU GAVE UP ON.
AFTER WE BOTH FAILED THE ENGINEERING EXAM...
...IT'S A MIRACLE WE WEREN'T SHIPPED OFF TO A BIRTHING CLINIC!
DON'T EVEN SAY THAT!

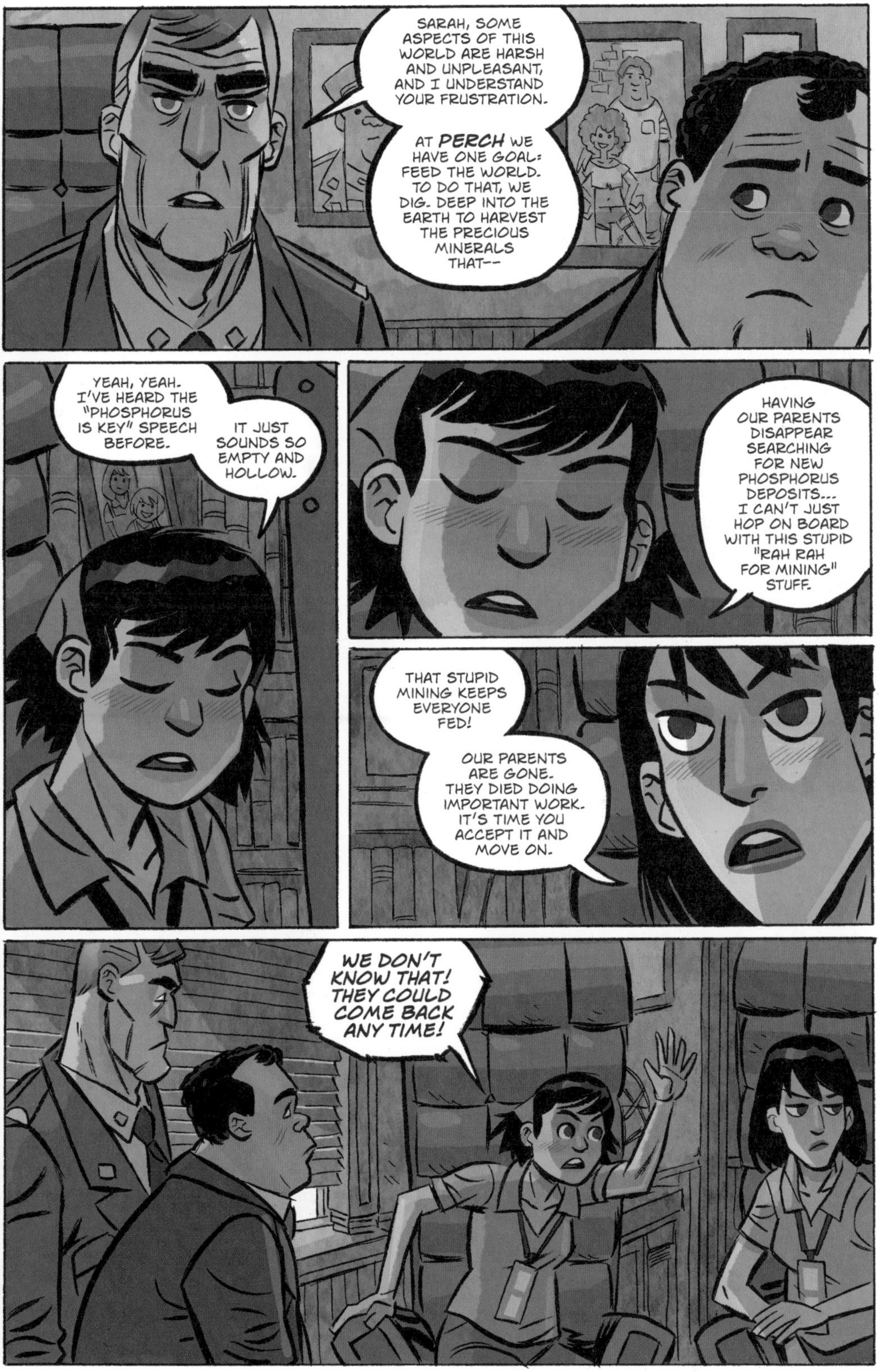
SARAH, SOME ASPECTS OF THIS WORLD ARE HARSH AND UNPLEASANT, AND I UNDERSTAND YOUR FRUSTRATION.
AT PERCH WE HAVE ONE GOAL: FEED THE WORLD. TO DO THAT, WE DIG. DEEP INTO THE EARTH TO HARVEST THE PRECIOUS MINERALS THAT--
YEAH, YEAH. I'VE HEARD THE "PHOSPHORUS IS KEY" SPEECH BEFORE.
IT JUST SOUNDS SO EMPTY AND HOLLOW.
HAVING OUR PARENTS DISAPPEAR SEARCHING FOR NEW PHOSPHORUS DEPOSITS... I CAN'T JUST HOP ON BOARD WITH THIS STUPID "RAH RAH FOR MINING" STUFF.
THAT STUPID MINING KEEPS EVERYONE FED!
OUR PARENTS ARE GONE. THEY DIED DOING IMPORTANT WORK. IT'S TIME YOU ACCEPT IT AND MOVE ON.
WE DON'T KNOW THAT! THEY COULD COME BACK ANY TIME!

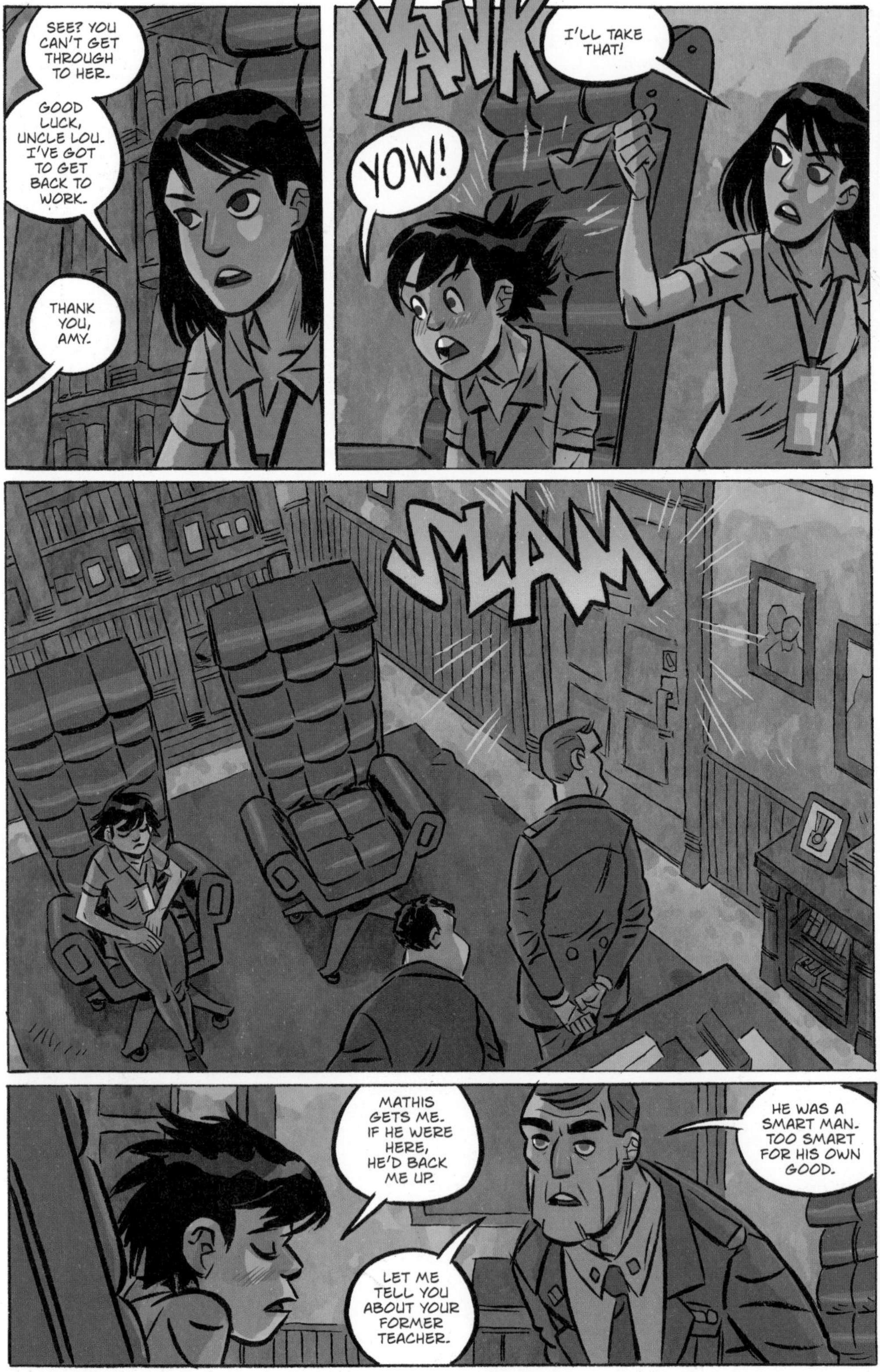
SEE? YOU CAN'T GET THROUGH TO HER.
GOOD LUCK, UNCLE LOU. I'VE GOT TO GET BACK TO WORK.
THANK YOU, AMY.
YANK
I'LL TAKE THAT!
YOW!
SLAM
MATHIS GETS ME. IF HE WERE HERE, HE'D BACK ME UP.
LET ME TELL YOU ABOUT YOUR FORMER TEACHER.
HE WAS A SMART MAN. TOO SMART FOR HIS OWN GOOD.

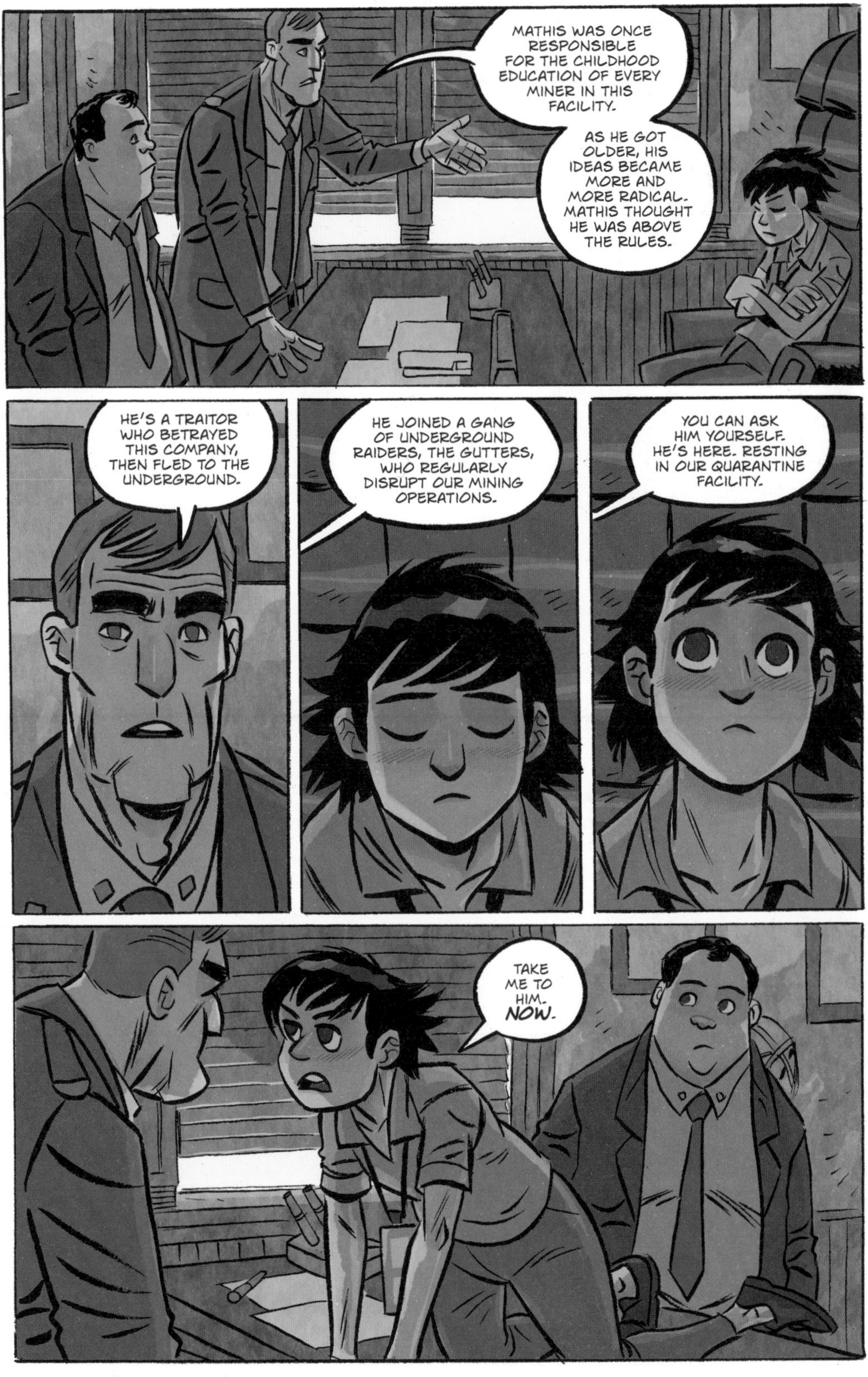
MATHIS WAS ONCE RESPONSIBLE FOR THE CHILDHOOD EDUCATION OF EVERY MINER IN THIS FACILITY.
AS HE GOT OLDER, HIS IDEAS BECAME MORE AND MORE RADICAL. MATHIS THOUGHT HE WAS ABOVE THE RULES.
HE'S A TRAITOR WHO BETRAYED THIS COMPANY, THEN FLED TO THE UNDERGROUND.
HE JOINED A GANG OF UNDERGROUND RAIDERS, THE GUTTERS, WHO REGULARLY DISRUPT OUR MINING OPERATIONS.
YOU CAN ASK HIM YOURSELF. HE'S HERE. RESTING IN OUR QUARANTINE FACILITY.
TAKE ME TO HIM. **NOW.**

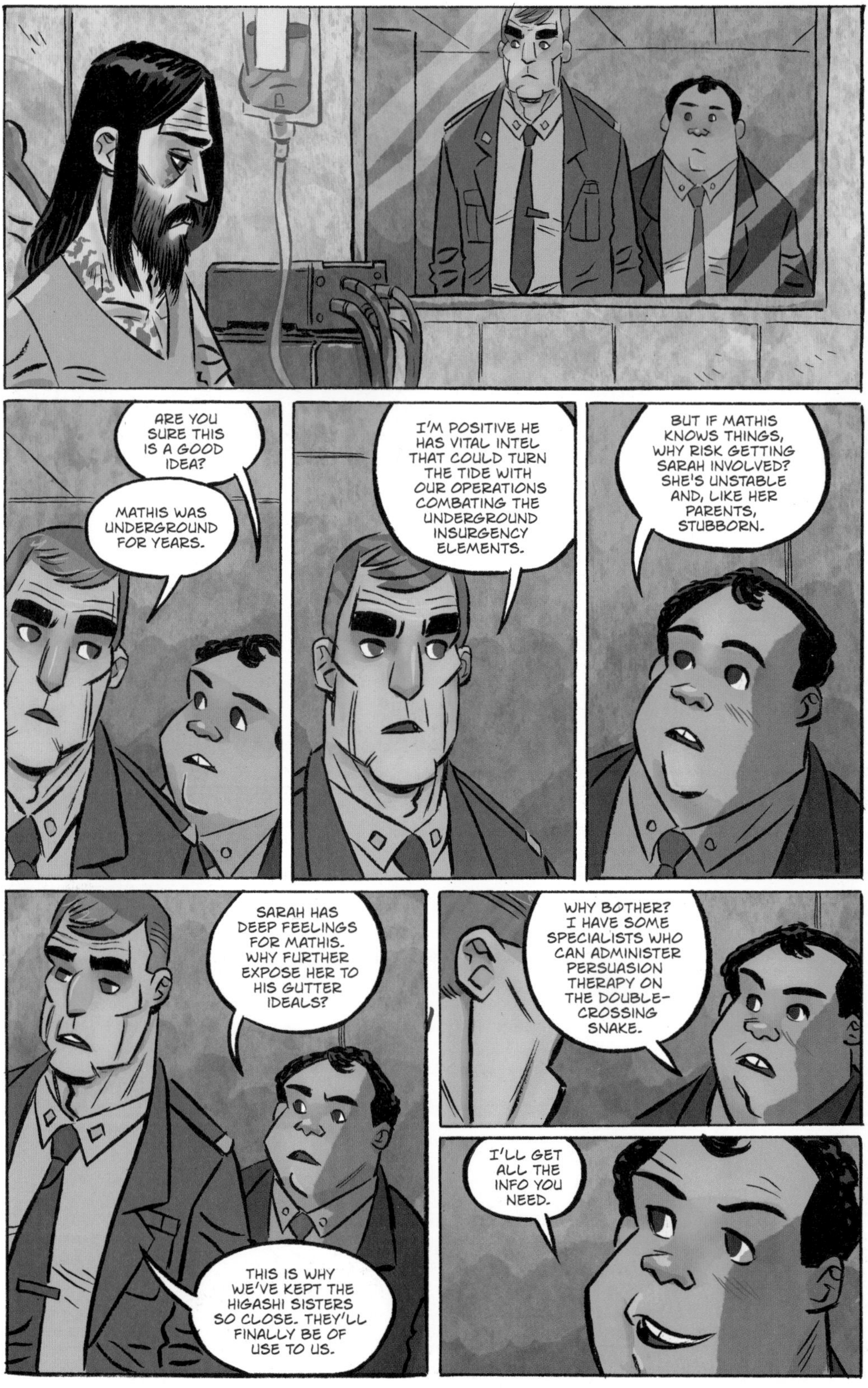
ARE YOU SURE THIS IS A GOOD IDEA?
MATHIS WAS UNDERGROUND FOR YEARS.
I'M POSITIVE HE HAS VITAL INTEL THAT COULD TURN THE TIDE WITH OUR OPERATIONS COMBATING THE UNDERGROUND INSURGENCY ELEMENTS.
BUT IF MATHIS KNOWS THINGS, WHY RISK GETTING SARAH INVOLVED? SHE'S UNSTABLE AND, LIKE HER PARENTS, STUBBORN.
SARAH HAS DEEP FEELINGS FOR MATHIS. WHY FURTHER EXPOSE HER TO HIS GUTTER IDEALS?
THIS IS WHY WE'VE KEPT THE HIGASHI SISTERS SO CLOSE. THEY'LL FINALLY BE OF USE TO US.
WHY BOTHER? I HAVE SOME SPECIALISTS WHO CAN ADMINISTER PERSUASION THERAPY ON THE DOUBLE-CROSSING SNAKE.
I'LL GET ALL THE INFO YOU NEED.

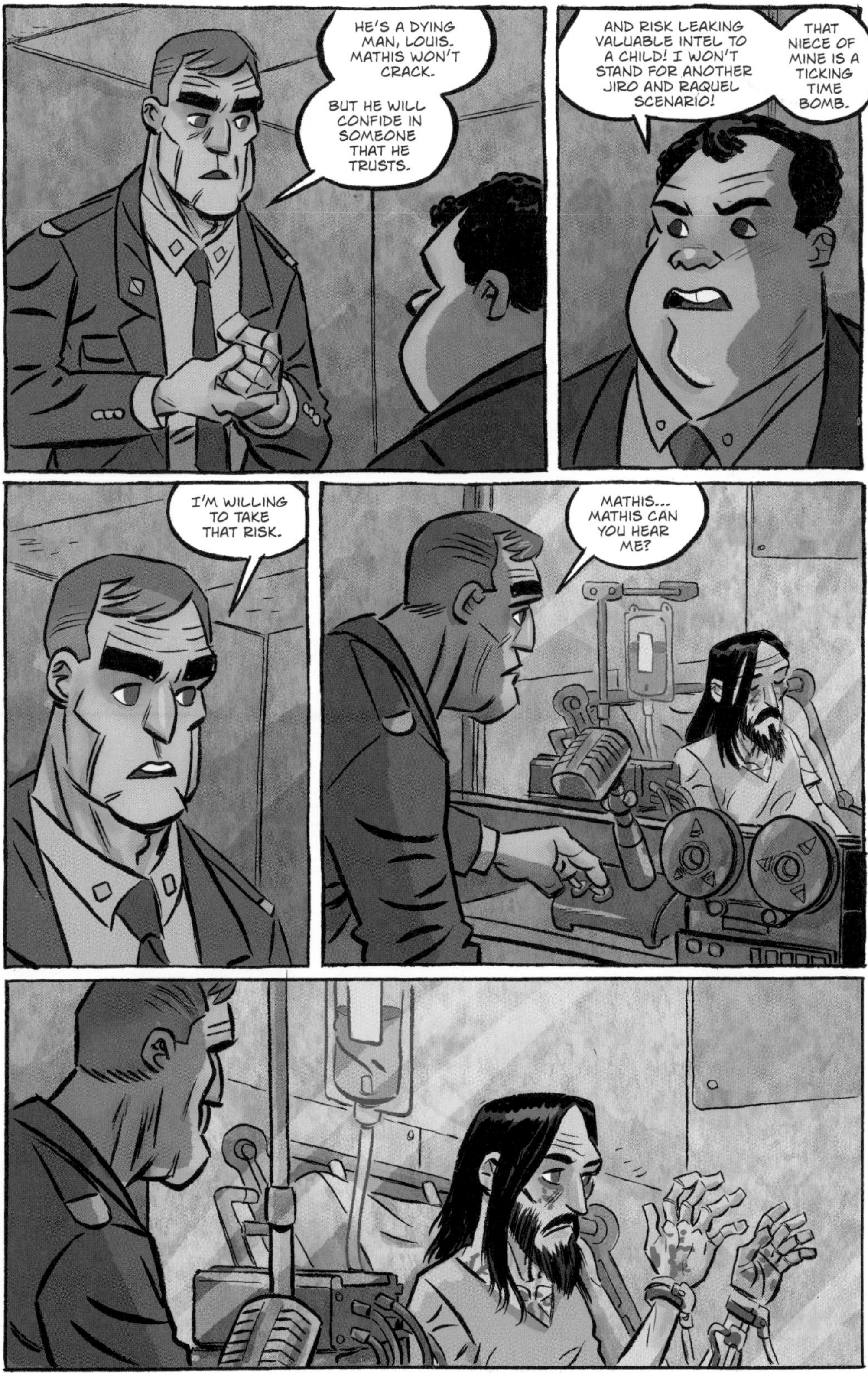
HE'S A DYING MAN, LOUIS. MATHIS WON'T CRACK.
BUT HE WILL CONFIDE IN SOMEONE THAT HE TRUSTS.
AND RISK LEAKING VALUABLE INTEL TO A CHILD! I WON'T STAND FOR ANOTHER JIRO AND RAQUEL SCENARIO!
THAT NIECE OF MINE IS A TICKING TIME BOMB.
I'M WILLING TO TAKE THAT RISK.
MATHIS... MATHIS CAN YOU HEAR ME?

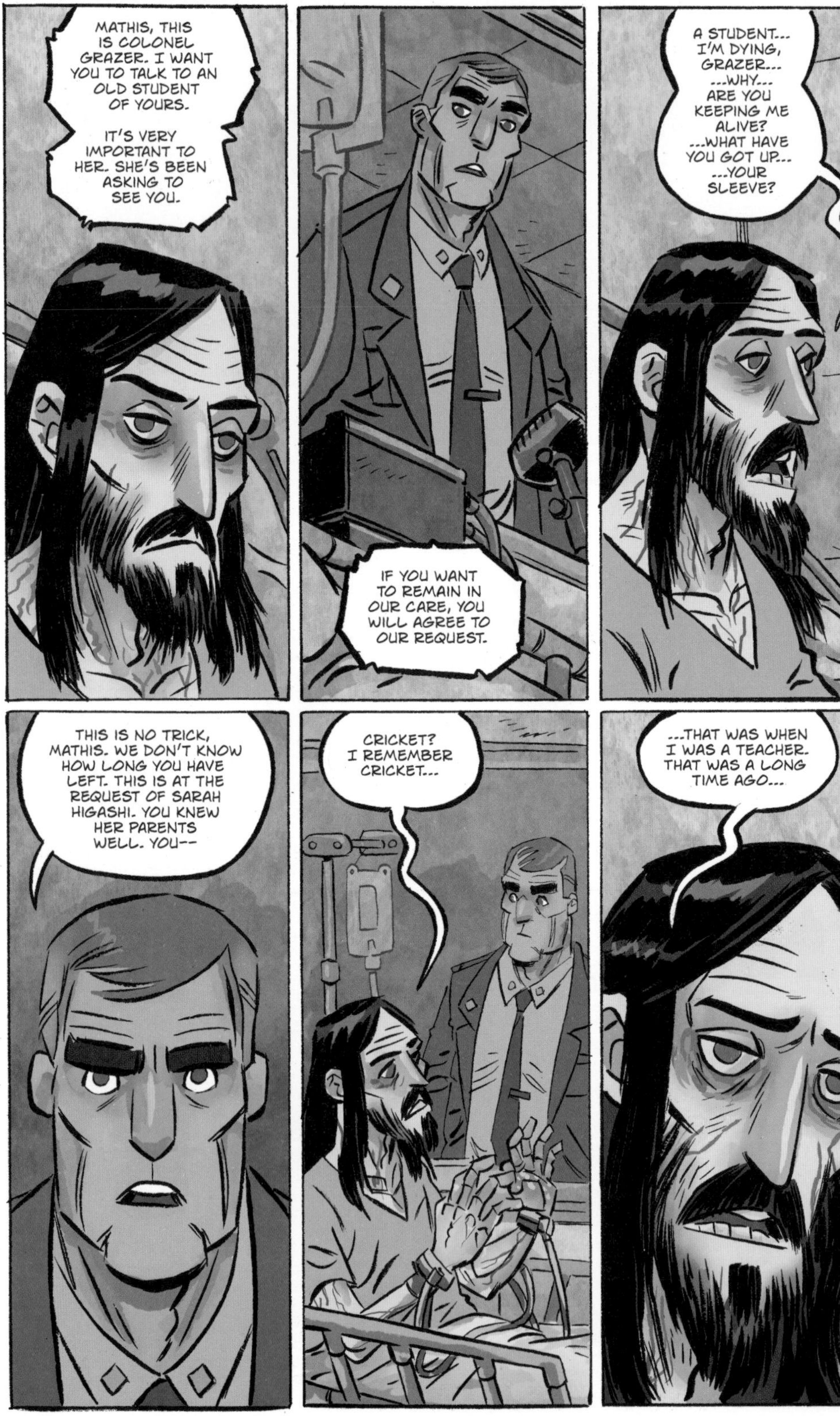
MATHIS, THIS IS COLONEL GRAZER. I WANT YOU TO TALK TO AN OLD STUDENT OF YOURS.
IT'S VERY IMPORTANT TO HER. SHE'S BEEN ASKING TO SEE YOU.
IF YOU WANT TO REMAIN IN OUR CARE, YOU WILL AGREE TO OUR REQUEST.
A STUDENT... I'M DYING, GRAZER... ...WHY... ARE YOU KEEPING ME ALIVE? ...WHAT HAVE YOU GOT UP... ...YOUR SLEEVE?
THIS IS NO TRICK, MATHIS. WE DON'T KNOW HOW LONG YOU HAVE LEFT. THIS IS AT THE REQUEST OF SARAH HIGASHI. YOU KNEW HER PARENTS WELL. YOU--
CRICKET? I REMEMBER CRICKET...
...THAT WAS WHEN I WAS A TEACHER. THAT WAS A LONG TIME AGO...

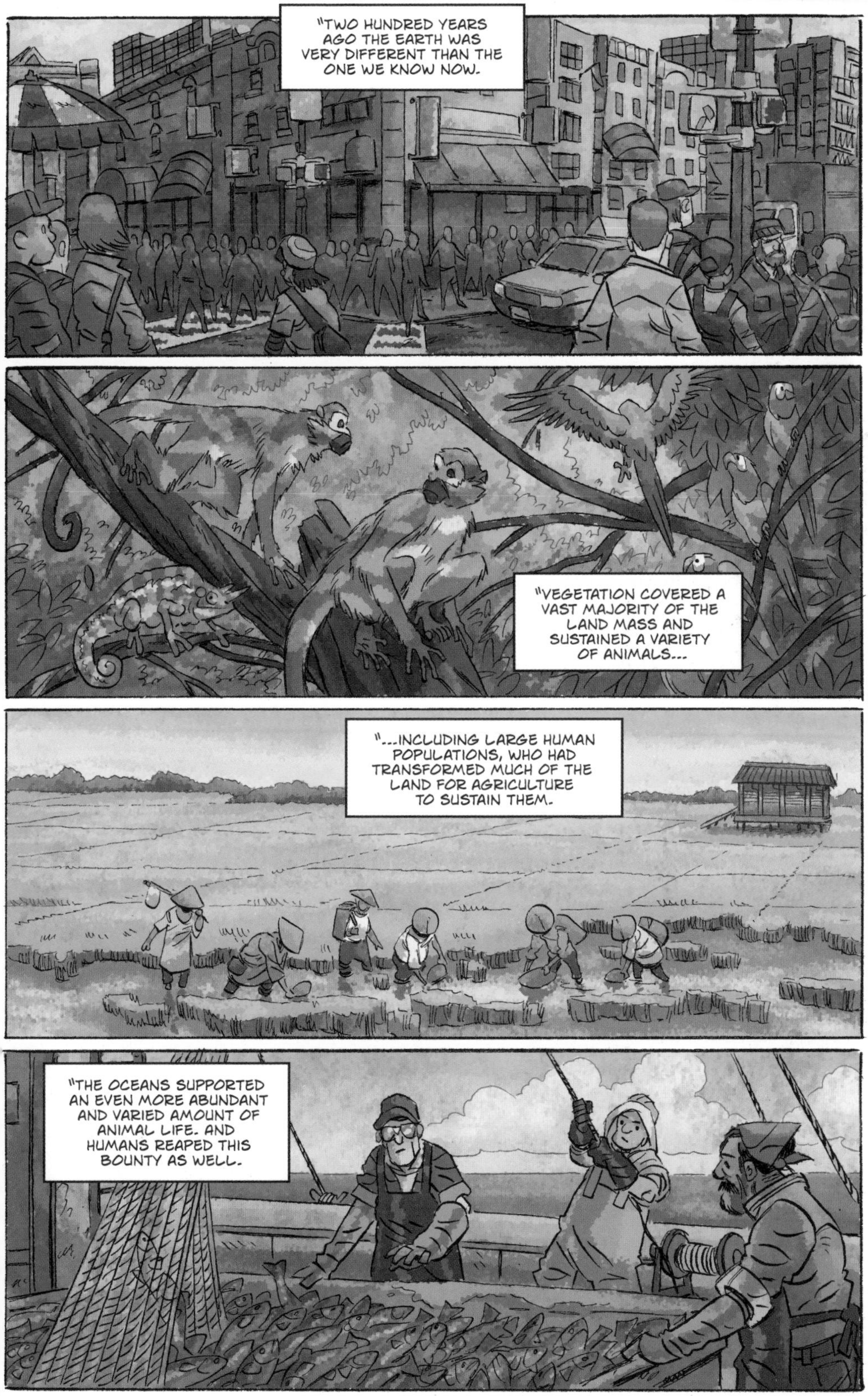
"TWO HUNDRED YEARS AGO THE EARTH WAS VERY DIFFERENT THAN THE ONE WE KNOW NOW.
"VEGETATION COVERED A VAST MAJORITY OF THE LAND MASS AND SUSTAINED A VARIETY OF ANIMALS...
"...INCLUDING LARGE HUMAN POPULATIONS, WHO HAD TRANSFORMED MUCH OF THE LAND FOR AGRICULTURE TO SUSTAIN THEM.
"THE OCEANS SUPPORTED AN EVEN MORE ABUNDANT AND VARIED AMOUNT OF ANIMAL LIFE. AND HUMANS REAPED THIS BOUNTY AS WELL.

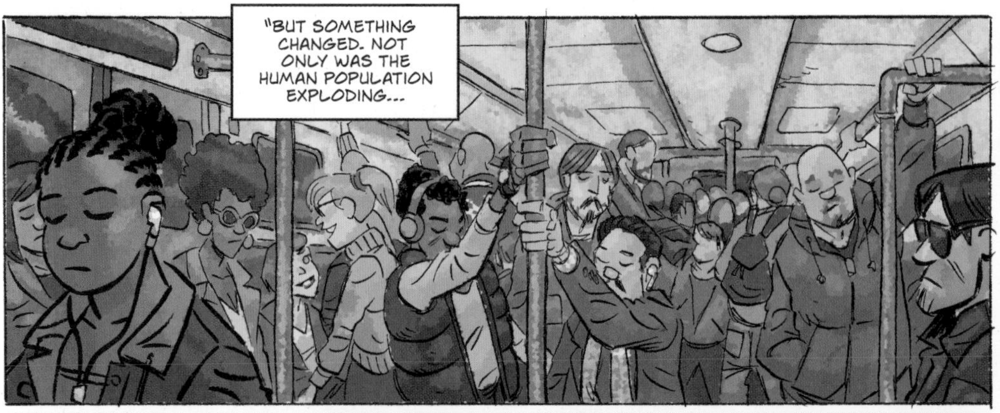
"BUT SOMETHING CHANGED. NOT ONLY WAS THE HUMAN POPULATION EXPLODING...

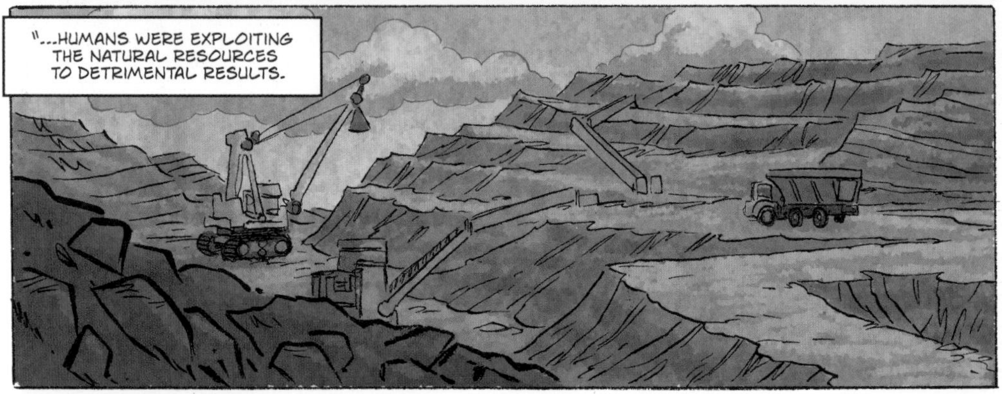
"...HUMANS WERE EXPLOITING THE NATURAL RESOURCES TO DETRIMENTAL RESULTS.

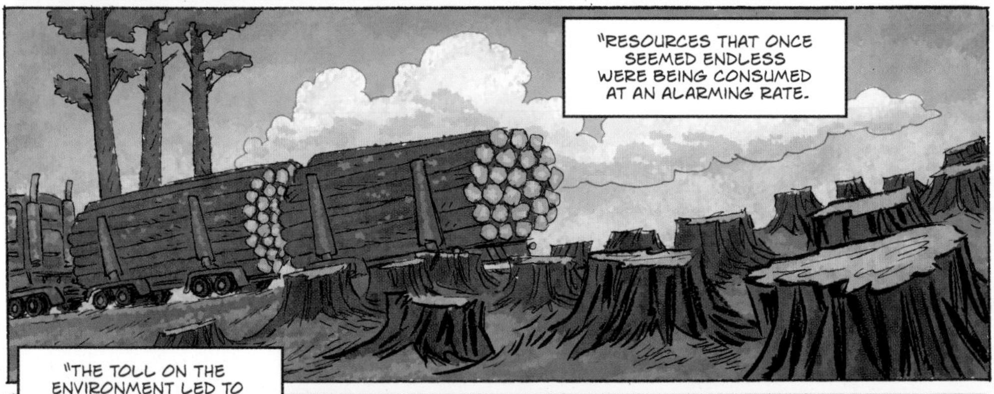
"RESOURCES THAT ONCE SEEMED ENDLESS WERE BEING CONSUMED AT AN ALARMING RATE.

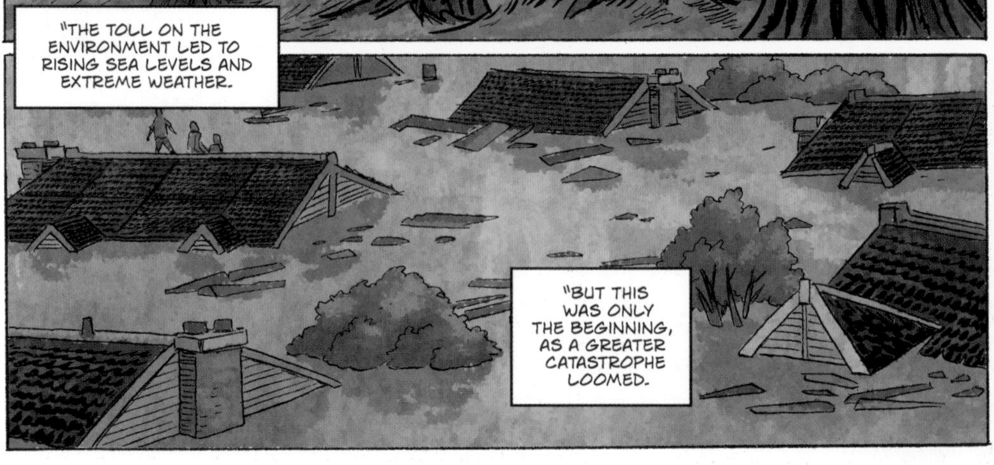
"THE TOLL ON THE ENVIRONMENT LED TO RISING SEA LEVELS AND EXTREME WEATHER.
"BUT THIS WAS ONLY THE BEGINNING, AS A GREATER CATASTROPHE LOOMED.

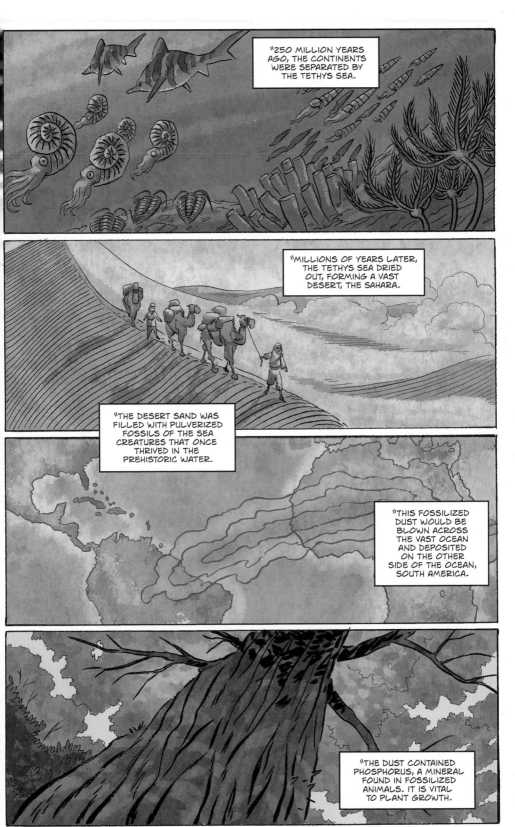

"250 MILLION YEARS AGO, THE CONTINENTS WERE SEPARATED BY THE TETHYS SEA.

"MILLIONS OF YEARS LATER, THE TETHYS SEA DRIED OUT, FORMING A VAST DESERT, THE SAHARA.

"THE DESERT SAND WAS FILLED WITH PULVERIZED FOSSILS OF THE SEA CREATURES THAT ONCE THRIVED IN THE PREHISTORIC WATER.

"THIS FOSSILIZED DUST WOULD BE BLOWN ACROSS THE VAST OCEAN AND DEPOSITED ON THE OTHER SIDE OF THE OCEAN, SOUTH AMERICA.

"THE DUST CONTAINED PHOSPHORUS, A MINERAL FOUND IN FOSSILIZED ANIMALS. IT IS VITAL TO PLANT GROWTH.

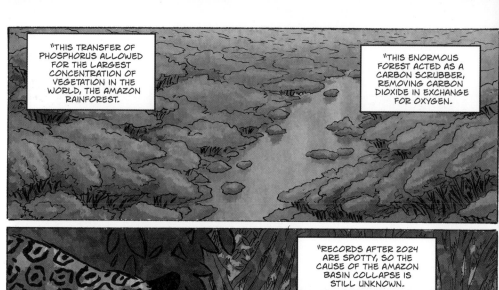

"THIS TRANSFER OF PHOSPHORUS ALLOWED FOR THE LARGEST CONCENTRATION OF VEGETATION IN THE WORLD, THE AMAZON RAINFOREST.

"THIS ENORMOUS FOREST ACTED AS A CARBON SCRUBBER, REMOVING CARBON DIOXIDE IN EXCHANGE FOR OXYGEN.

"RECORDS AFTER 2024 ARE SPOTTY, SO THE CAUSE OF THE AMAZON BASIN COLLAPSE IS STILL UNKNOWN.

"SCIENTISTS ARE UNSURE WHETHER IT WAS A CHANGE IN WEATHER PATTERNS OR IF THE LAYER OF FOSSILIZED DUST WAS DEPLETED, BUT THE RAINFOREST COLLAPSED IN LESS THAN A DECADE.

"THE LOSS OF THE AMAZON CAUSED CARBON DIOXIDE RATES IN THE ATMOSHPERE TO SKYROCKET. COMBINED WITH MAN-MADE CARBON, THIS HAD RIPPLE EFFECTS ALL OVER THE GLOBE.

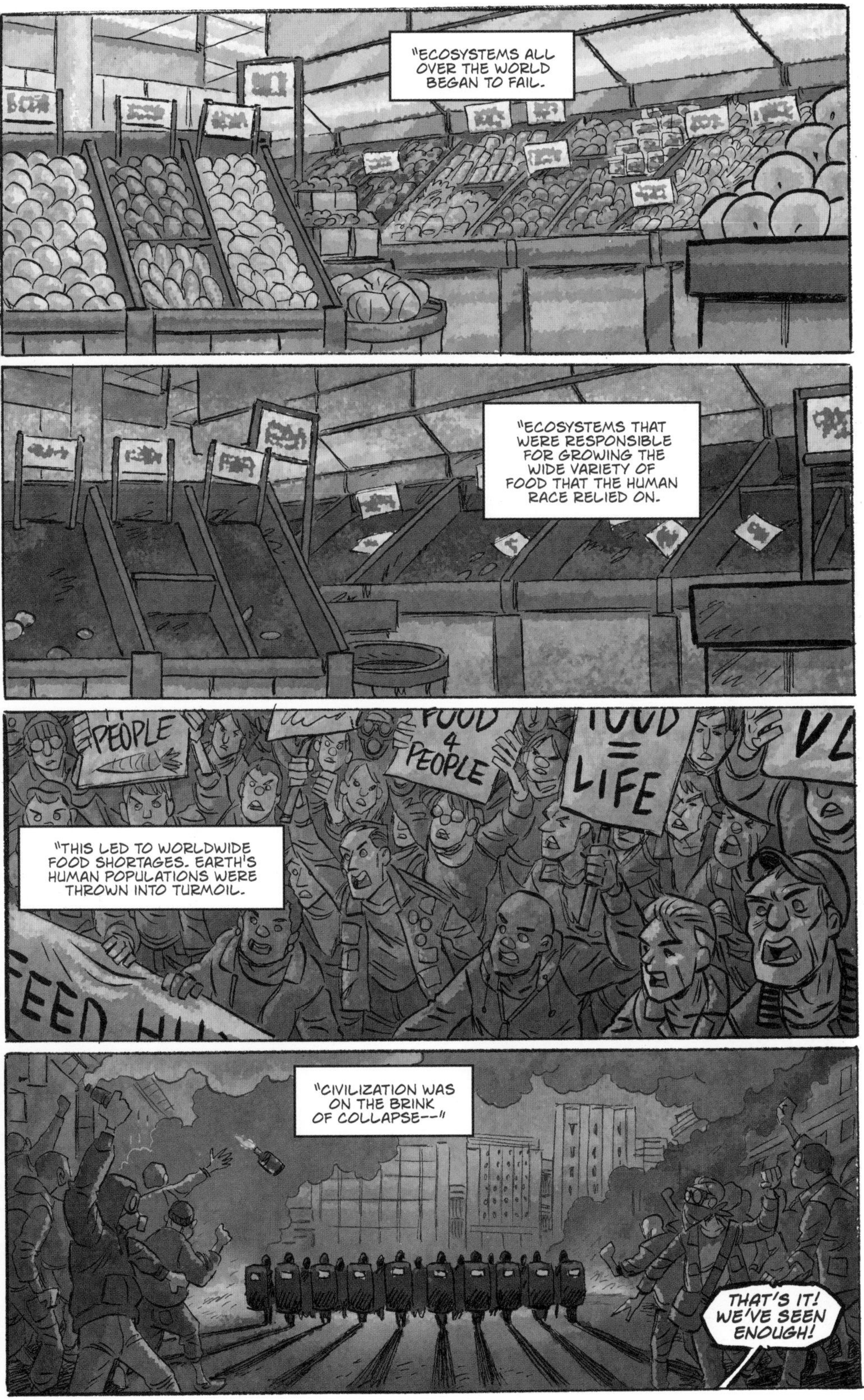
"ECOSYSTEMS ALL OVER THE WORLD BEGAN TO FAIL.
"ECOSYSTEMS THAT WERE RESPONSIBLE FOR GROWING THE WIDE VARIETY OF FOOD THAT THE HUMAN RACE RELIED ON.
PEOPLE
4 PEOPLE
= LIFE
"THIS LED TO WORLDWIDE FOOD SHORTAGES. EARTH'S HUMAN POPULATIONS WERE THROWN INTO TURMOIL.
"CIVILIZATION WAS ON THE BRINK OF COLLAPSE--"
THAT'S IT! WE'VE SEEN ENOUGH!

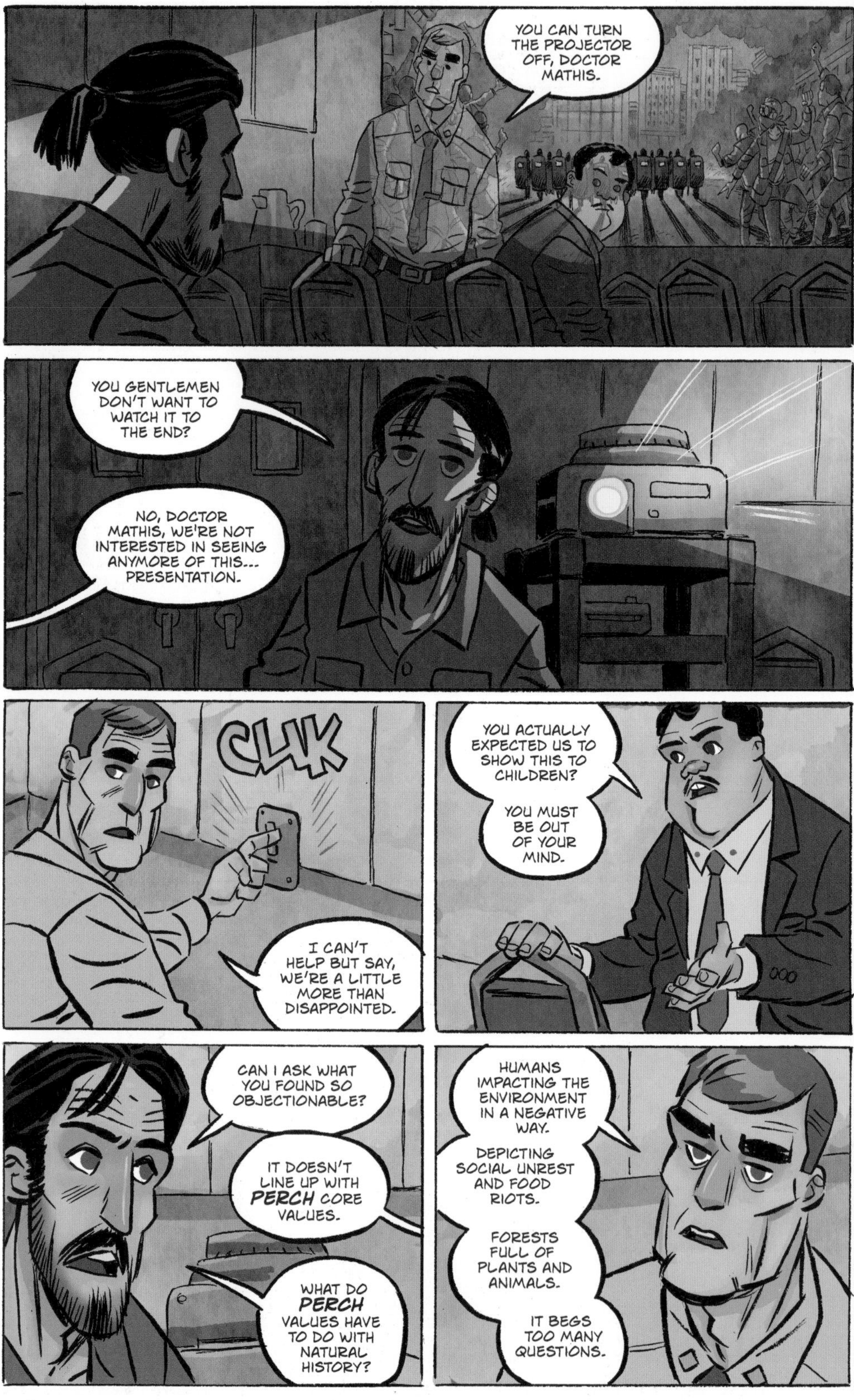
YOU CAN TURN THE PROJECTOR OFF, DOCTOR MATHIS.
YOU GENTLEMEN DON'T WANT TO WATCH IT TO THE END?
NO, DOCTOR MATHIS, WE'RE NOT INTERESTED IN SEEING ANYMORE OF THIS... PRESENTATION.
CLIK
I CAN'T HELP BUT SAY, WE'RE A LITTLE MORE THAN DISAPPOINTED.
YOU ACTUALLY EXPECTED US TO SHOW THIS TO CHILDREN?
YOU MUST BE OUT OF YOUR MIND.
CAN I ASK WHAT YOU FOUND SO OBJECTIONABLE?
IT DOESN'T LINE UP WITH PERCH CORE VALUES.
WHAT DO PERCH VALUES HAVE TO DO WITH NATURAL HISTORY?
HUMANS IMPACTING THE ENVIRONMENT IN A NEGATIVE WAY.
DEPICTING SOCIAL UNREST AND FOOD RIOTS.
FORESTS FULL OF PLANTS AND ANIMALS.
IT BEGS TOO MANY QUESTIONS.

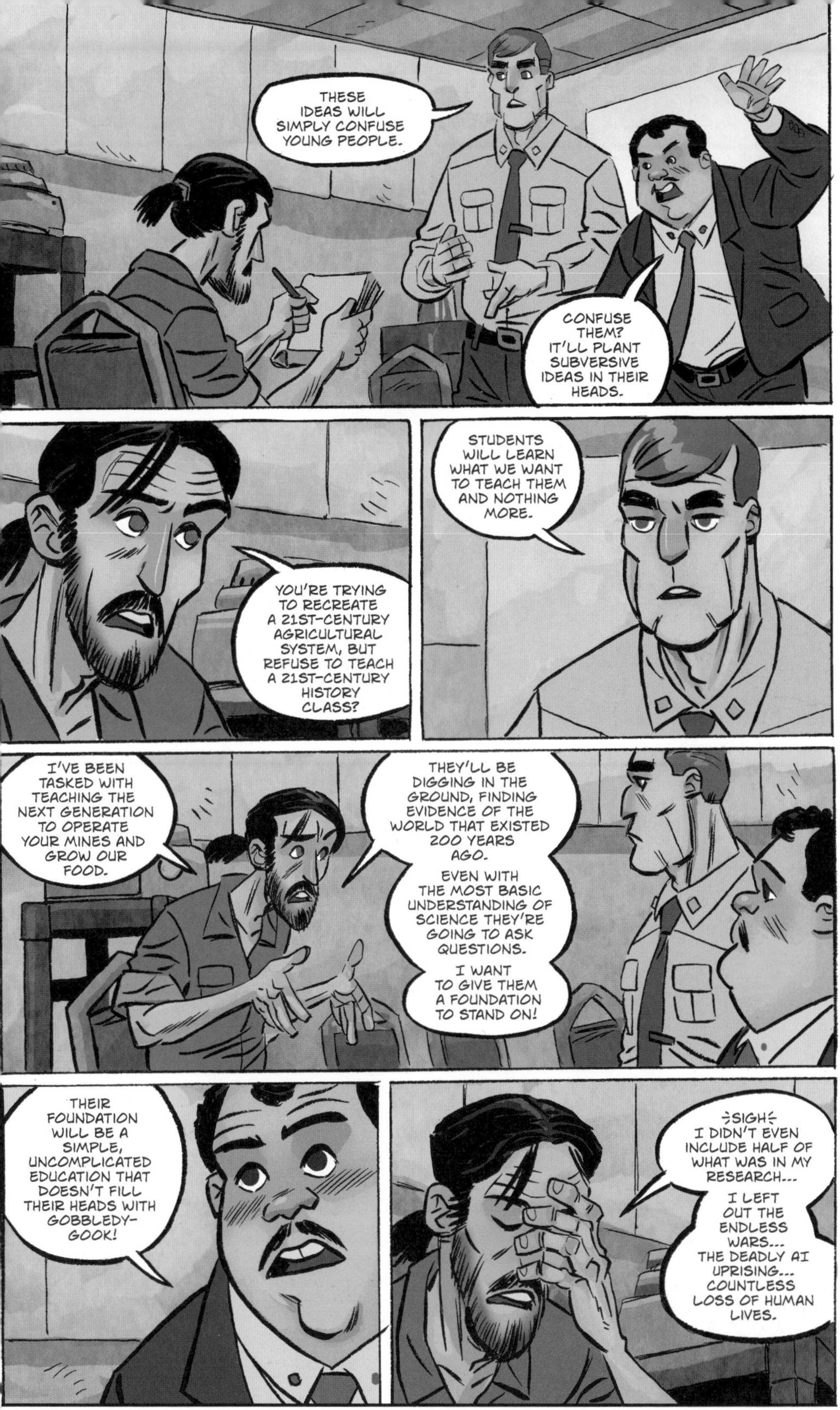
THESE IDEAS WILL SIMPLY CONFUSE YOUNG PEOPLE.
CONFUSE THEM? IT'LL PLANT SUBVERSIVE IDEAS IN THEIR HEADS.
YOU'RE TRYING TO RECREATE A 21ST-CENTURY AGRICULTURAL SYSTEM, BUT REFUSE TO TEACH A 21ST-CENTURY HISTORY CLASS?
STUDENTS WILL LEARN WHAT WE WANT TO TEACH THEM AND NOTHING MORE.
I'VE BEEN TASKED WITH TEACHING THE NEXT GENERATION TO OPERATE YOUR MINES AND GROW OUR FOOD.
THEY'LL BE DIGGING IN THE GROUND, FINDING EVIDENCE OF THE WORLD THAT EXISTED 200 YEARS AGO.
EVEN WITH THE MOST BASIC UNDERSTANDING OF SCIENCE THEY'RE GOING TO ASK QUESTIONS.
I WANT TO GIVE THEM A FOUNDATION TO STAND ON!
THEIR FOUNDATION WILL BE A SIMPLE, UNCOMPLICATED EDUCATION THAT DOESN'T FILL THEIR HEADS WITH GOBBLEDY-GOOK!
SIGH
I DIDN'T EVEN INCLUDE HALF OF WHAT WAS IN MY RESEARCH...
I LEFT OUT THE ENDLESS WARS... THE DEADLY AI UPRISING... COUNTLESS LOSS OF HUMAN LIVES.

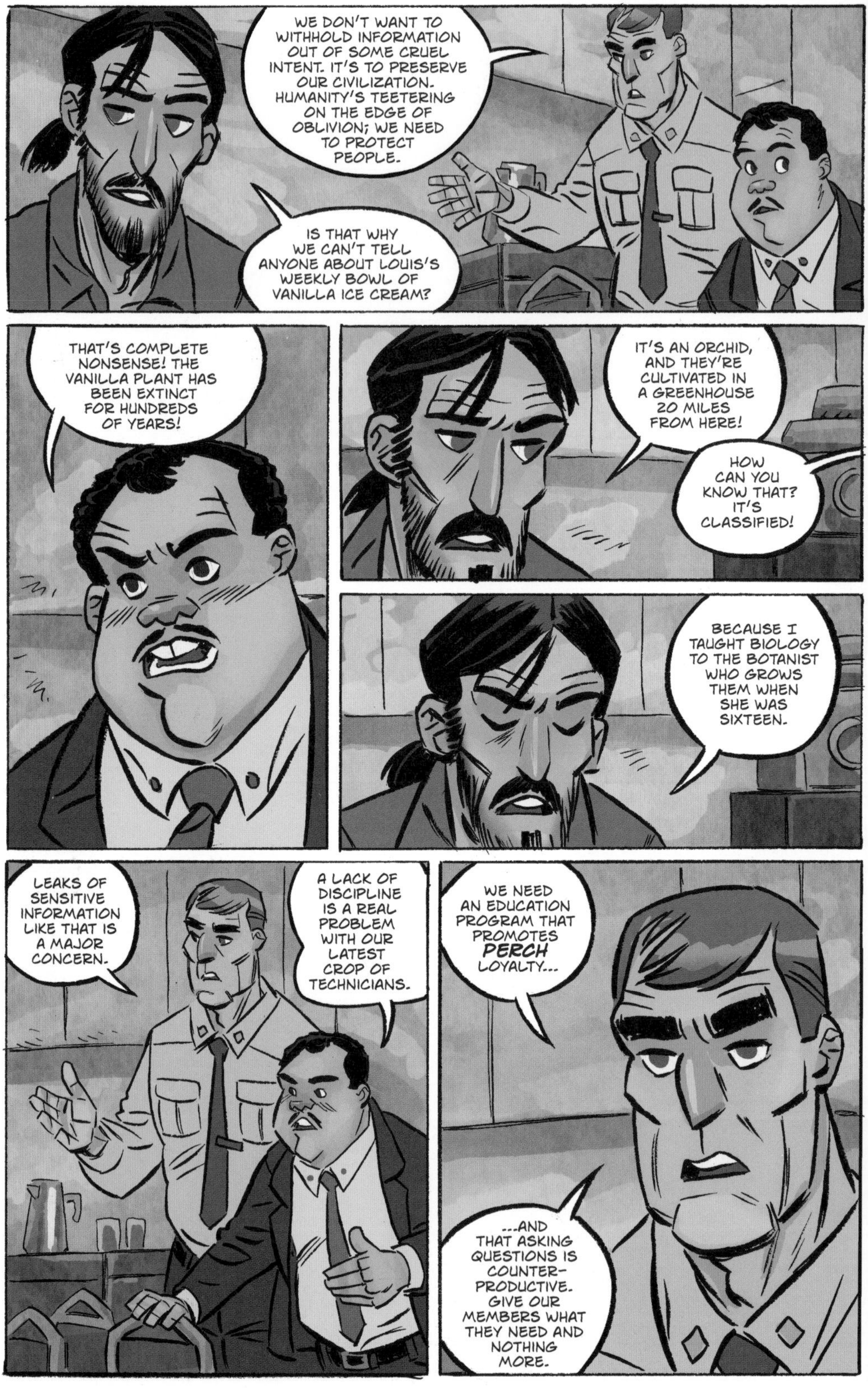
WE DON'T WANT TO WITHHOLD INFORMATION OUT OF SOME CRUEL INTENT. IT'S TO PRESERVE OUR CIVILIZATION. HUMANITY'S TEETERING ON THE EDGE OF OBLIVION; WE NEED TO PROTECT PEOPLE.
IS THAT WHY WE CAN'T TELL ANYONE ABOUT LOUIS'S WEEKLY BOWL OF VANILLA ICE CREAM?
THAT'S COMPLETE NONSENSE! THE VANILLA PLANT HAS BEEN EXTINCT FOR HUNDREDS OF YEARS!
IT'S AN ORCHID, AND THEY'RE CULTIVATED IN A GREENHOUSE 20 MILES FROM HERE!
HOW CAN YOU KNOW THAT? IT'S CLASSIFIED!
BECAUSE I TAUGHT BIOLOGY TO THE BOTANIST WHO GROWS THEM WHEN SHE WAS SIXTEEN.
LEAKS OF SENSITIVE INFORMATION LIKE THAT IS A MAJOR CONCERN.
A LACK OF DISCIPLINE IS A REAL PROBLEM WITH OUR LATEST CROP OF TECHNICIANS.
WE NEED AN EDUCATION PROGRAM THAT PROMOTES **PERCH** LOYALTY...
...AND THAT ASKING QUESTIONS IS COUNTER-PRODUCTIVE. GIVE OUR MEMBERS WHAT THEY NEED AND NOTHING MORE.

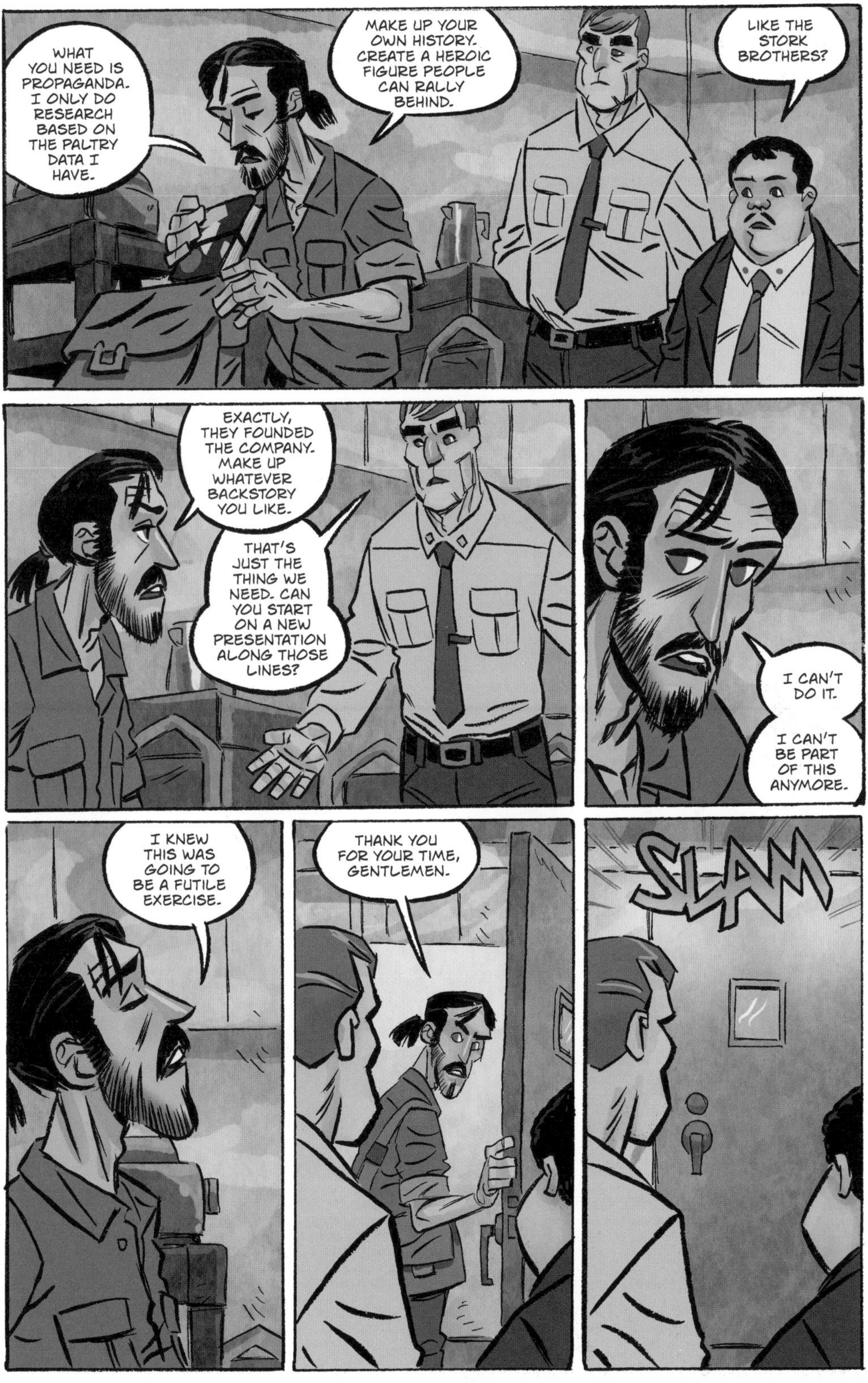
WHAT YOU NEED IS PROPAGANDA. I ONLY DO RESEARCH BASED ON THE PALTRY DATA I HAVE.
MAKE UP YOUR OWN HISTORY. CREATE A HEROIC FIGURE PEOPLE CAN RALLY BEHIND.
LIKE THE STORK BROTHERS?
EXACTLY, THEY FOUNDED THE COMPANY. MAKE UP WHATEVER BACKSTORY YOU LIKE.
THAT'S JUST THE THING WE NEED. CAN YOU START ON A NEW PRESENTATION ALONG THOSE LINES?
I CAN'T DO IT.
I CAN'T BE PART OF THIS ANYMORE.
I KNEW THIS WAS GOING TO BE A FUTILE EXERCISE.
THANK YOU FOR YOUR TIME, GENTLEMEN.
SLAM

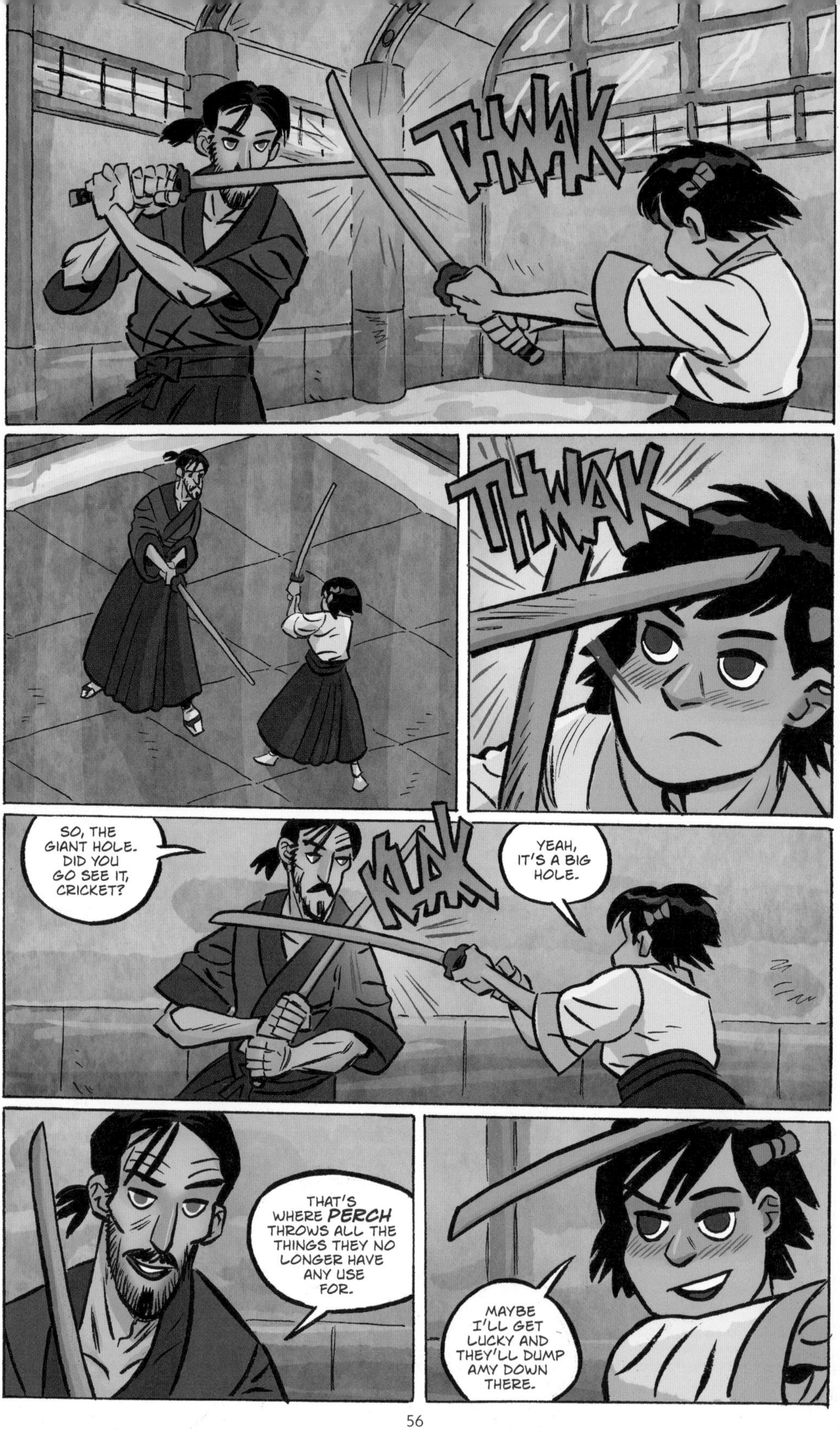
THWAK
THWAK
SO, THE GIANT HOLE. DID YOU GO SEE IT, CRICKET?
KLAK
YEAH, IT'S A BIG HOLE.
THAT'S WHERE PERCH THROWS ALL THE THINGS THEY NO LONGER HAVE ANY USE FOR.
MAYBE I'LL GET LUCKY AND THEY'LL DUMP AMY DOWN THERE.

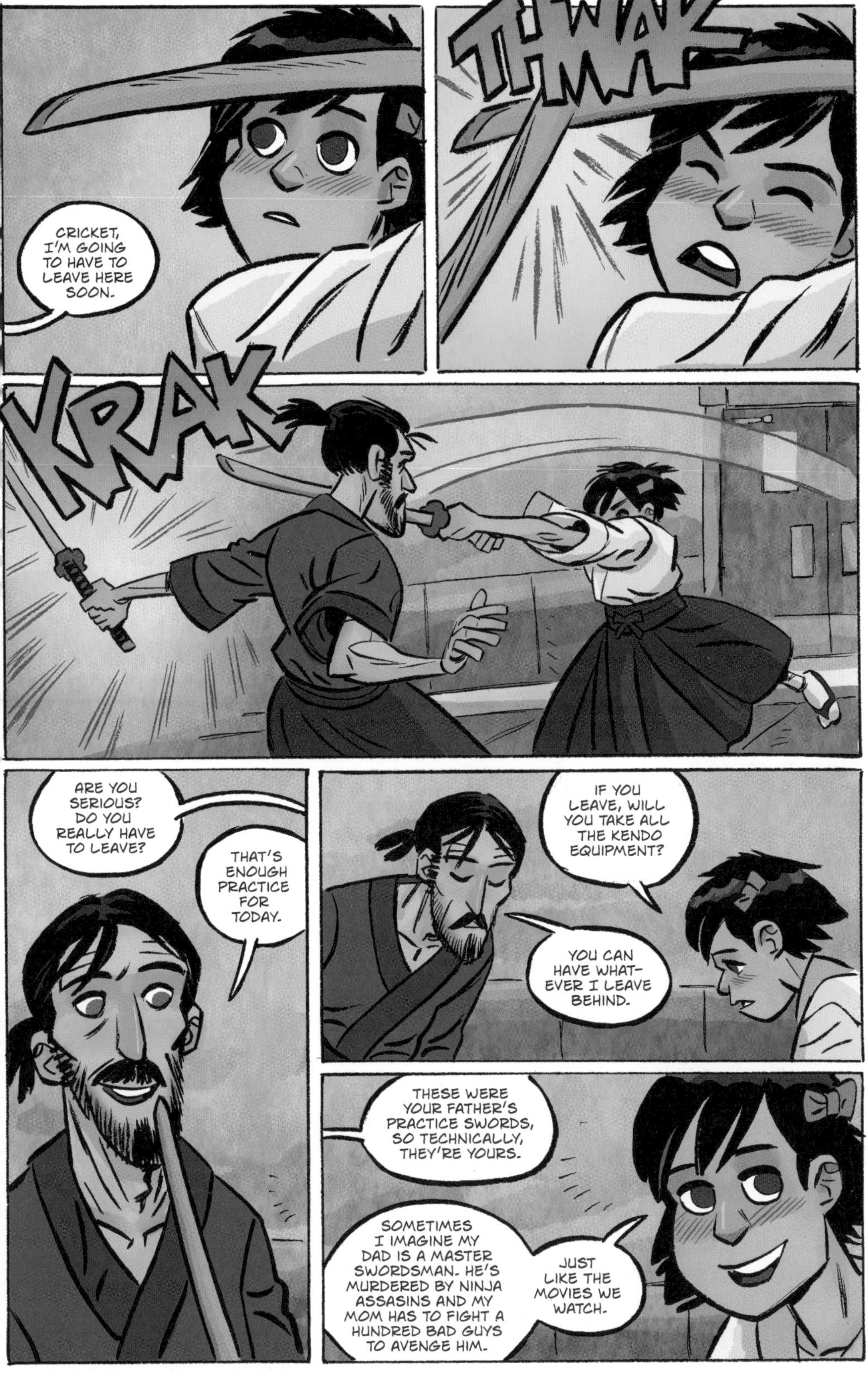
CRICKET, I'M GOING TO HAVE TO LEAVE HERE SOON.
THWAK
KRAK
ARE YOU SERIOUS? DO YOU REALLY HAVE TO LEAVE?
THAT'S ENOUGH PRACTICE FOR TODAY.
IF YOU LEAVE, WILL YOU TAKE ALL THE KENDO EQUIPMENT?
YOU CAN HAVE WHAT-EVER I LEAVE BEHIND.
THESE WERE YOUR FATHER'S PRACTICE SWORDS, SO TECHNICALLY, THEY'RE YOURS.
SOMETIMES I IMAGINE MY DAD IS A MASTER SWORDSMAN. HE'S MURDERED BY NINJA ASSASINS AND MY MOM HAS TO FIGHT A HUNDRED BAD GUYS TO AVENGE HIM.
JUST LIKE THE MOVIES WE WATCH.

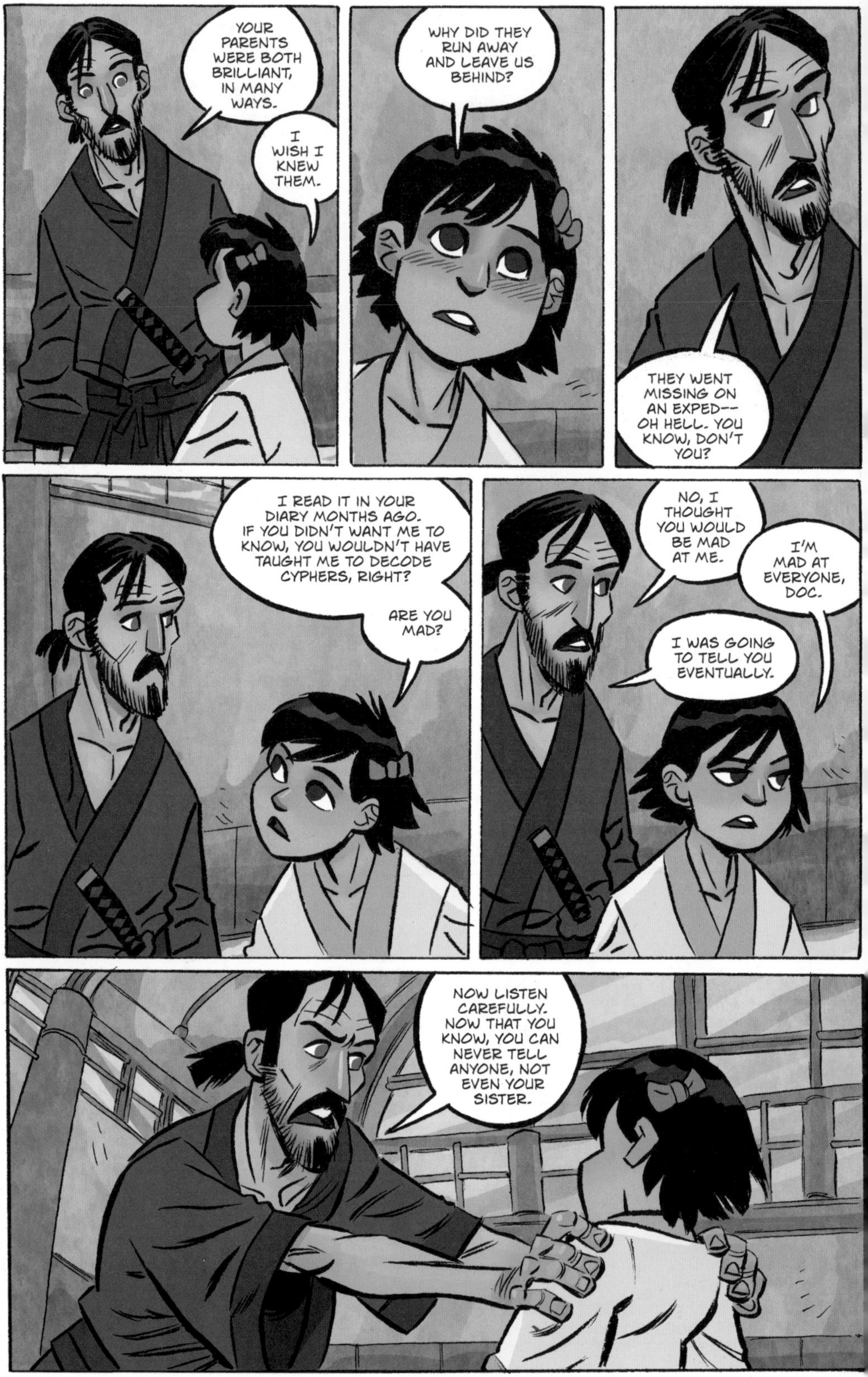
YOUR PARENTS WERE BOTH BRILLIANT, IN MANY WAYS.
I WISH I KNEW THEM.
WHY DID THEY RUN AWAY AND LEAVE US BEHIND?
THEY WENT MISSING ON AN EXPED-- OH HELL. YOU KNOW, DON'T YOU?
I READ IT IN YOUR DIARY MONTHS AGO. IF YOU DIDN'T WANT ME TO KNOW, YOU WOULDN'T HAVE TAUGHT ME TO DECODE CYPHERS, RIGHT?
ARE YOU MAD?
NO, I THOUGHT YOU WOULD BE MAD AT ME.
I'M MAD AT EVERYONE, DOC.
I WAS GOING TO TELL YOU EVENTUALLY.
NOW LISTEN CAREFULLY. NOW THAT YOU KNOW, YOU CAN NEVER TELL ANYONE, NOT EVEN YOUR SISTER.

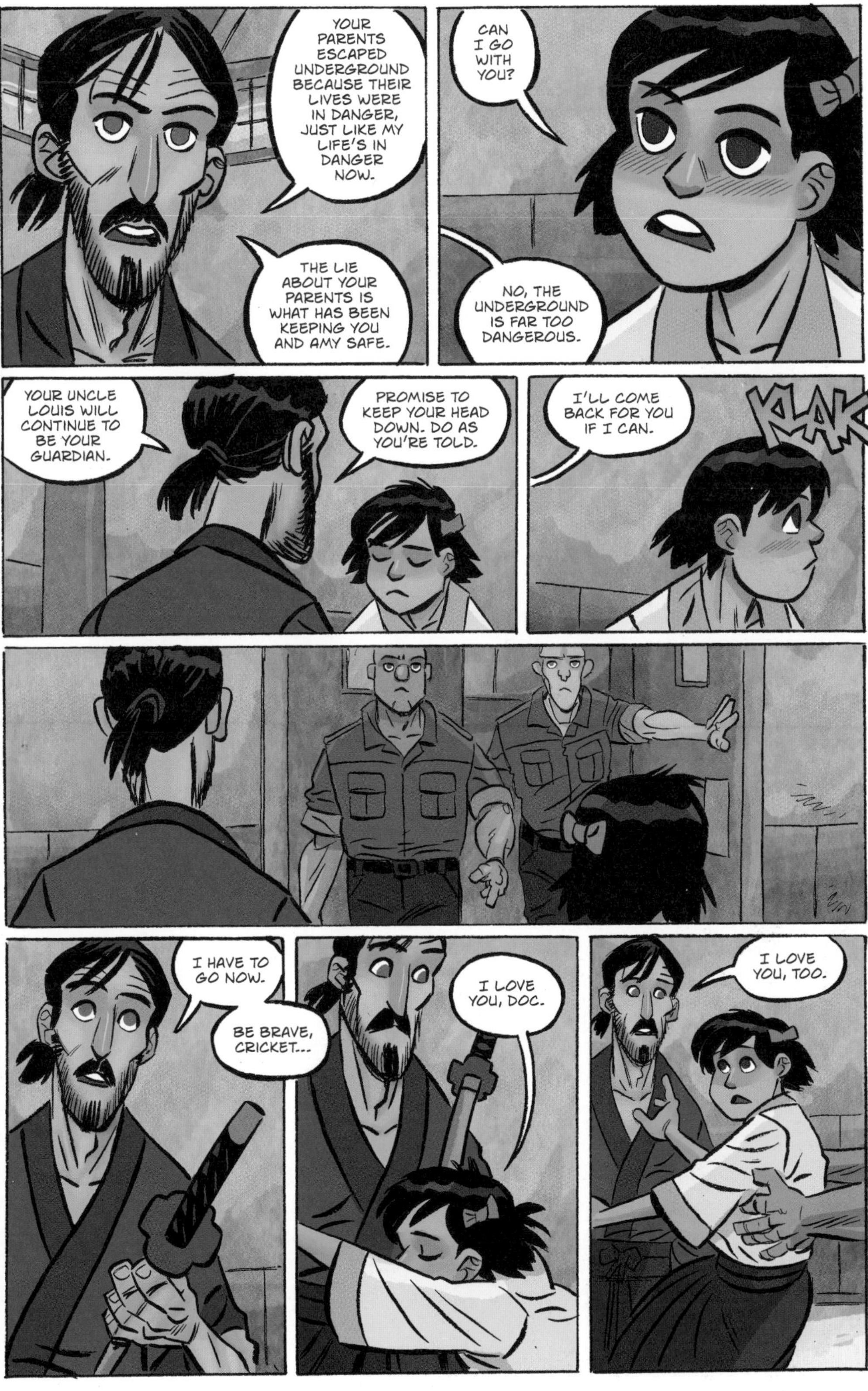

YOUR PARENTS ESCAPED UNDERGROUND BECAUSE THEIR LIVES WERE IN DANGER, JUST LIKE MY LIFE'S IN DANGER NOW.
THE LIE ABOUT YOUR PARENTS IS WHAT HAS BEEN KEEPING YOU AND AMY SAFE.
CAN I GO WITH YOU?
NO, THE UNDERGROUND IS FAR TOO DANGEROUS.
YOUR UNCLE LOUIS WILL CONTINUE TO BE YOUR GUARDIAN.
PROMISE TO KEEP YOUR HEAD DOWN. DO AS YOU'RE TOLD.
I'LL COME BACK FOR YOU IF I CAN.
KLAK
I HAVE TO GO NOW.
BE BRAVE, CRICKET...
I LOVE YOU, DOC.
I LOVE YOU, TOO.

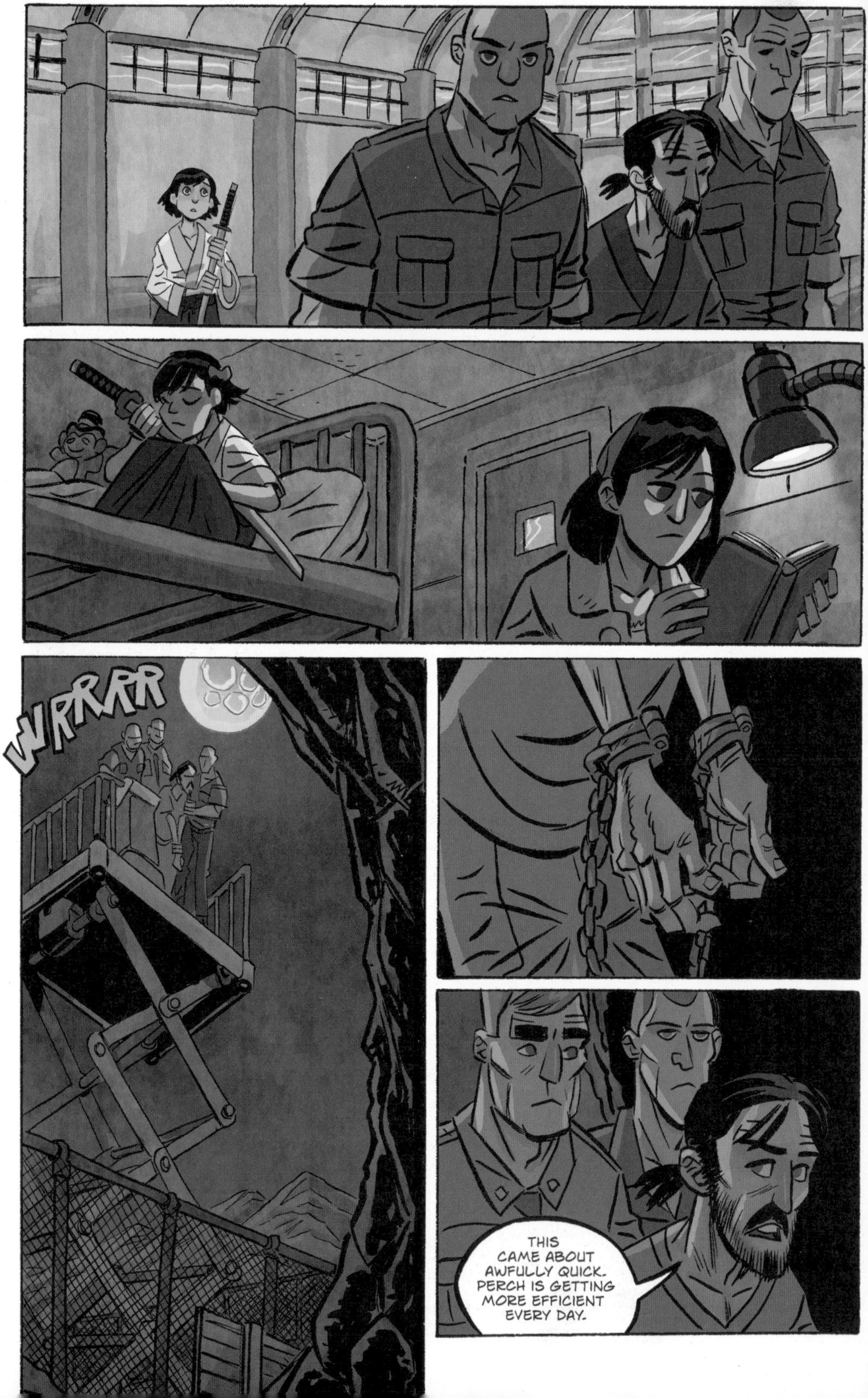
WRRRR
THIS CAME ABOUT AWFULLY QUICK. PERCH IS GETTING MORE EFFICIENT EVERY DAY.

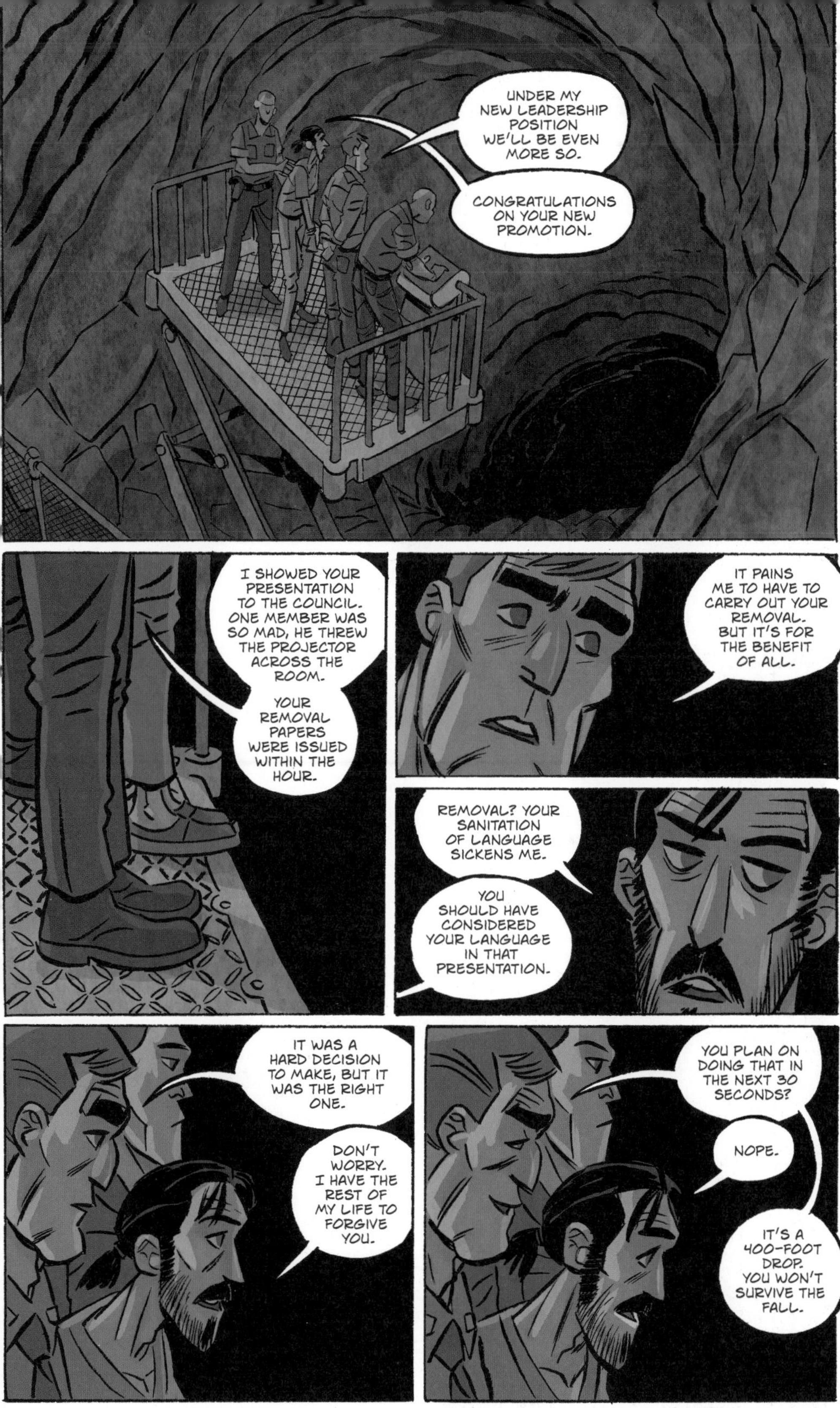
UNDER MY NEW LEADERSHIP POSITION WE'LL BE EVEN MORE SO.
CONGRATULATIONS ON YOUR NEW PROMOTION.
I SHOWED YOUR PRESENTATION TO THE COUNCIL. ONE MEMBER WAS SO MAD, HE THREW THE PROJECTOR ACROSS THE ROOM.
YOUR REMOVAL PAPERS WERE ISSUED WITHIN THE HOUR.
IT PAINS ME TO HAVE TO CARRY OUT YOUR REMOVAL. BUT IT'S FOR THE BENEFIT OF ALL.
REMOVAL? YOUR SANITATION OF LANGUAGE SICKENS ME.
YOU SHOULD HAVE CONSIDERED YOUR LANGUAGE IN THAT PRESENTATION.
IT WAS A HARD DECISION TO MAKE, BUT IT WAS THE RIGHT ONE.
DON'T WORRY. I HAVE THE REST OF MY LIFE TO FORGIVE YOU.
YOU PLAN ON DOING THAT IN THE NEXT 30 SECONDS?
NOPE.
IT'S A 400-FOOT DROP. YOU WON'T SURVIVE THE FALL.

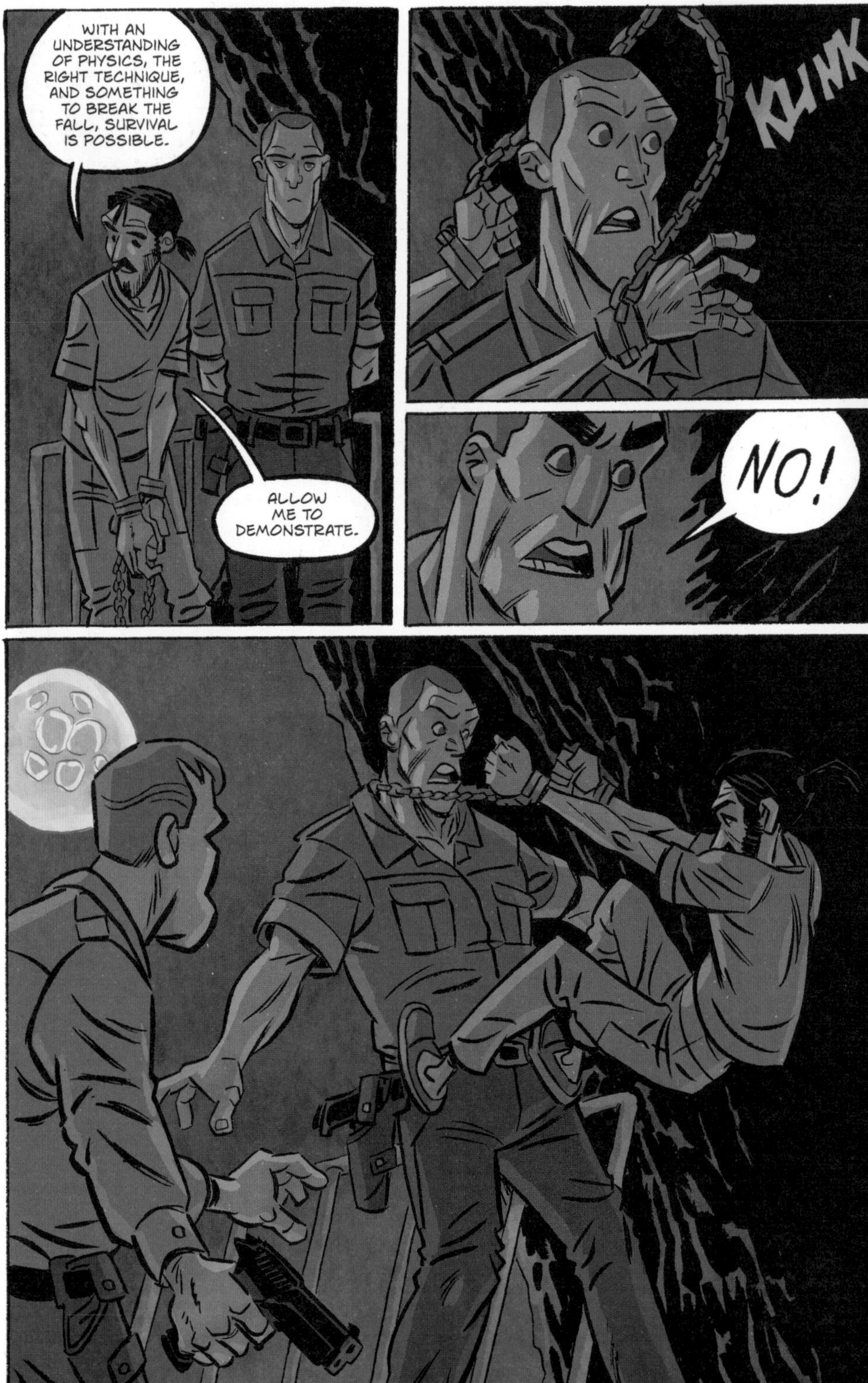
WITH AN UNDERSTANDING OF PHYSICS, THE RIGHT TECHNIQUE, AND SOMETHING TO BREAK THE FALL, SURVIVAL IS POSSIBLE.
ALLOW ME TO DEMONSTRATE.
KLINK
NO!

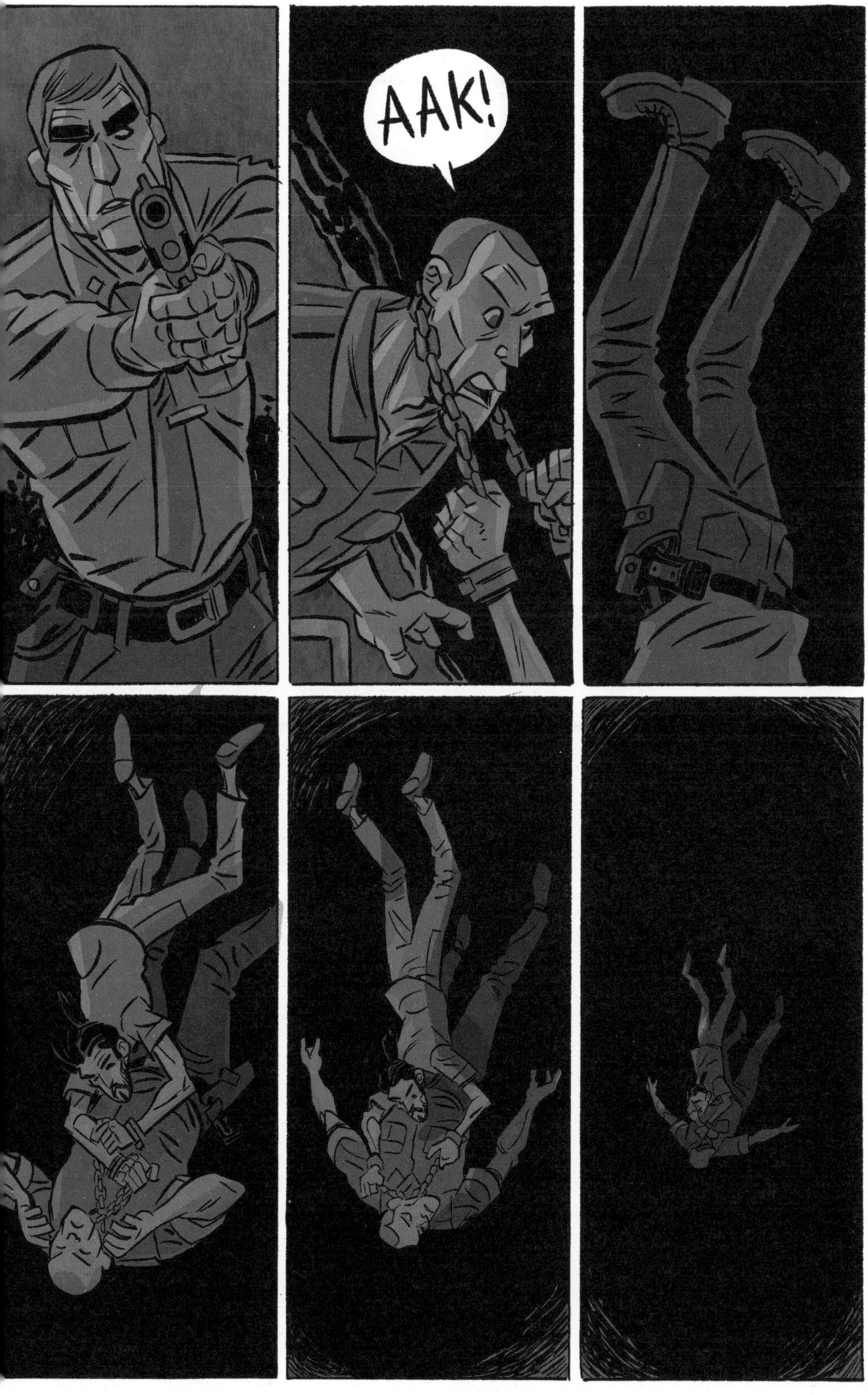
AAK!

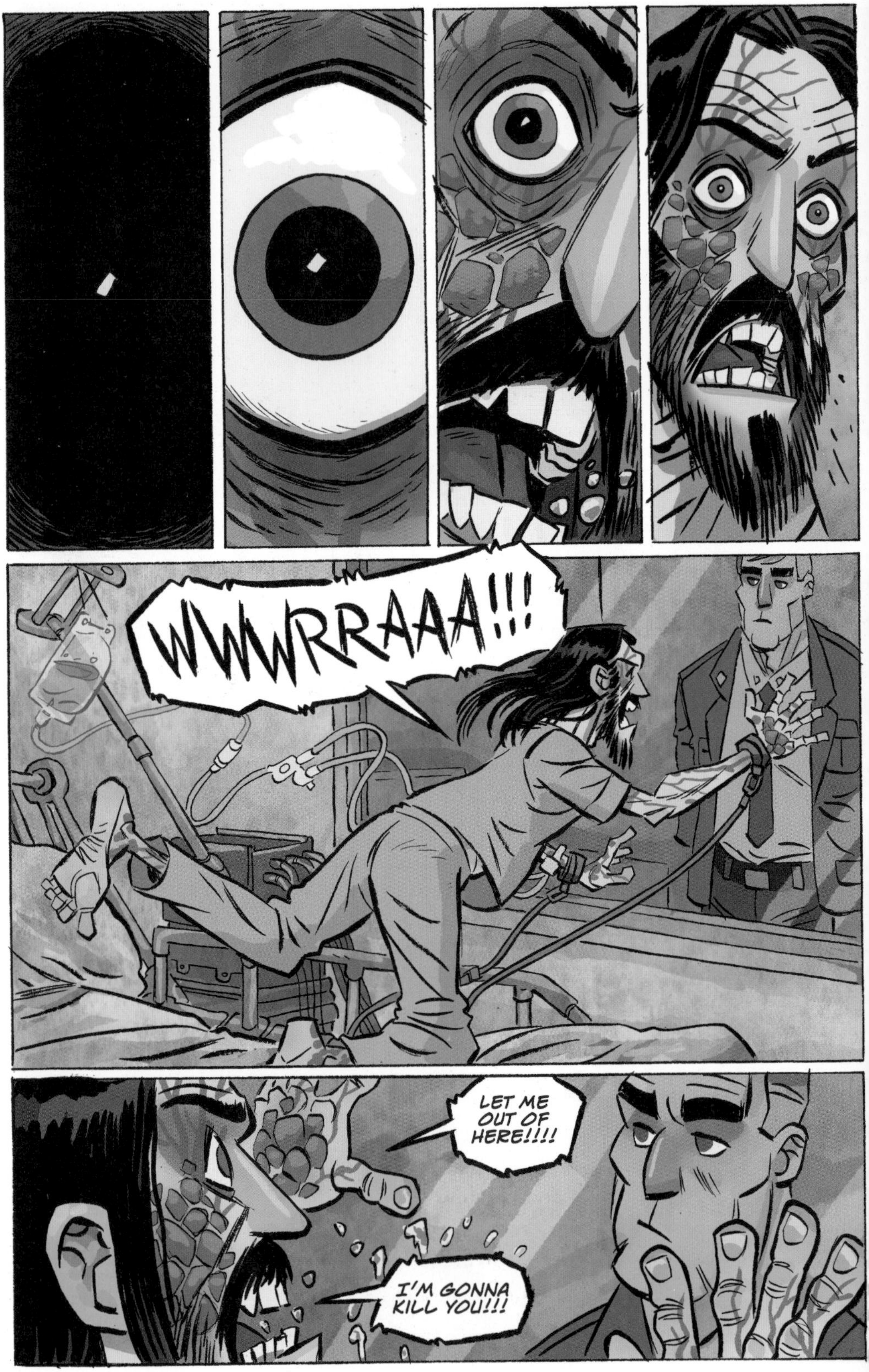
WWWRRAAA!!!
LET ME OUT OF HERE!!!!
I'M GONNA KILL YOU!!!

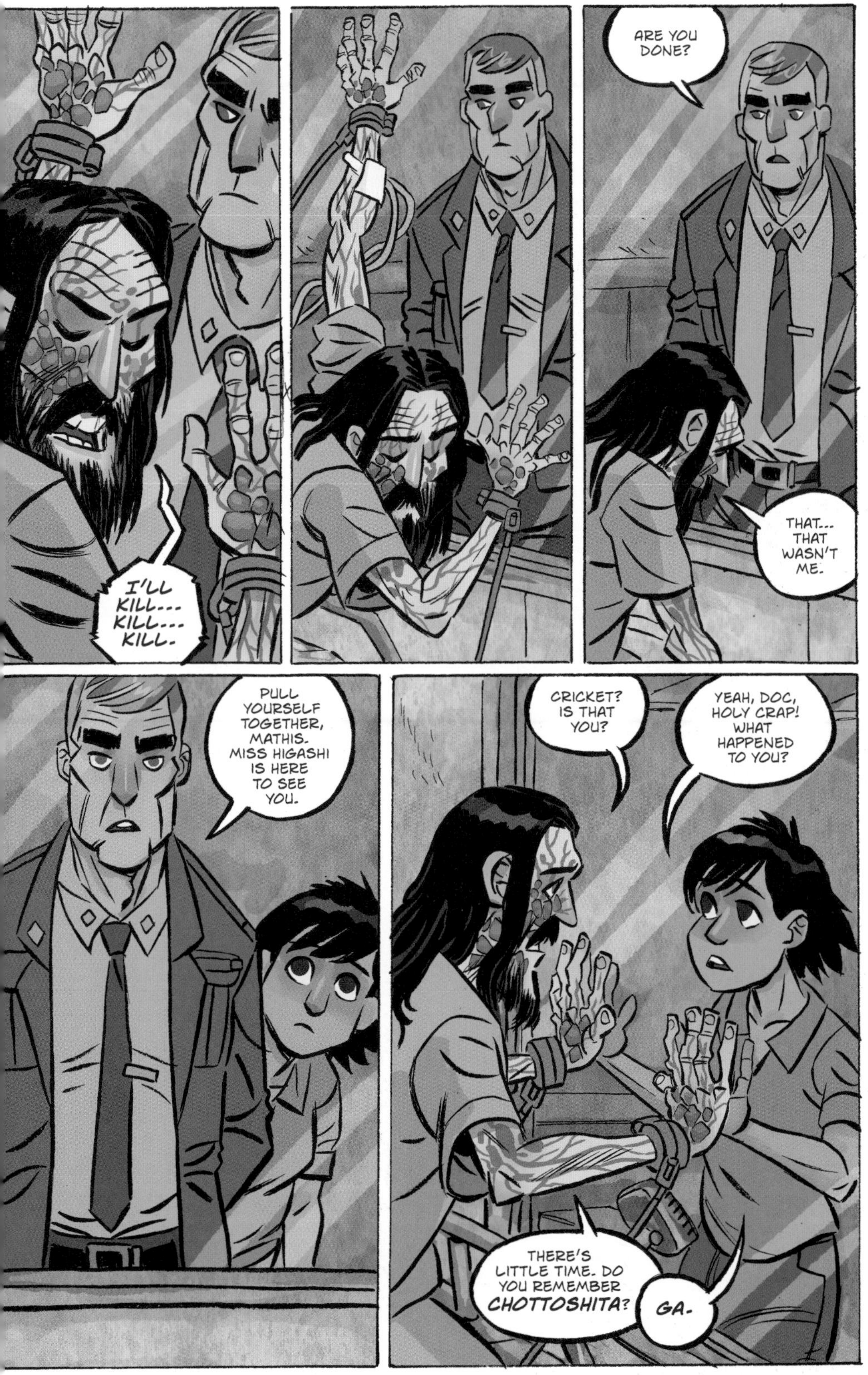
I'LL KILL... KILL... KILL.
ARE YOU DONE?
THAT... THAT WASN'T ME.
PULL YOURSELF TOGETHER, MATHIS. MISS HIGASHI IS HERE TO SEE YOU.
CRICKET? IS THAT YOU?
YEAH, DOC, HOLY CRAP! WHAT HAPPENED TO YOU?
THERE'S LITTLE TIME. DO YOU REMEMBER CHOTTOSHITA?
GA.

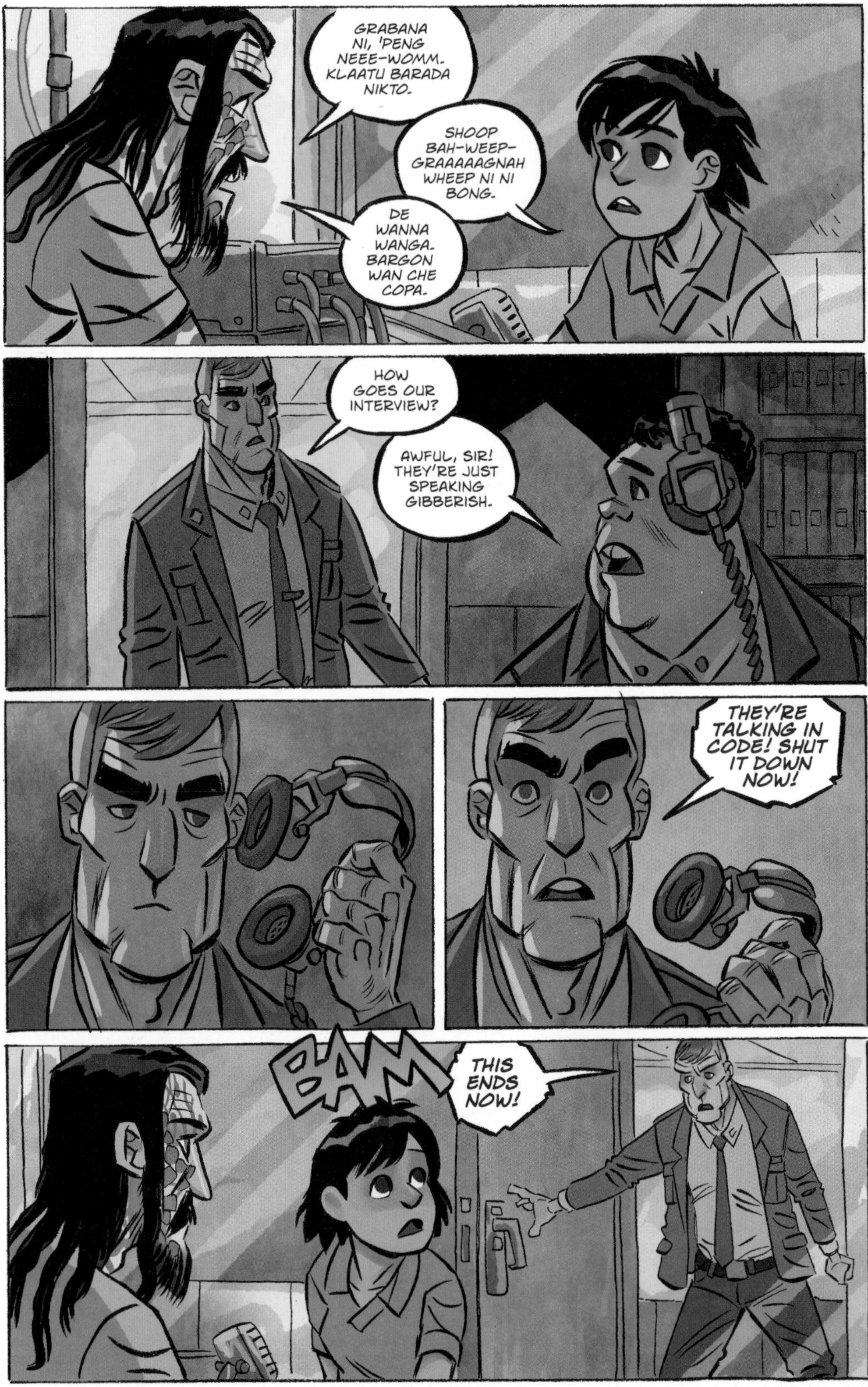
GRABANA NI, 'PENG NEEE-WOMM. KLAATU BARADA NIKTO.
SHOOP BAH-WEEP-GRAAAAAGNAH WHEEP NI NI BONG.
DE WANNA WANGA. BARGON WAN CHE COPA.
HOW GOES OUR INTERVIEW?
AWFUL, SIR! THEY'RE JUST SPEAKING GIBBERISH.
THEY'RE TALKING IN CODE! SHUT IT DOWN NOW!
BAM
THIS ENDS NOW!

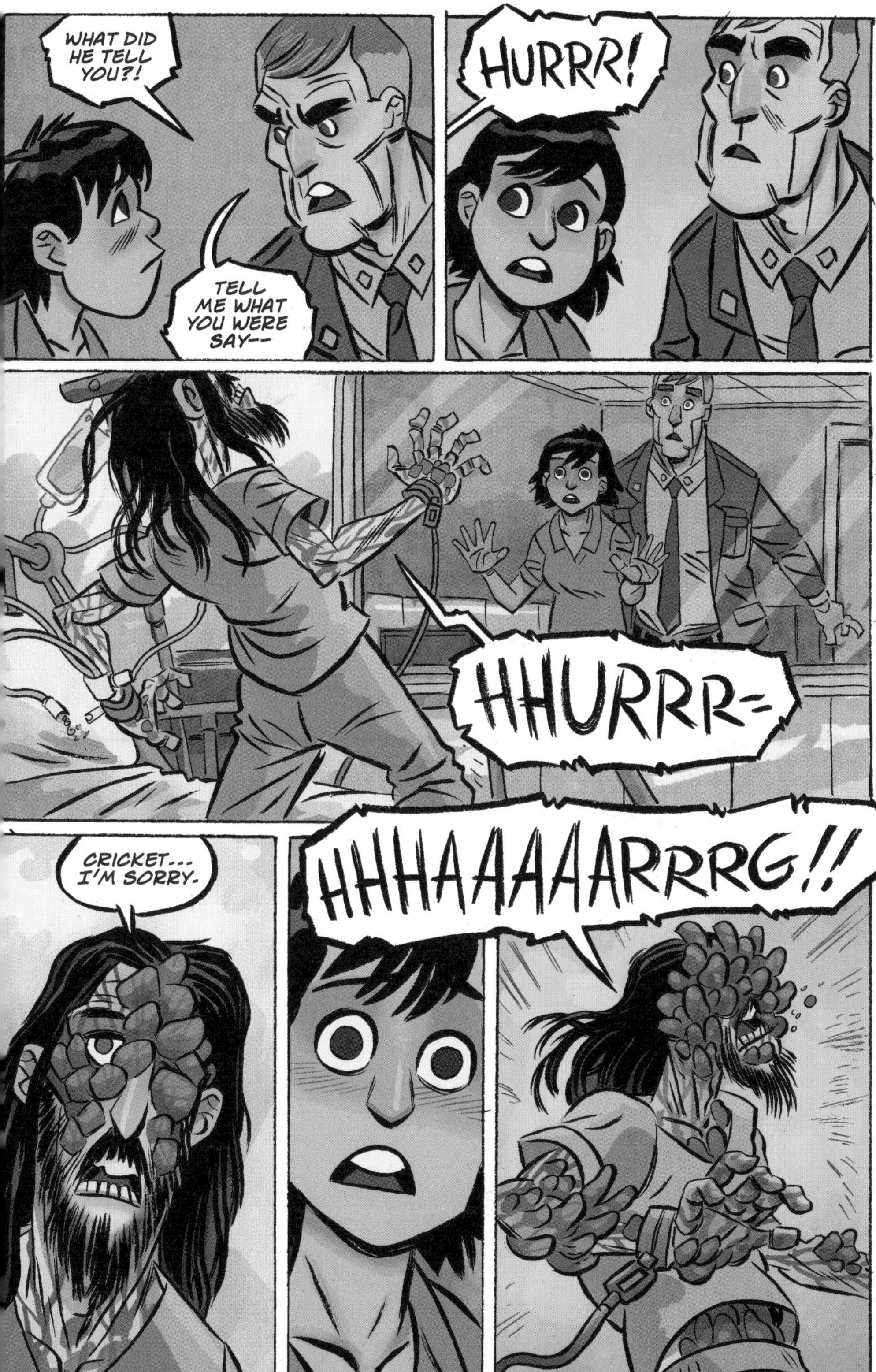
WHAT DID HE TELL YOU?!
TELL ME WHAT YOU WERE SAY--
HURRR!
HHURRR=
CRICKET... I'M SORRY.
HHHAAAAARRRG!!

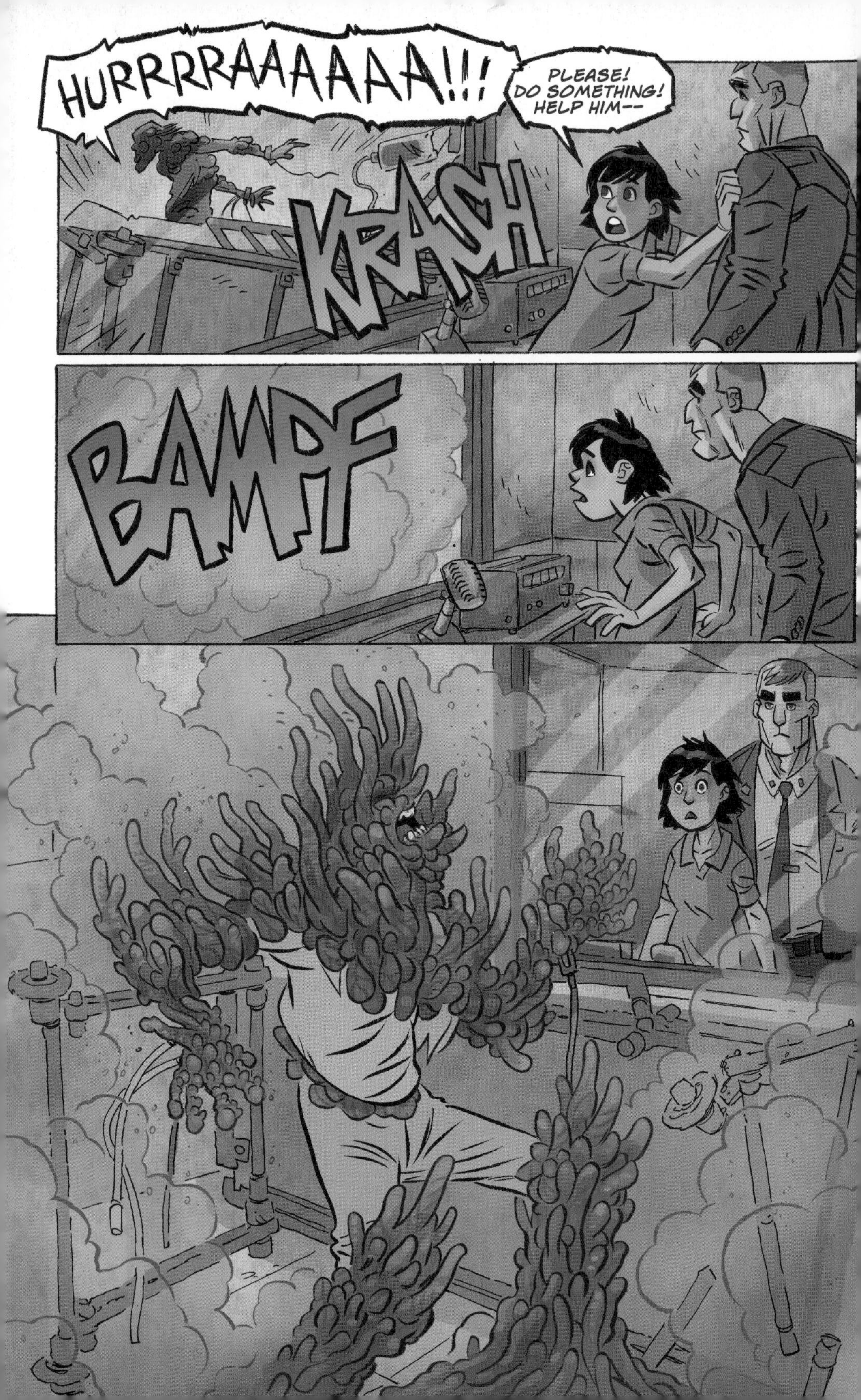
HURRRRAAAAAAA!!!
PLEASE! DO SOMETHING! HELP HIM--
KRASH
BAMPF

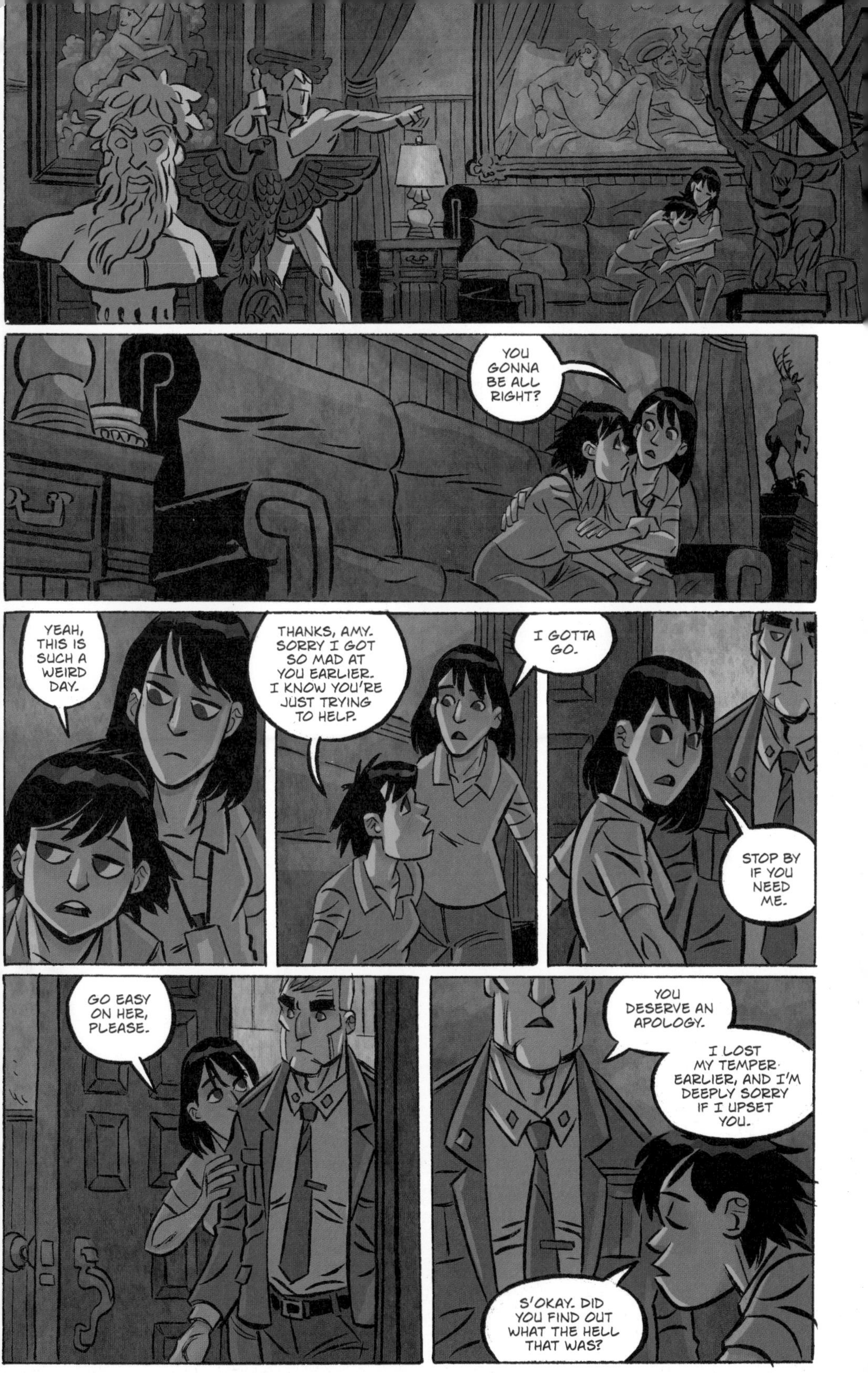
YOU GONNA BE ALL RIGHT?
YEAH, THIS IS SUCH A WEIRD DAY.
THANKS, AMY. SORRY I GOT SO MAD AT YOU EARLIER. I KNOW YOU'RE JUST TRYING TO HELP.
I GOTTA GO.
STOP BY IF YOU NEED ME.
GO EASY ON HER, PLEASE.
YOU DESERVE AN APOLOGY.
I LOST MY TEMPER EARLIER, AND I'M DEEPLY SORRY IF I UPSET YOU.
S'OKAY. DID YOU FIND OUT WHAT THE HELL THAT WAS?

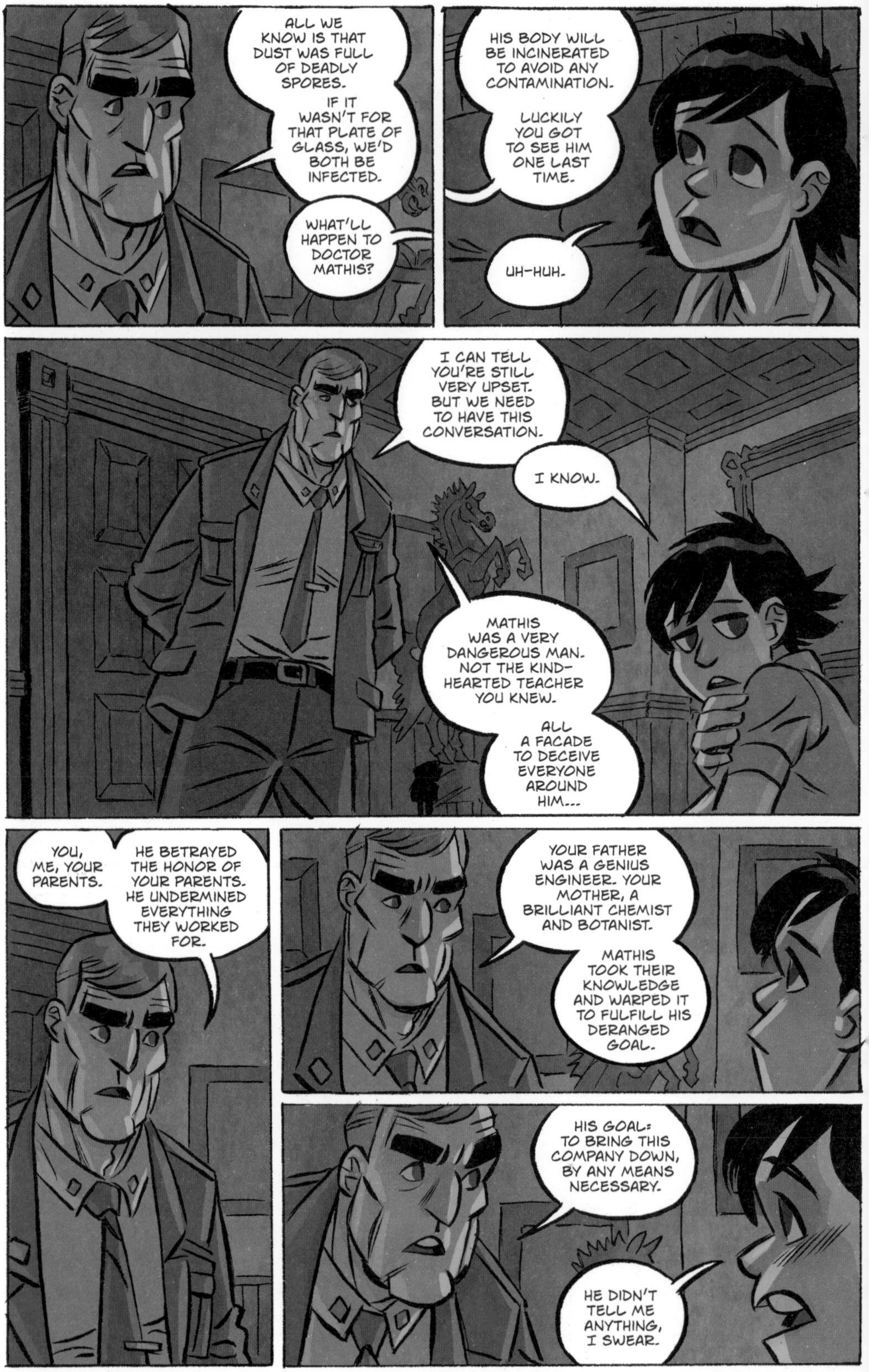
ALL WE KNOW IS THAT DUST WAS FULL OF DEADLY SPORES.
IF IT WASN'T FOR THAT PLATE OF GLASS, WE'D BOTH BE INFECTED.
WHAT'LL HAPPEN TO DOCTOR MATHIS?
HIS BODY WILL BE INCINERATED TO AVOID ANY CONTAMINATION.
LUCKILY YOU GOT TO SEE HIM ONE LAST TIME.
UH-HUH.
I CAN TELL YOU'RE STILL VERY UPSET. BUT WE NEED TO HAVE THIS CONVERSATION.
I KNOW.
MATHIS WAS A VERY DANGEROUS MAN. NOT THE KIND-HEARTED TEACHER YOU KNEW.
ALL A FACADE TO DECEIVE EVERYONE AROUND HIM...
YOU, ME, YOUR PARENTS.
HE BETRAYED THE HONOR OF YOUR PARENTS. HE UNDERMINED EVERYTHING THEY WORKED FOR.
YOUR FATHER WAS A GENIUS ENGINEER. YOUR MOTHER, A BRILLIANT CHEMIST AND BOTANIST.
MATHIS TOOK THEIR KNOWLEDGE AND WARPED IT TO FULFILL HIS DERANGED GOAL.
HIS GOAL: TO BRING THIS COMPANY DOWN, BY ANY MEANS NECESSARY.
HE DIDN'T TELL ME ANYTHING, I SWEAR.

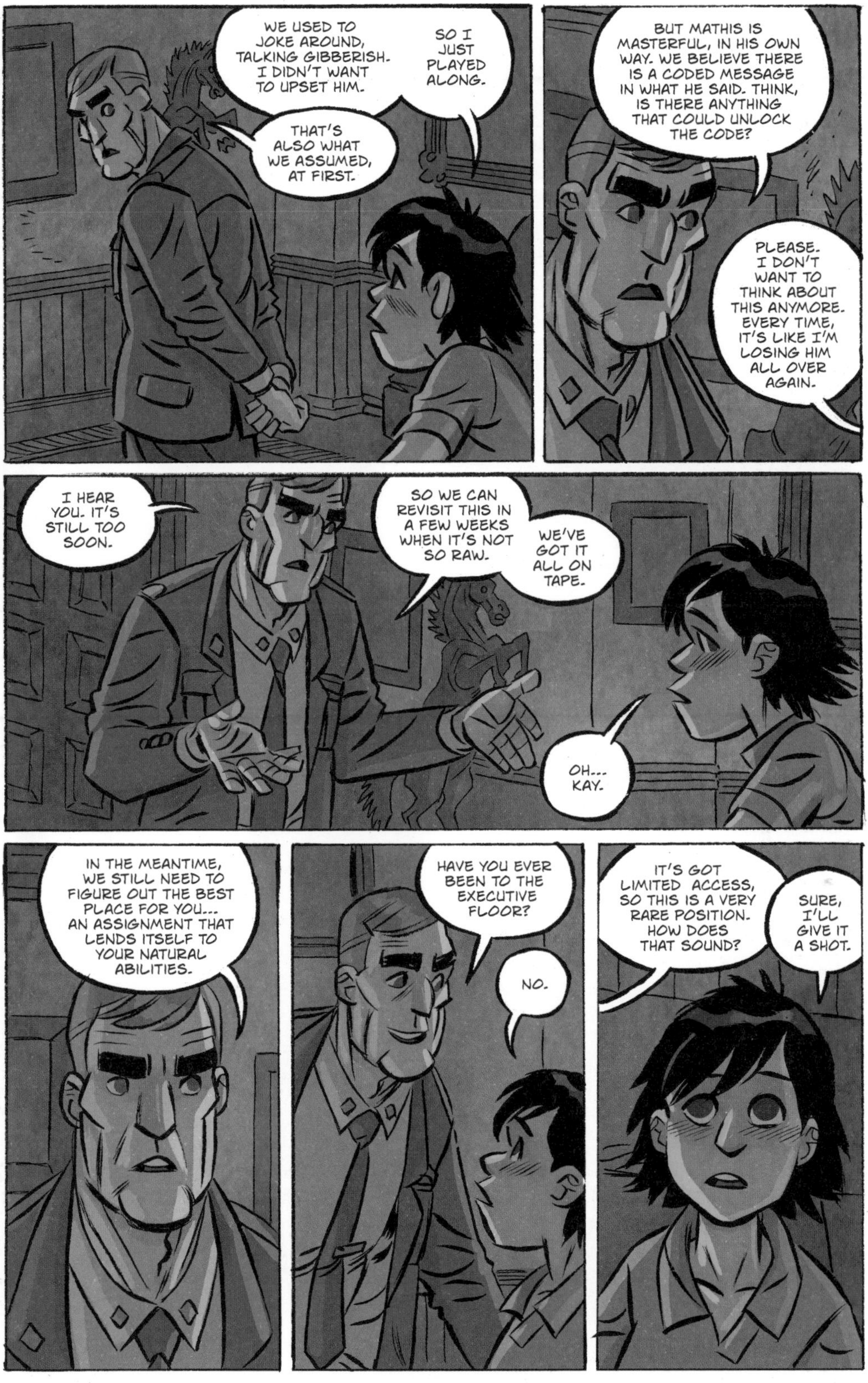
WE USED TO JOKE AROUND, TALKING GIBBERISH. I DIDN'T WANT TO UPSET HIM.
SO I JUST PLAYED ALONG.
THAT'S ALSO WHAT WE ASSUMED, AT FIRST.
BUT MATHIS IS MASTERFUL, IN HIS OWN WAY. WE BELIEVE THERE IS A CODED MESSAGE IN WHAT HE SAID. THINK, IS THERE ANYTHING THAT COULD UNLOCK THE CODE?
PLEASE. I DON'T WANT TO THINK ABOUT THIS ANYMORE. EVERY TIME, IT'S LIKE I'M LOSING HIM ALL OVER AGAIN.
I HEAR YOU. IT'S STILL TOO SOON.
SO WE CAN REVISIT THIS IN A FEW WEEKS WHEN IT'S NOT SO RAW.
WE'VE GOT IT ALL ON TAPE.
OH... KAY.
IN THE MEANTIME, WE STILL NEED TO FIGURE OUT THE BEST PLACE FOR YOU... AN ASSIGNMENT THAT LENDS ITSELF TO YOUR NATURAL ABILITIES.
HAVE YOU EVER BEEN TO THE EXECUTIVE FLOOR?
NO.
IT'S GOT LIMITED ACCESS, SO THIS IS A VERY RARE POSITION. HOW DOES THAT SOUND?
SURE, I'LL GIVE IT A SHOT.

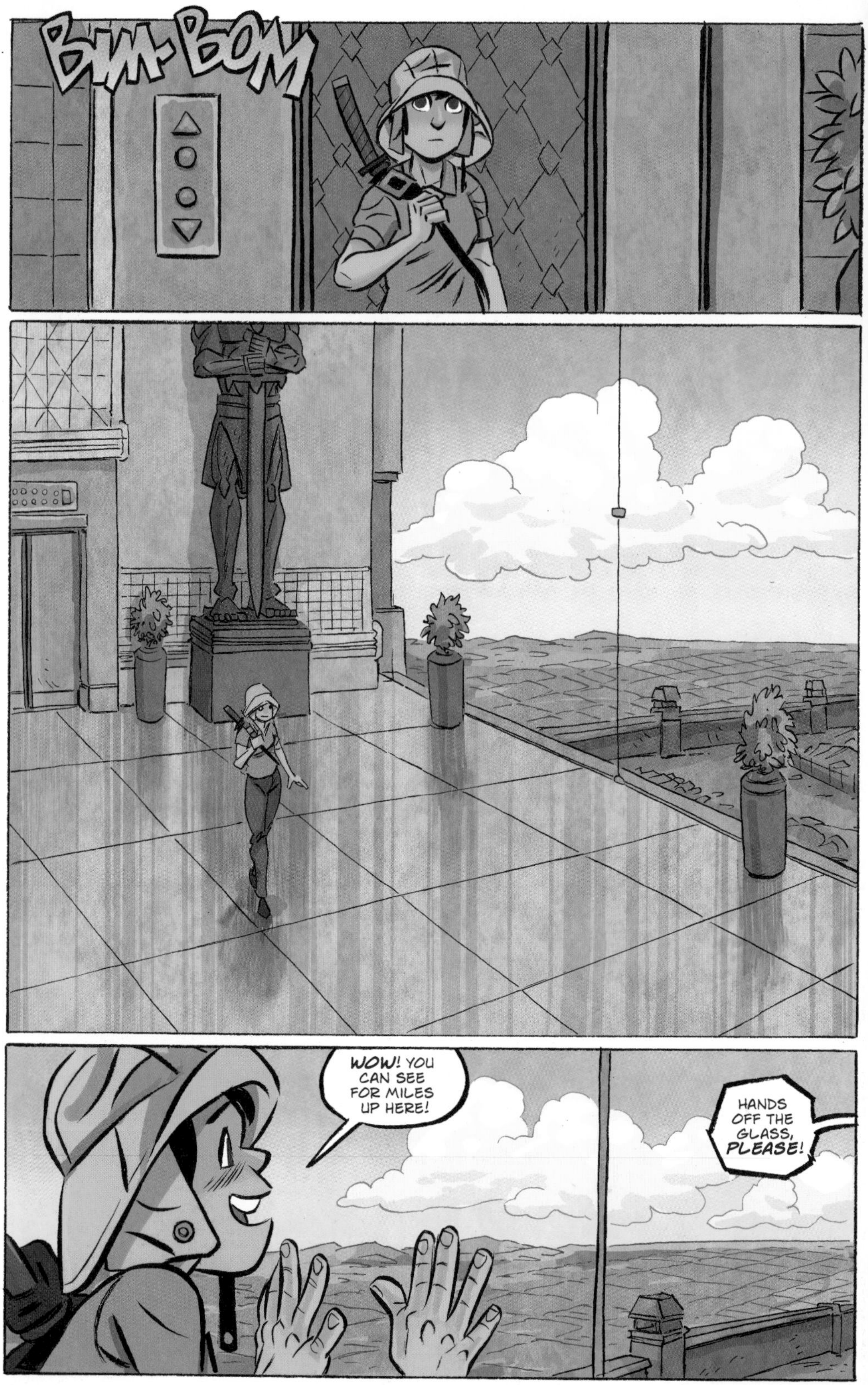
BIM-BOM
WOW! YOU CAN SEE FOR MILES UP HERE!
HANDS OFF THE GLASS, PLEASE!

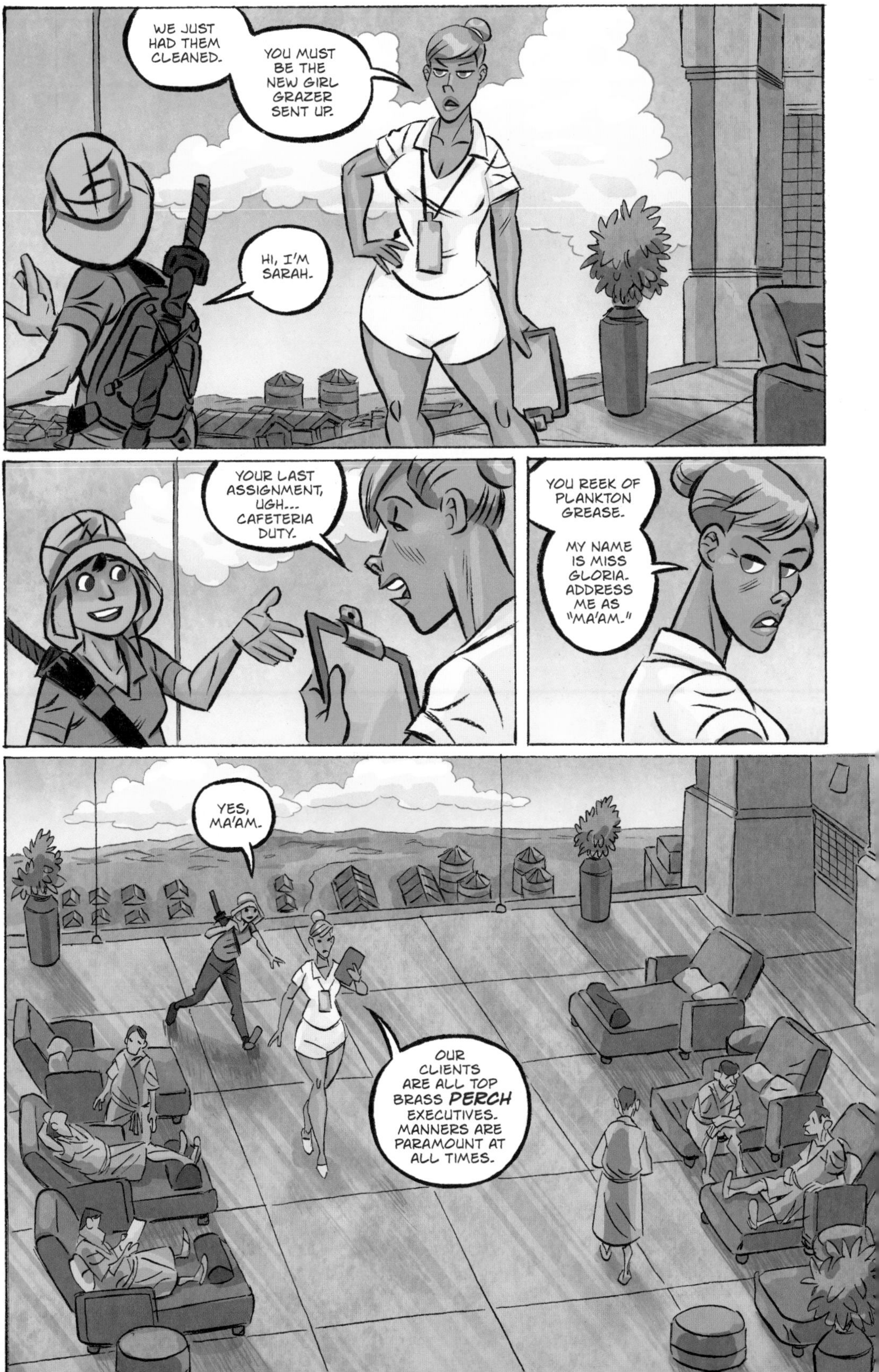
WE JUST HAD THEM CLEANED.
YOU MUST BE THE NEW GIRL GRAZER SENT UP.
HI, I'M SARAH.
YOUR LAST ASSIGNMENT, UGH... CAFETERIA DUTY.
YOU REEK OF PLANKTON GREASE.
MY NAME IS MISS GLORIA. ADDRESS ME AS "MA'AM."
YES, MA'AM.
OUR CLIENTS ARE ALL TOP BRASS PERCH EXECUTIVES. MANNERS ARE PARAMOUNT AT ALL TIMES.

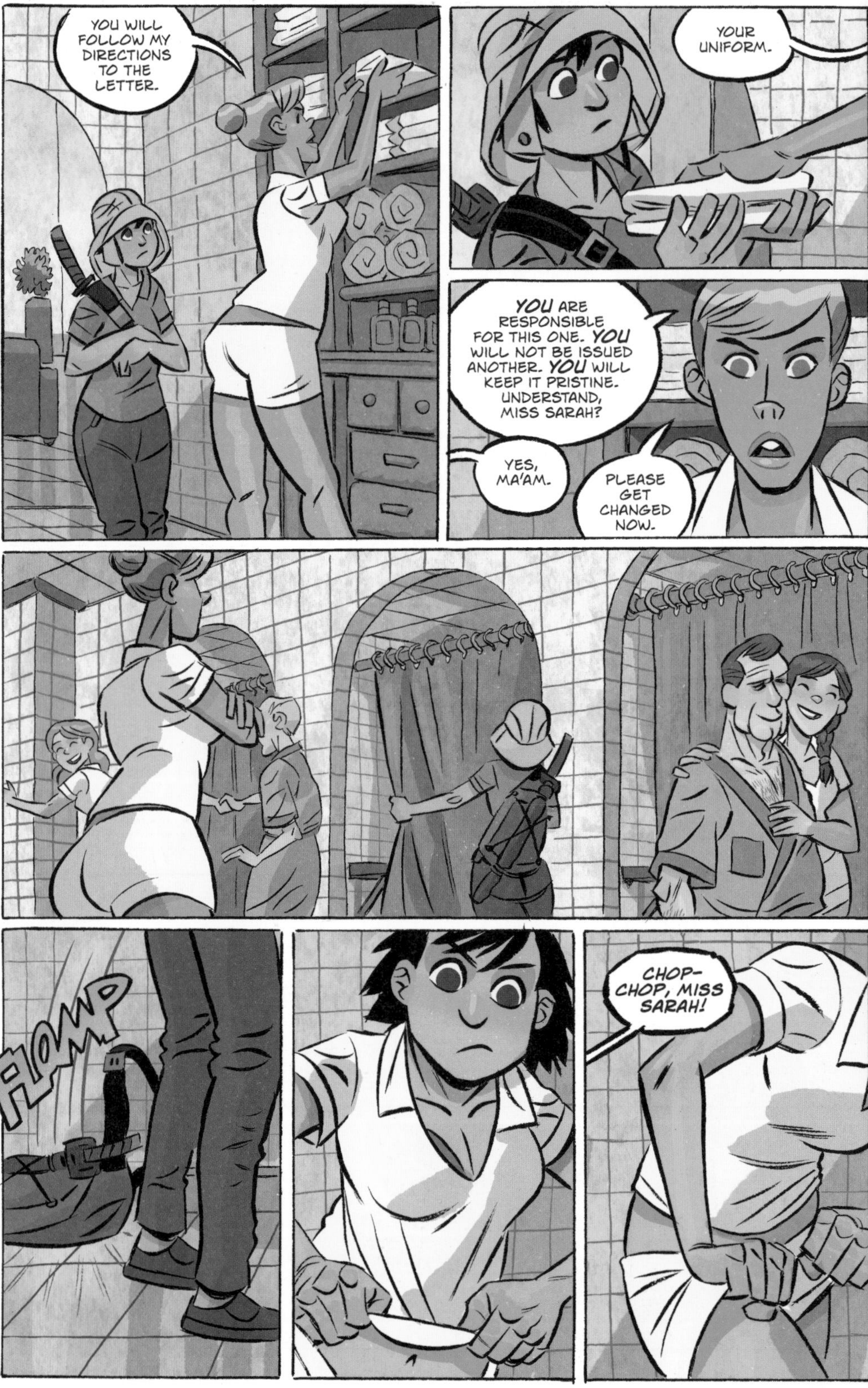
YOU WILL FOLLOW MY DIRECTIONS TO THE LETTER.
YOUR UNIFORM.
YOU ARE RESPONSIBLE FOR THIS ONE. YOU WILL NOT BE ISSUED ANOTHER. YOU WILL KEEP IT PRISTINE. UNDERSTAND, MISS SARAH?
YES, MA'AM.
PLEASE GET CHANGED NOW.
FLOMP
CHOP-CHOP, MISS SARAH!

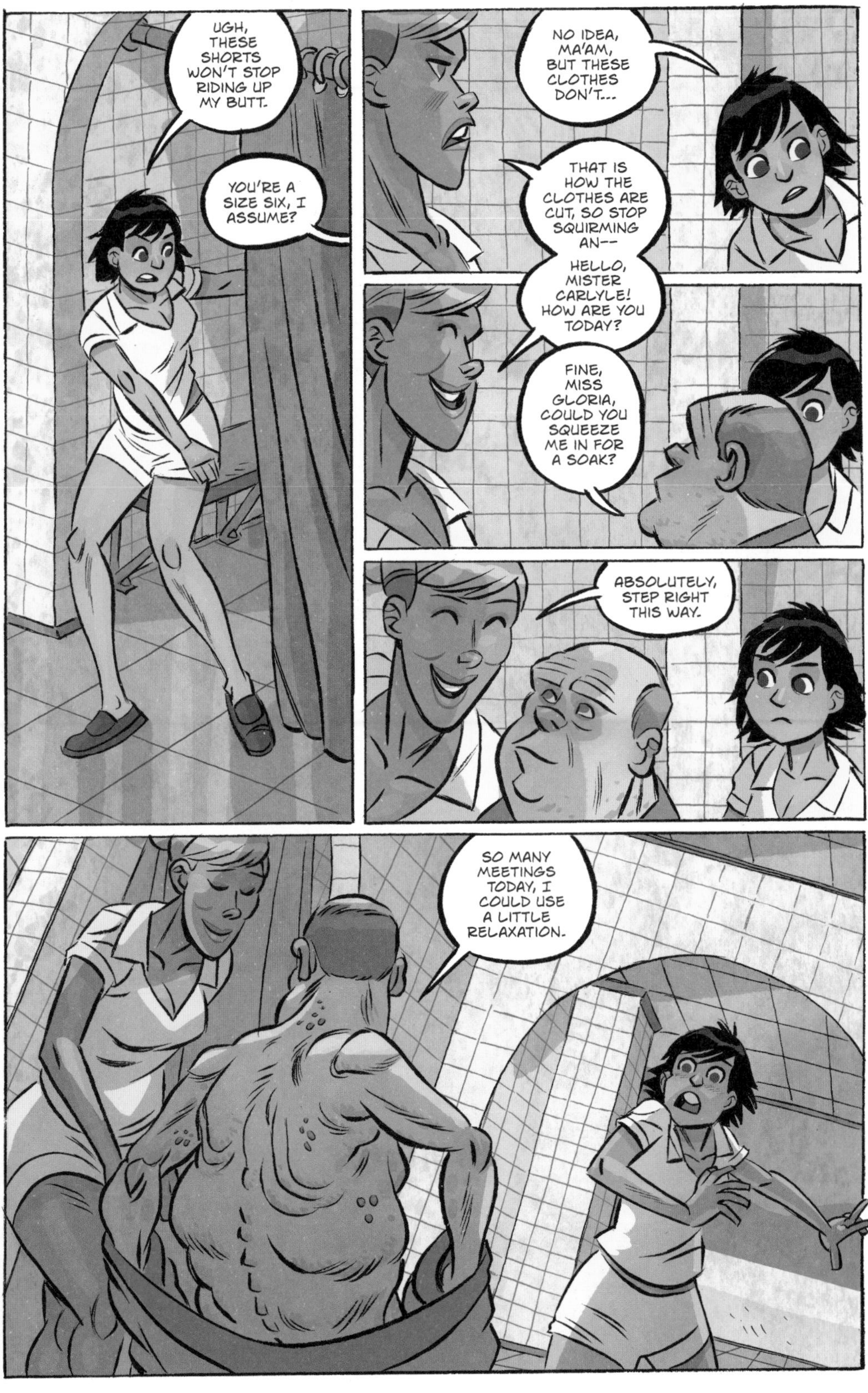
UGH, THESE SHORTS WON'T STOP RIDING UP MY BUTT.
YOU'RE A SIZE SIX, I ASSUME?
NO IDEA, MA'AM, BUT THESE CLOTHES DON'T...
THAT IS HOW THE CLOTHES ARE CUT, SO STOP SQUIRMING AN--
HELLO, MISTER CARLYLE! HOW ARE YOU TODAY?
FINE, MISS GLORIA, COULD YOU SQUEEZE ME IN FOR A SOAK?
ABSOLUTELY, STEP RIGHT THIS WAY.
SO MANY MEETINGS TODAY, I COULD USE A LITTLE RELAXATION.

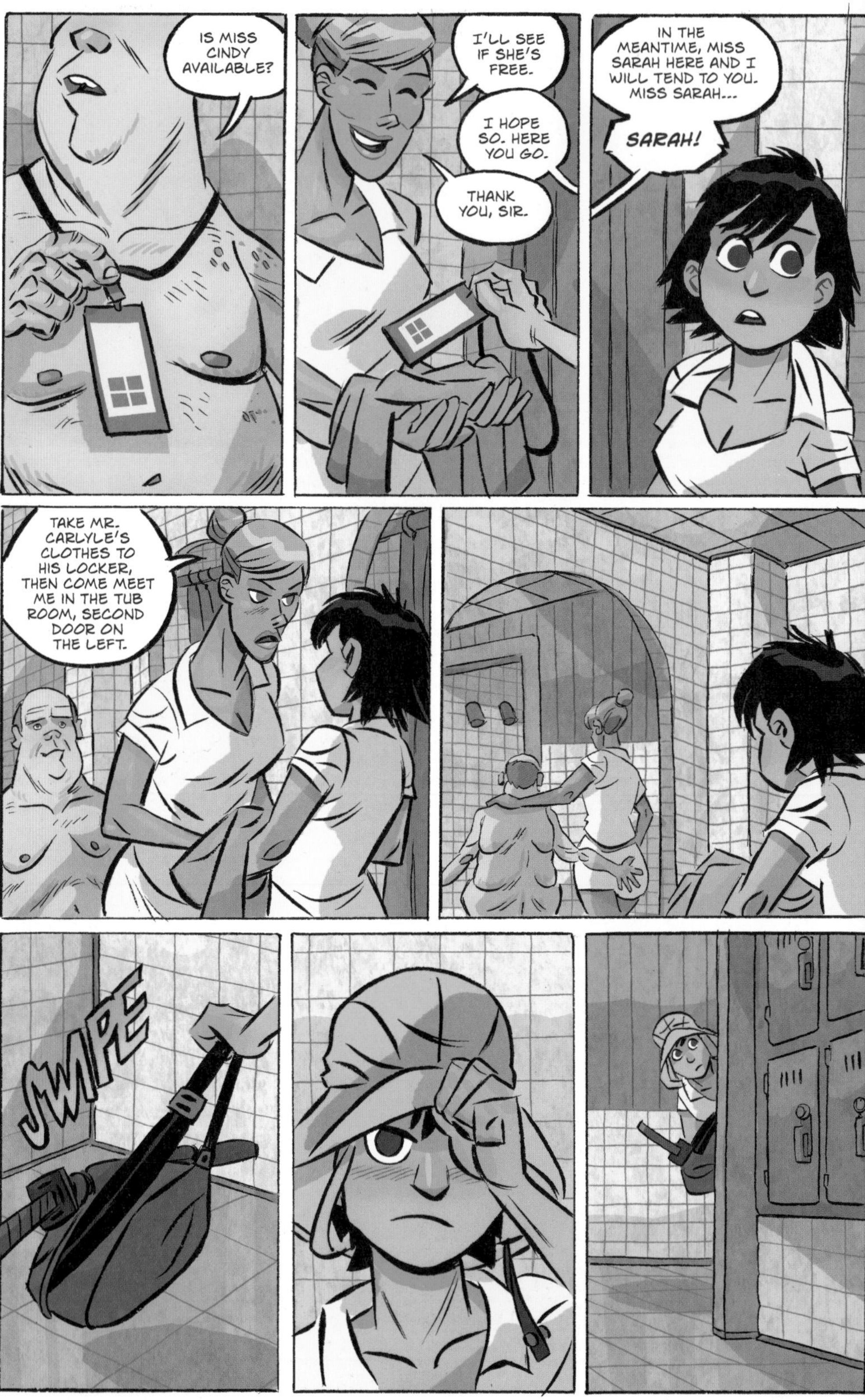
IS MISS CINDY AVAILABLE?
I'LL SEE IF SHE'S FREE.
I HOPE SO. HERE YOU GO.
THANK YOU, SIR.
IN THE MEANTIME, MISS SARAH HERE AND I WILL TEND TO YOU. MISS SARAH...
SARAH!
TAKE MR. CARLYLE'S CLOTHES TO HIS LOCKER, THEN COME MEET ME IN THE TUB ROOM, SECOND DOOR ON THE LEFT.
SWIPE

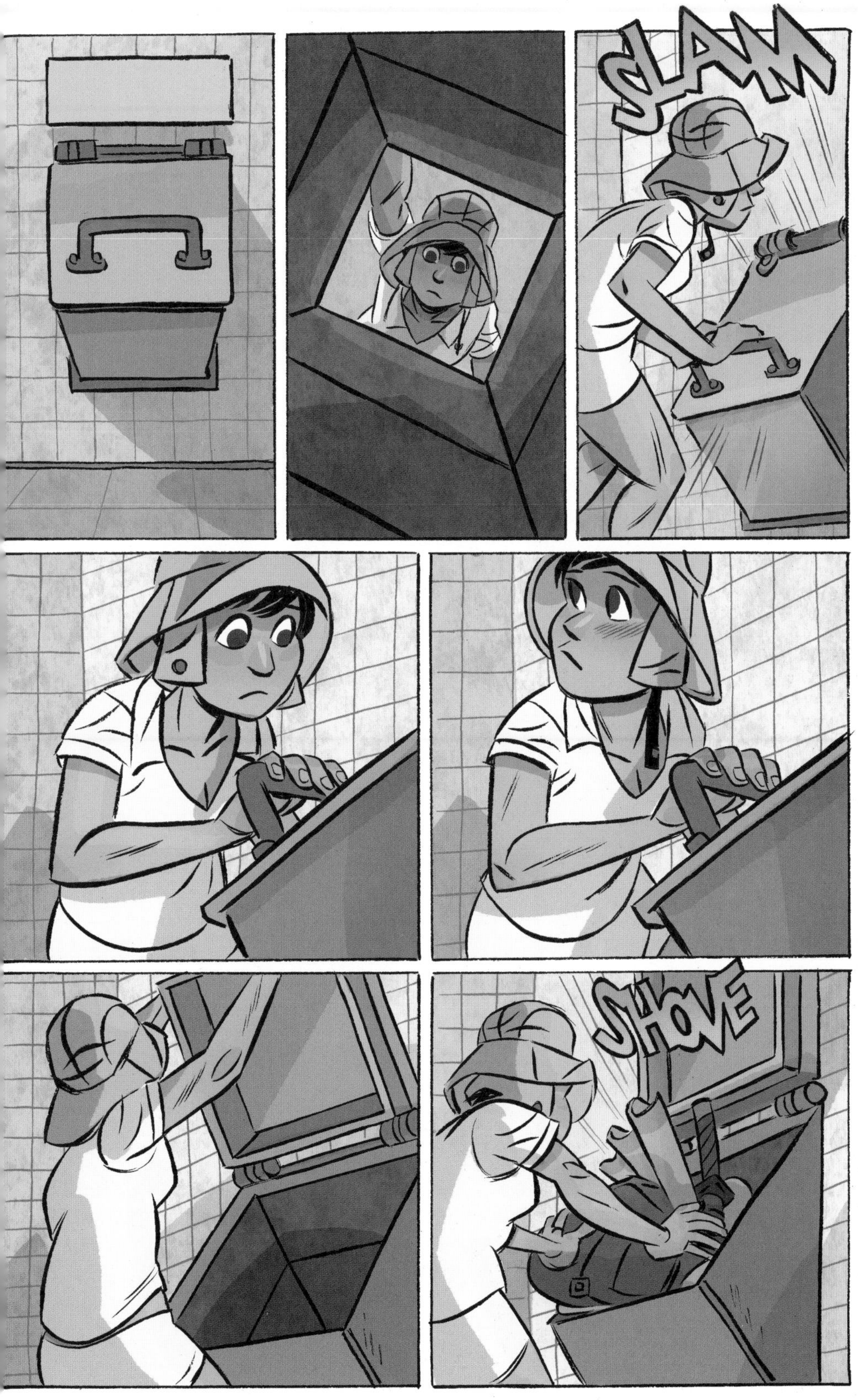
SLAM
SHOVE

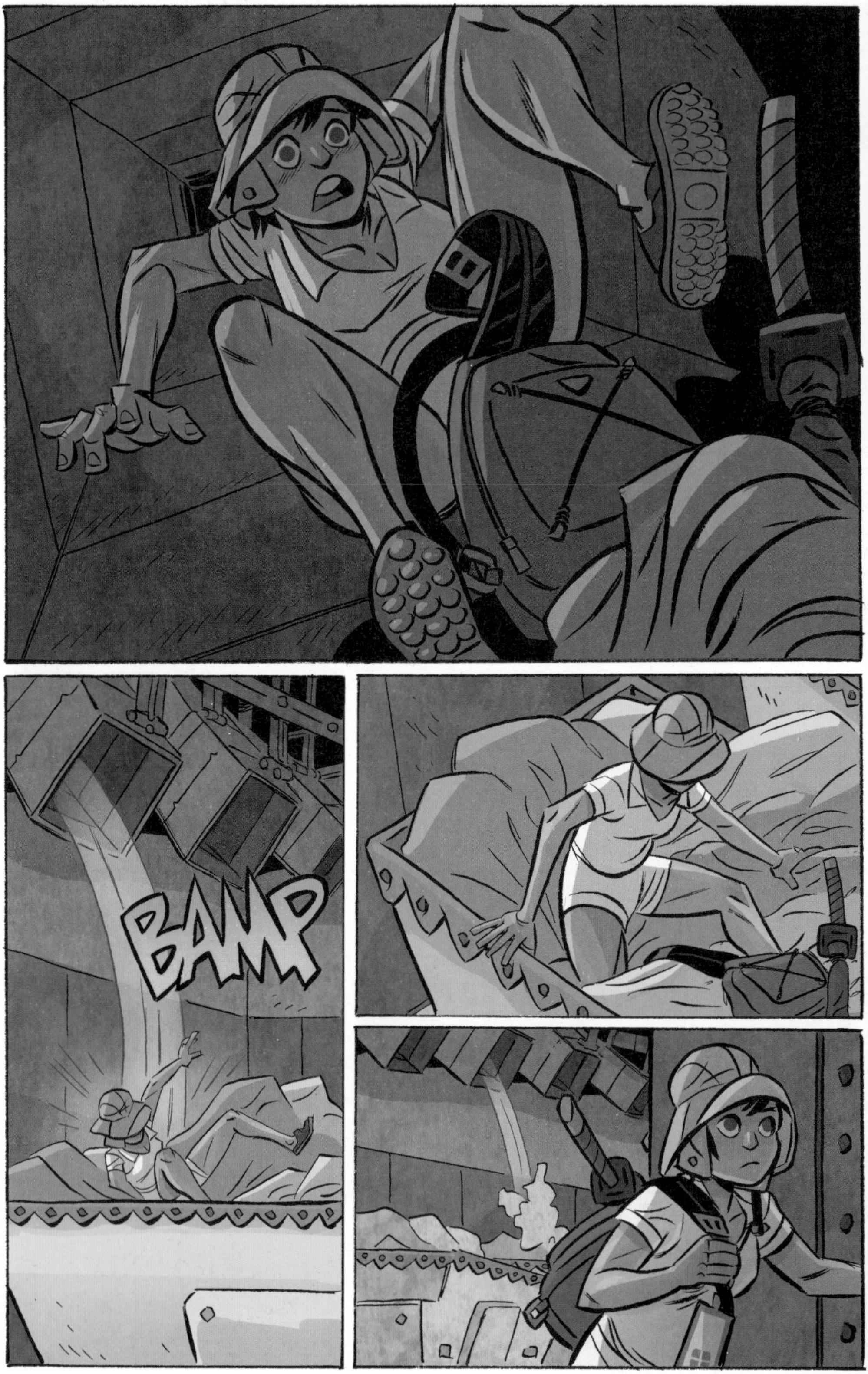
BAMP

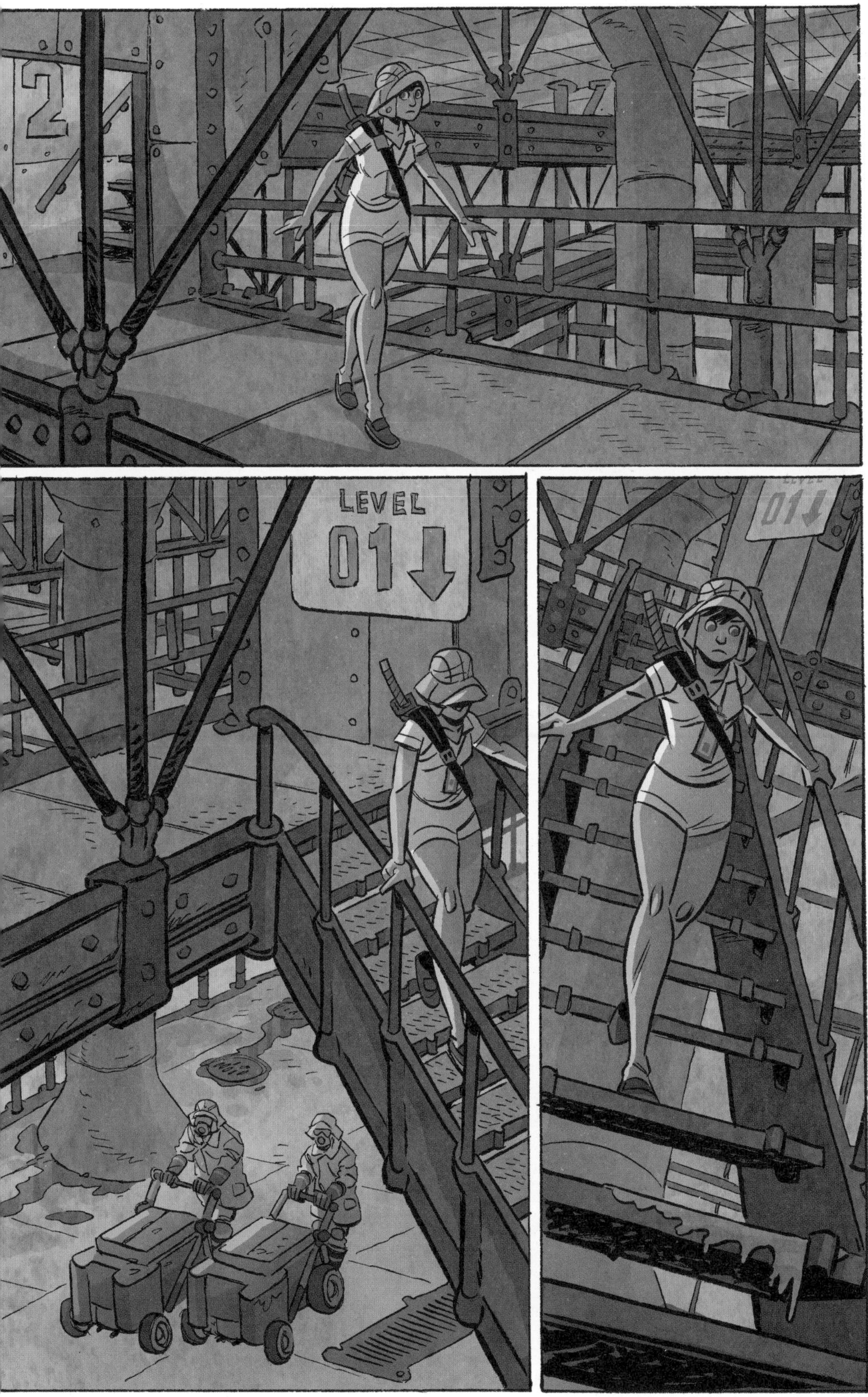
2
LEVEL
01
LEVEL
01

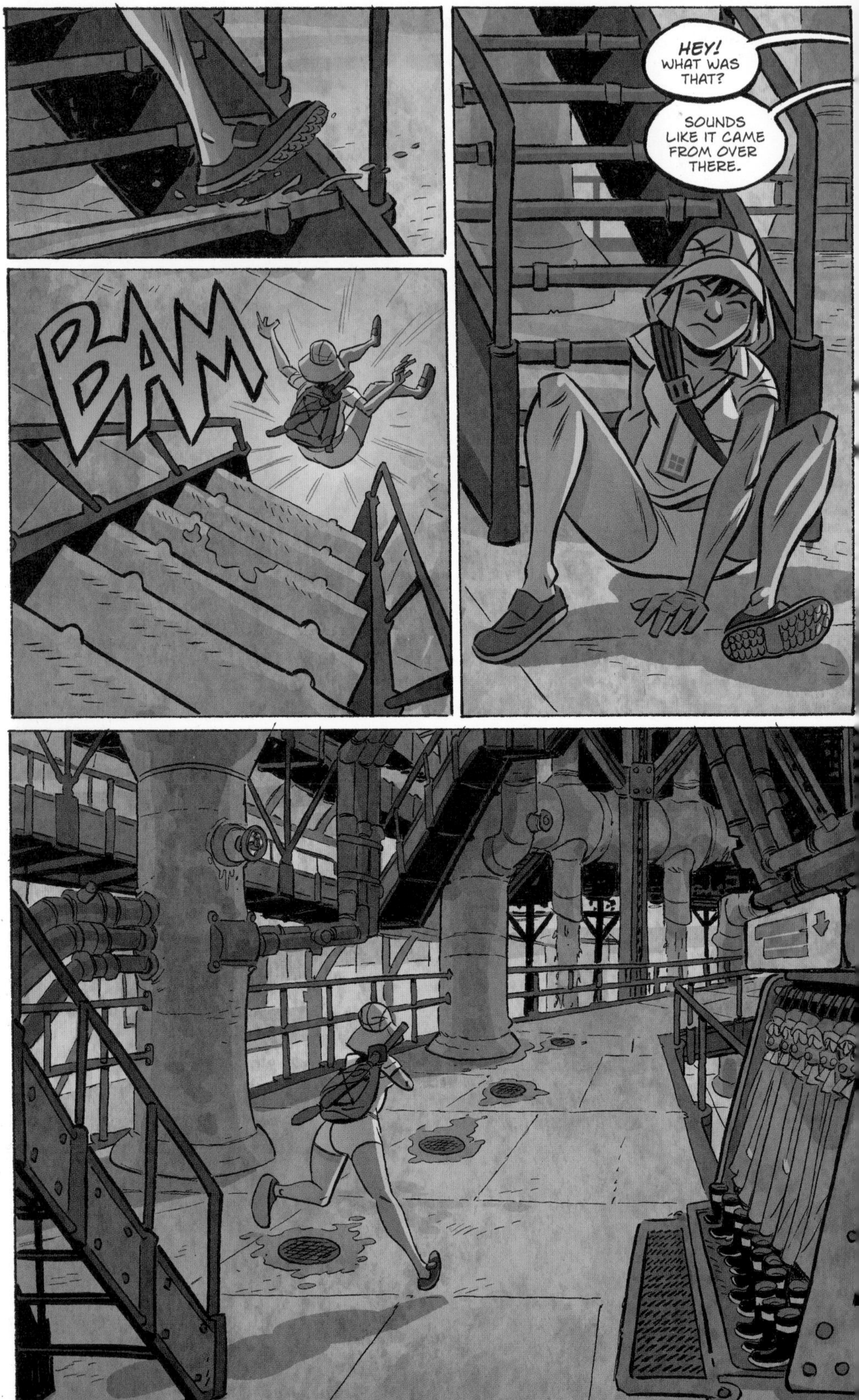
HEY! WHAT WAS THAT?
SOUNDS LIKE IT CAME FROM OVER THERE.
BAM

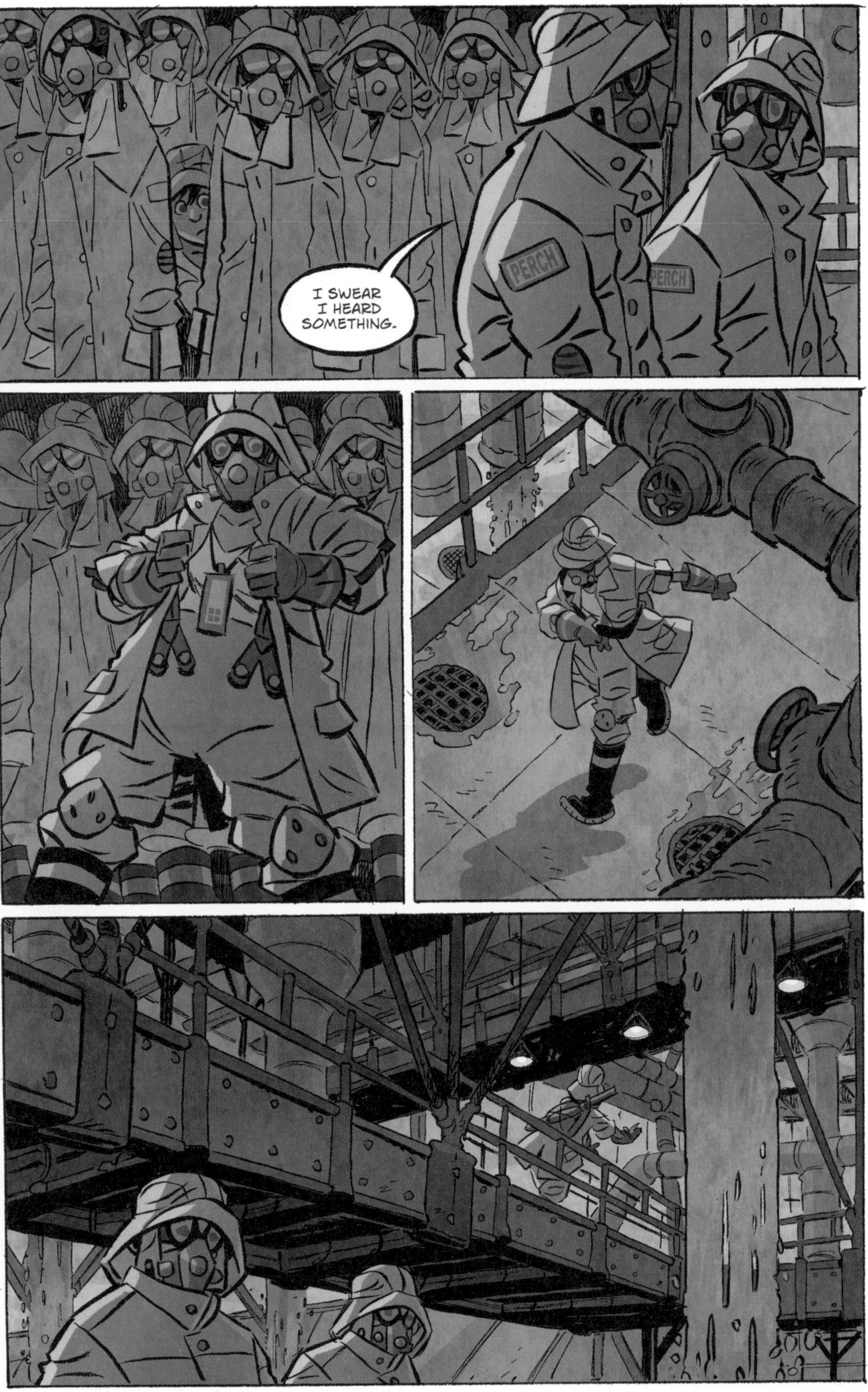
I SWEAR I HEARD SOMETHING.
PERCH
PERCH

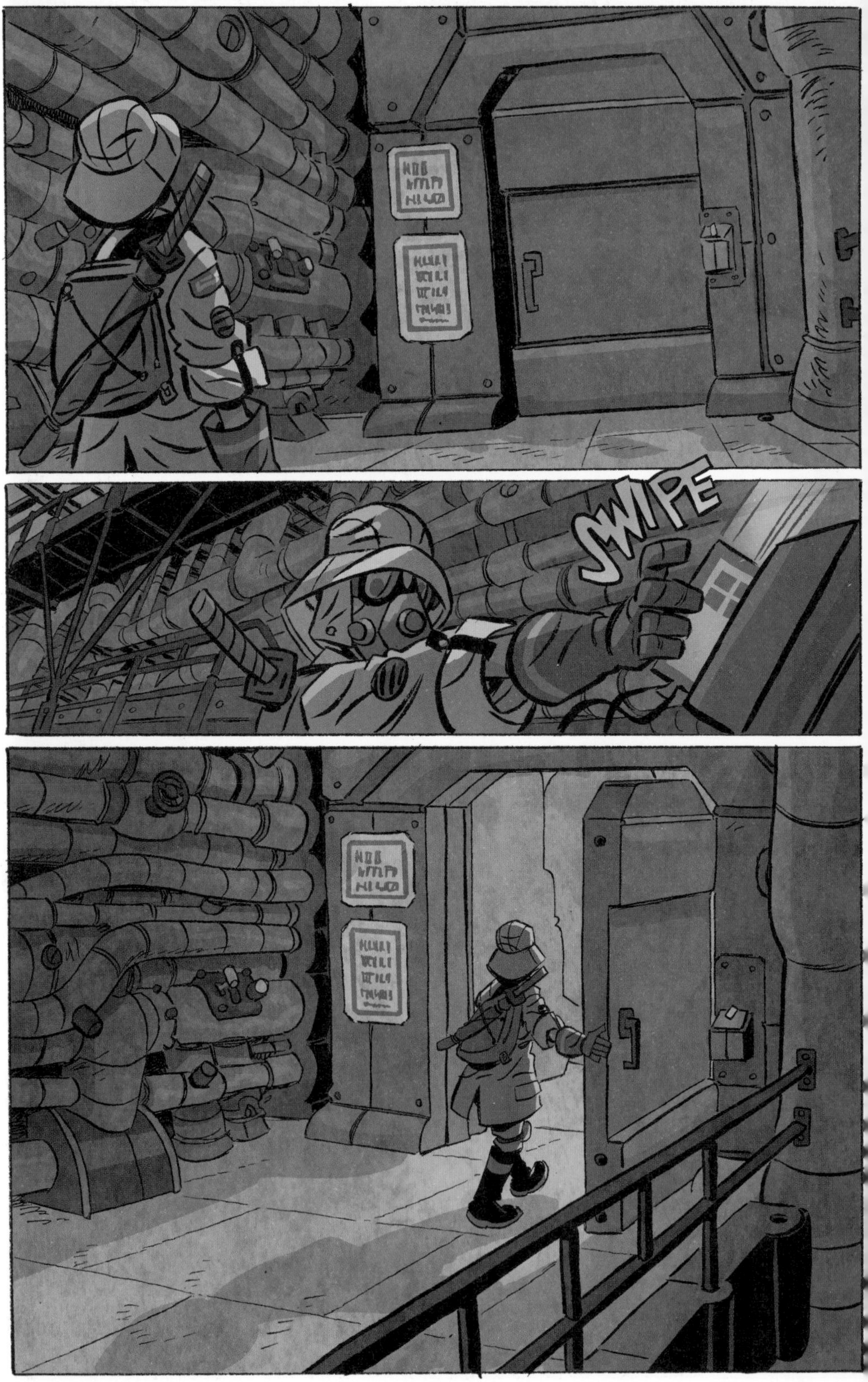
SWIPE

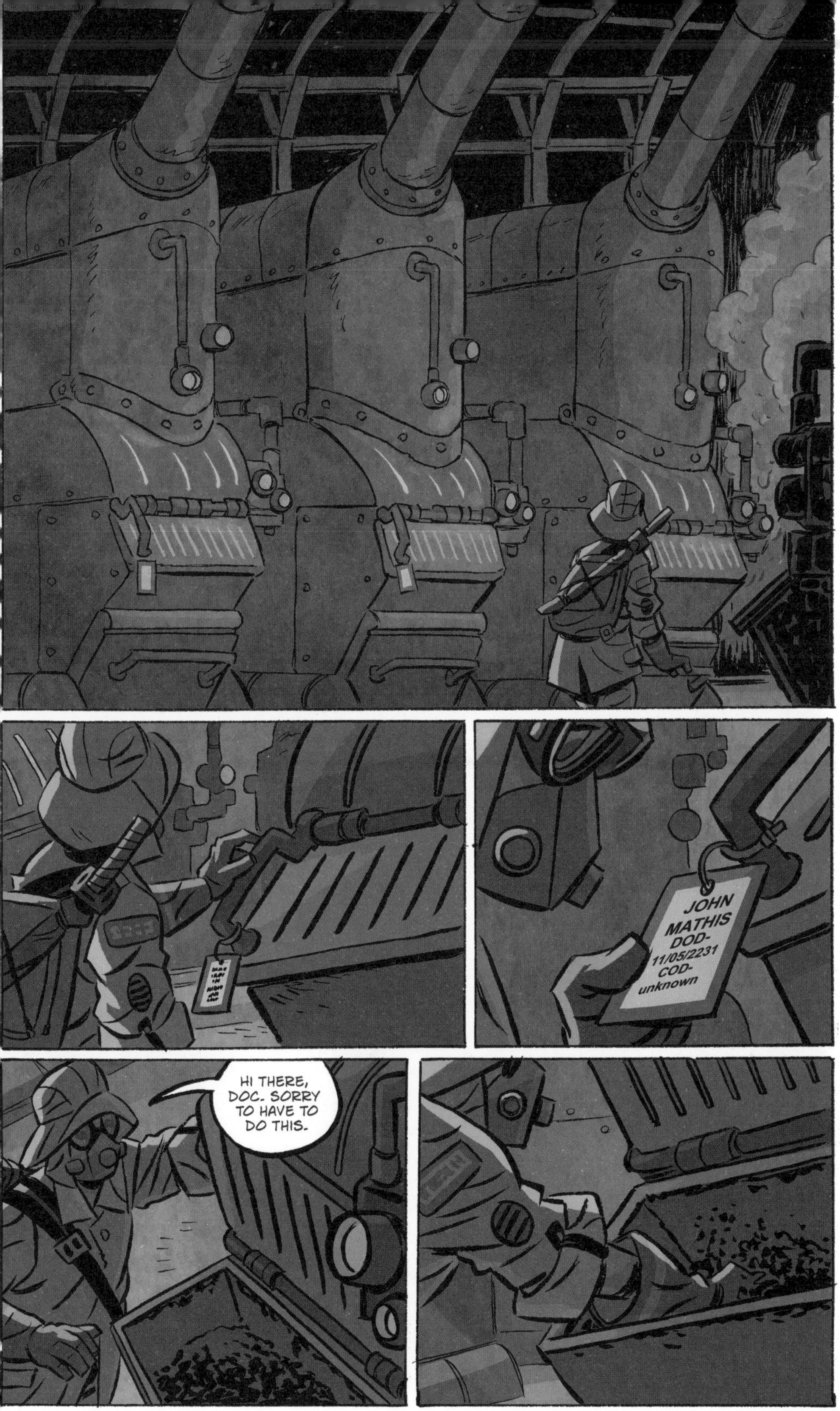
JOHN MATHIS DOD- 11/05/2231 COD- unknown
HI THERE, DOC. SORRY TO HAVE TO DO THIS.

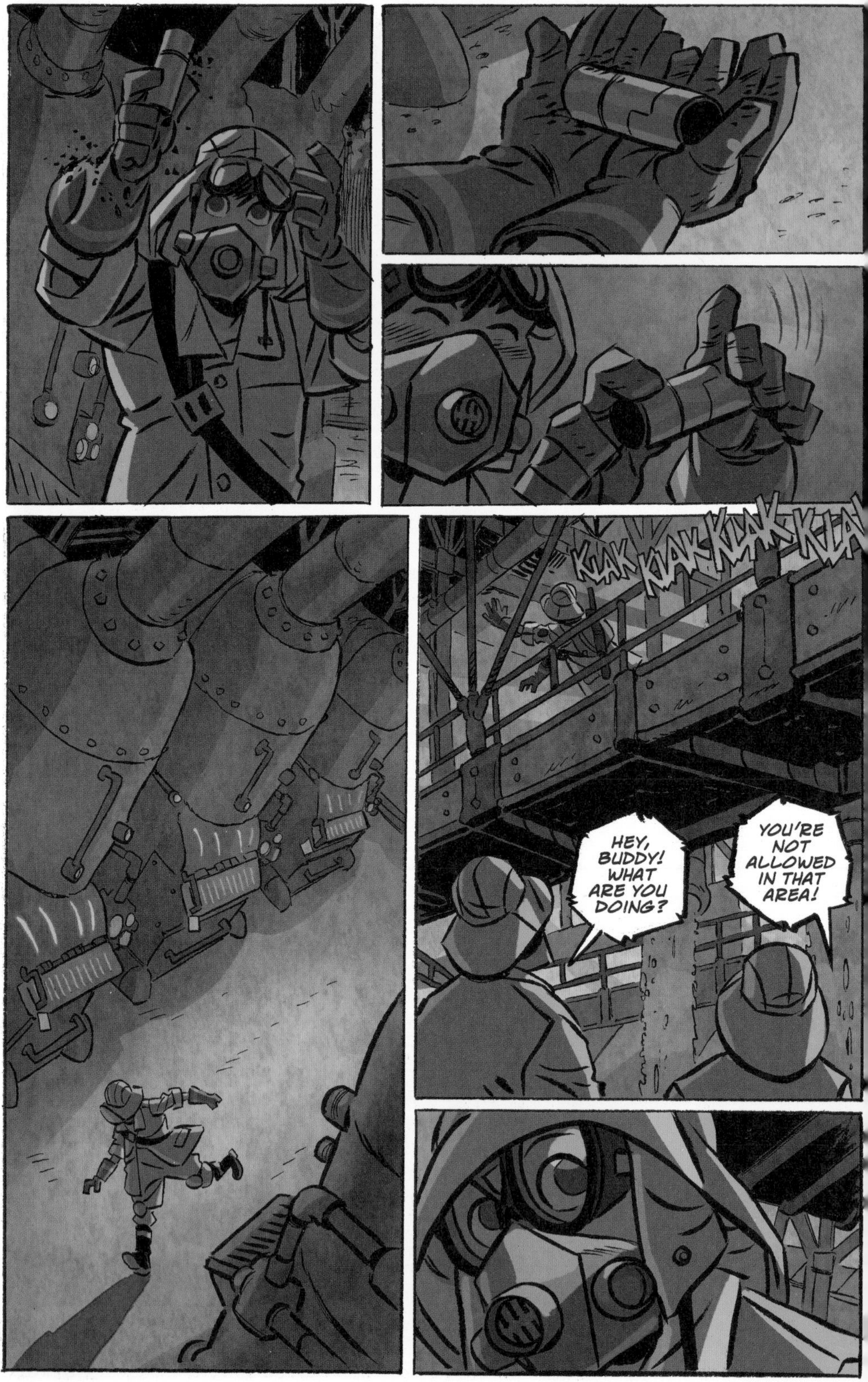
KLAK KLAK KLAK KLA
HEY, BUDDY! WHAT ARE YOU DOING?
YOU'RE NOT ALLOWED IN THAT AREA!

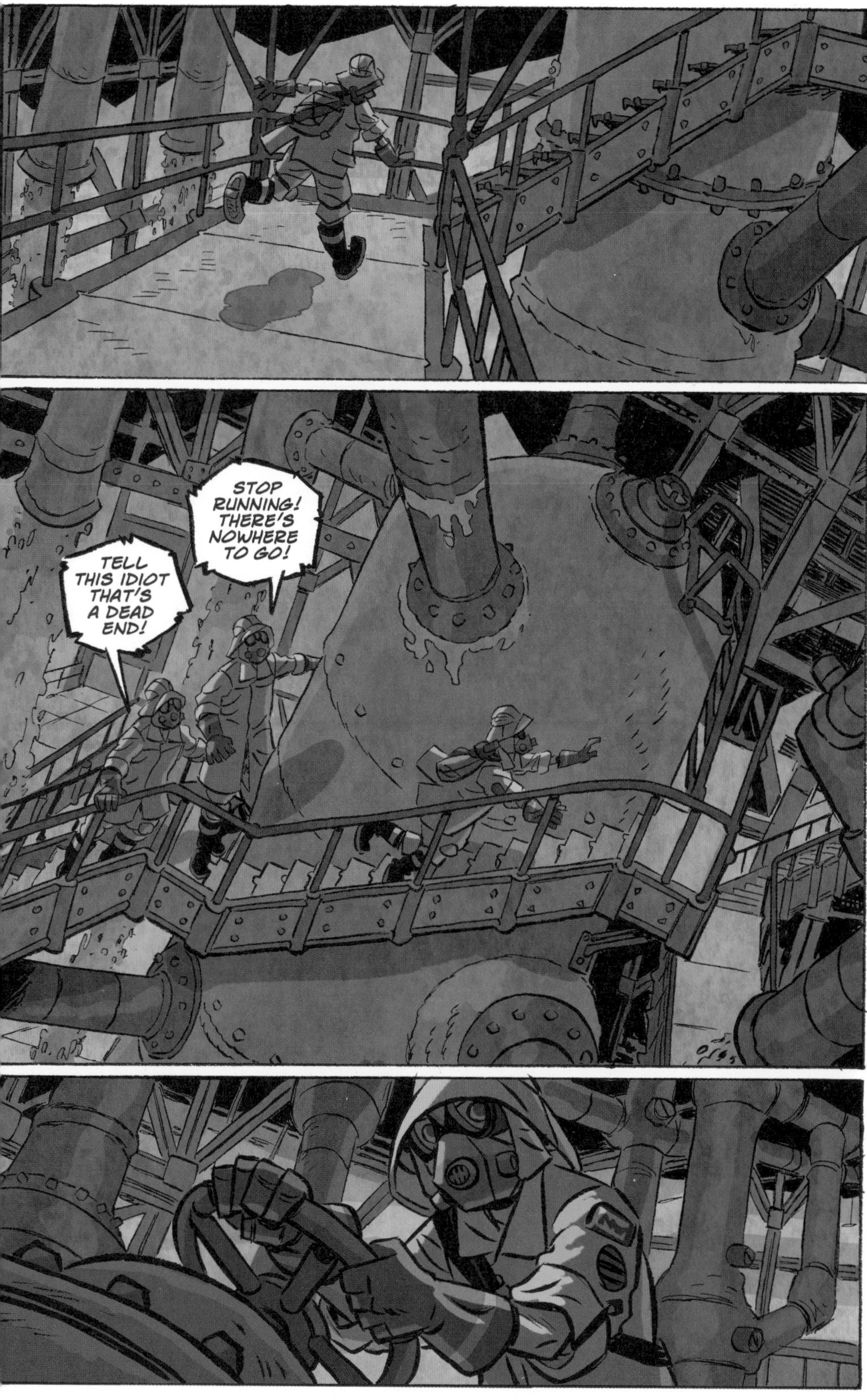
TELL THIS IDIOT THAT'S A DEAD END!
STOP RUNNING! THERE'S NOWHERE TO GO!

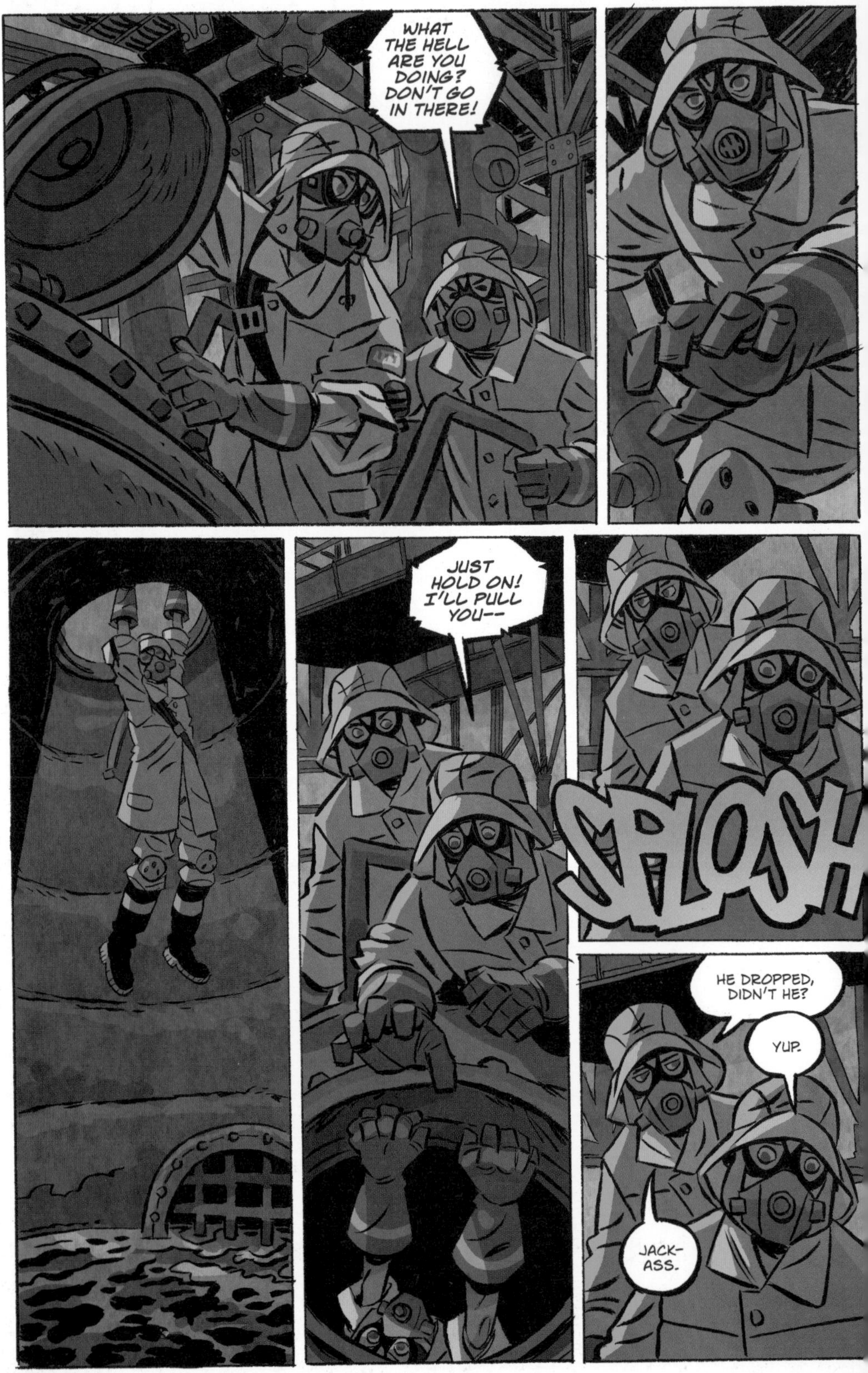
WHAT THE HELL ARE YOU DOING? DON'T GO IN THERE!
JUST HOLD ON! I'LL PULL YOU--
SPLOSH
HE DROPPED, DIDN'T HE?
YUP.
JACK-ASS.

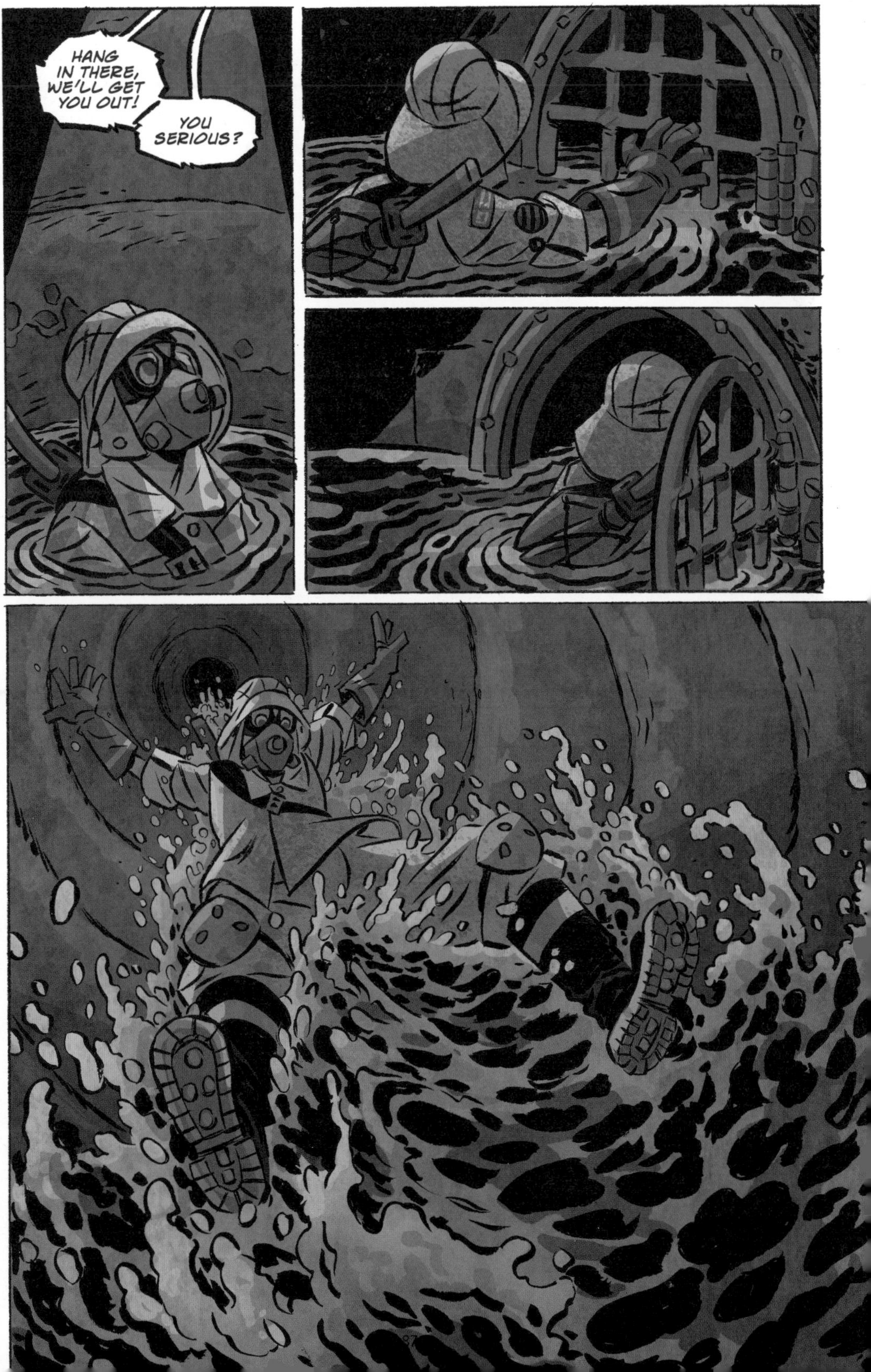
HANG IN THERE, WE'LL GET YOU OUT!
YOU SERIOUS?

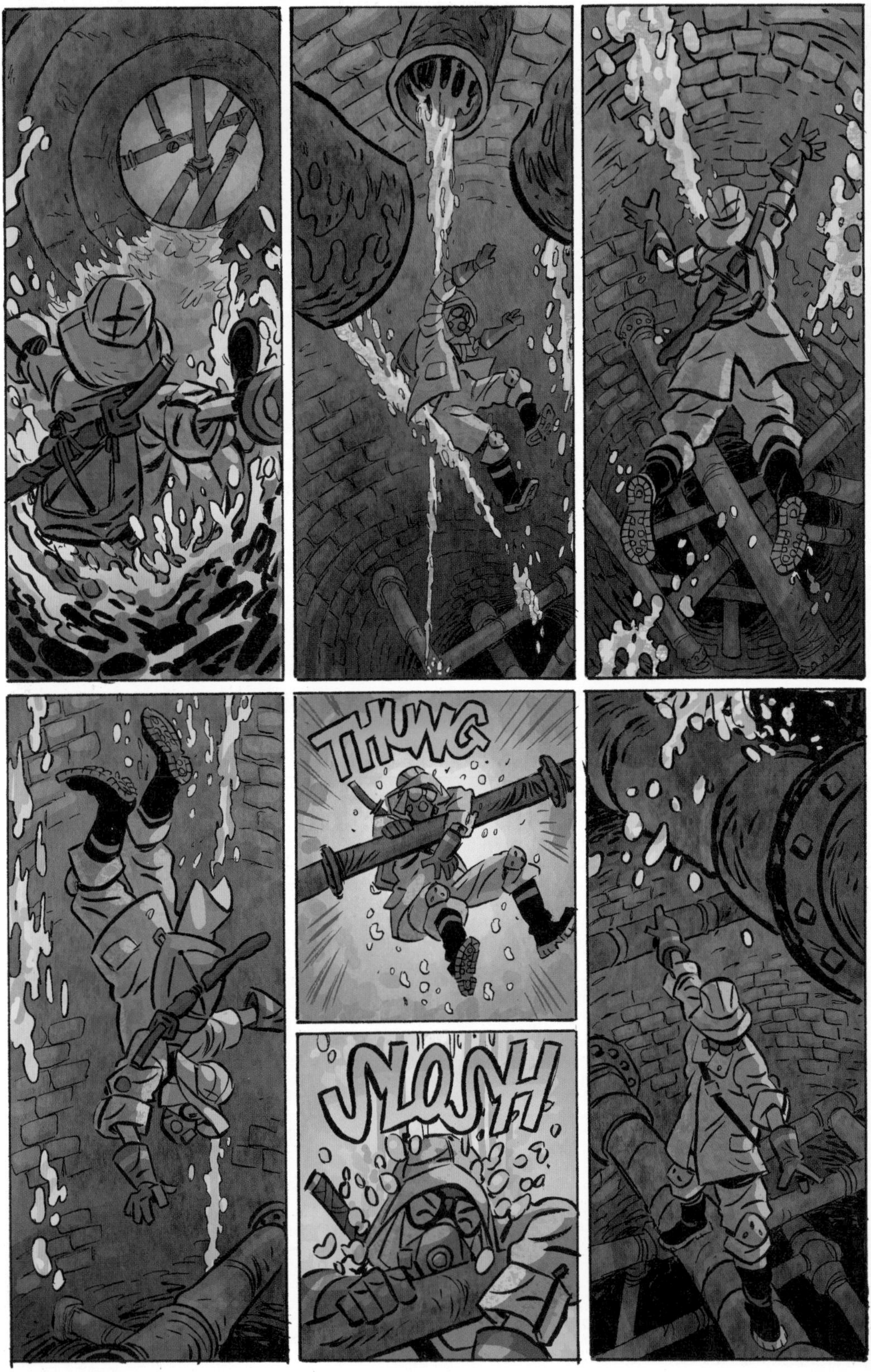
THUNG
SLOSH

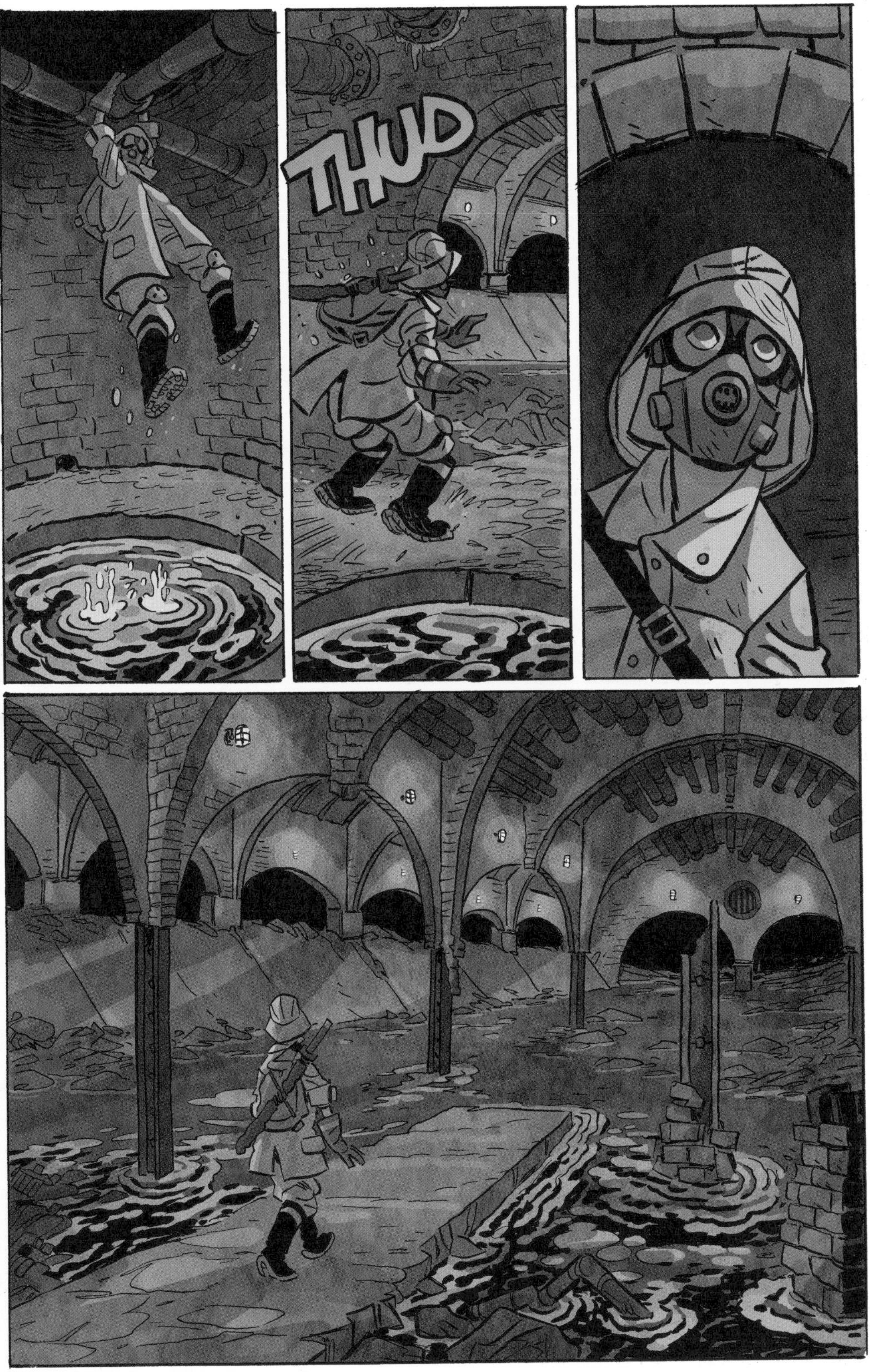
THUD

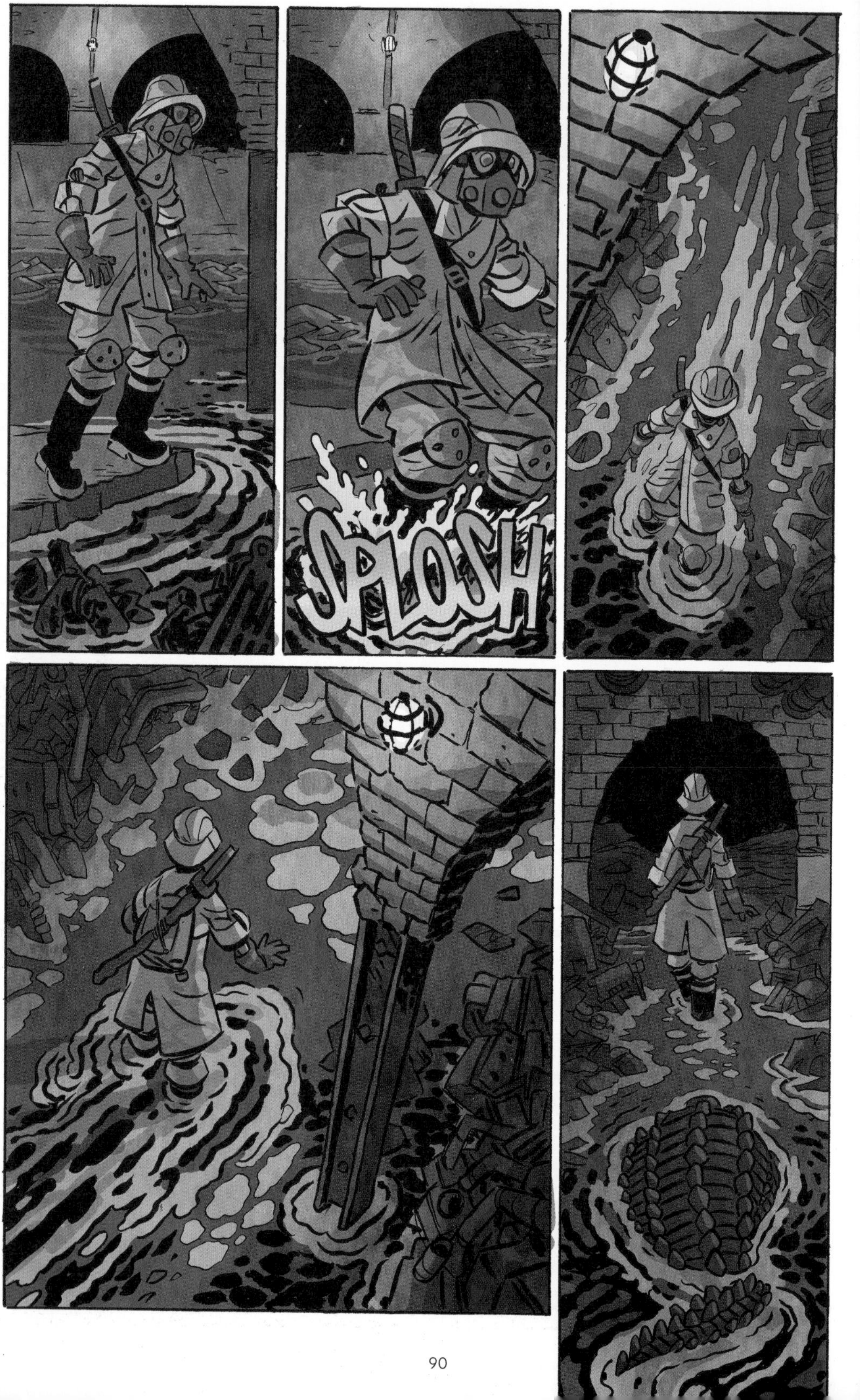
SPLOSH

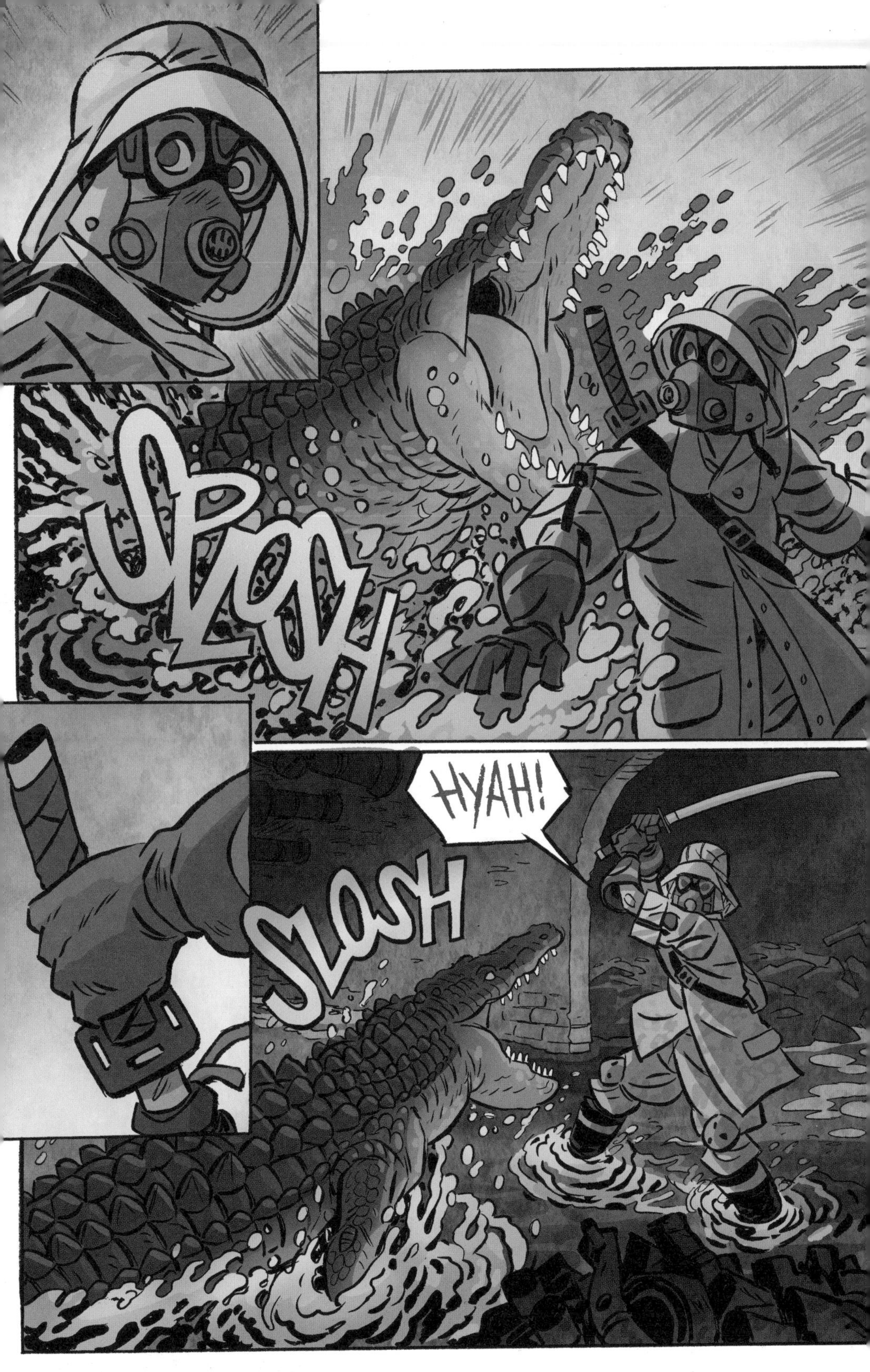
SPLOOSH
HYAH!
SLOSH

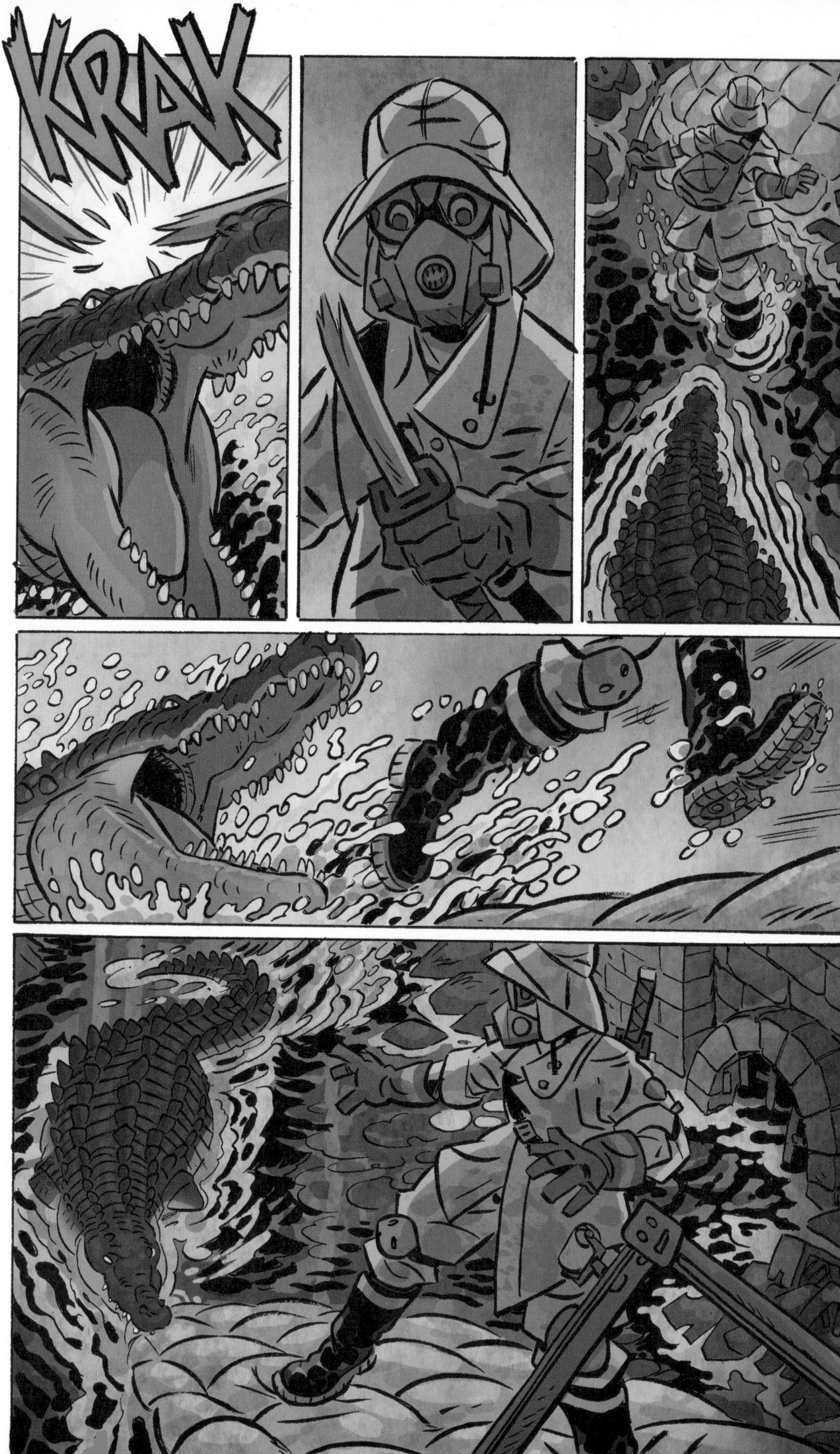
KRAK

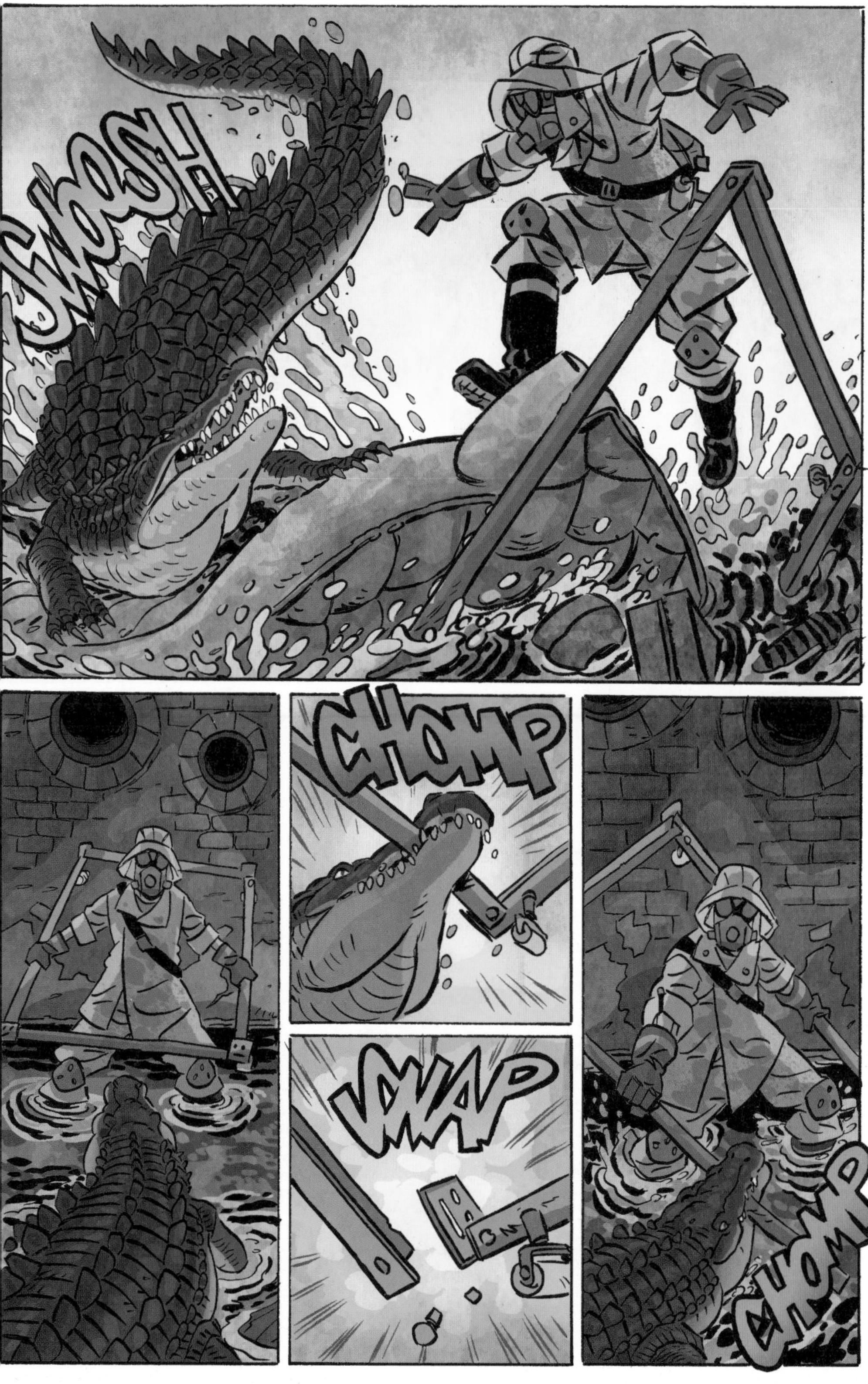
SWOOSH
CHOMP
SNAP
CHOMP

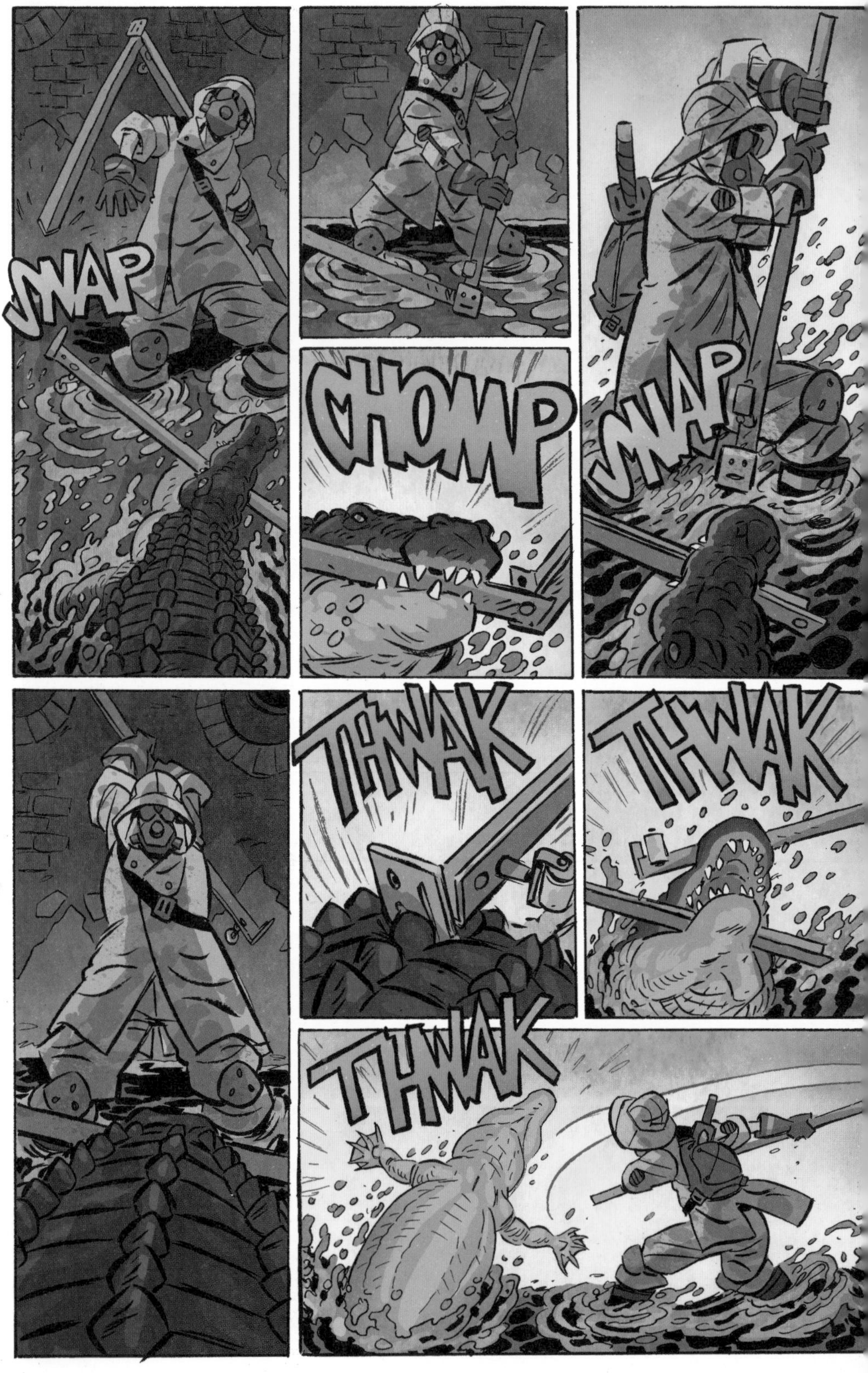
SNAP
CHOMP
SNAP
THWAK
THWAK
THWAK

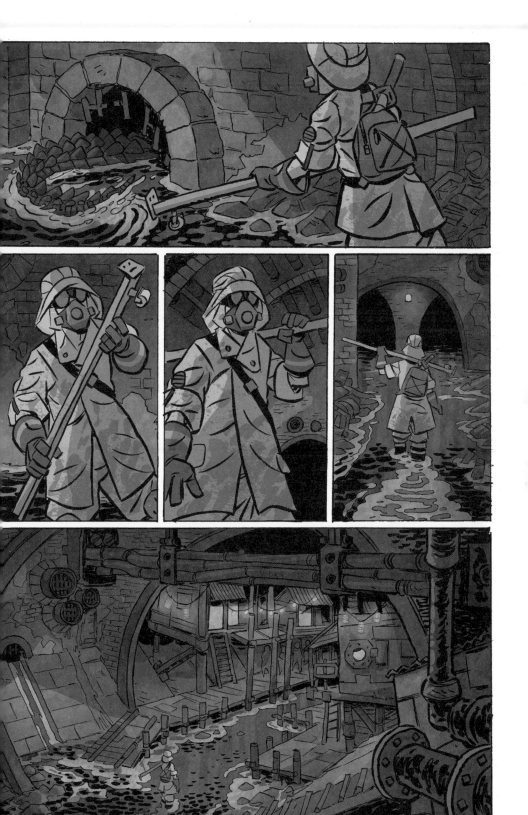

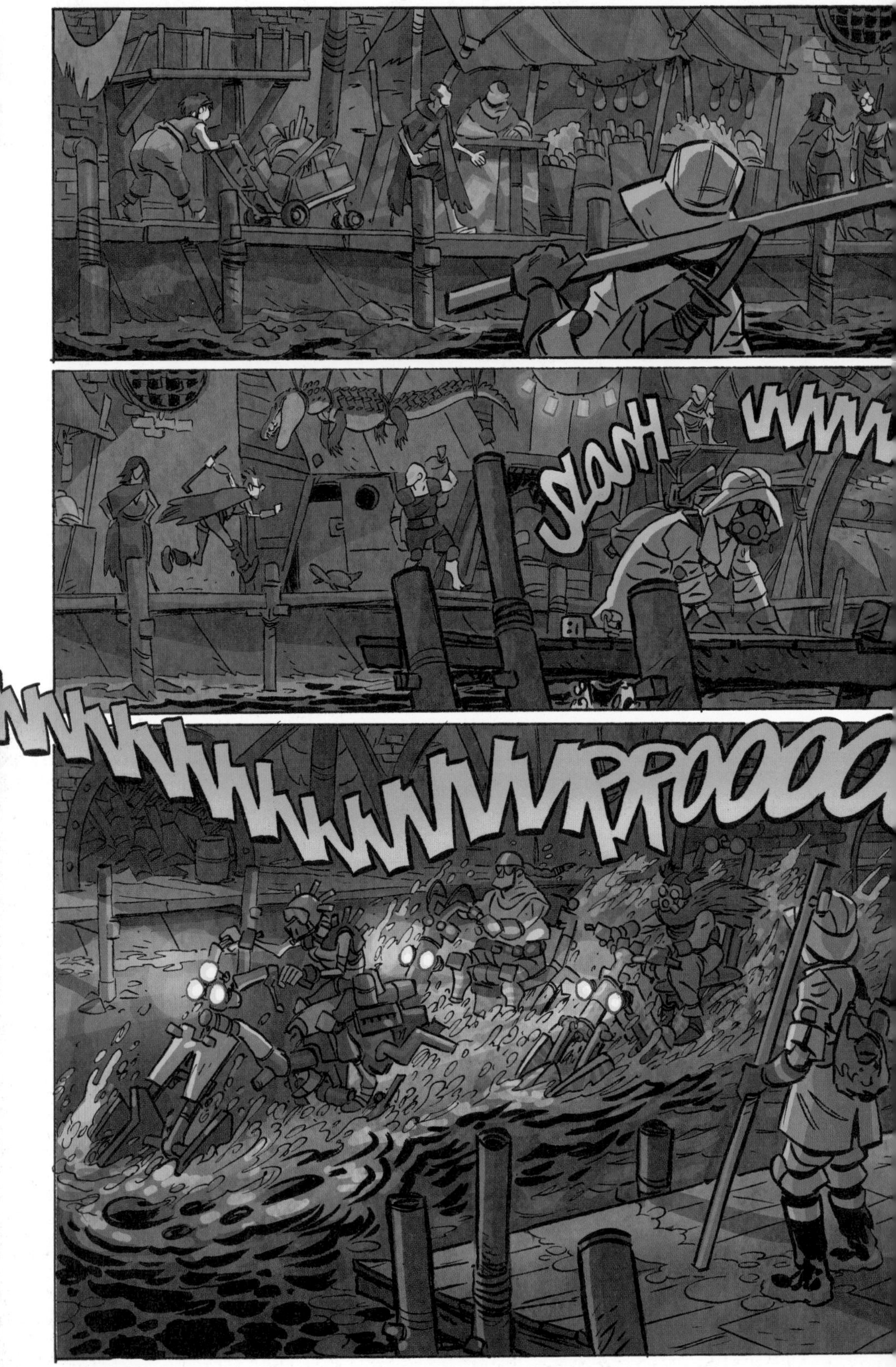
SPLASH
VVVVV
VVVVVVVVVVVVVVRROOOO

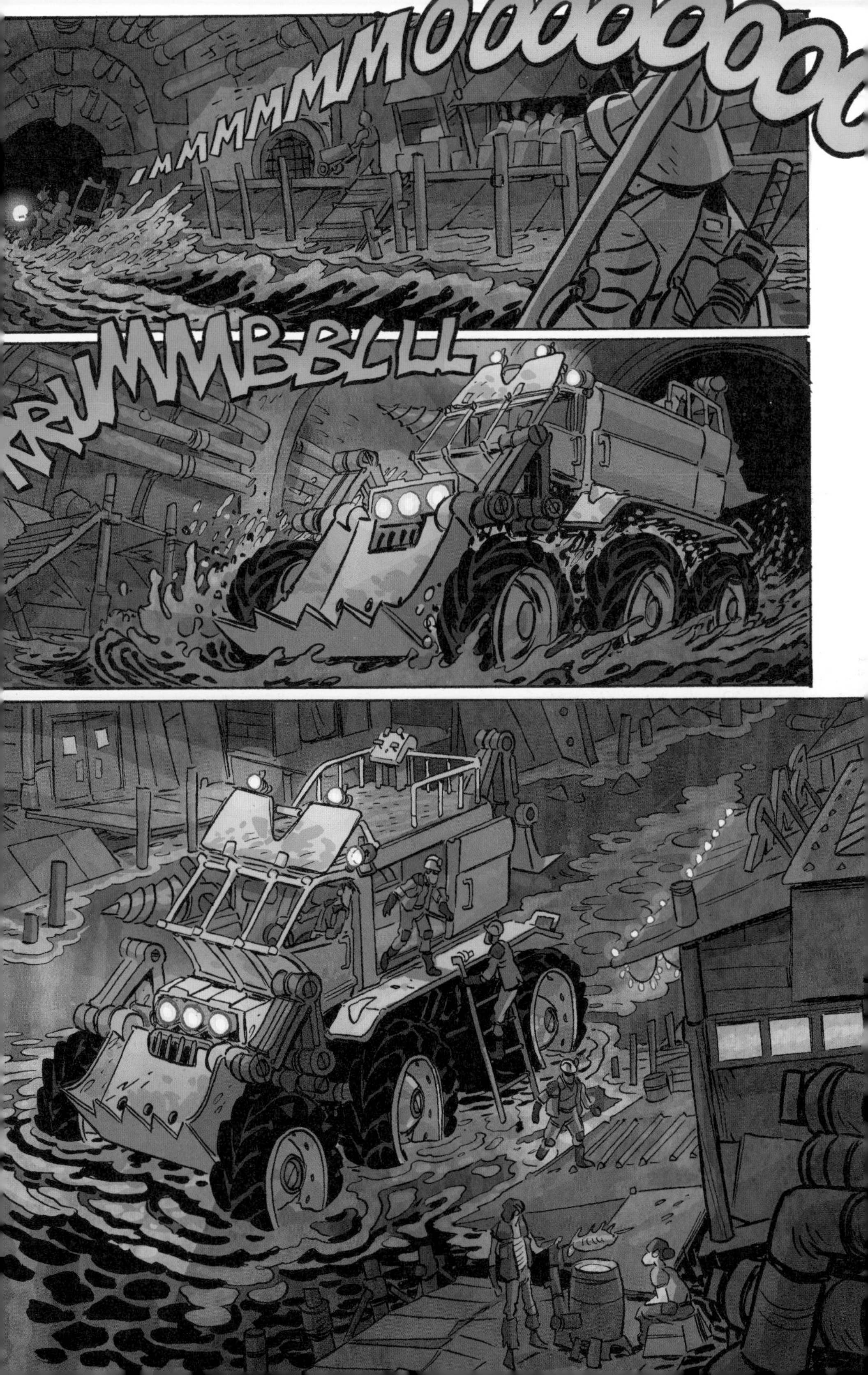
MMMMMMMOOOOOOOOO
VRUMMBBLLL

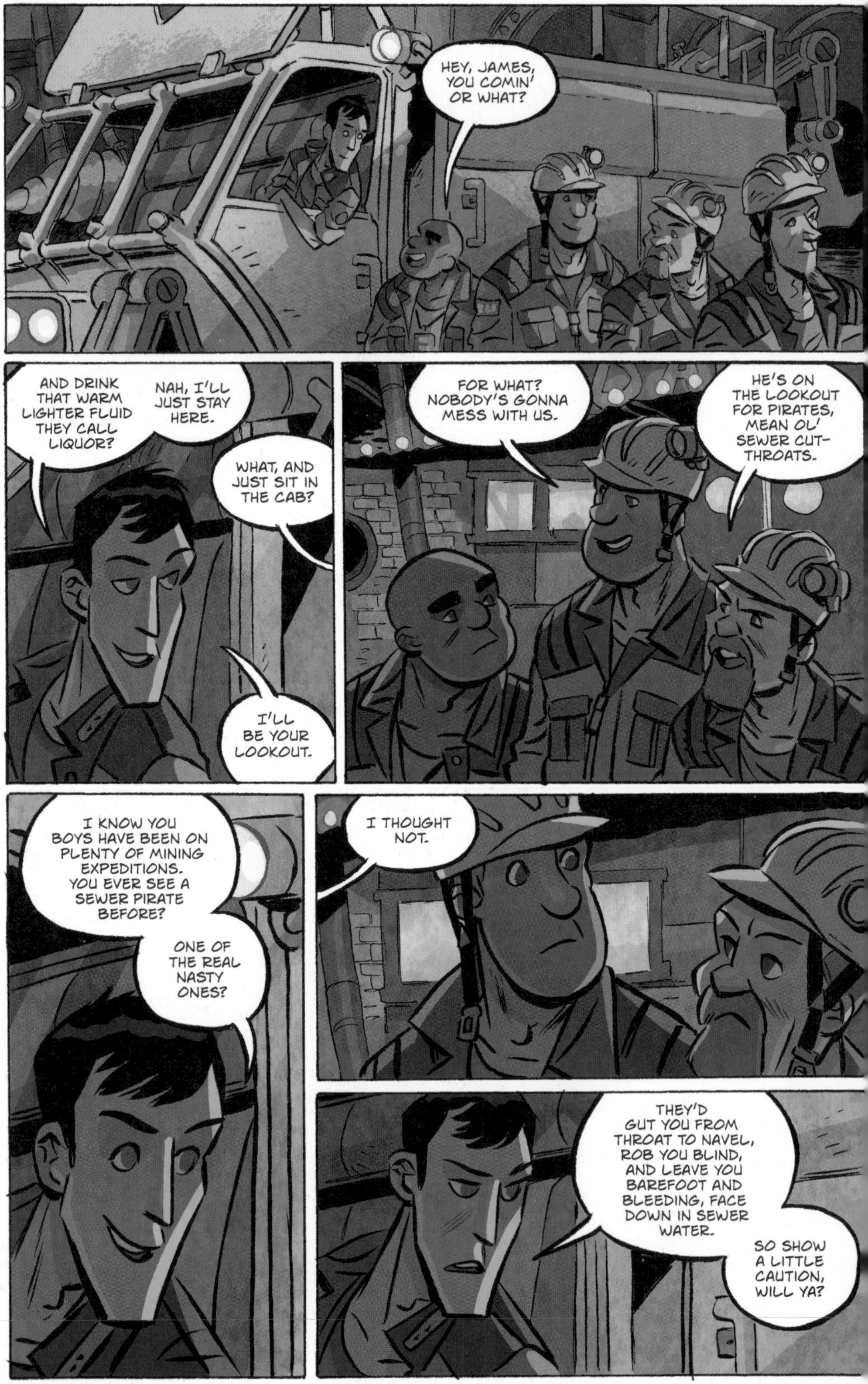
HEY, JAMES, YOU COMIN' OR WHAT?
NAH, I'LL JUST STAY HERE.
AND DRINK THAT WARM LIGHTER FLUID THEY CALL LIQUOR?
WHAT, AND JUST SIT IN THE CAB?
I'LL BE YOUR LOOKOUT.
FOR WHAT? NOBODY'S GONNA MESS WITH US.
HE'S ON THE LOOKOUT FOR PIRATES, MEAN OL' SEWER CUT-THROATS.
I KNOW YOU BOYS HAVE BEEN ON PLENTY OF MINING EXPEDITIONS. YOU EVER SEE A SEWER PIRATE BEFORE?
ONE OF THE REAL NASTY ONES?
I THOUGHT NOT.
THEY'D GUT YOU FROM THROAT TO NAVEL, ROB YOU BLIND, AND LEAVE YOU BAREFOOT AND BLEEDING, FACE DOWN IN SEWER WATER.
SO SHOW A LITTLE CAUTION, WILL YA?

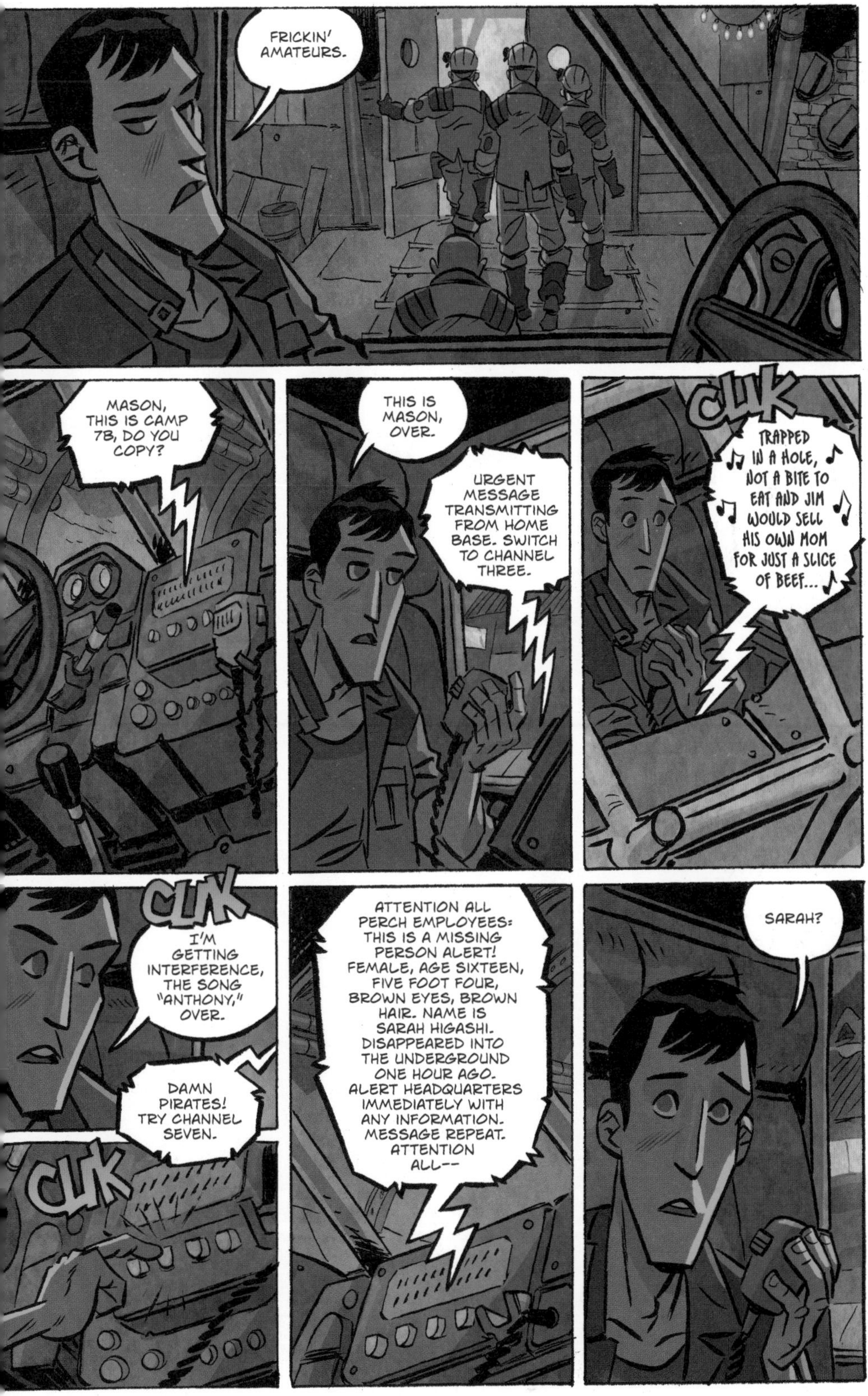
FRICKIN' AMATEURS.
MASON, THIS IS CAMP 7B, DO YOU COPY?
THIS IS MASON, OVER.
URGENT MESSAGE TRANSMITTING FROM HOME BASE. SWITCH TO CHANNEL THREE.
CLIK
TRAPPED IN A HOLE, NOT A BITE TO EAT AND JIM WOULD SELL HIS OWN MOM FOR JUST A SLICE OF BEEF...
CLIK
I'M GETTING INTERFERENCE, THE SONG "ANTHONY," OVER.
DAMN PIRATES! TRY CHANNEL SEVEN.
CLIK
ATTENTION ALL PERCH EMPLOYEES: THIS IS A MISSING PERSON ALERT! FEMALE, AGE SIXTEEN, FIVE FOOT FOUR, BROWN EYES, BROWN HAIR. NAME IS SARAH HIGASHI. DISAPPEARED INTO THE UNDERGROUND ONE HOUR AGO. ALERT HEADQUARTERS IMMEDIATELY WITH ANY INFORMATION. MESSAGE REPEAT. ATTENTION ALL--
SARAH?

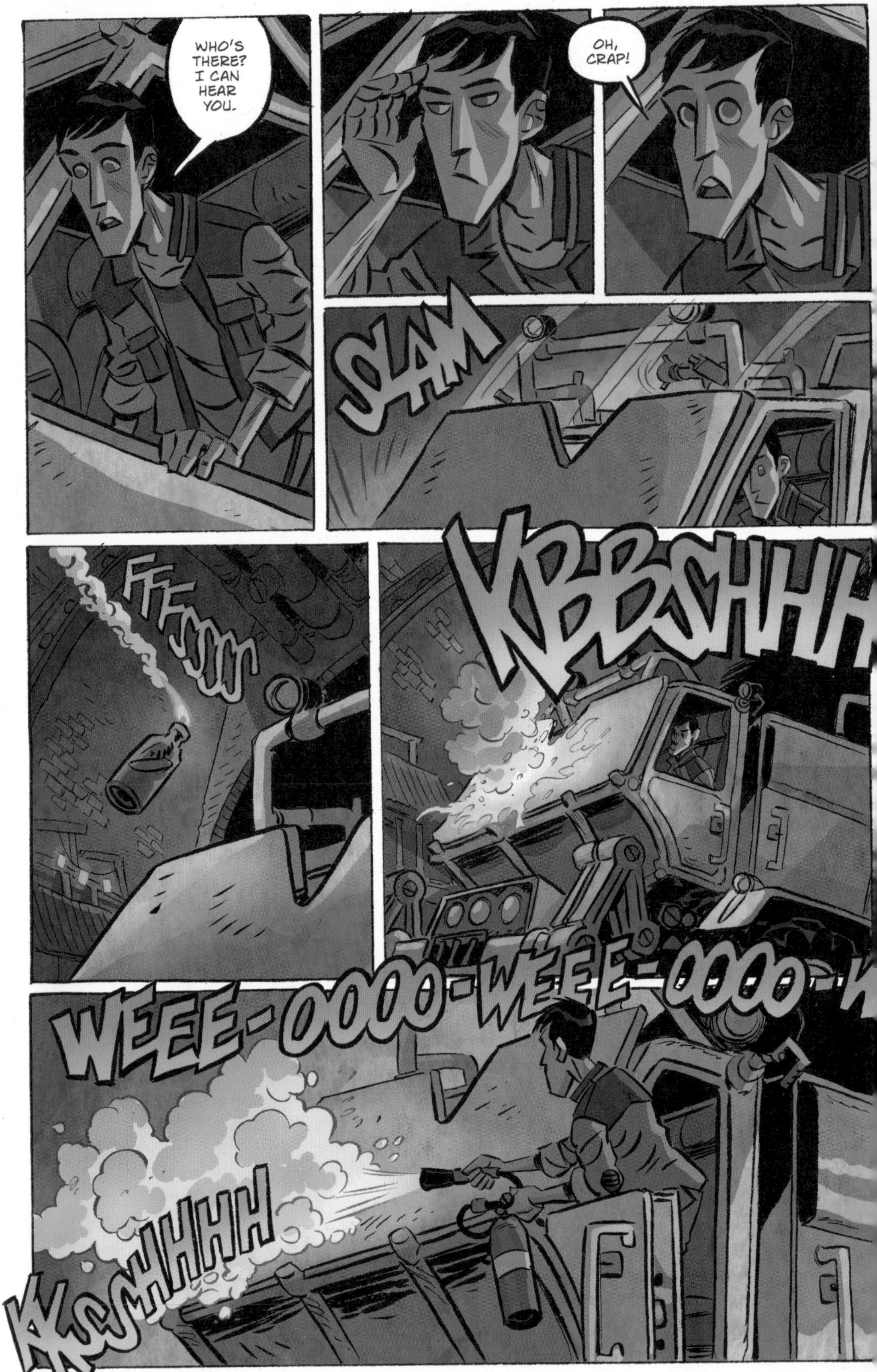
WHO'S THERE? I CAN HEAR YOU.
OH, CRAP!
SLAM
FFFSSSSS
KBBSHHH
WEEE-OOOO-WEEE-OOOO
KKSSHHHHH

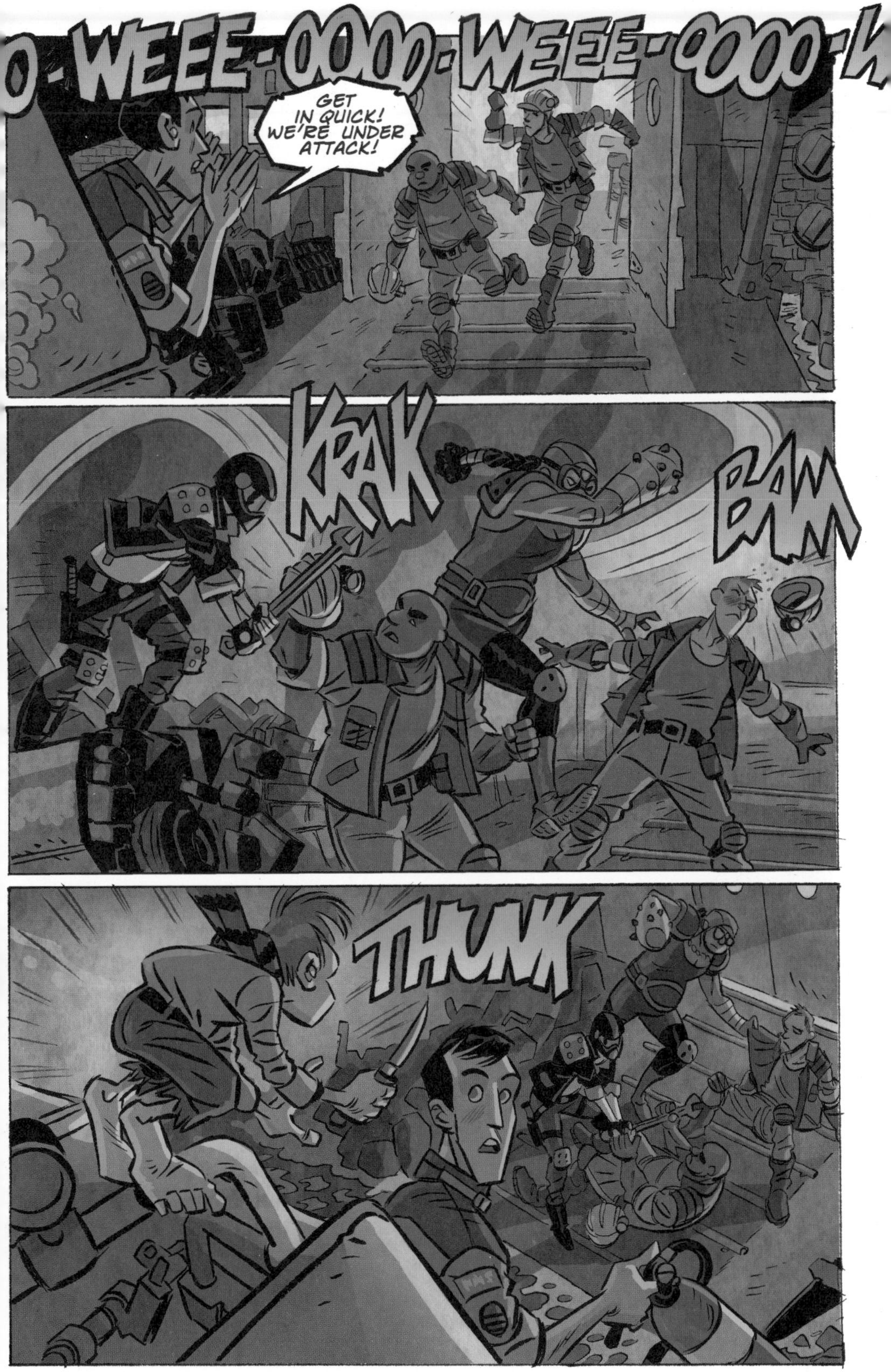
O-WEEE-OOOO-WEEE-OOOO-K
GET IN QUICK! WE'RE UNDER ATTACK!
KRAK
BAM
THUNK

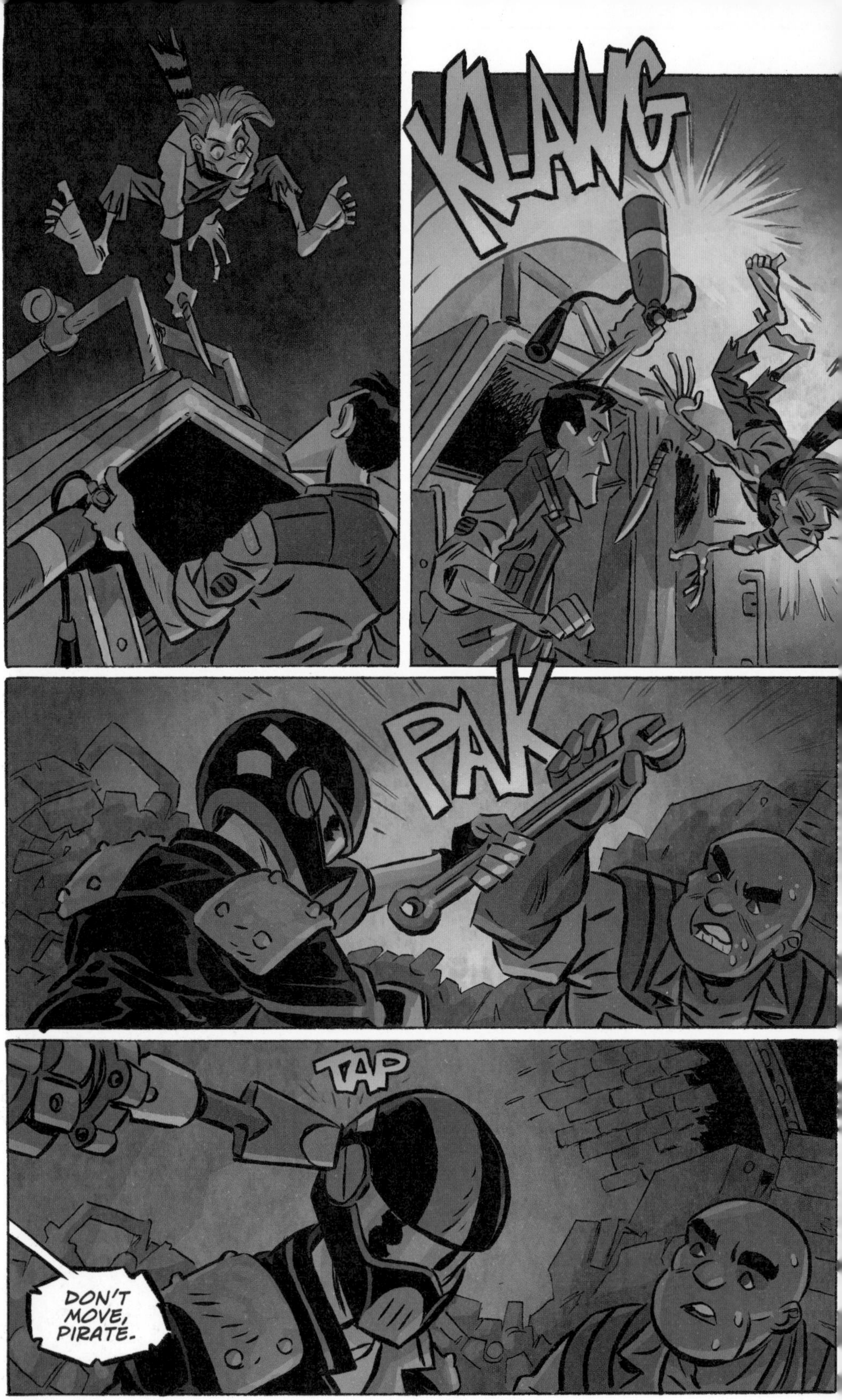
KLANG
PAK
TAP
DON'T MOVE, PIRATE.

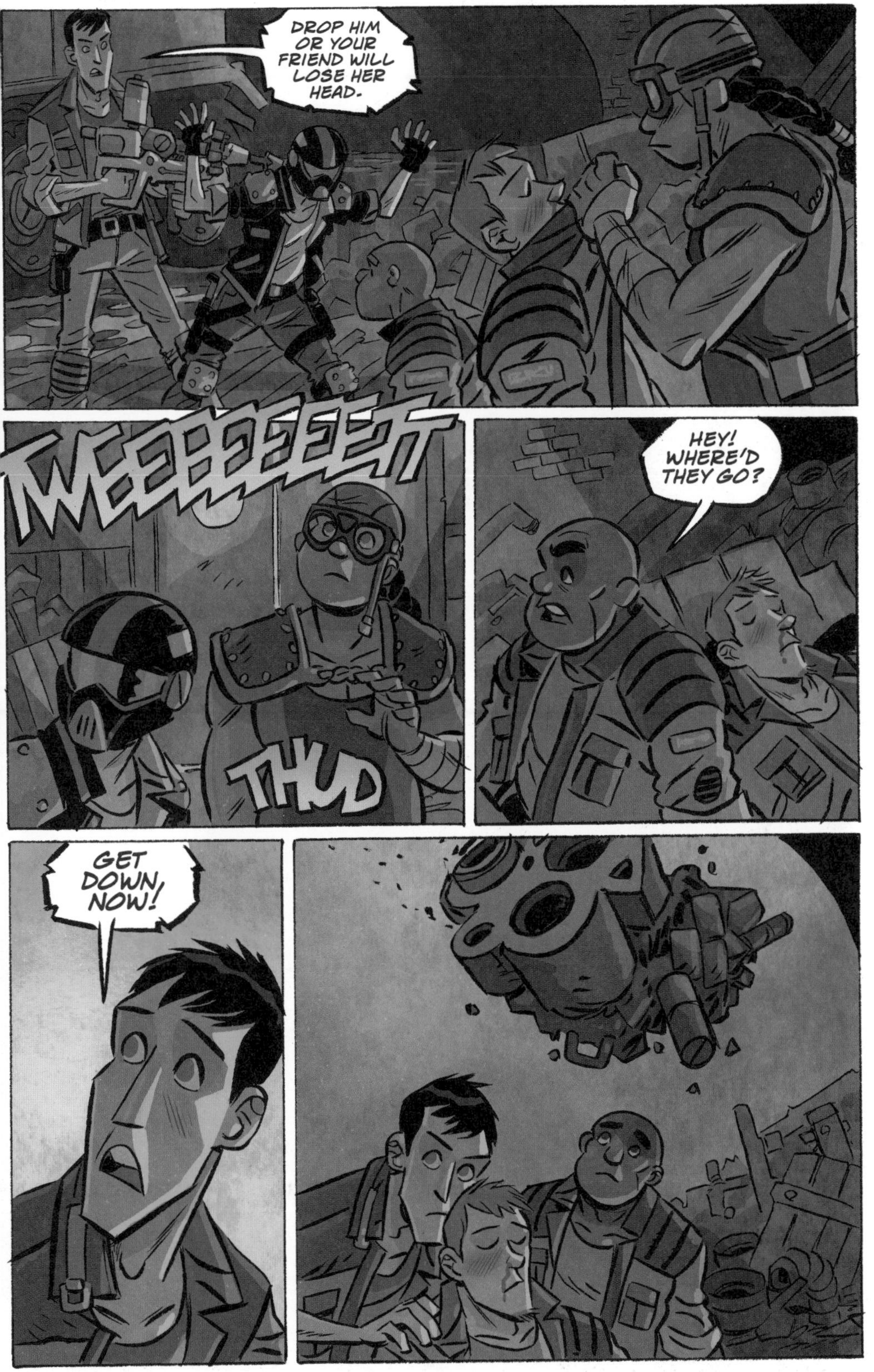
DROP HIM OR YOUR FRIEND WILL LOSE HER HEAD.
TWEEEEEEEET
THUD
HEY! WHERE'D THEY GO?
GET DOWN, NOW!

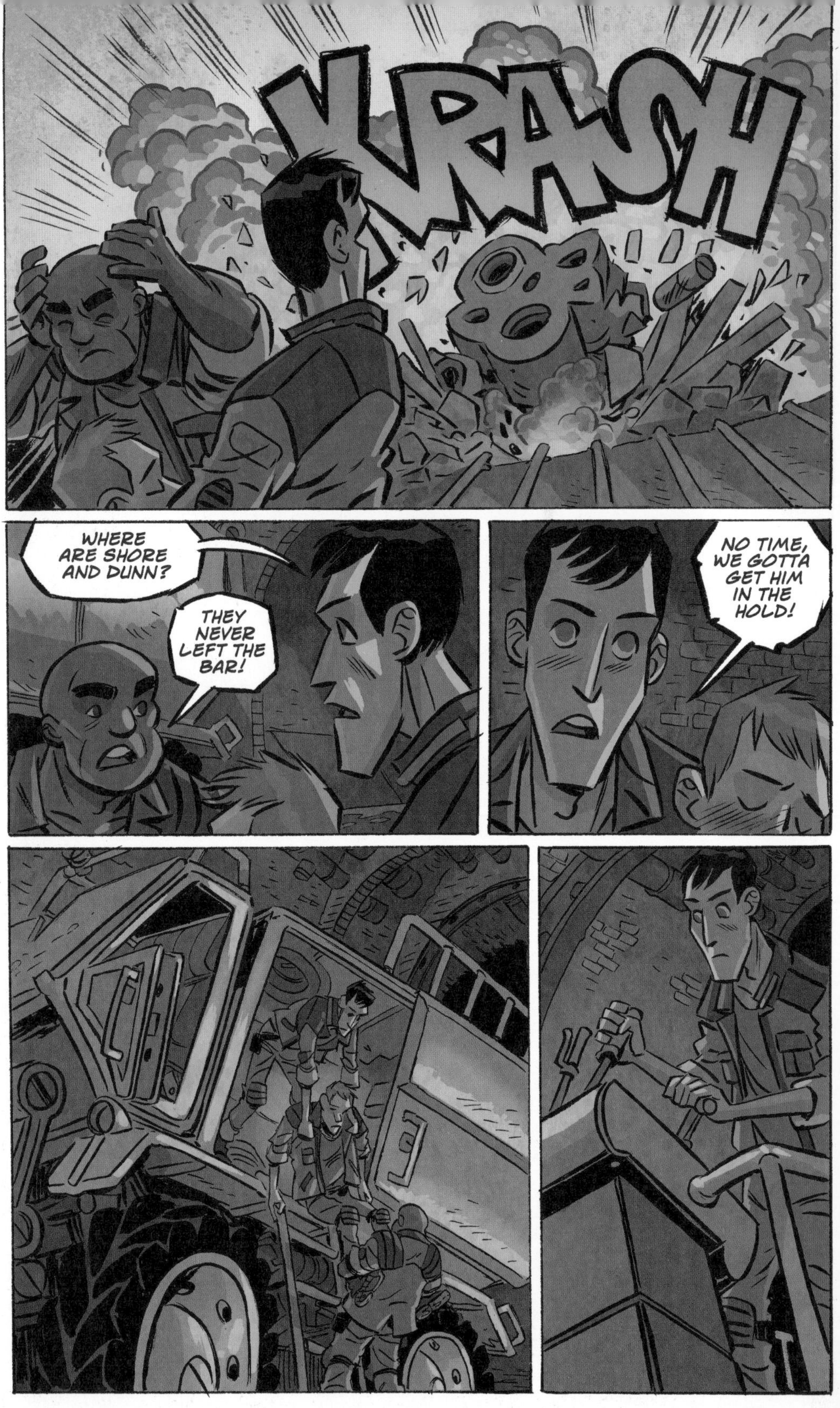
KRASH
WHERE ARE SHORE AND DUNN?
THEY NEVER LEFT THE BAR!
NO TIME, WE GOTTA GET HIM IN THE HOLD!

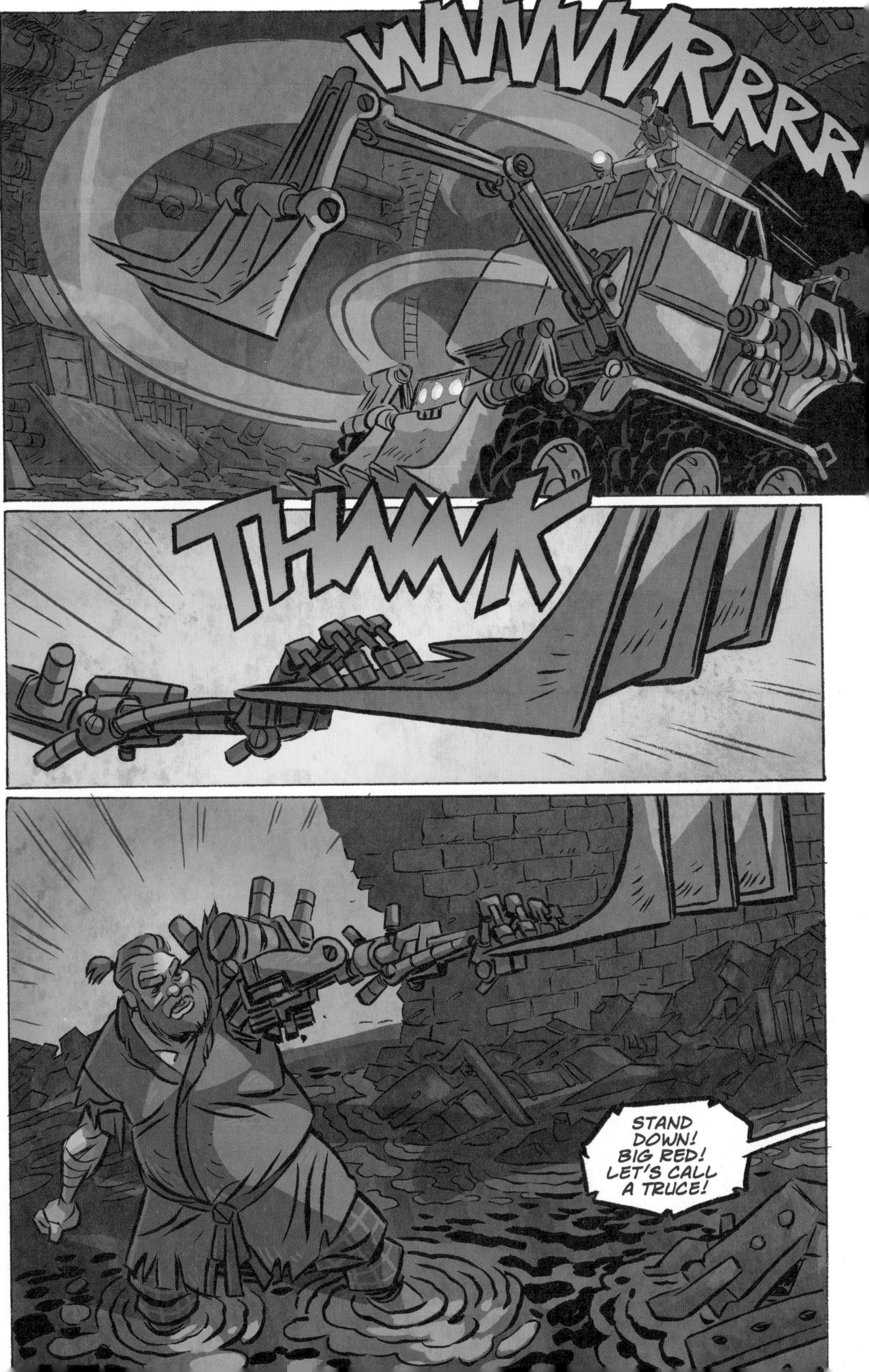
WHHHHRRRR
THUNK
STAND DOWN! BIG RED! LET'S CALL A TRUCE!

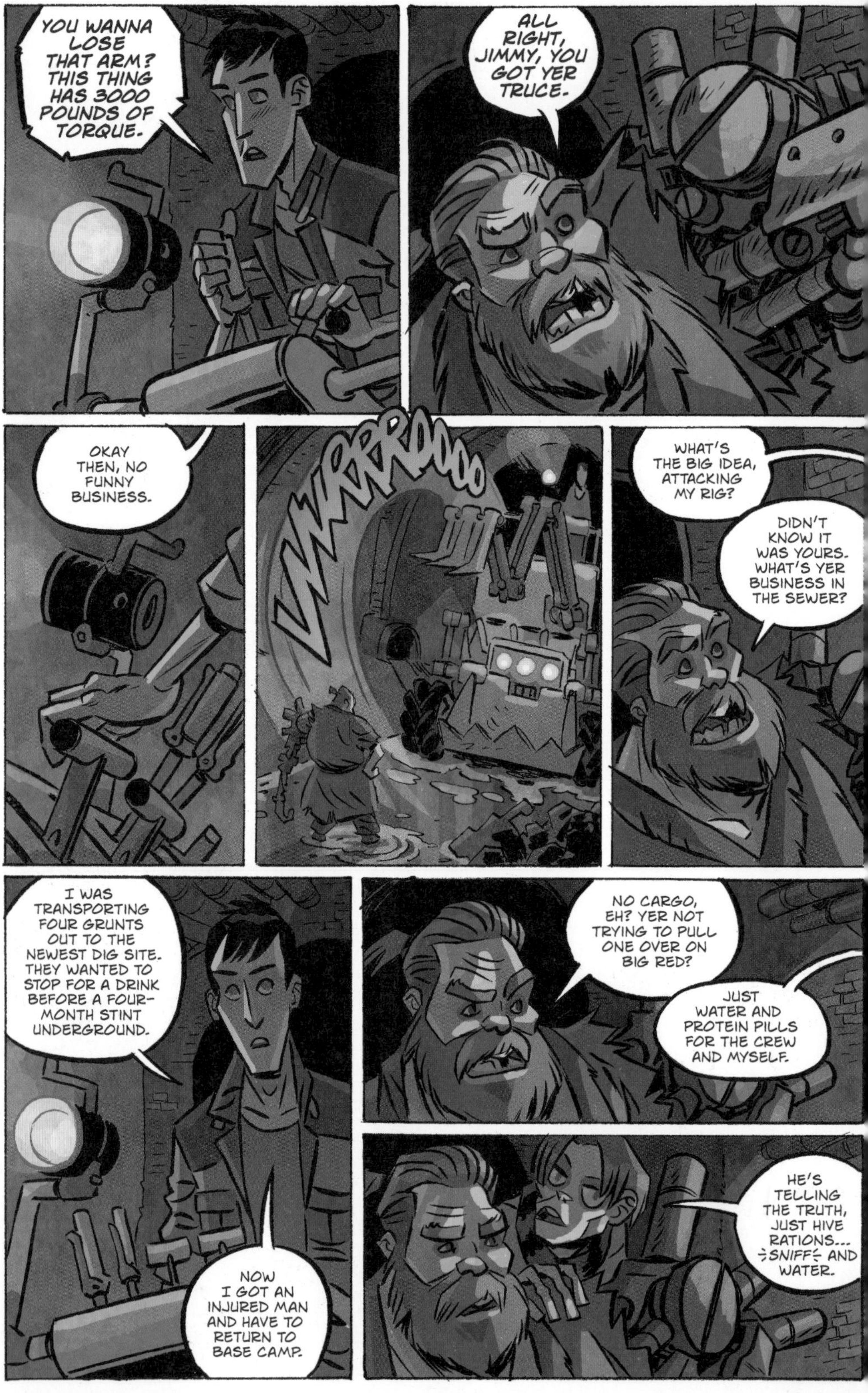
YOU WANNA LOSE THAT ARM? THIS THING HAS 3000 POUNDS OF TORQUE.
ALL RIGHT, JIMMY, YOU GOT YER TRUCE.
OKAY THEN, NO FUNNY BUSINESS.
WWRRRDOOO
WHAT'S THE BIG IDEA, ATTACKING MY RIG?
DIDN'T KNOW IT WAS YOURS. WHAT'S YER BUSINESS IN THE SEWER?
I WAS TRANSPORTING FOUR GRUNTS OUT TO THE NEWEST DIG SITE. THEY WANTED TO STOP FOR A DRINK BEFORE A FOUR-MONTH STINT UNDERGROUND.
NOW I GOT AN INJURED MAN AND HAVE TO RETURN TO BASE CAMP.
NO CARGO, EH? YER NOT TRYING TO PULL ONE OVER ON BIG RED?
JUST WATER AND PROTEIN PILLS FOR THE CREW AND MYSELF.
HE'S TELLING THE TRUTH, JUST HIVE RATIONS... SNIFF AND WATER.

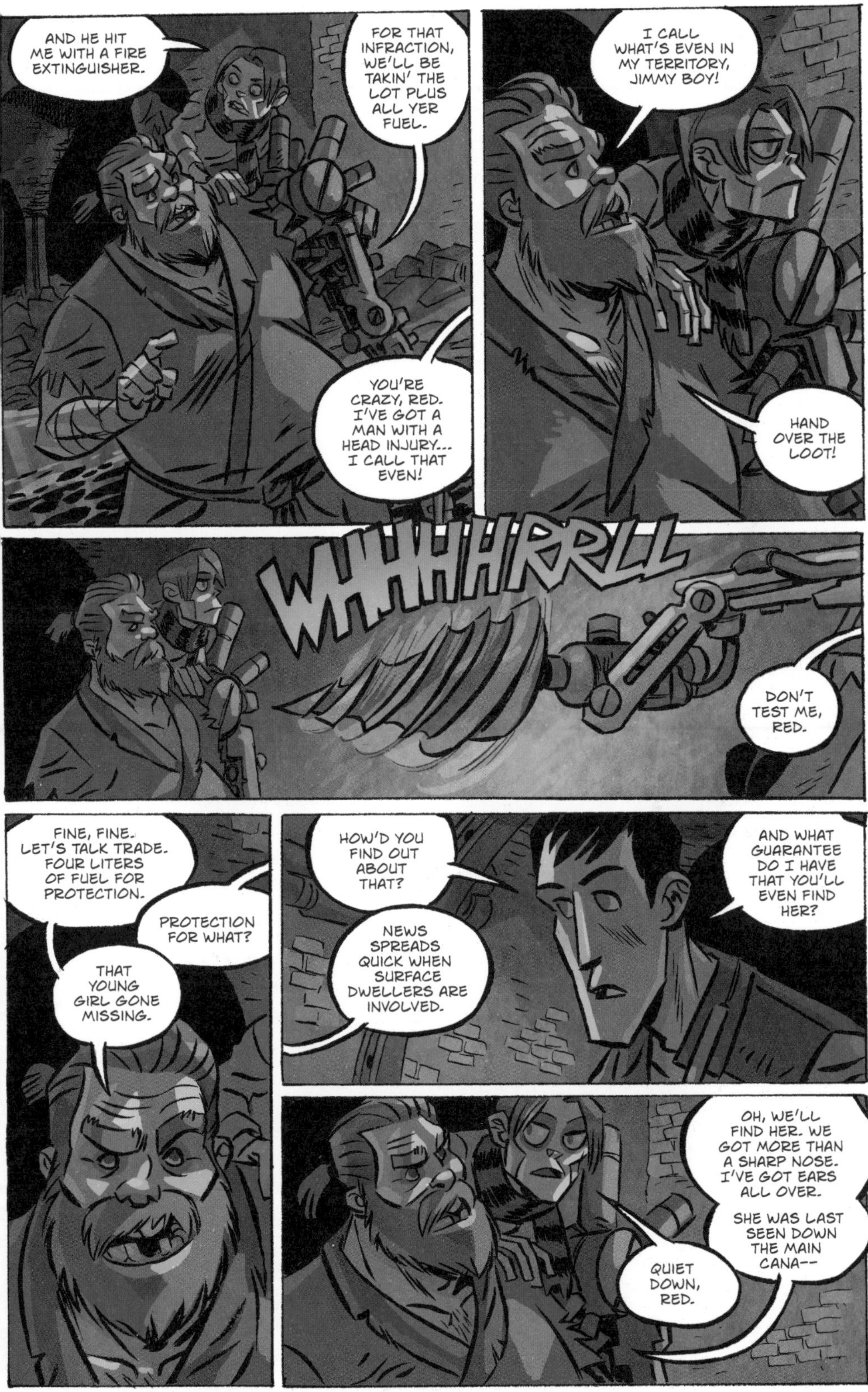
AND HE HIT ME WITH A FIRE EXTINGUISHER.
FOR THAT INFRACTION, WE'LL BE TAKIN' THE LOT PLUS ALL YER FUEL.
YOU'RE CRAZY, RED. I'VE GOT A MAN WITH A HEAD INJURY... I CALL THAT EVEN!
I CALL WHAT'S EVEN IN MY TERRITORY, JIMMY BOY!
HAND OVER THE LOOT!
WHHHHRRLL
DON'T TEST ME, RED.
FINE, FINE. LET'S TALK TRADE. FOUR LITERS OF FUEL FOR PROTECTION.
PROTECTION FOR WHAT?
THAT YOUNG GIRL GONE MISSING.
HOW'D YOU FIND OUT ABOUT THAT?
NEWS SPREADS QUICK WHEN SURFACE DWELLERS ARE INVOLVED.
AND WHAT GUARANTEE DO I HAVE THAT YOU'LL EVEN FIND HER?
OH, WE'LL FIND HER. WE GOT MORE THAN A SHARP NOSE. I'VE GOT EARS ALL OVER.
SHE WAS LAST SEEN DOWN THE MAIN CANA--
QUIET DOWN, RED.

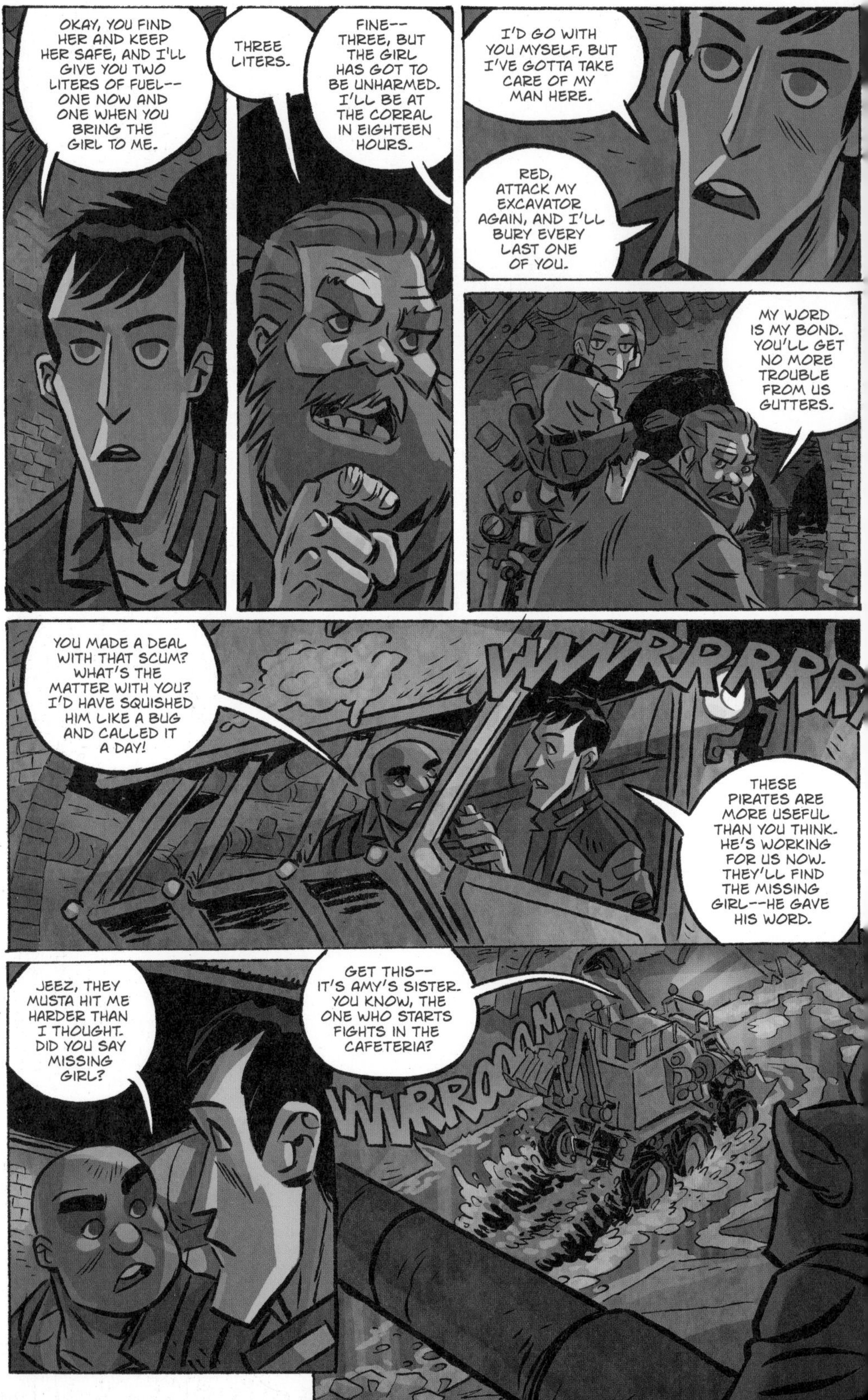
OKAY, YOU FIND HER AND KEEP HER SAFE, AND I'LL GIVE YOU TWO LITERS OF FUEL--ONE NOW AND ONE WHEN YOU BRING THE GIRL TO ME.
THREE LITERS.
FINE--THREE, BUT THE GIRL HAS GOT TO BE UNHARMED. I'LL BE AT THE CORRAL IN EIGHTEEN HOURS.
I'D GO WITH YOU MYSELF, BUT I'VE GOTTA TAKE CARE OF MY MAN HERE.
RED, ATTACK MY EXCAVATOR AGAIN, AND I'LL BURY EVERY LAST ONE OF YOU.
MY WORD IS MY BOND. YOU'LL GET NO MORE TROUBLE FROM US GUTTERS.
YOU MADE A DEAL WITH THAT SCUM? WHAT'S THE MATTER WITH YOU? I'D HAVE SQUISHED HIM LIKE A BUG AND CALLED IT A DAY!
VVVRRRRR
THESE PIRATES ARE MORE USEFUL THAN YOU THINK. HE'S WORKING FOR US NOW. THEY'LL FIND THE MISSING GIRL--HE GAVE HIS WORD.
JEEZ, THEY MUSTA HIT ME HARDER THAN I THOUGHT. DID YOU SAY MISSING GIRL?
GET THIS--IT'S AMY'S SISTER. YOU KNOW, THE ONE WHO STARTS FIGHTS IN THE CAFETERIA?
VVRRoooM

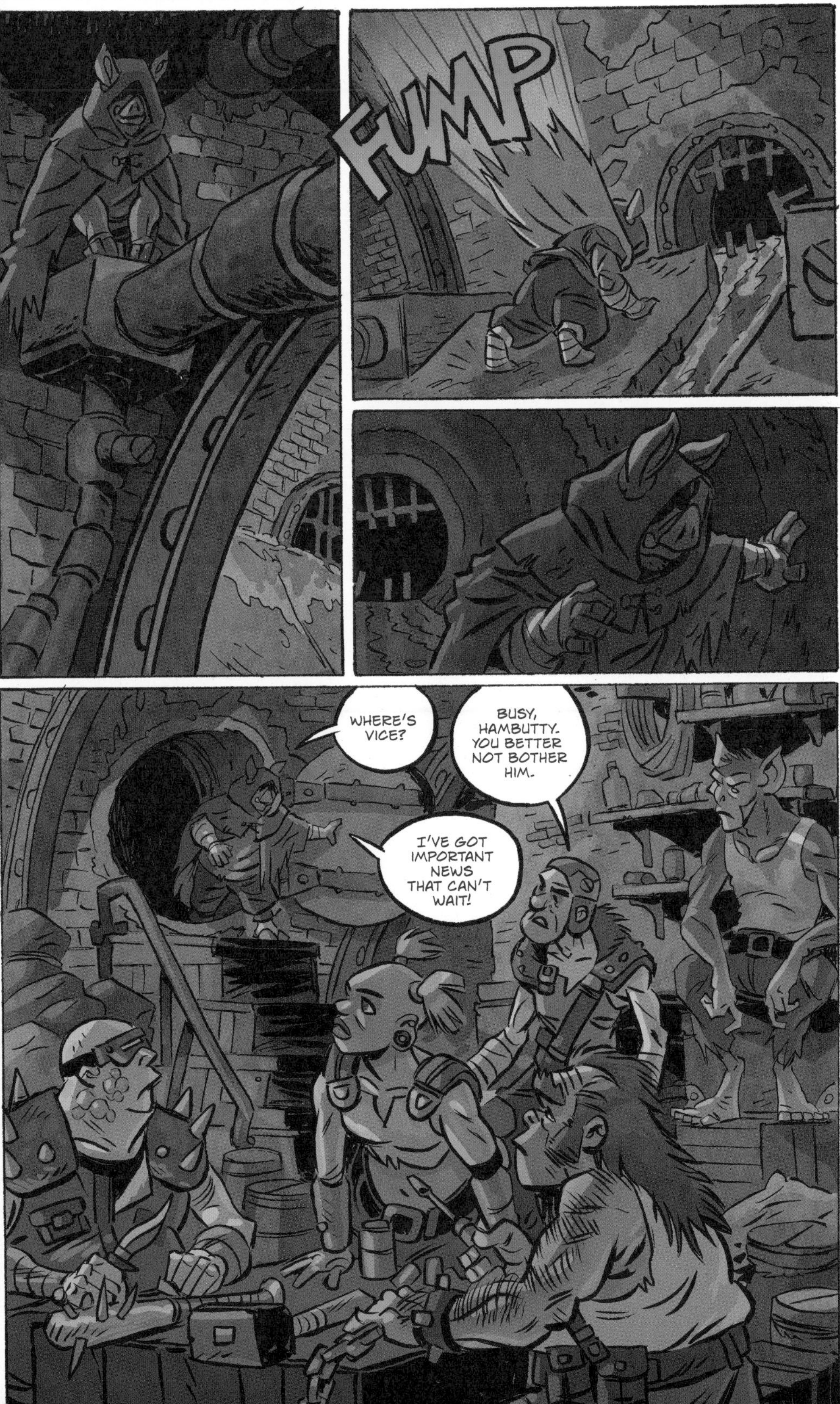
FUMP
WHERE'S VICE?
BUSY, HAMBUTTY. YOU BETTER NOT BOTHER HIM.
I'VE GOT IMPORTANT NEWS THAT CAN'T WAIT!

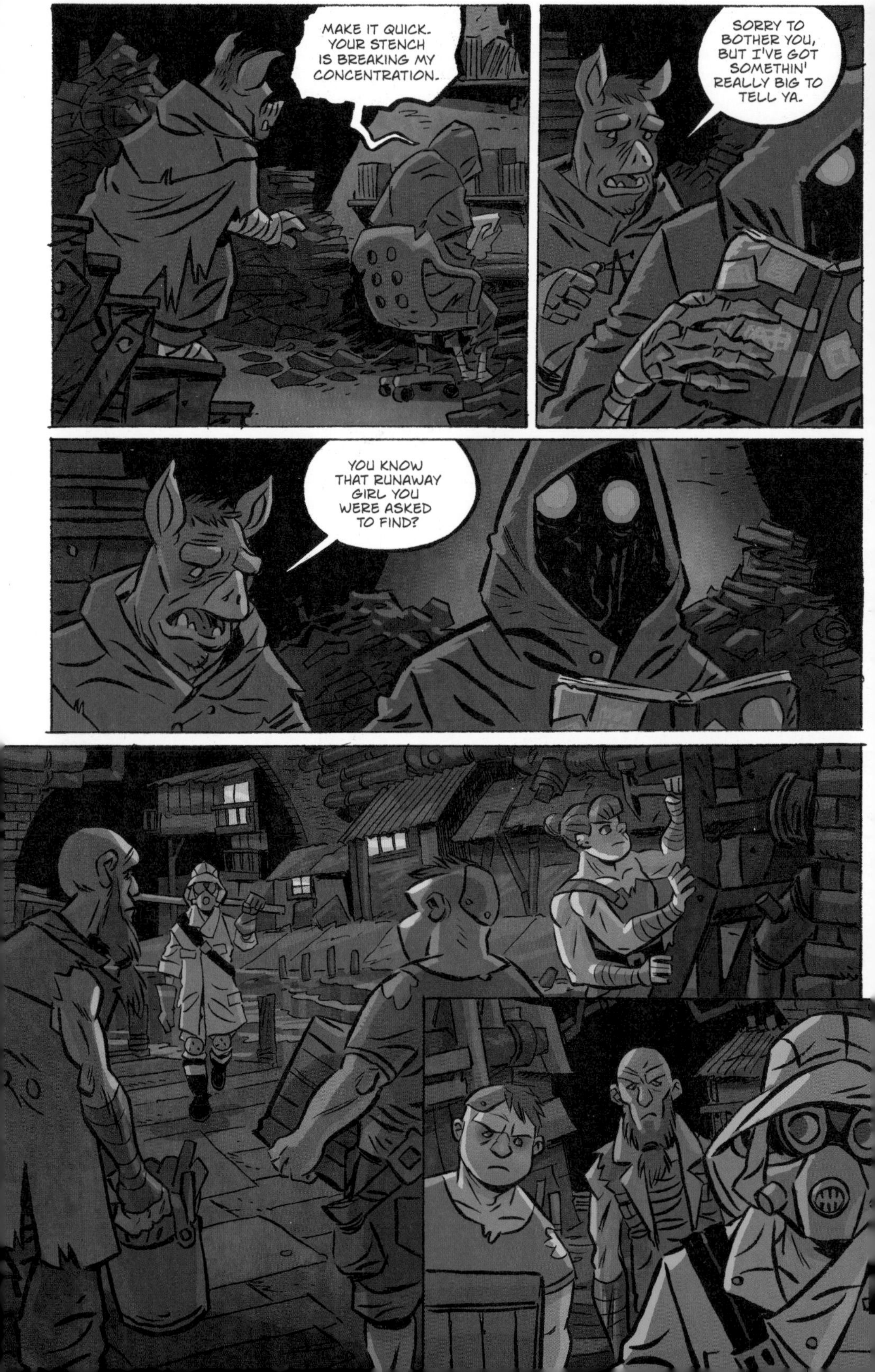
MAKE IT QUICK. YOUR STENCH IS BREAKING MY CONCENTRATION.
SORRY TO BOTHER YOU, BUT I'VE GOT SOMETHIN' REALLY BIG TO TELL YA.
YOU KNOW THAT RUNAWAY GIRL YOU WERE ASKED TO FIND?

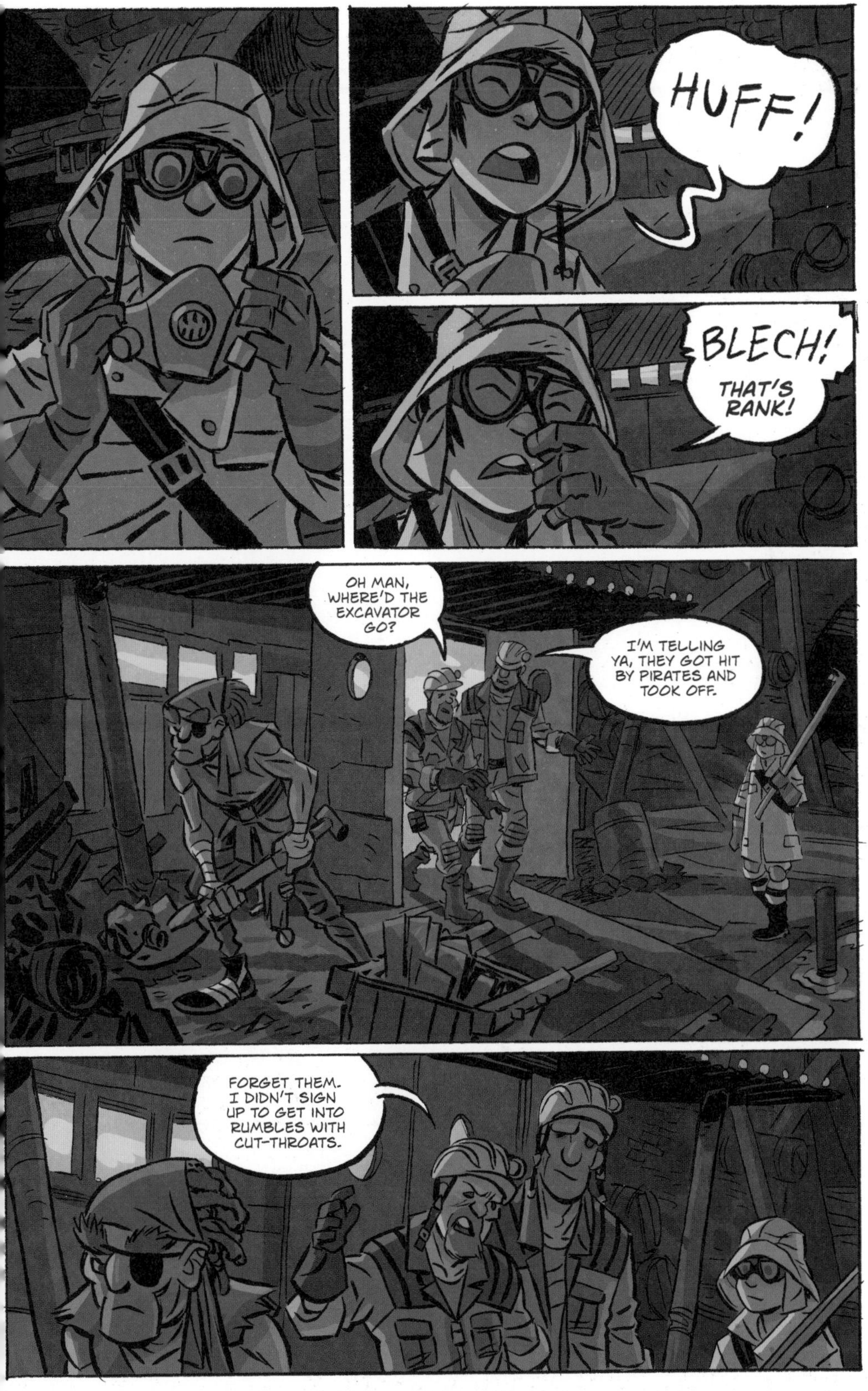
HUFF!
BLECH!
THAT'S RANK!
OH MAN, WHERE'D THE EXCAVATOR GO?
I'M TELLING YA, THEY GOT HIT BY PIRATES AND TOOK OFF.
FORGET THEM. I DIDN'T SIGN UP TO GET INTO RUMBLES WITH CUT-THROATS.

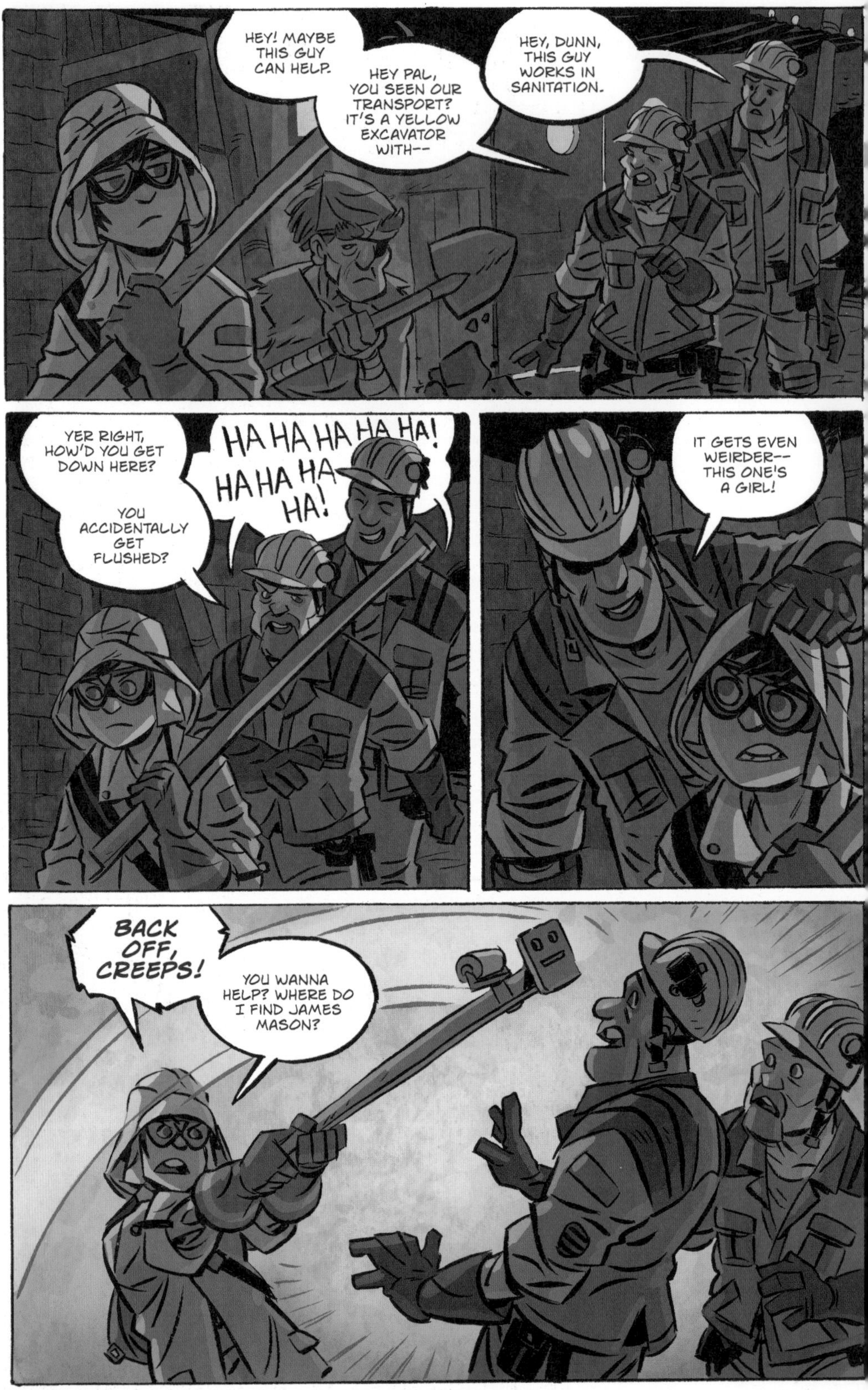
HEY! MAYBE THIS GUY CAN HELP.
HEY PAL, YOU SEEN OUR TRANSPORT? IT'S A YELLOW EXCAVATOR WITH--
HEY, DUNN, THIS GUY WORKS IN SANITATION.
YER RIGHT, HOW'D YOU GET DOWN HERE?
YOU ACCIDENTALLY GET FLUSHED?
HA HA HA HA HA HA! HA HA HA HA!
IT GETS EVEN WEIRDER-- THIS ONE'S A GIRL!
BACK OFF, CREEPS!
YOU WANNA HELP? WHERE DO I FIND JAMES MASON?

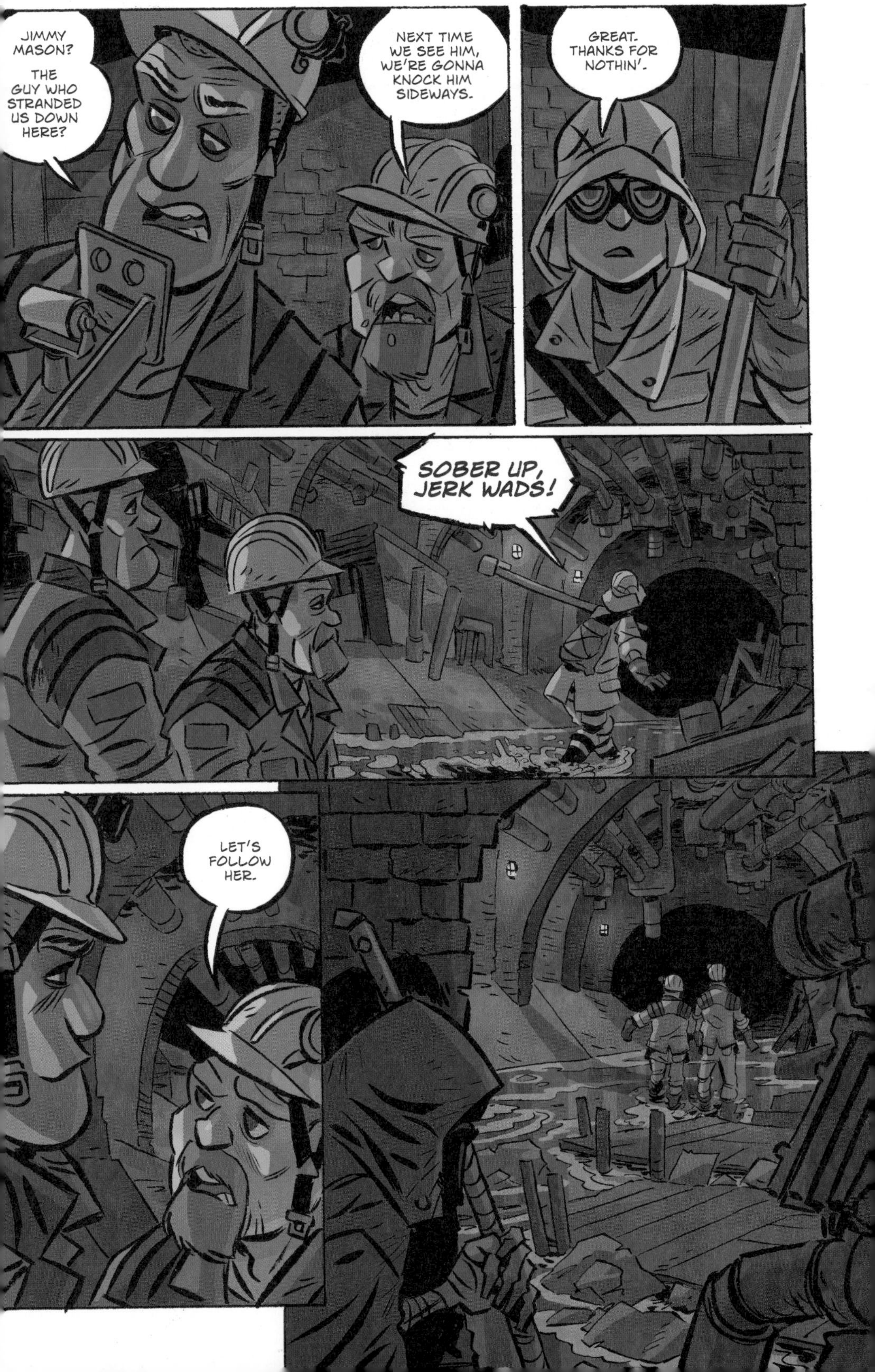
JIMMY MASON?
THE GUY WHO STRANDED US DOWN HERE?
NEXT TIME WE SEE HIM, WE'RE GONNA KNOCK HIM SIDEWAYS.
GREAT. THANKS FOR NOTHIN'.
SOBER UP, JERK WADS!
LET'S FOLLOW HER.

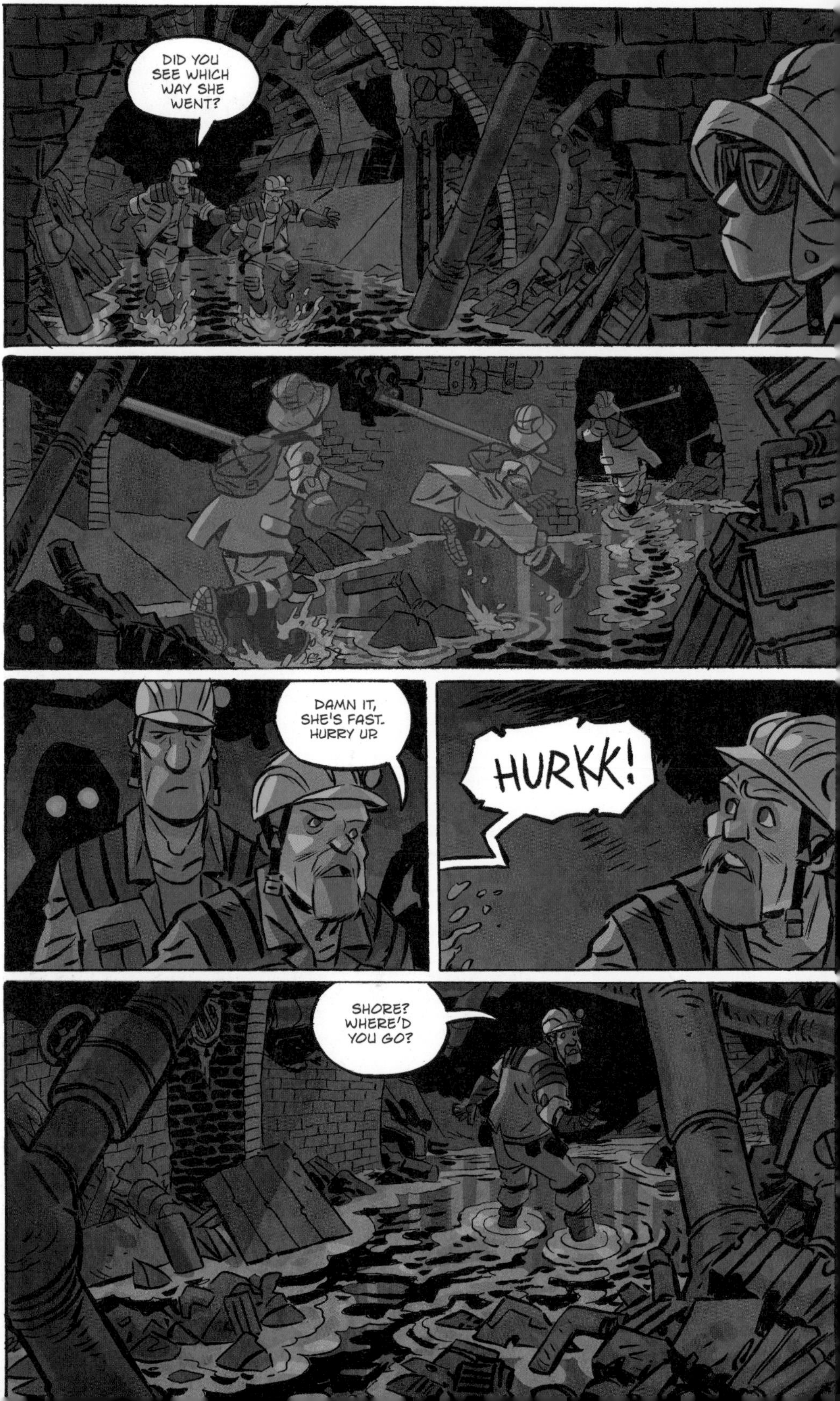
DID YOU SEE WHICH WAY SHE WENT?
DAMN IT, SHE'S FAST. HURRY UP.
HURKK!
SHORE? WHERE'D YOU GO?

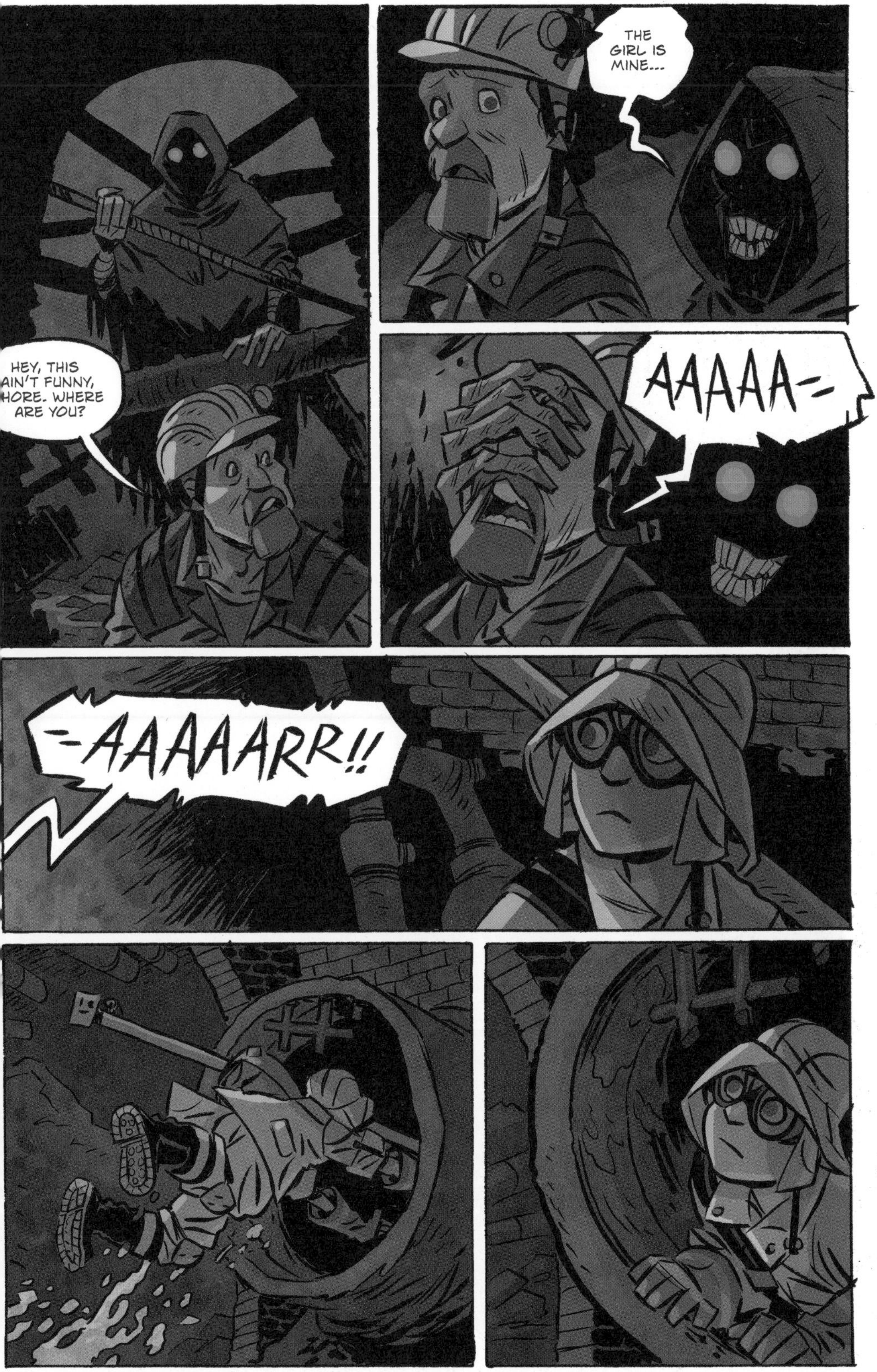
HEY, THIS AIN'T FUNNY, HORE. WHERE ARE YOU?
THE GIRL IS MINE...
AAAAA-
-AAAAARR!!

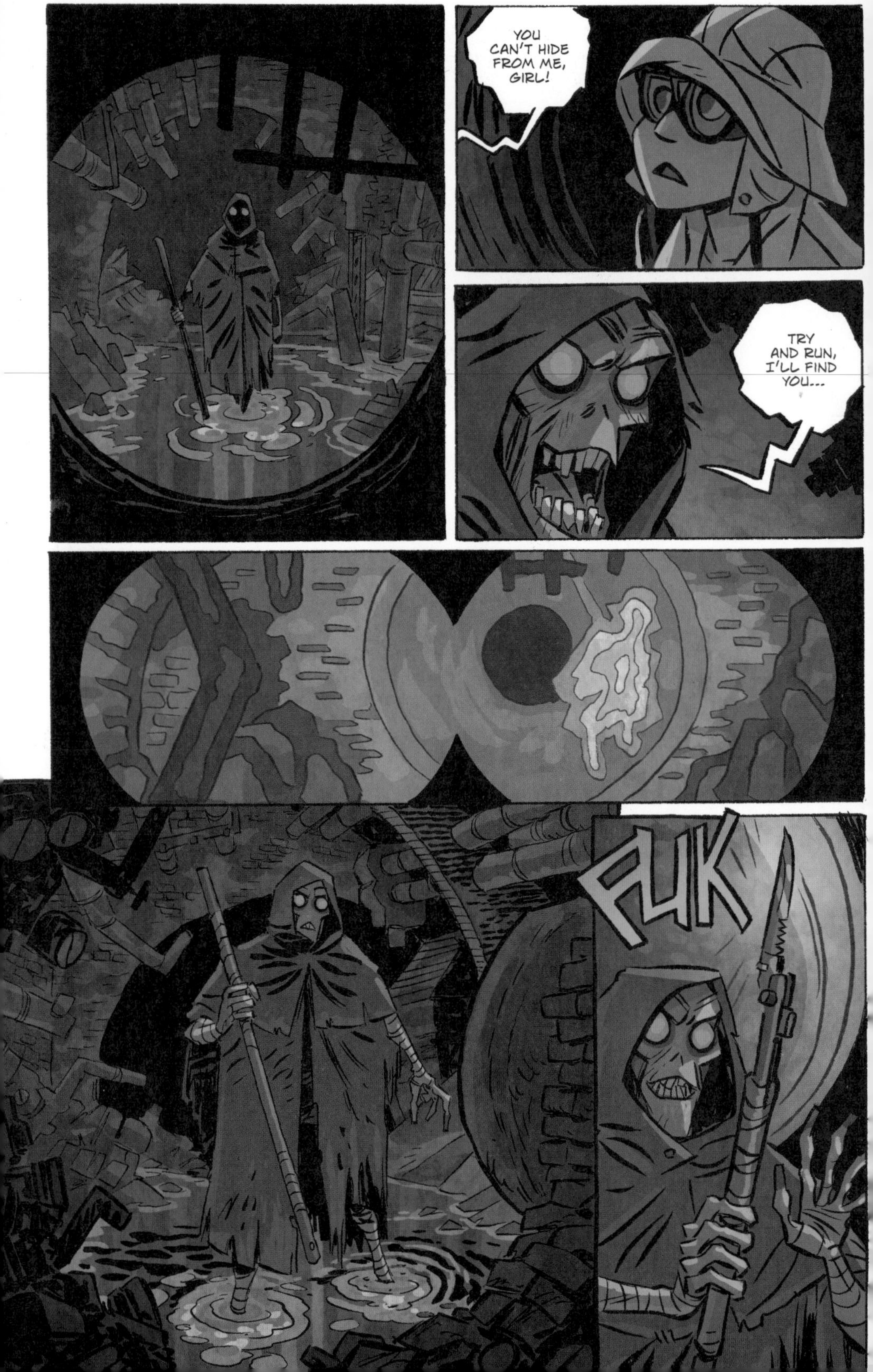

YOU CAN'T HIDE FROM ME, GIRL!
TRY AND RUN, I'LL FIND YOU...
FUK

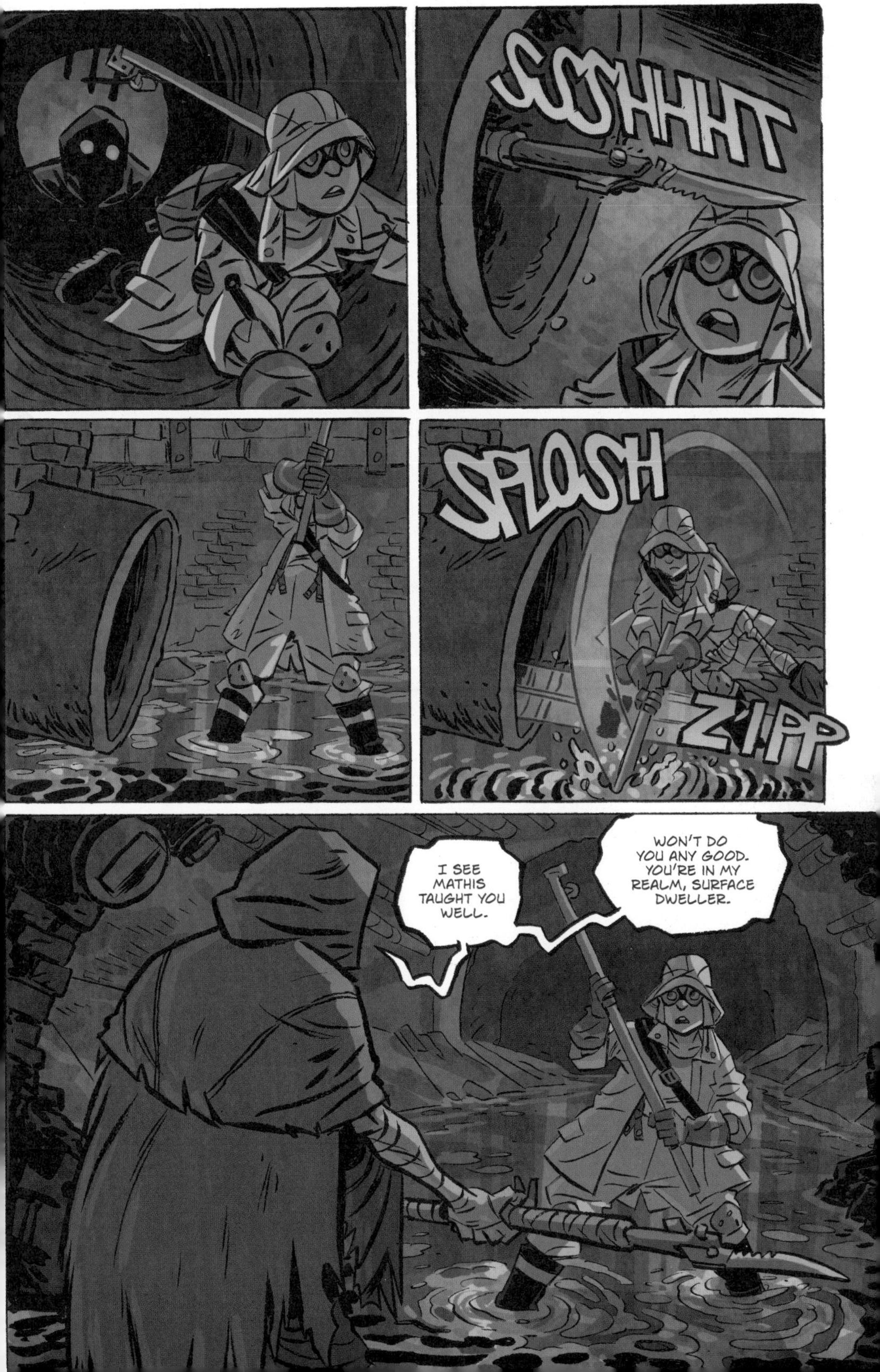
SSSHHHT
SPLOSH
ZIPP
I SEE MATHIS TAUGHT YOU WELL.
WON'T DO YOU ANY GOOD. YOU'RE IN MY REALM, SURFACE DWELLER.

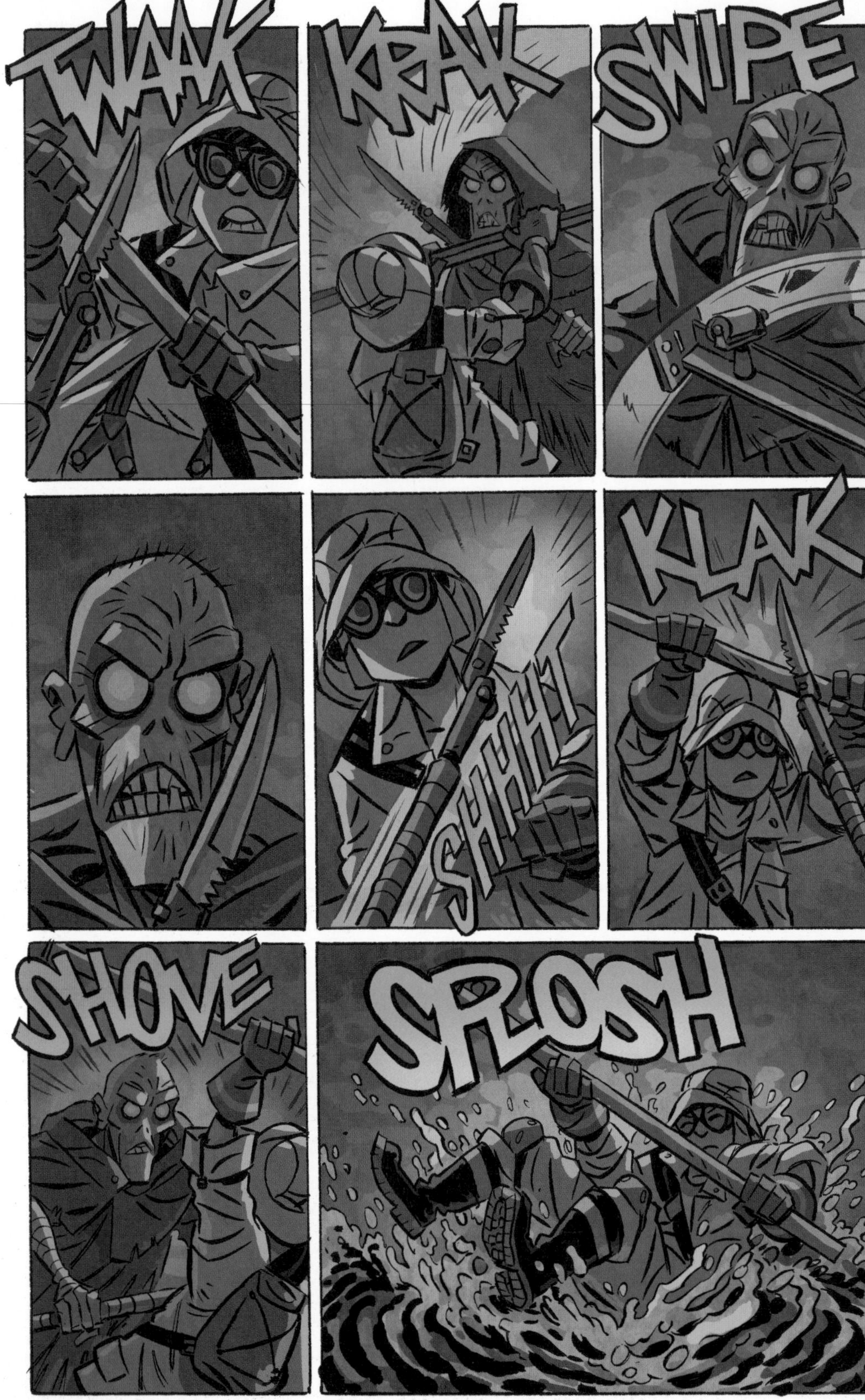
TWAAK
KRAK
SWIPE
SHHHT
KLAK
SHOVE
SPLOSH

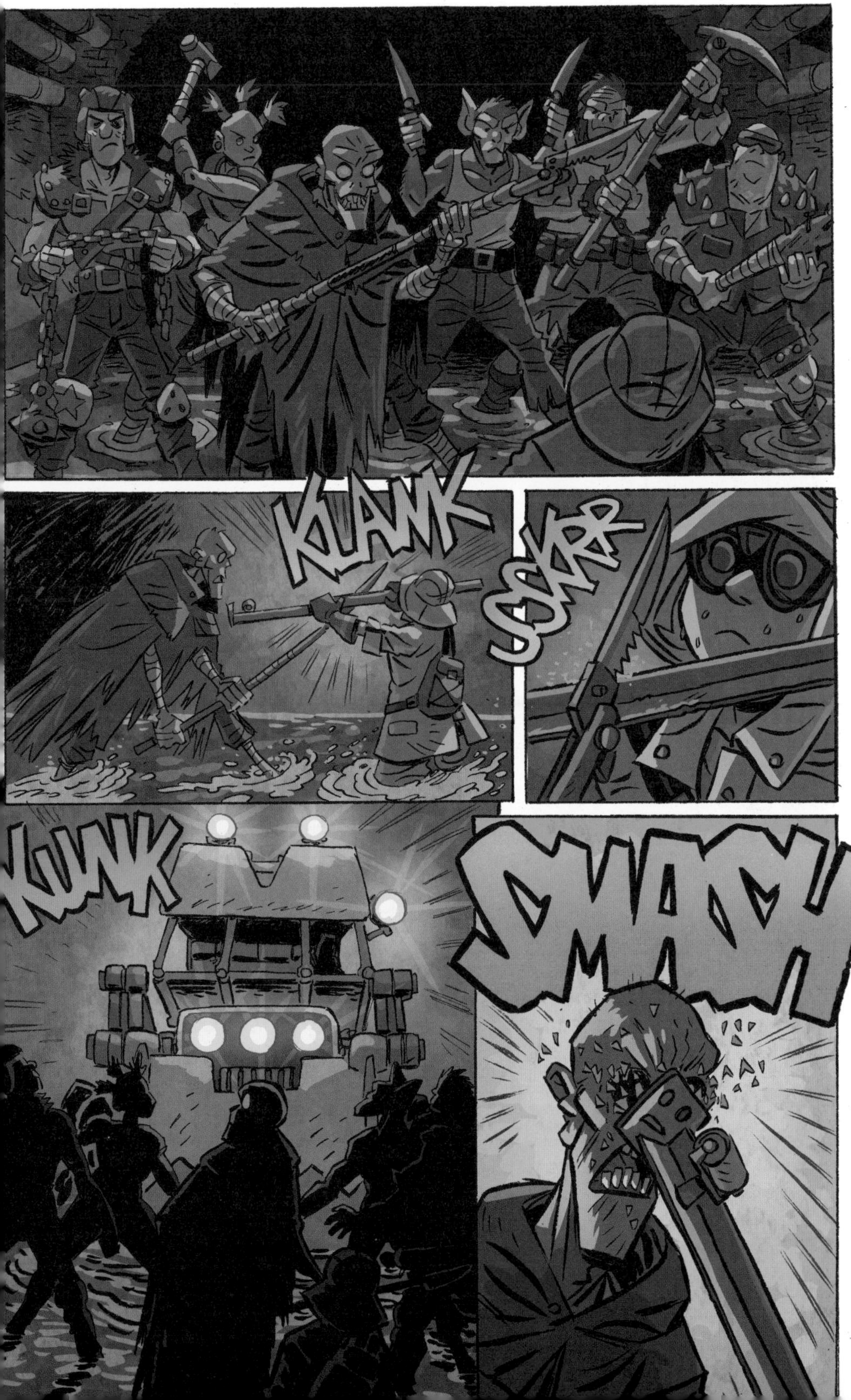
KLANK
SSKRR
KLUNK
SMASH

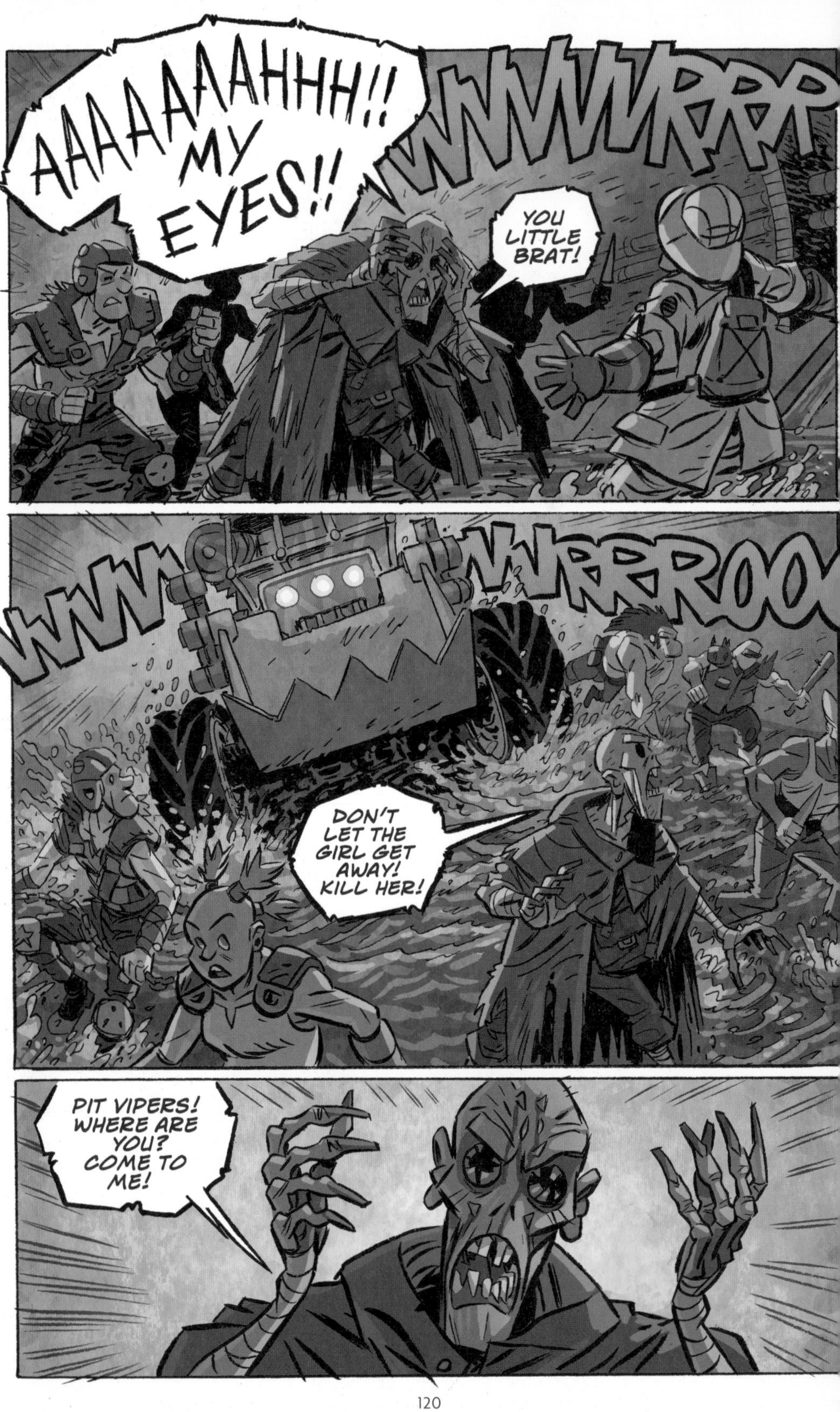
AAAAAAAHHHH!! MY EYES!!
YOU LITTLE BRAT!
DON'T LET THE GIRL GET AWAY! KILL HER!
PIT VIPERS! WHERE ARE YOU? COME TO ME!

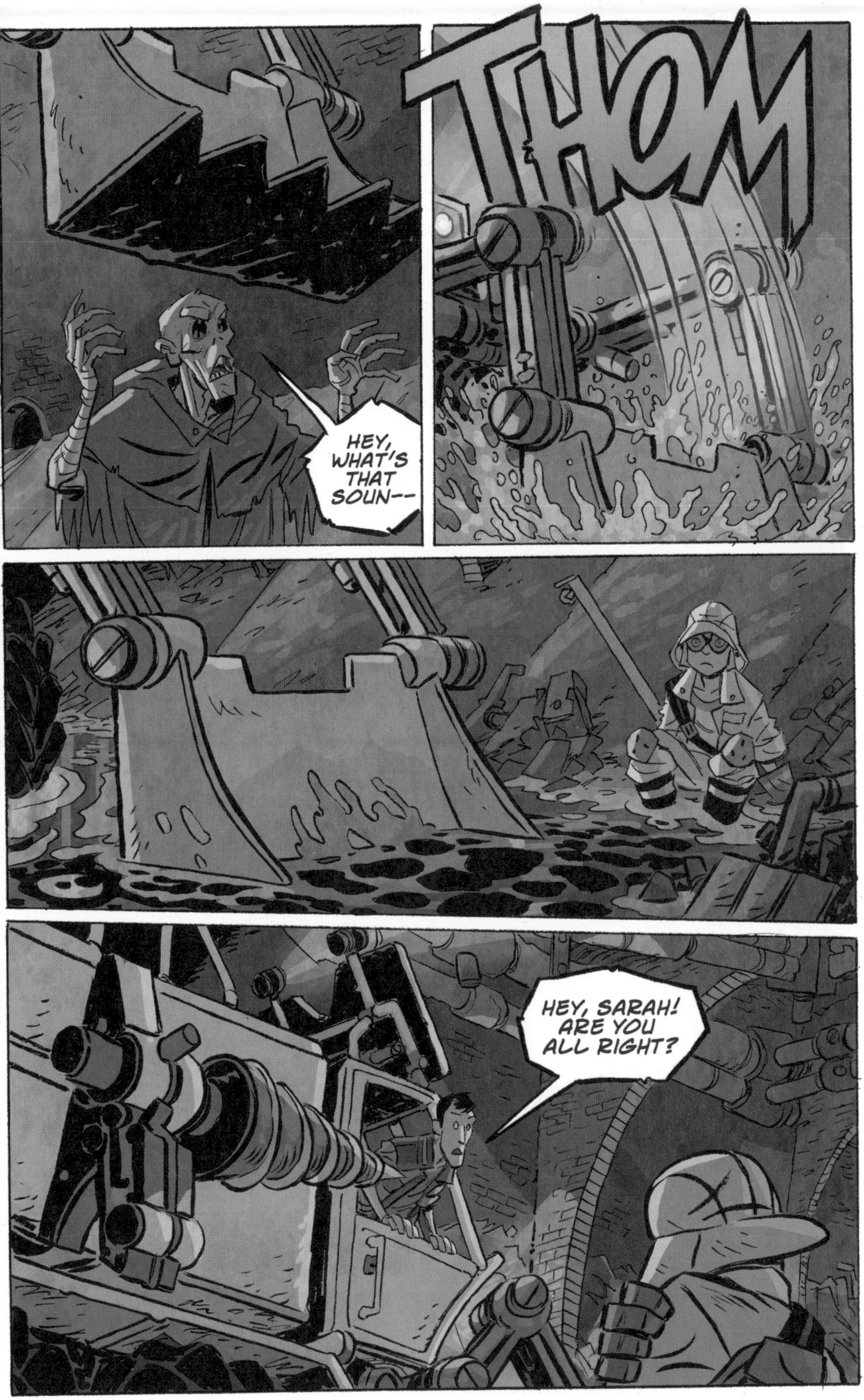
HEY, WHAT'S THAT SOUN--
THOM
HEY, SARAH! ARE YOU ALL RIGHT?

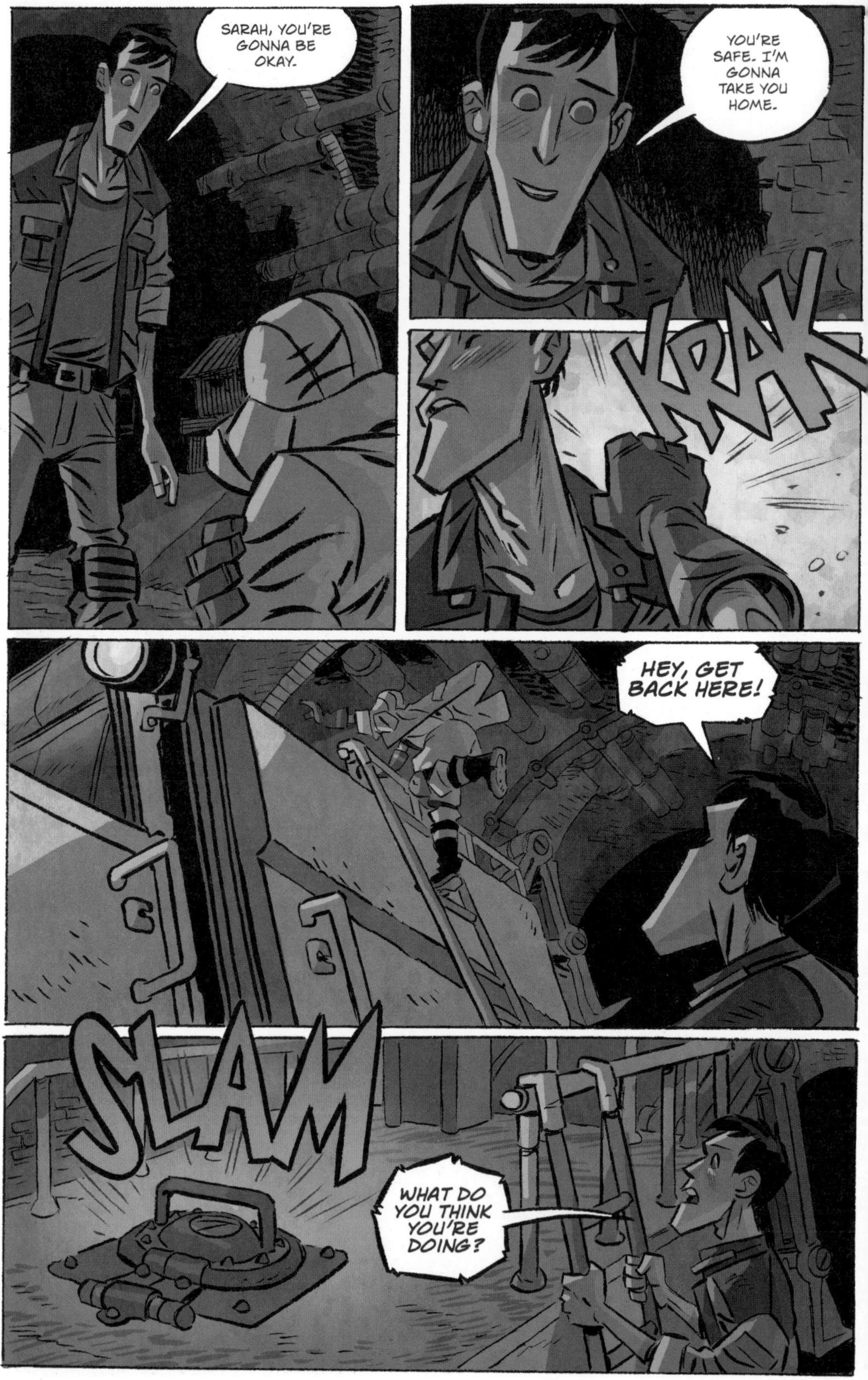
SARAH, YOU'RE GONNA BE OKAY.
YOU'RE SAFE. I'M GONNA TAKE YOU HOME.
KRAK
HEY, GET BACK HERE!
SLAM
WHAT DO YOU THINK YOU'RE DOING?

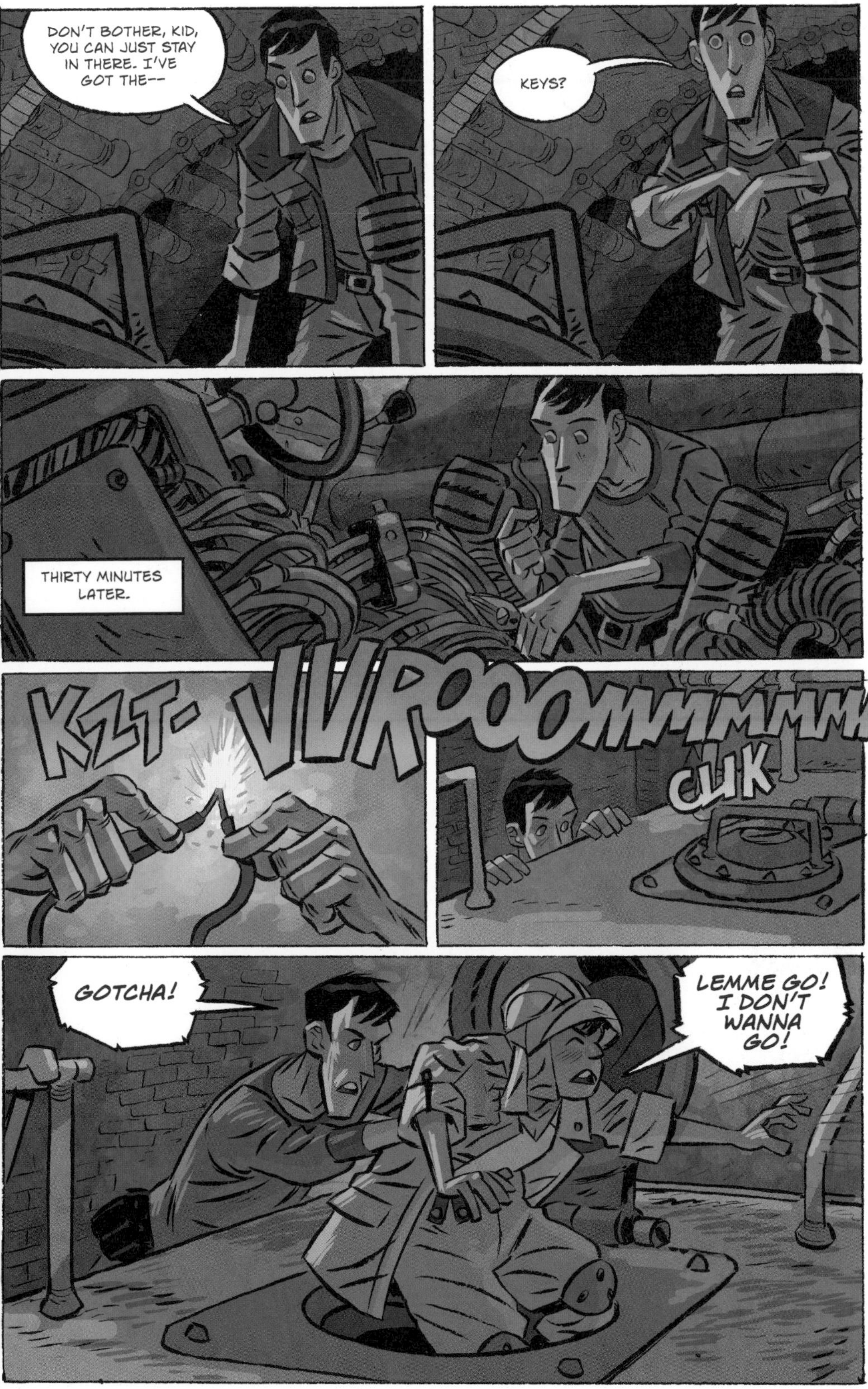
DON'T BOTHER, KID, YOU CAN JUST STAY IN THERE. I'VE GOT THE--
KEYS?
THIRTY MINUTES LATER.
KZT-
VVROOOMMMMMMM
CLIK
GOTCHA!
LEMME GO! I DON'T WANNA GO!

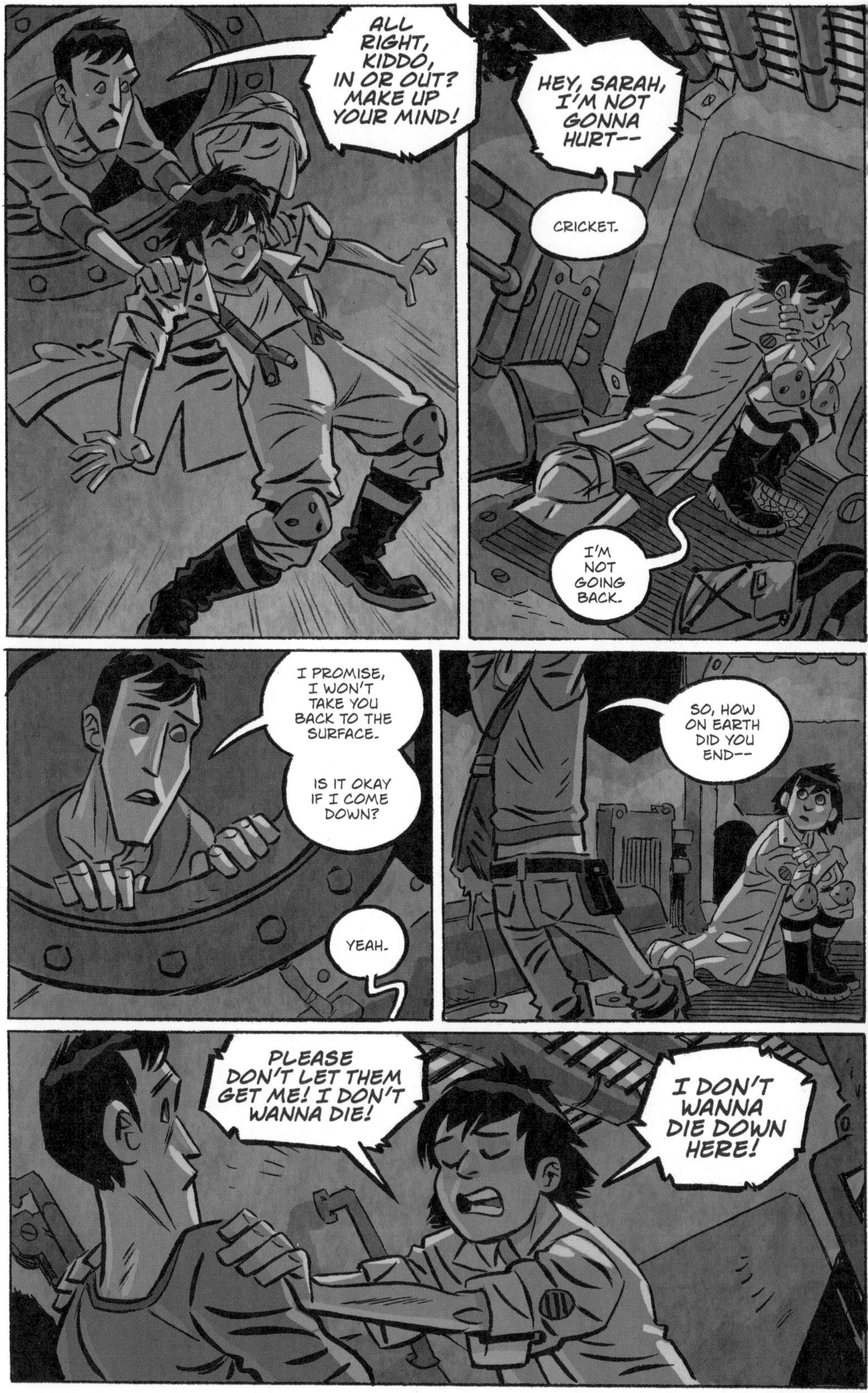
ALL RIGHT, KIDDO, IN OR OUT? MAKE UP YOUR MIND!
HEY, SARAH, I'M NOT GONNA HURT--
CRICKET.
I'M NOT GOING BACK.
I PROMISE, I WON'T TAKE YOU BACK TO THE SURFACE.
IS IT OKAY IF I COME DOWN?
YEAH.
SO, HOW ON EARTH DID YOU END--
PLEASE DON'T LET THEM GET ME! I DON'T WANNA DIE!
I DON'T WANNA DIE DOWN HERE!

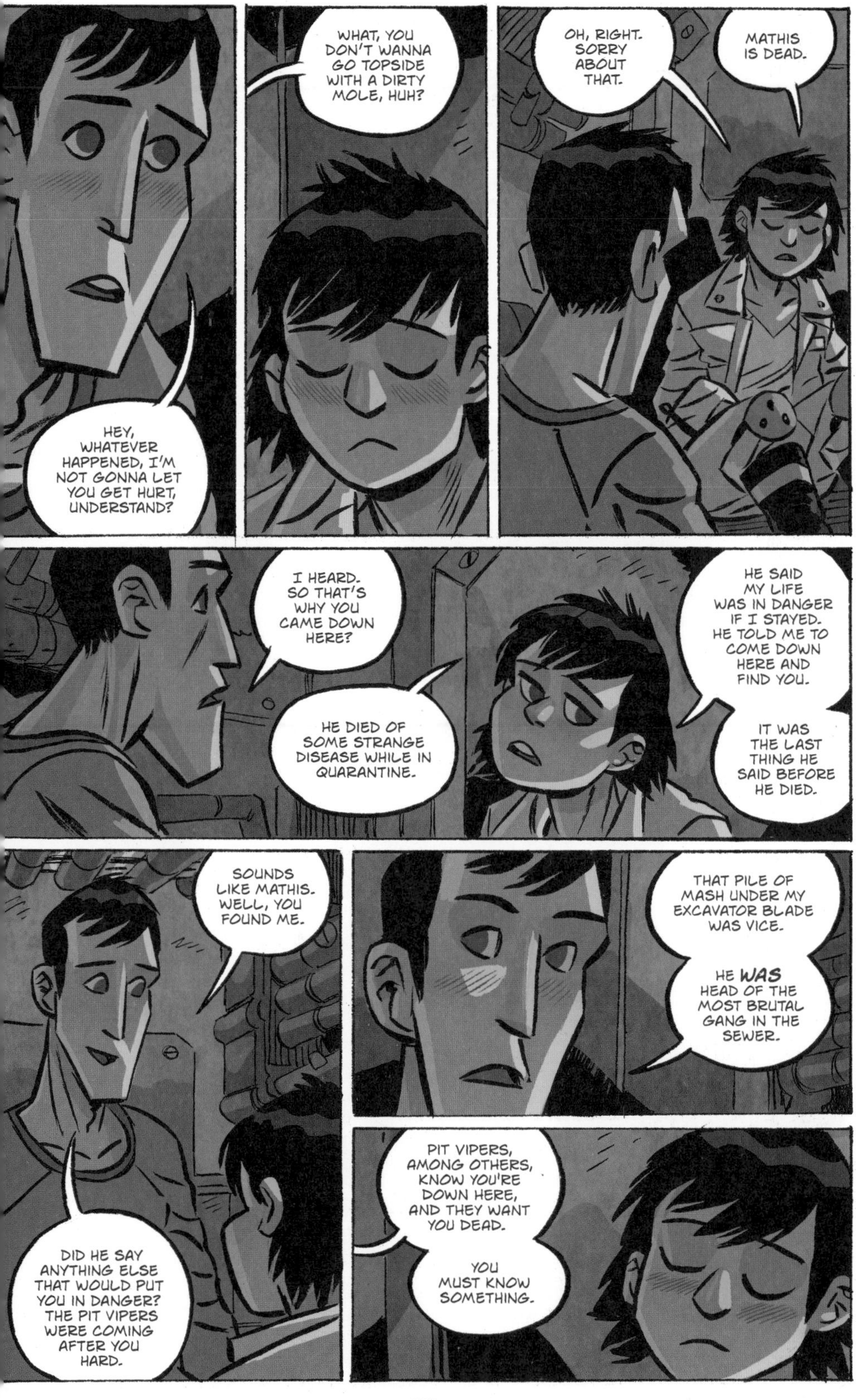
HEY, WHATEVER HAPPENED, I'M NOT GONNA LET YOU GET HURT, UNDERSTAND?
WHAT, YOU DON'T WANNA GO TOPSIDE WITH A DIRTY MOLE, HUH?
OH, RIGHT. SORRY ABOUT THAT.
MATHIS IS DEAD.
I HEARD. SO THAT'S WHY YOU CAME DOWN HERE?
HE DIED OF SOME STRANGE DISEASE WHILE IN QUARANTINE.
HE SAID MY LIFE WAS IN DANGER IF I STAYED. HE TOLD ME TO COME DOWN HERE AND FIND YOU.
IT WAS THE LAST THING HE SAID BEFORE HE DIED.
SOUNDS LIKE MATHIS. WELL, YOU FOUND ME.
DID HE SAY ANYTHING ELSE THAT WOULD PUT YOU IN DANGER? THE PIT VIPERS WERE COMING AFTER YOU HARD.
THAT PILE OF MASH UNDER MY EXCAVATOR BLADE WAS VICE.
HE **WAS** HEAD OF THE MOST BRUTAL GANG IN THE SEWER.
PIT VIPERS, AMONG OTHERS, KNOW YOU'RE DOWN HERE, AND THEY WANT YOU DEAD.
YOU MUST KNOW SOMETHING.

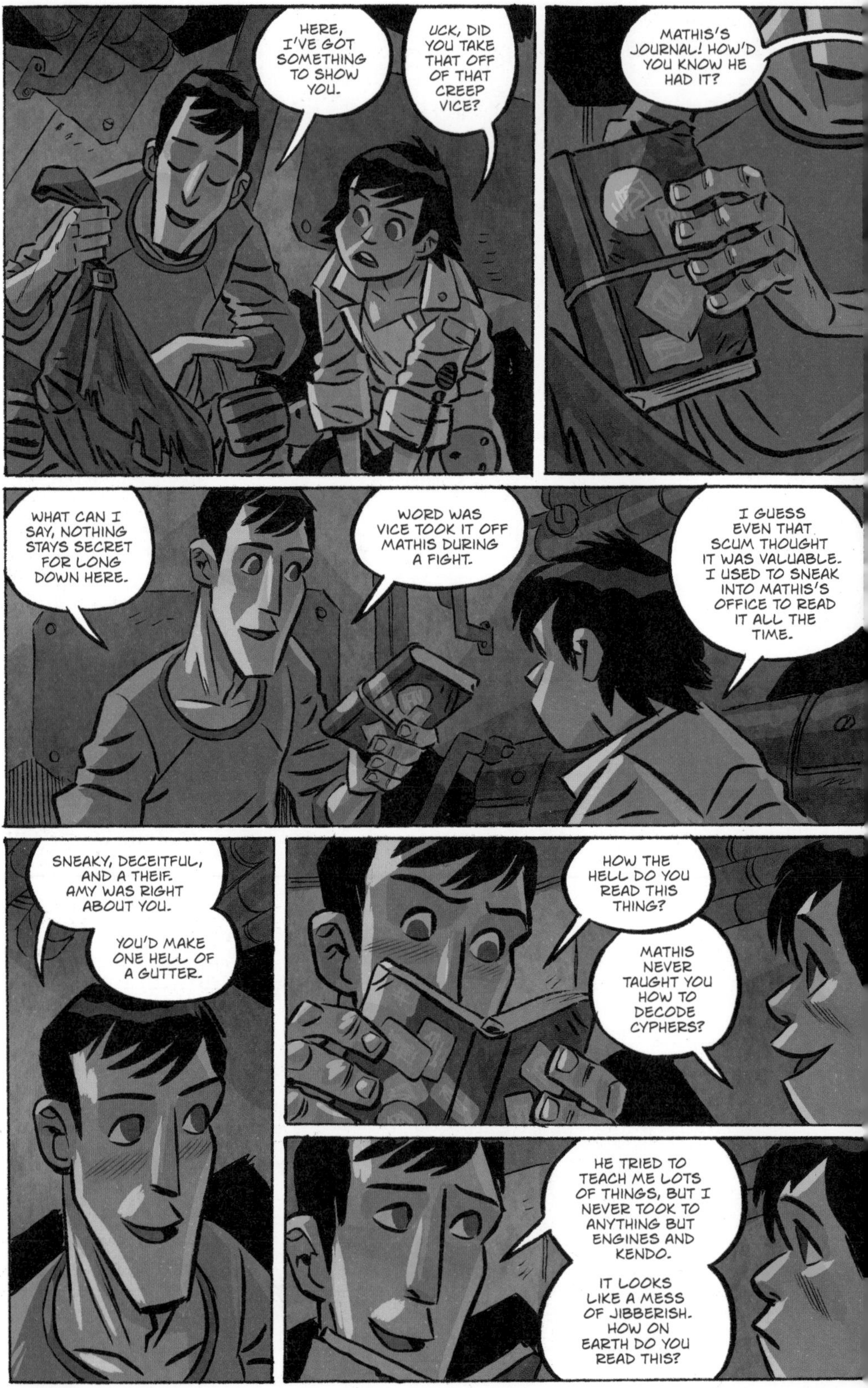
HERE, I'VE GOT SOMETHING TO SHOW YOU.
UCK, DID YOU TAKE THAT OFF OF THAT CREEP VICE?
MATHIS'S JOURNAL! HOW'D YOU KNOW HE HAD IT?
WHAT CAN I SAY, NOTHING STAYS SECRET FOR LONG DOWN HERE.
WORD WAS VICE TOOK IT OFF MATHIS DURING A FIGHT.
I GUESS EVEN THAT SCUM THOUGHT IT WAS VALUABLE. I USED TO SNEAK INTO MATHIS'S OFFICE TO READ IT ALL THE TIME.
SNEAKY, DECEITFUL, AND A THEIF. AMY WAS RIGHT ABOUT YOU.
YOU'D MAKE ONE HELL OF A GUTTER.
HOW THE HELL DO YOU READ THIS THING?
MATHIS NEVER TAUGHT YOU HOW TO DECODE CYPHERS?
HE TRIED TO TEACH ME LOTS OF THINGS, BUT I NEVER TOOK TO ANYTHING BUT ENGINES AND KENDO.
IT LOOKS LIKE A MESS OF JIBBERISH. HOW ON EARTH DO YOU READ THIS?

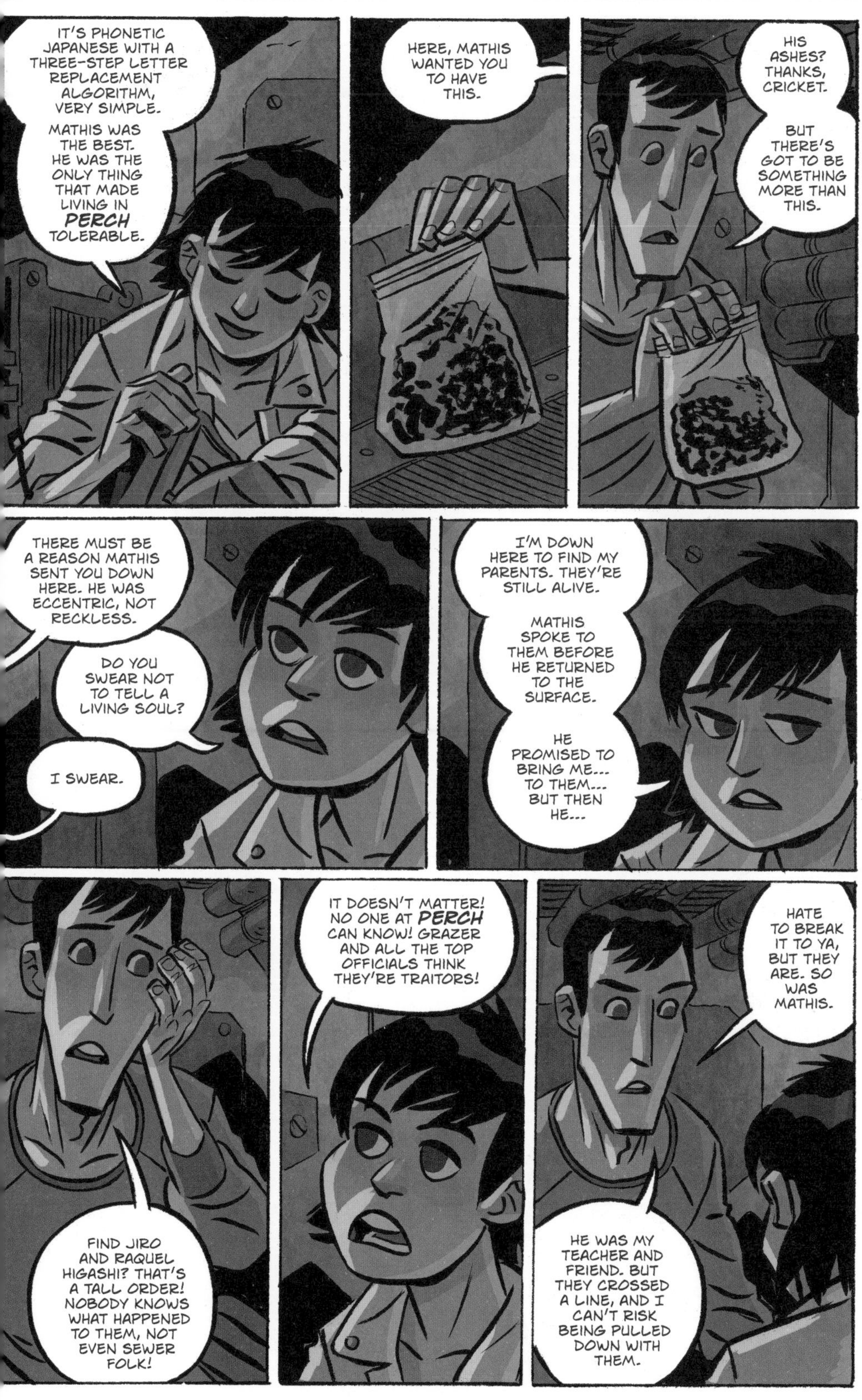
IT'S PHONETIC JAPANESE WITH A THREE-STEP LETTER REPLACEMENT ALGORITHM, VERY SIMPLE.
MATHIS WAS THE BEST. HE WAS THE ONLY THING THAT MADE LIVING IN PERCH TOLERABLE.
HERE, MATHIS WANTED YOU TO HAVE THIS.
HIS ASHES? THANKS, CRICKET.
BUT THERE'S GOT TO BE SOMETHING MORE THAN THIS.
THERE MUST BE A REASON MATHIS SENT YOU DOWN HERE. HE WAS ECCENTRIC, NOT RECKLESS.
DO YOU SWEAR NOT TO TELL A LIVING SOUL?
I SWEAR.
I'M DOWN HERE TO FIND MY PARENTS. THEY'RE STILL ALIVE.
MATHIS SPOKE TO THEM BEFORE HE RETURNED TO THE SURFACE.
HE PROMISED TO BRING ME... TO THEM... BUT THEN HE...
FIND JIRO AND RAQUEL HIGASHI? THAT'S A TALL ORDER! NOBODY KNOWS WHAT HAPPENED TO THEM, NOT EVEN SEWER FOLK!
IT DOESN'T MATTER! NO ONE AT PERCH CAN KNOW! GRAZER AND ALL THE TOP OFFICIALS THINK THEY'RE TRAITORS!
HATE TO BREAK IT TO YA, BUT THEY ARE. SO WAS MATHIS.
HE WAS MY TEACHER AND FRIEND. BUT THEY CROSSED A LINE, AND I CAN'T RISK BEING PULLED DOWN WITH THEM.

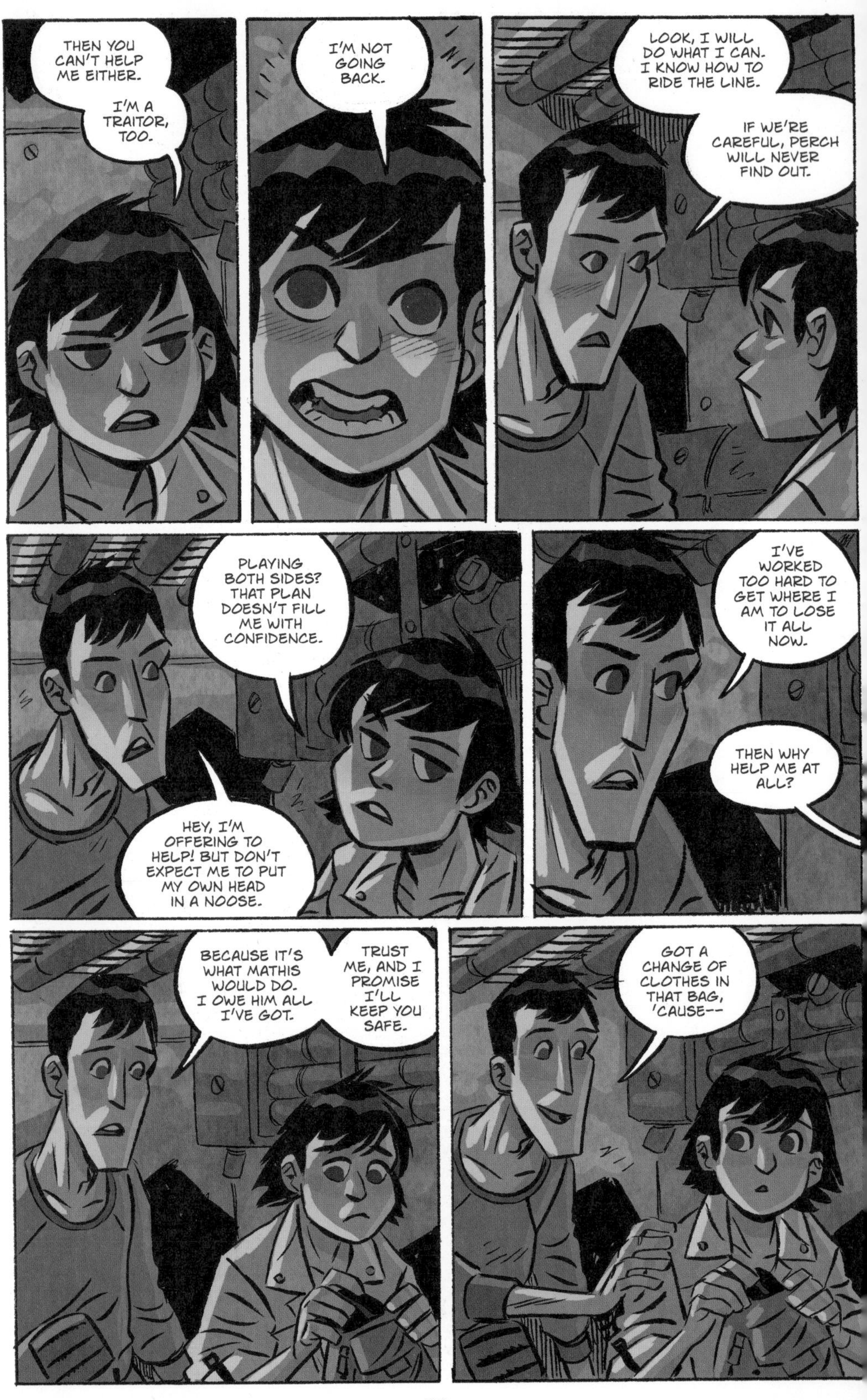
THEN YOU CAN'T HELP ME EITHER.
I'M A TRAITOR, TOO.
I'M NOT GOING BACK.
LOOK, I WILL DO WHAT I CAN. I KNOW HOW TO RIDE THE LINE.
IF WE'RE CAREFUL, PERCH WILL NEVER FIND OUT.
PLAYING BOTH SIDES? THAT PLAN DOESN'T FILL ME WITH CONFIDENCE.
HEY, I'M OFFERING TO HELP! BUT DON'T EXPECT ME TO PUT MY OWN HEAD IN A NOOSE.
I'VE WORKED TOO HARD TO GET WHERE I AM TO LOSE IT ALL NOW.
THEN WHY HELP ME AT ALL?
BECAUSE IT'S WHAT MATHIS WOULD DO. I OWE HIM ALL I'VE GOT.
TRUST ME, AND I PROMISE I'LL KEEP YOU SAFE.
GOT A CHANGE OF CLOTHES IN THAT BAG, 'CAUSE--

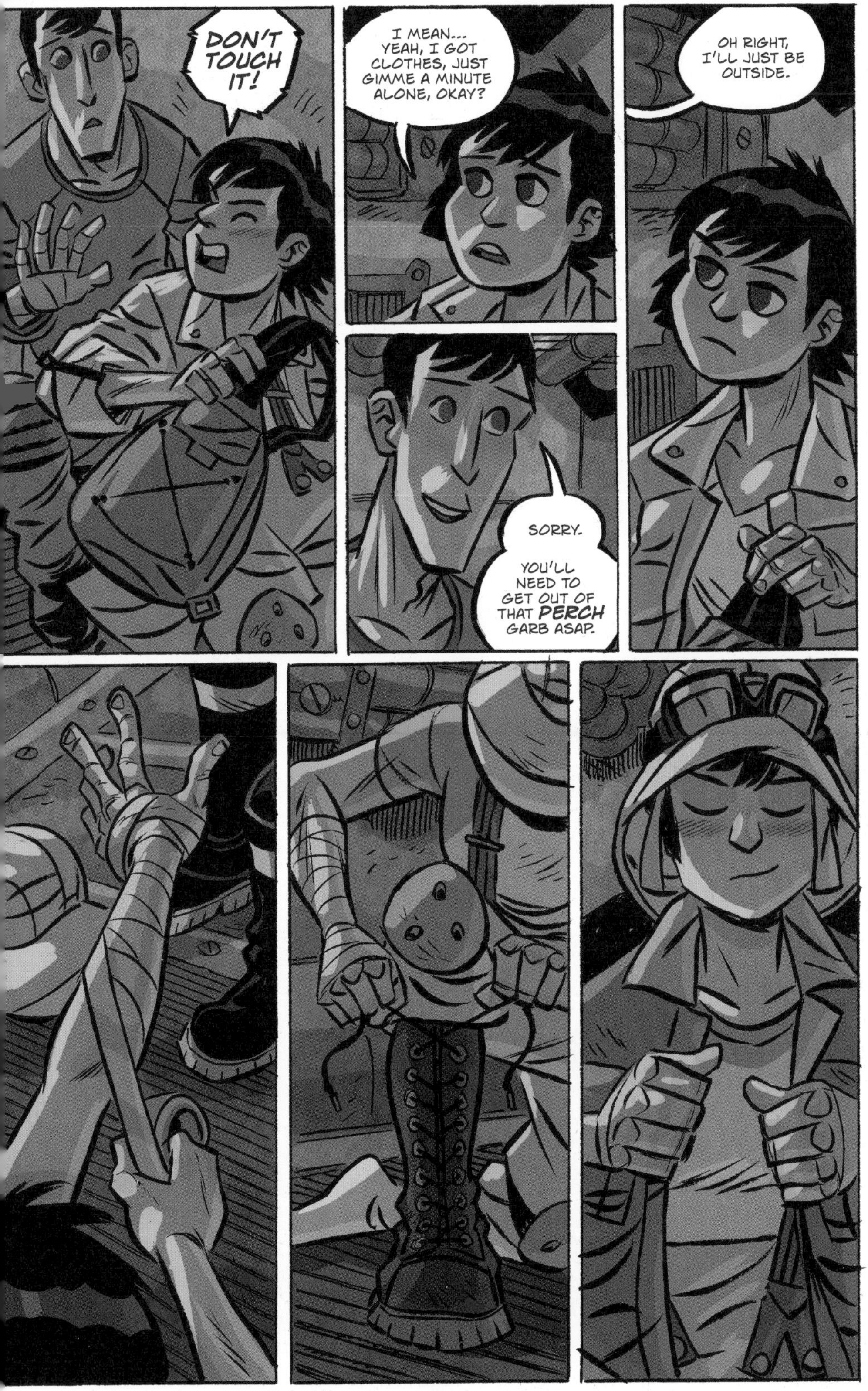
DON'T TOUCH IT!
I MEAN... YEAH, I GOT CLOTHES, JUST GIMME A MINUTE ALONE, OKAY?
OH RIGHT, I'LL JUST BE OUTSIDE.
SORRY.
YOU'LL NEED TO GET OUT OF THAT PERCH GARB ASAP.

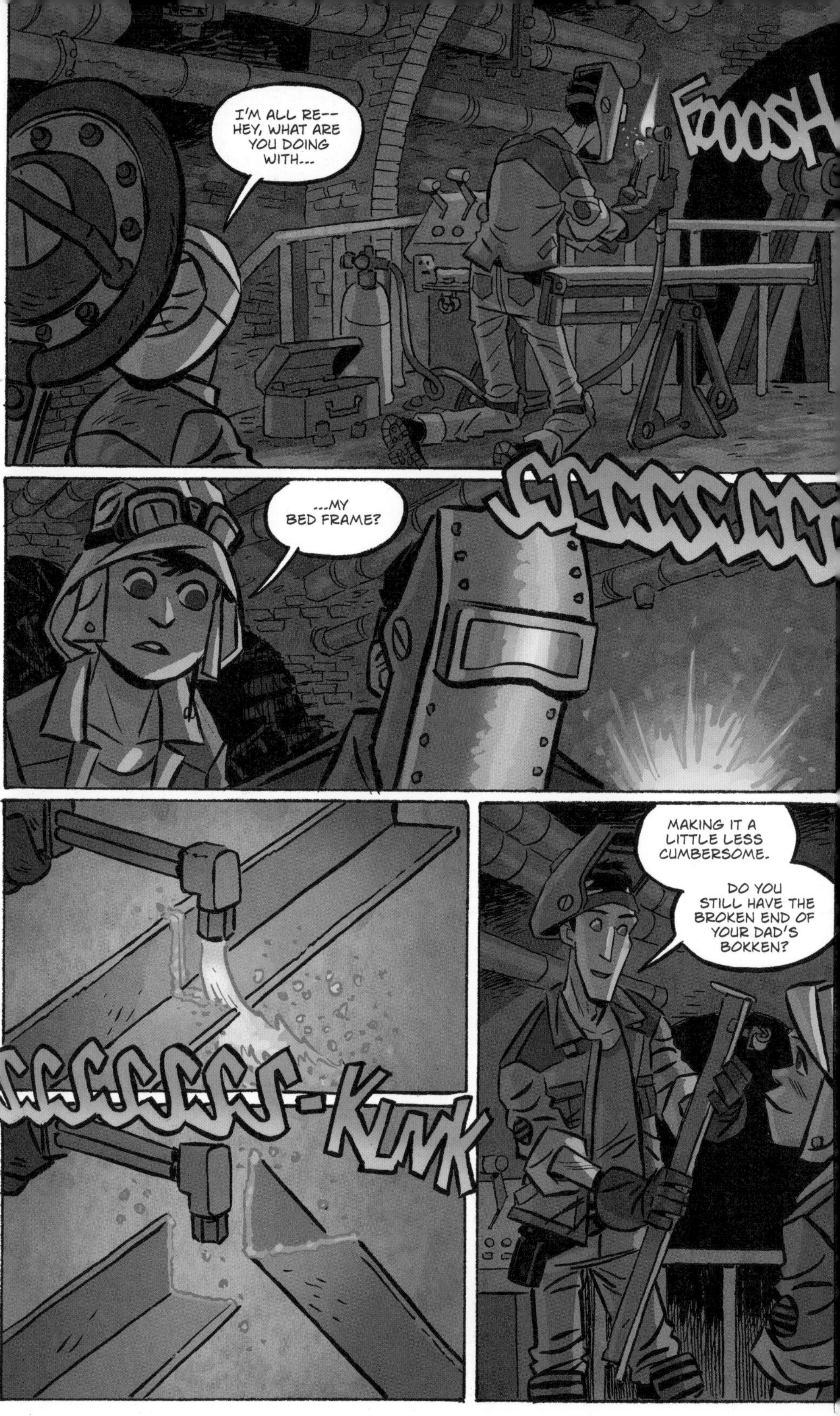
I'M ALL RE-- HEY, WHAT ARE YOU DOING WITH...
FOOOSH
...MY BED FRAME?
SCCCCCCC
SCCCCCS-KLINK
MAKING IT A LITTLE LESS CUMBERSOME.
DO YOU STILL HAVE THE BROKEN END OF YOUR DAD'S BOKKEN?

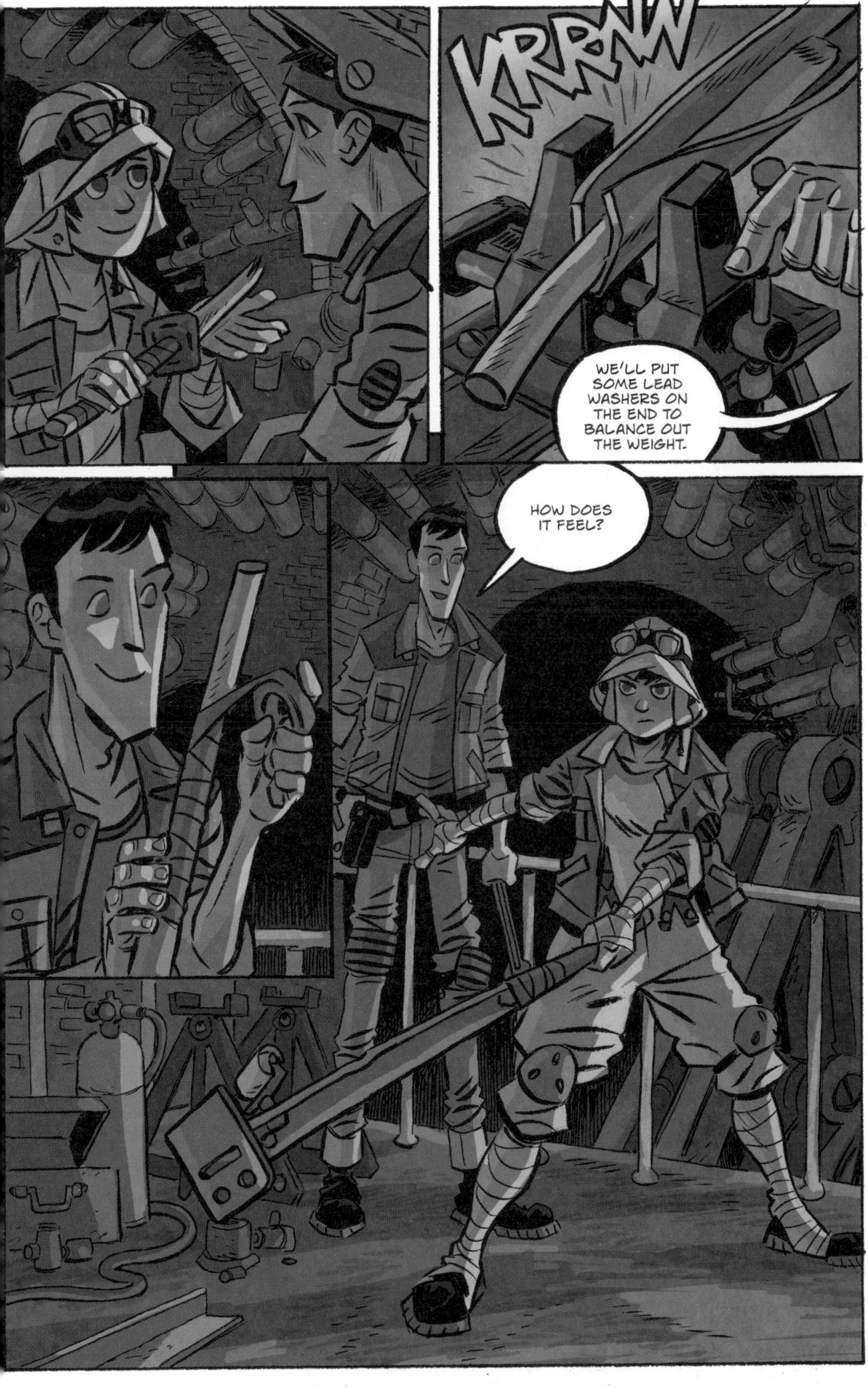
KRRNW
WE'LL PUT SOME LEAD WASHERS ON THE END TO BALANCE OUT THE WEIGHT.
HOW DOES IT FEEL?

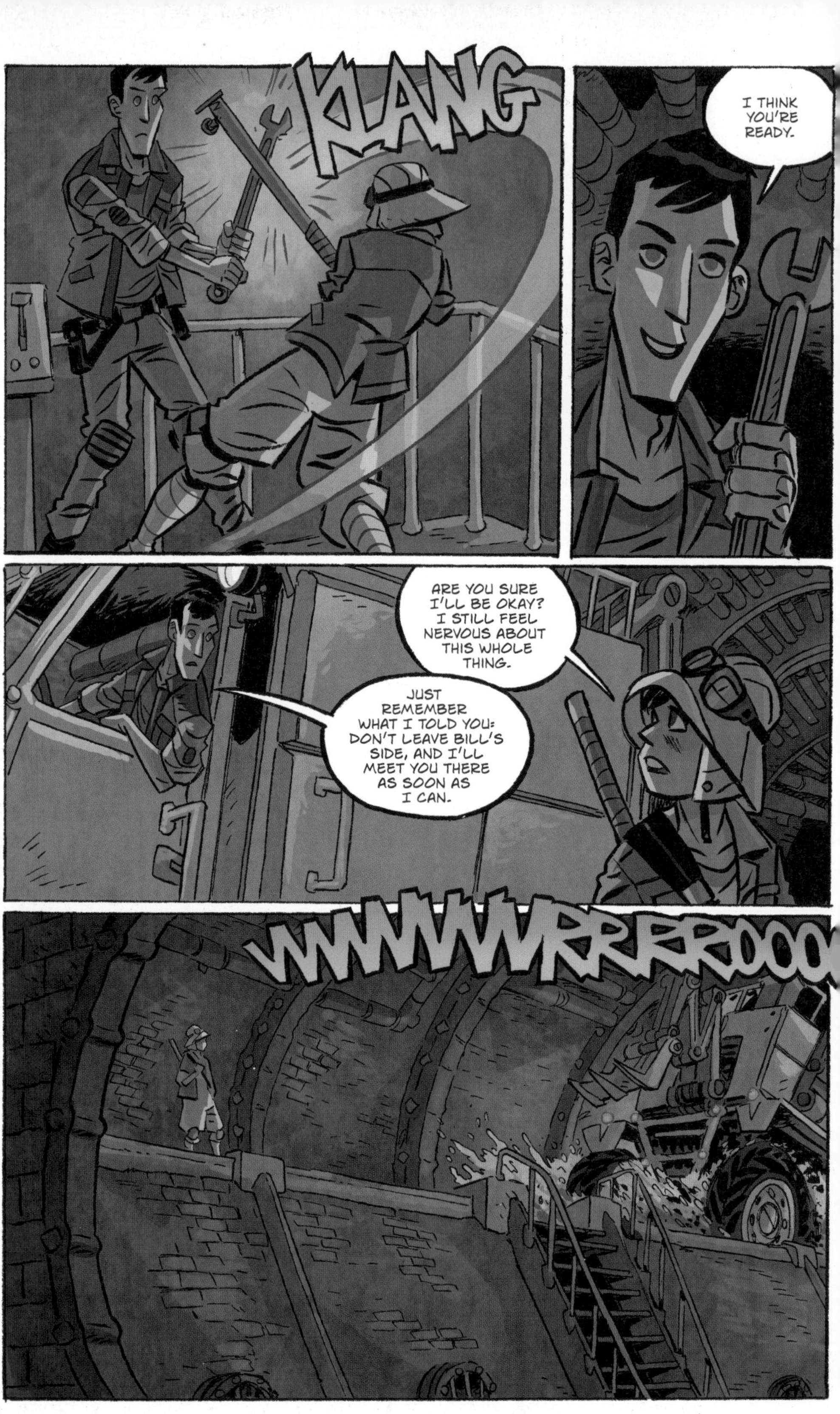
KLANG
I THINK YOU'RE READY.
ARE YOU SURE I'LL BE OKAY? I STILL FEEL NERVOUS ABOUT THIS WHOLE THING.
JUST REMEMBER WHAT I TOLD YOU: DON'T LEAVE BILL'S SIDE, AND I'LL MEET YOU THERE AS SOON AS I CAN.
WWWWVRRRROOO

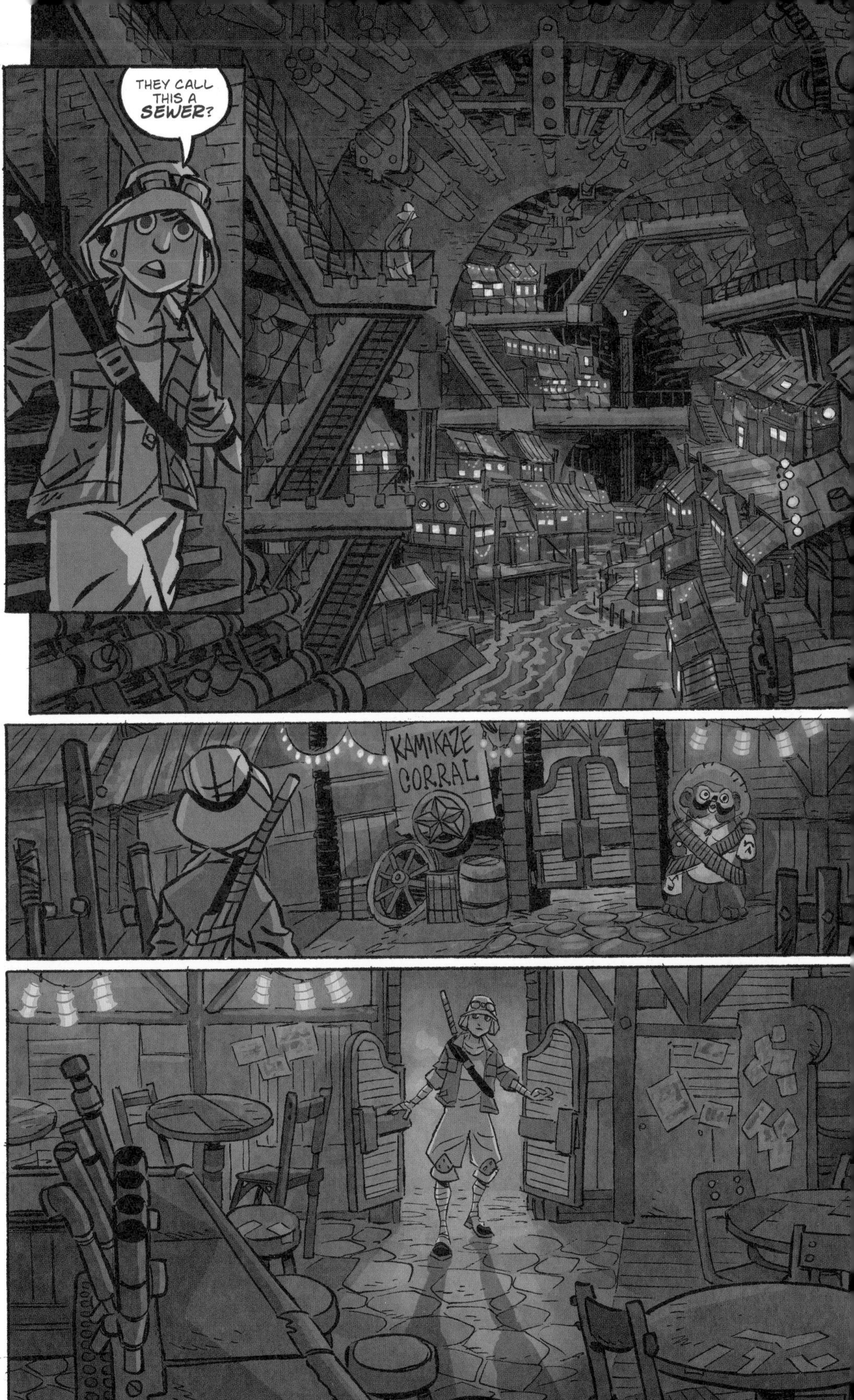
THEY CALL THIS A SEWER?
KAMIKAZE CORRAL

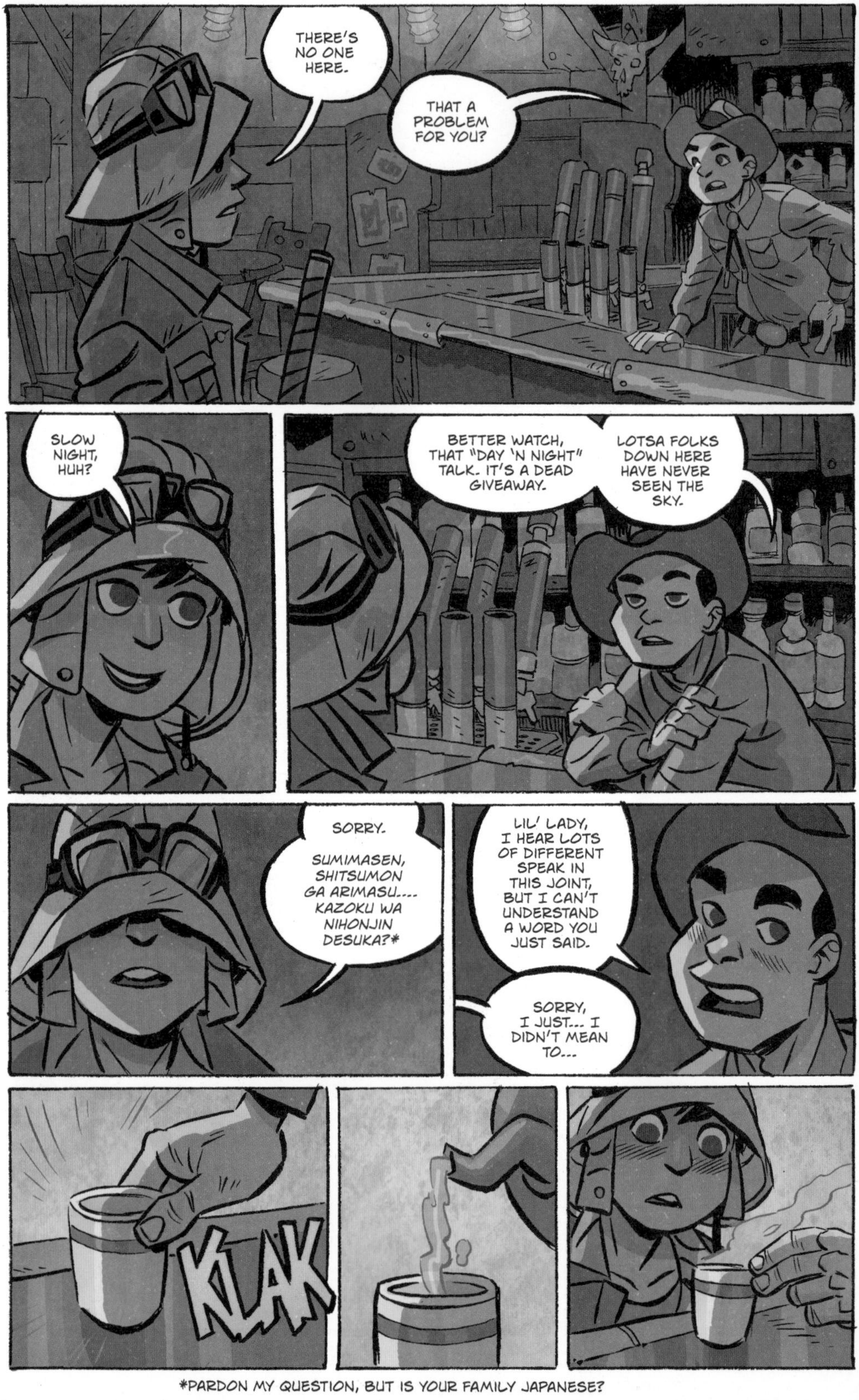
THERE'S NO ONE HERE.
THAT A PROBLEM FOR YOU?
SLOW NIGHT, HUH?
BETTER WATCH, THAT "DAY 'N NIGHT" TALK. IT'S A DEAD GIVEAWAY.
LOTSA FOLKS DOWN HERE HAVE NEVER SEEN THE SKY.
SORRY.
SUMIMASEN, SHITSUMON GA ARIMASU.... KAZOKU WA NIHONJIN DESUKA?*
LIL' LADY, I HEAR LOTS OF DIFFERENT SPEAK IN THIS JOINT, BUT I CAN'T UNDERSTAND A WORD YOU JUST SAID.
SORRY, I JUST... I DIDN'T MEAN TO...
KLAK

*PARDON MY QUESTION, BUT IS YOUR FAMILY JAPANESE?

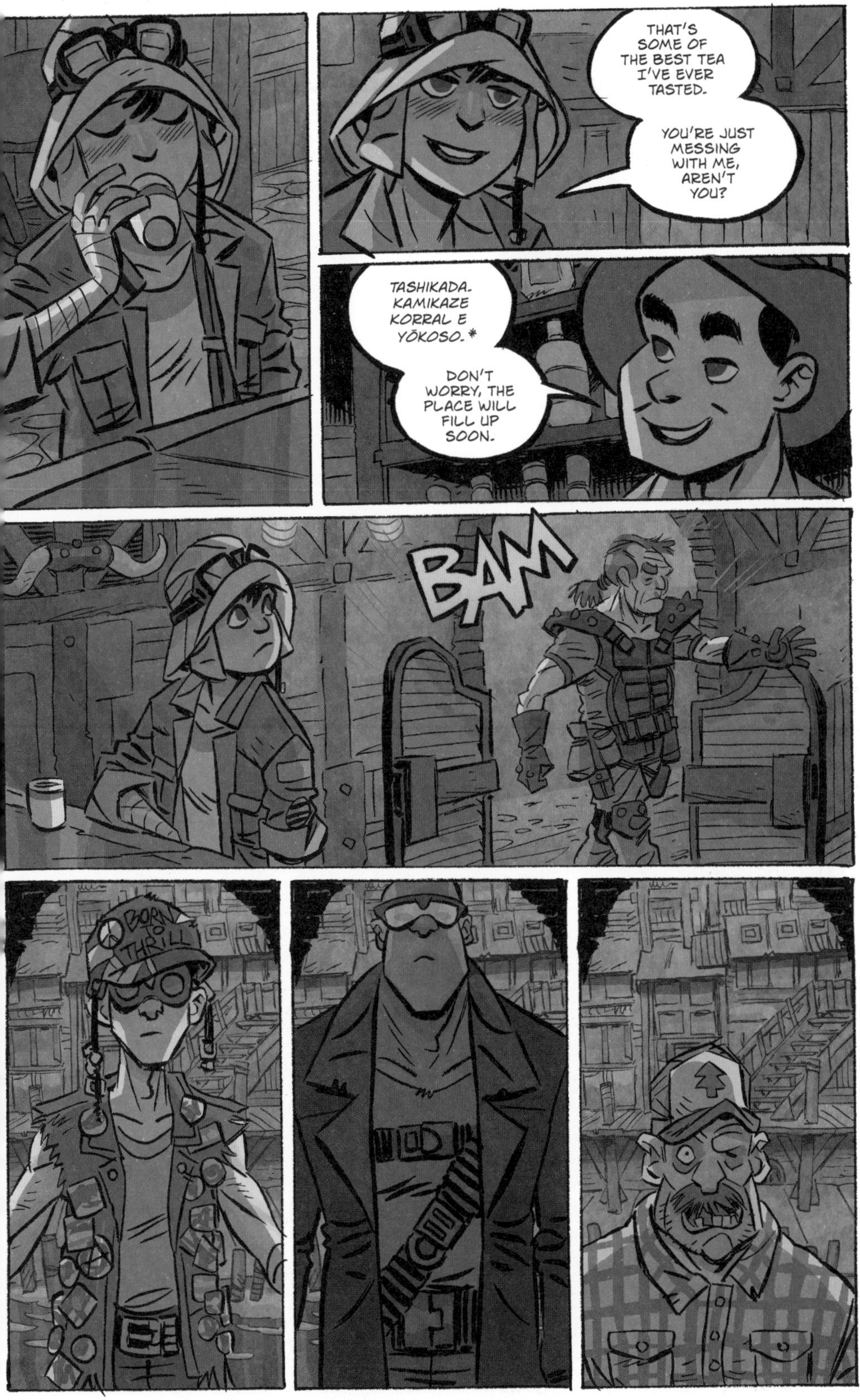
THAT'S SOME OF THE BEST TEA I'VE EVER TASTED.
YOU'RE JUST MESSING WITH ME, AREN'T YOU?
TASHIKADA. KAMIKAZE KORRAL E YŌKOSO.*
DON'T WORRY, THE PLACE WILL FILL UP SOON.
BAM
BORN TO THRILL

* I MOST CERTAINLY AM. WELCOME TO THE KAMIKAZE CORRAL.

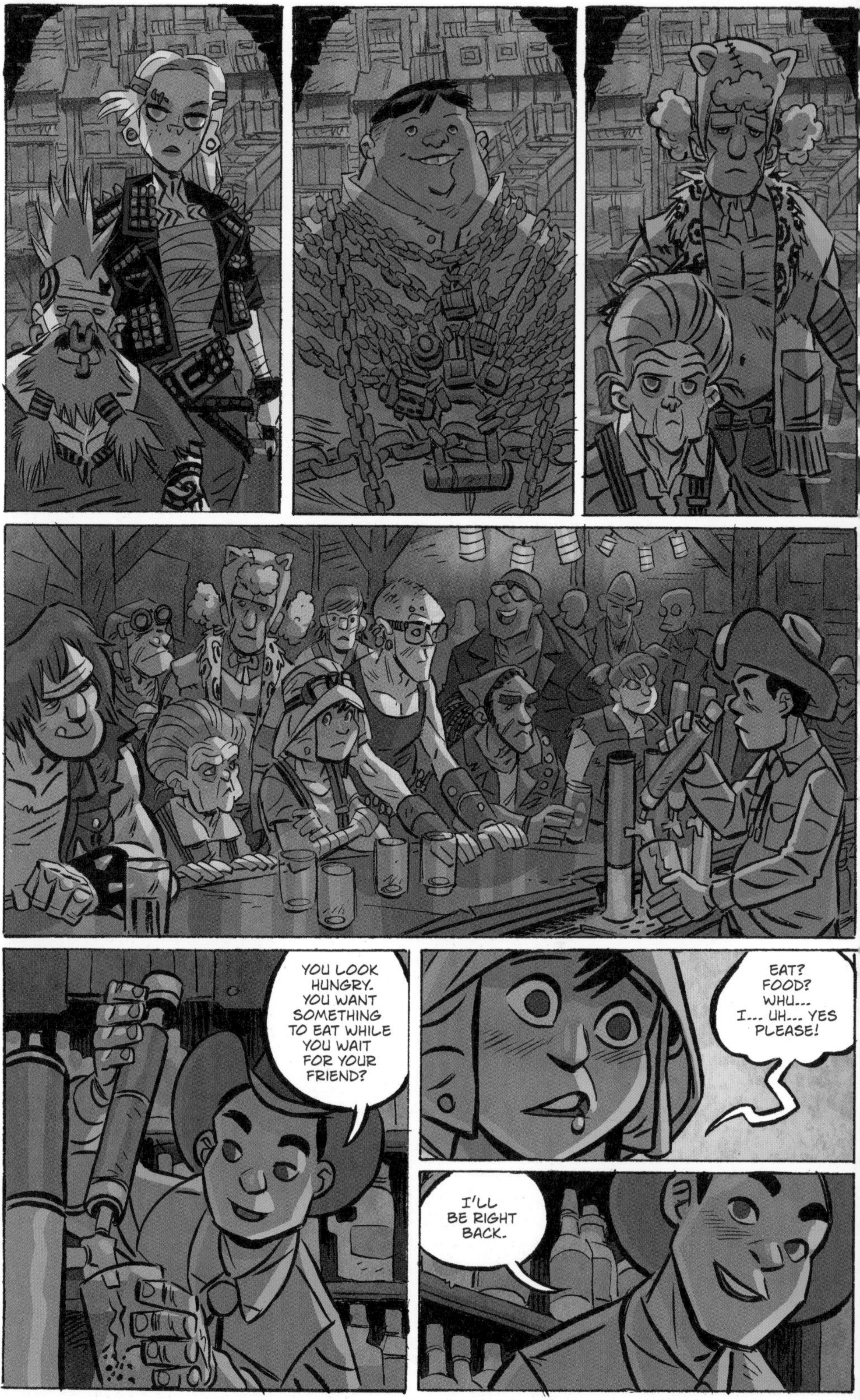
YOU LOOK HUNGRY. YOU WANT SOMETHING TO EAT WHILE YOU WAIT FOR YOUR FRIEND?
EAT? FOOD? WHU... I... UH... YES PLEASE!
I'LL BE RIGHT BACK.

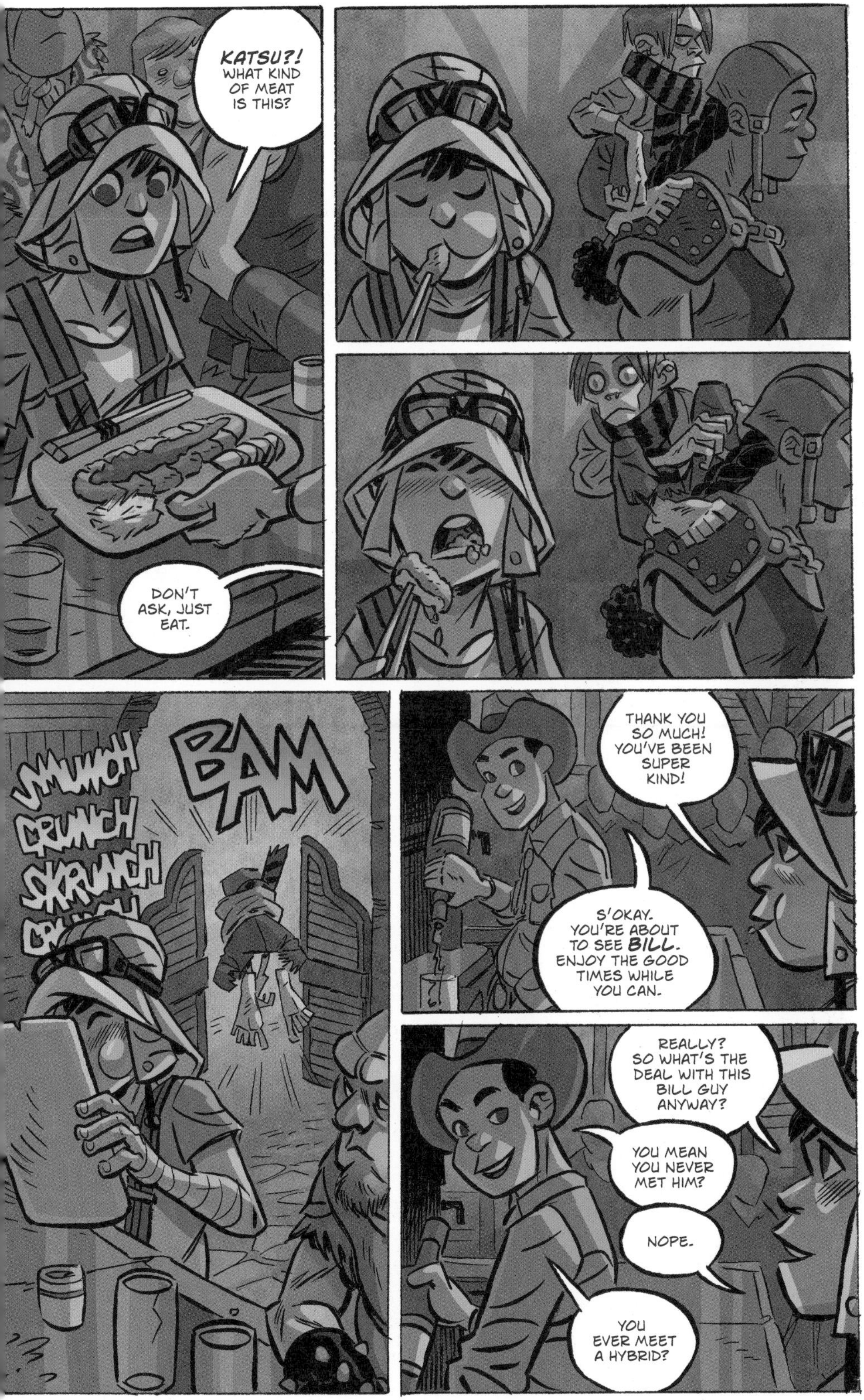
KATSU?! WHAT KIND OF MEAT IS THIS?
DON'T ASK, JUST EAT.
SMUNCH
CRUNCH
SKRUNCH
BAM
THANK YOU SO MUCH! YOU'VE BEEN SUPER KIND!
S'OKAY. YOU'RE ABOUT TO SEE BILL. ENJOY THE GOOD TIMES WHILE YOU CAN.
REALLY? SO WHAT'S THE DEAL WITH THIS BILL GUY ANYWAY?
YOU MEAN YOU NEVER MET HIM?
NOPE.
YOU EVER MEET A HYBRID?

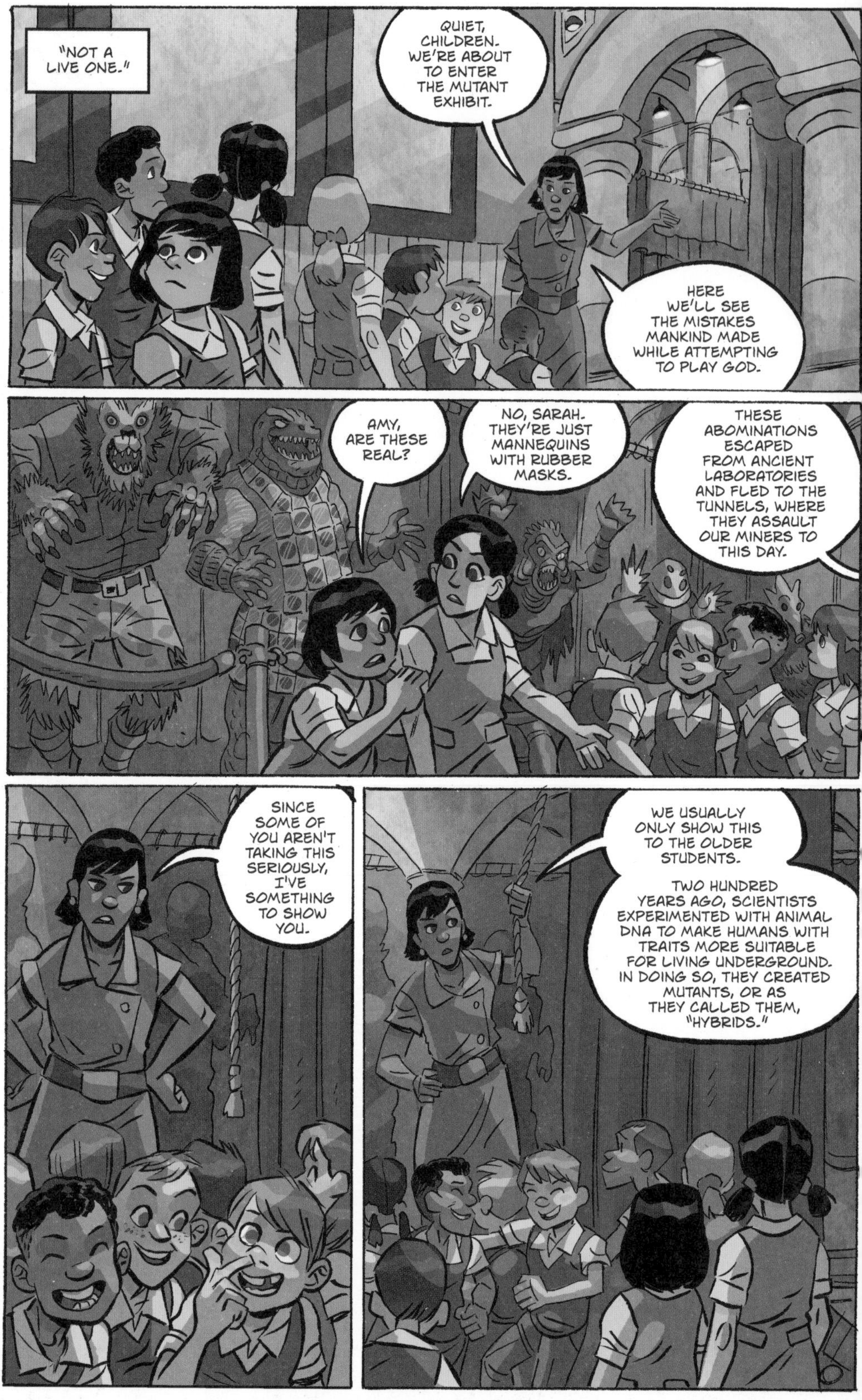
"NOT A LIVE ONE."
QUIET, CHILDREN. WE'RE ABOUT TO ENTER THE MUTANT EXHIBIT.
HERE WE'LL SEE THE MISTAKES MANKIND MADE WHILE ATTEMPTING TO PLAY GOD.
AMY, ARE THESE REAL?
NO, SARAH. THEY'RE JUST MANNEQUINS WITH RUBBER MASKS.
THESE ABOMINATIONS ESCAPED FROM ANCIENT LABORATORIES AND FLED TO THE TUNNELS, WHERE THEY ASSAULT OUR MINERS TO THIS DAY.
SINCE SOME OF YOU AREN'T TAKING THIS SERIOUSLY, I'VE SOMETHING TO SHOW YOU.
WE USUALLY ONLY SHOW THIS TO THE OLDER STUDENTS.
TWO HUNDRED YEARS AGO, SCIENTISTS EXPERIMENTED WITH ANIMAL DNA TO MAKE HUMANS WITH TRAITS MORE SUITABLE FOR LIVING UNDERGROUND. IN DOING SO, THEY CREATED MUTANTS, OR AS THEY CALLED THEM, "HYBRIDS."

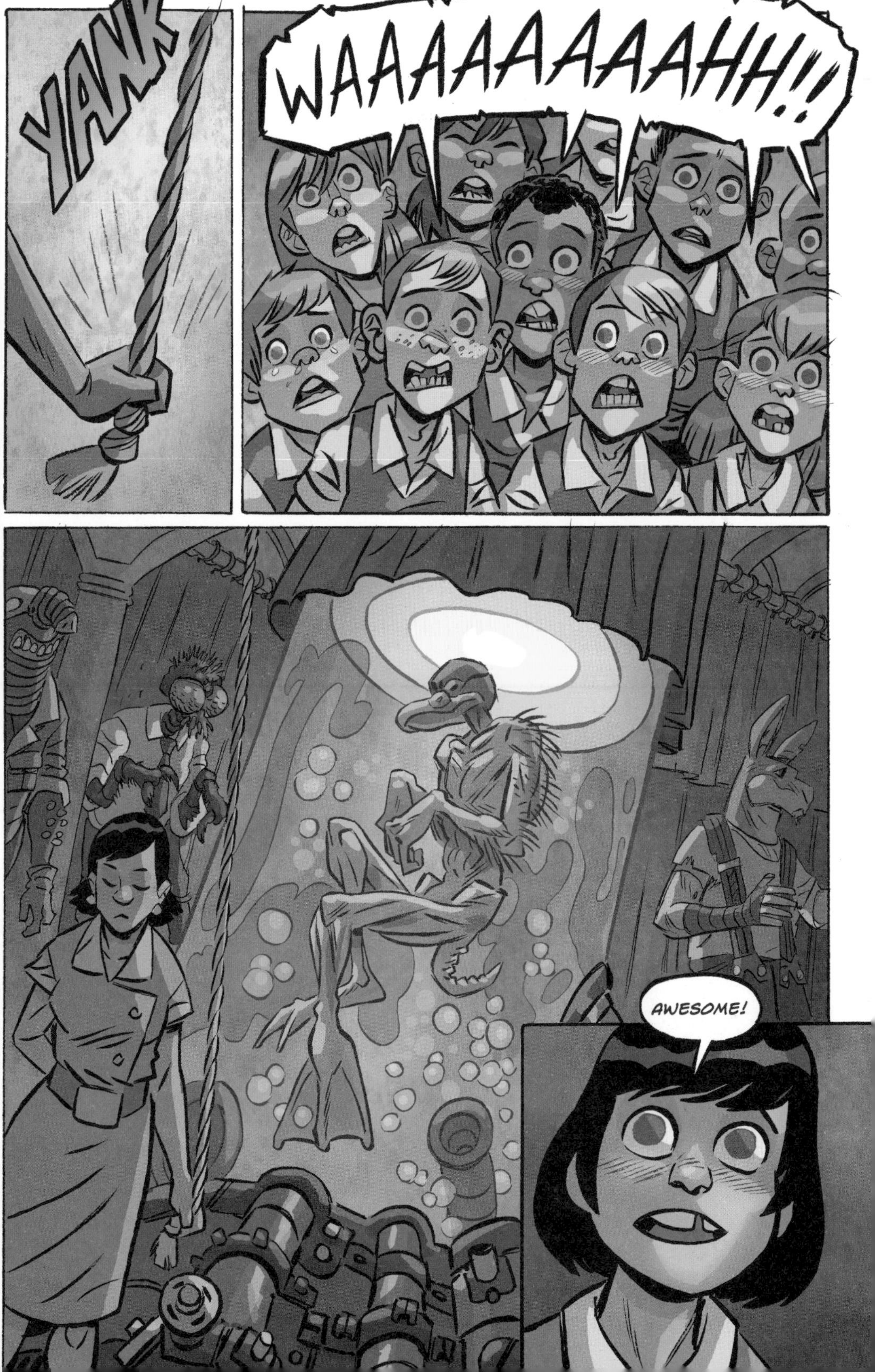
YANK
WAAAAAAAAAHH!!
AWESOME!

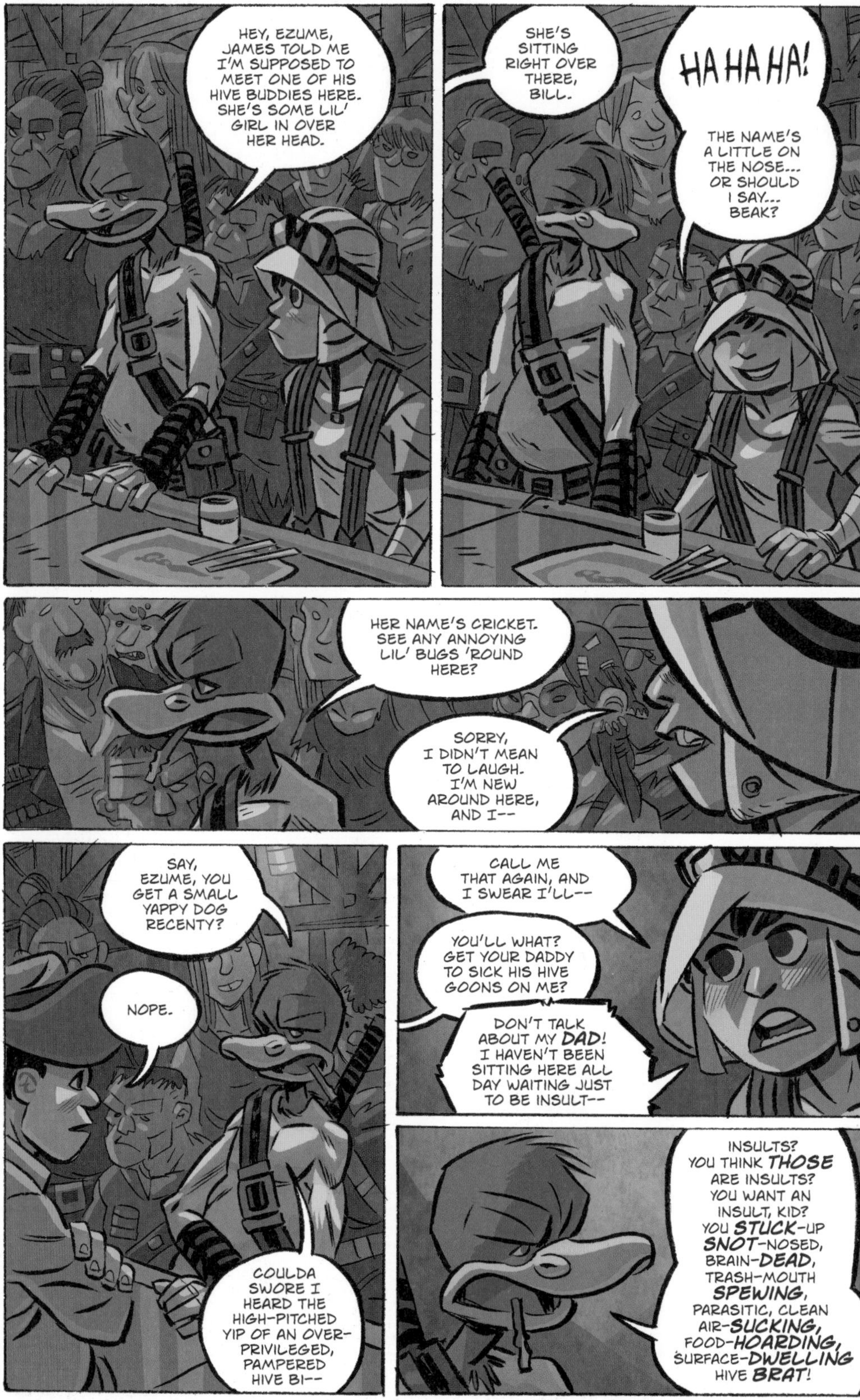
HEY, EZUME, JAMES TOLD ME I'M SUPPOSED TO MEET ONE OF HIS HIVE BUDDIES HERE. SHE'S SOME LIL' GIRL IN OVER HER HEAD.
SHE'S SITTING RIGHT OVER THERE, BILL.
HA HA HA!
THE NAME'S A LITTLE ON THE NOSE... OR SHOULD I SAY... BEAK?
HER NAME'S CRICKET. SEE ANY ANNOYING LIL' BUGS 'ROUND HERE?
SORRY, I DIDN'T MEAN TO LAUGH. I'M NEW AROUND HERE, AND I--
SAY, EZUME, YOU GET A SMALL YAPPY DOG RECENTY?
NOPE.
COULDA SWORE I HEARD THE HIGH-PITCHED YIP OF AN OVER-PRIVILEGED, PAMPERED HIVE BI--
CALL ME THAT AGAIN, AND I SWEAR I'LL--
YOU'LL WHAT? GET YOUR DADDY TO SICK HIS HIVE GOONS ON ME?
DON'T TALK ABOUT MY DAD! I HAVEN'T BEEN SITTING HERE ALL DAY WAITING JUST TO BE INSULT--
INSULTS? YOU THINK THOSE ARE INSULTS? YOU WANT AN INSULT, KID? YOU STUCK-UP SNOT-NOSED, BRAIN-DEAD, TRASH-MOUTH SPEWING, PARASITIC, CLEAN AIR-SUCKING, FOOD-HOARDING, SURFACE-DWELLING HIVE BRAT!

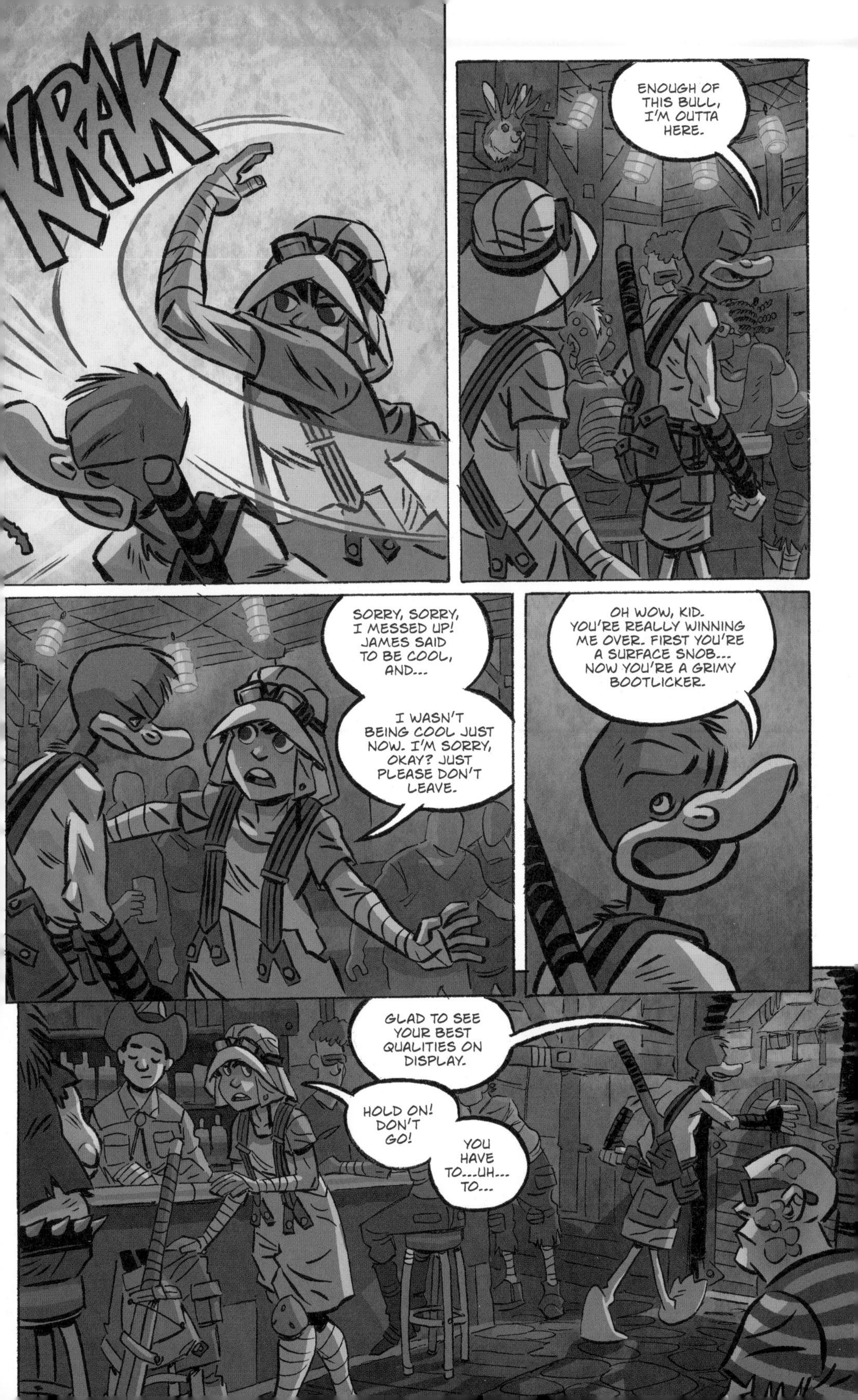
KRAK
ENOUGH OF THIS BULL, I'M OUTTA HERE.
SORRY, SORRY, I MESSED UP! JAMES SAID TO BE COOL, AND...
I WASN'T BEING COOL JUST NOW. I'M SORRY, OKAY? JUST PLEASE DON'T LEAVE.
OH WOW, KID. YOU'RE REALLY WINNING ME OVER. FIRST YOU'RE A SURFACE SNOB... NOW YOU'RE A GRIMY BOOTLICKER.
GLAD TO SEE YOUR BEST QUALITIES ON DISPLAY.
HOLD ON! DON'T GO!
YOU HAVE TO...UH... TO...

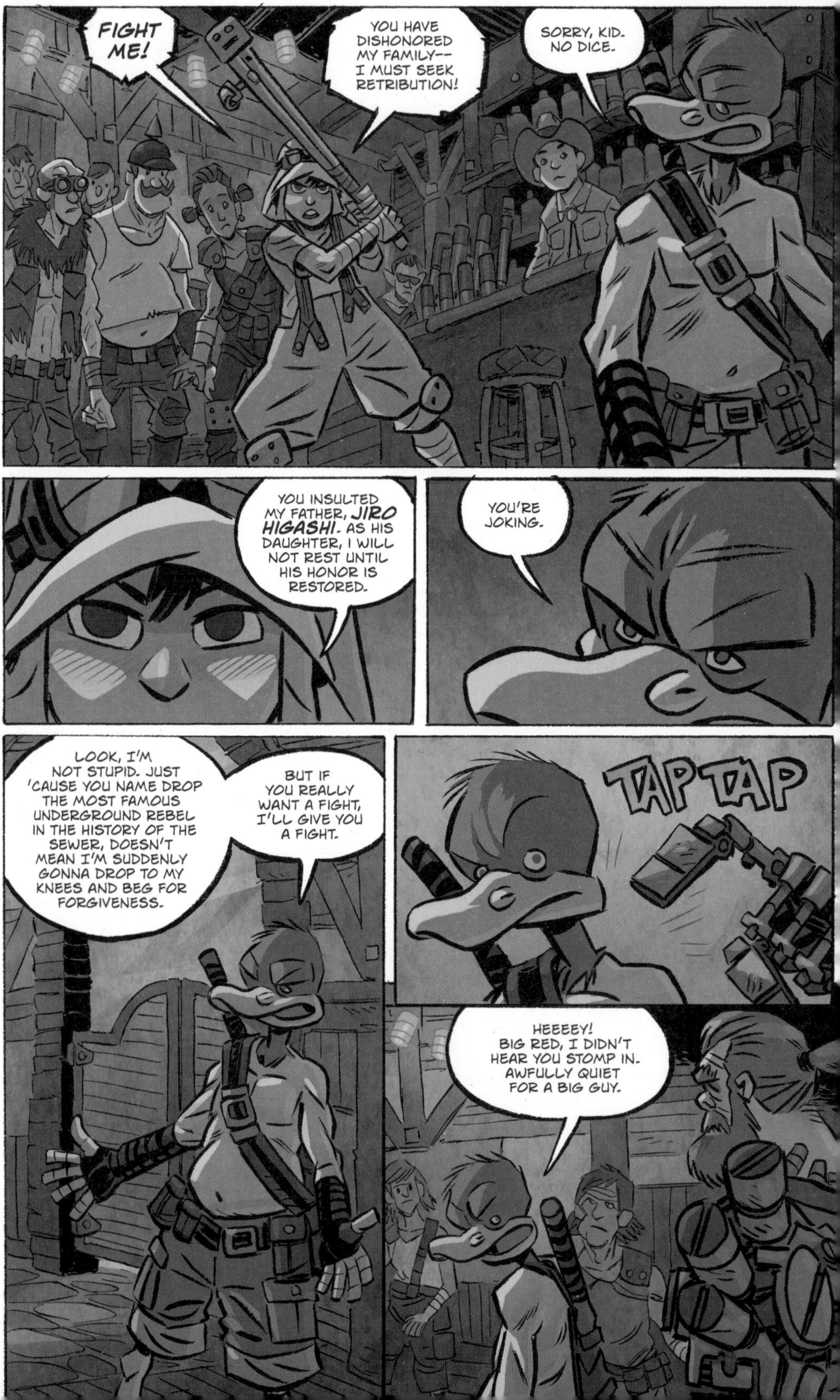
FIGHT ME!
YOU HAVE DISHONORED MY FAMILY-- I MUST SEEK RETRIBUTION!
SORRY, KID. NO DICE.
YOU INSULTED MY FATHER, JIRO HIGASHI. AS HIS DAUGHTER, I WILL NOT REST UNTIL HIS HONOR IS RESTORED.
YOU'RE JOKING.
LOOK, I'M NOT STUPID. JUST 'CAUSE YOU NAME DROP THE MOST FAMOUS UNDERGROUND REBEL IN THE HISTORY OF THE SEWER, DOESN'T MEAN I'M SUDDENLY GONNA DROP TO MY KNEES AND BEG FOR FORGIVENESS.
BUT IF YOU REALLY WANT A FIGHT, I'LL GIVE YOU A FIGHT.
TAP TAP
HEEEEY! BIG RED, I DIDN'T HEAR YOU STOMP IN. AWFULLY QUIET FOR A BIG GUY.

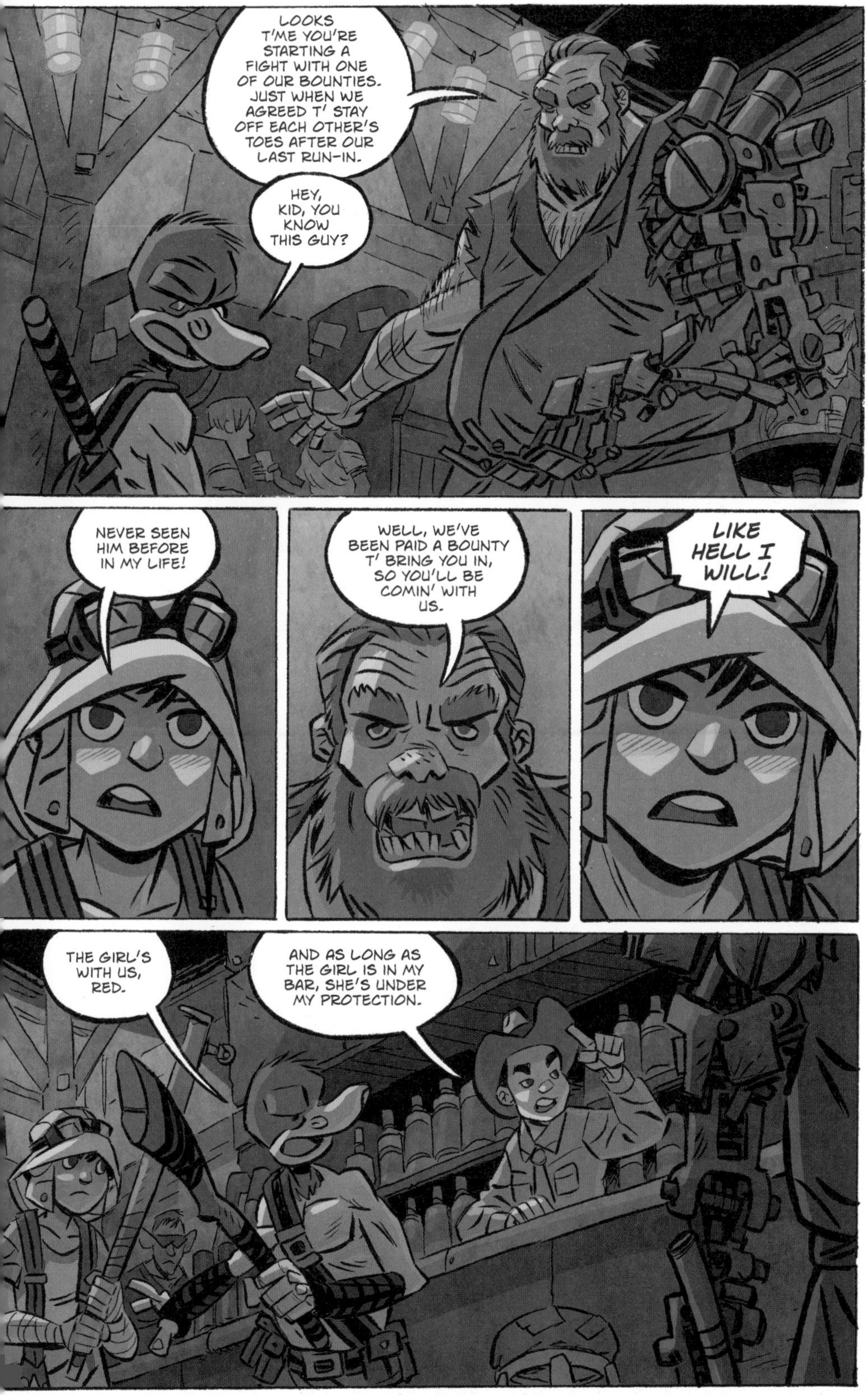
LOOKS T'ME YOU'RE STARTING A FIGHT WITH ONE OF OUR BOUNTIES. JUST WHEN WE AGREED T' STAY OFF EACH OTHER'S TOES AFTER OUR LAST RUN-IN.
HEY, KID, YOU KNOW THIS GUY?
NEVER SEEN HIM BEFORE IN MY LIFE!
WELL, WE'VE BEEN PAID A BOUNTY T' BRING YOU IN, SO YOU'LL BE COMIN' WITH US.
LIKE HELL I WILL!
THE GIRL'S WITH US, RED.
AND AS LONG AS THE GIRL IS IN MY BAR, SHE'S UNDER MY PROTECTION.

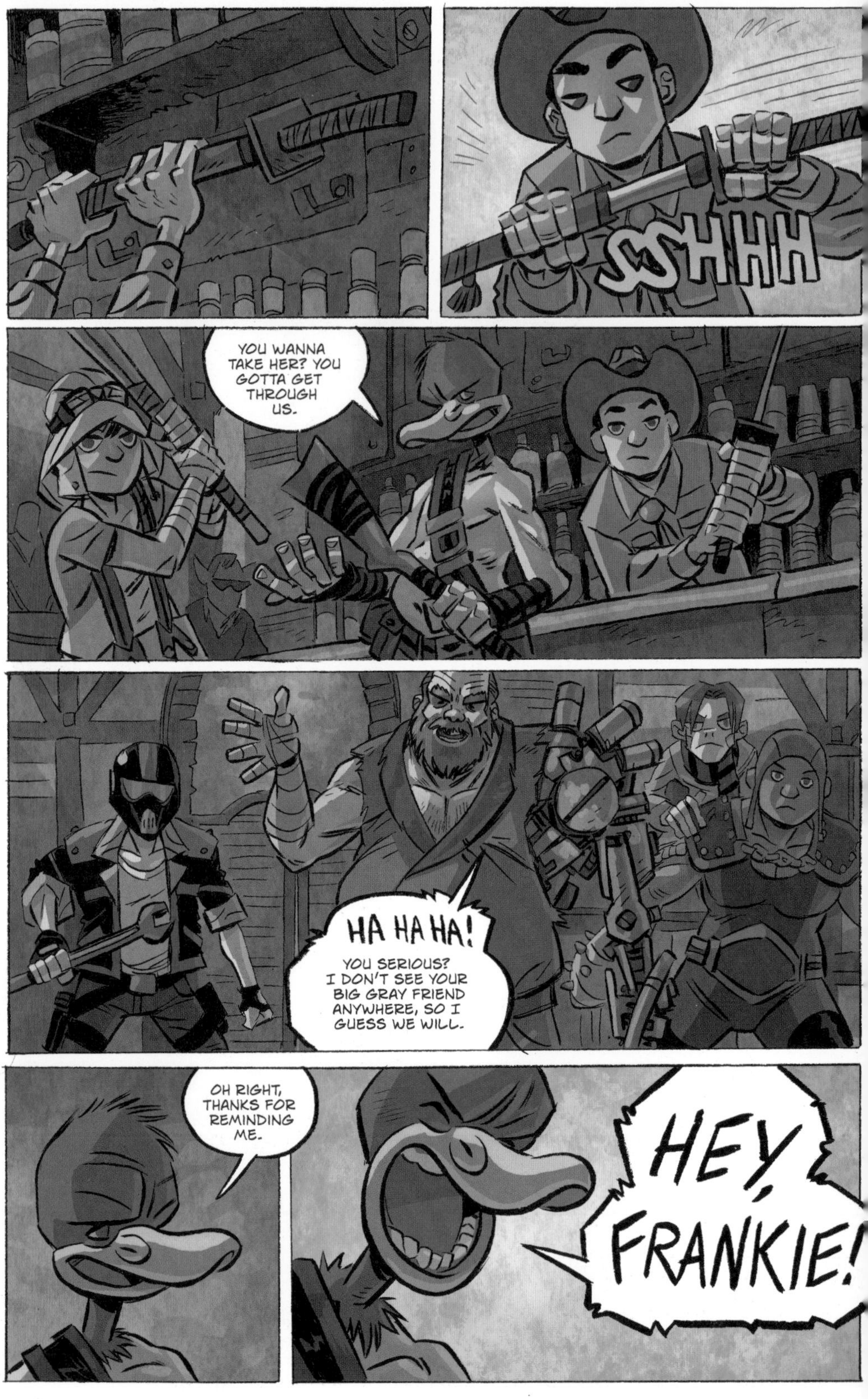
SSHHH
YOU WANNA TAKE HER? YOU GOTTA GET THROUGH US.
HA HA HA!
YOU SERIOUS? I DON'T SEE YOUR BIG GRAY FRIEND ANYWHERE, SO I GUESS WE WILL.
OH RIGHT, THANKS FOR REMINDING ME.
HEY, FRANKIE!

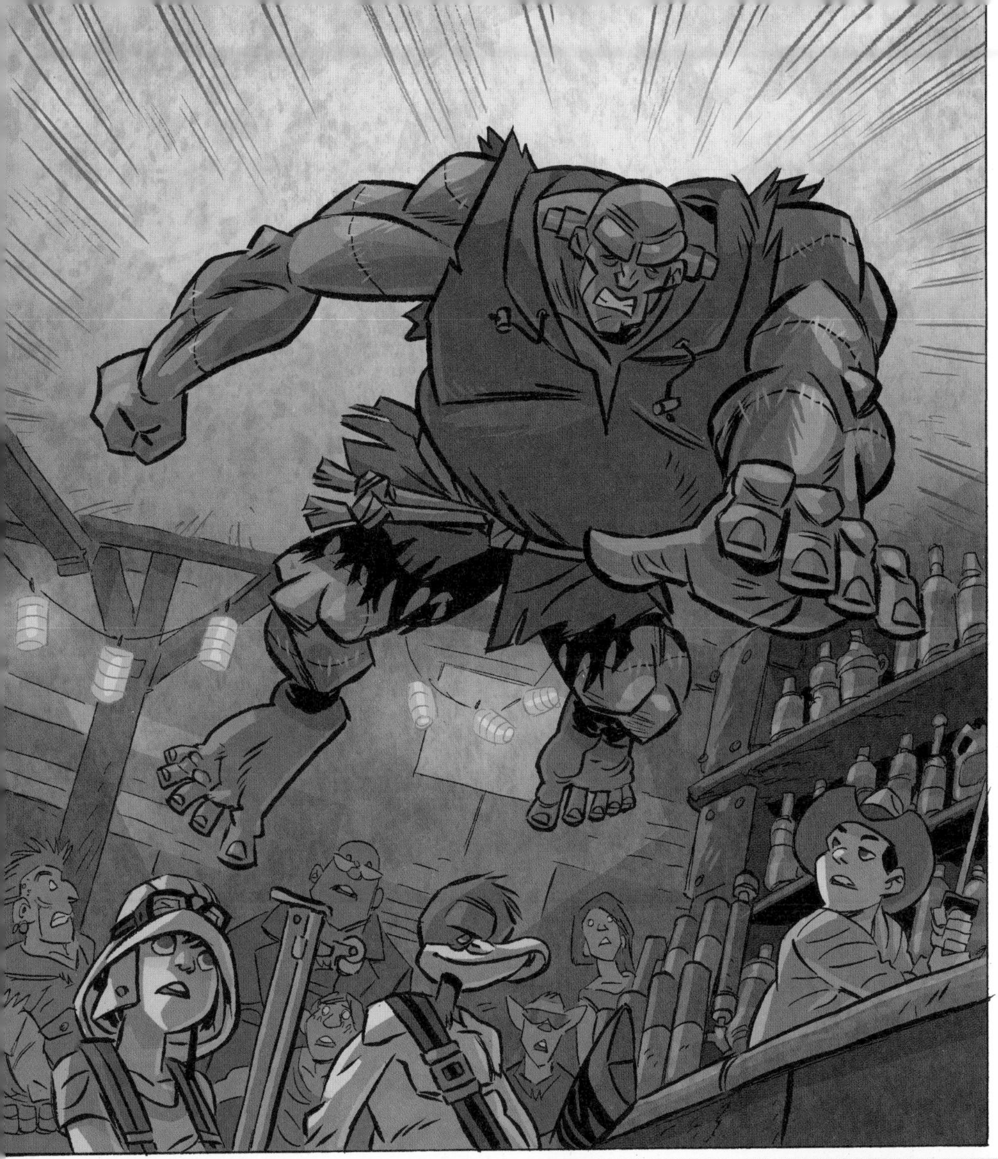

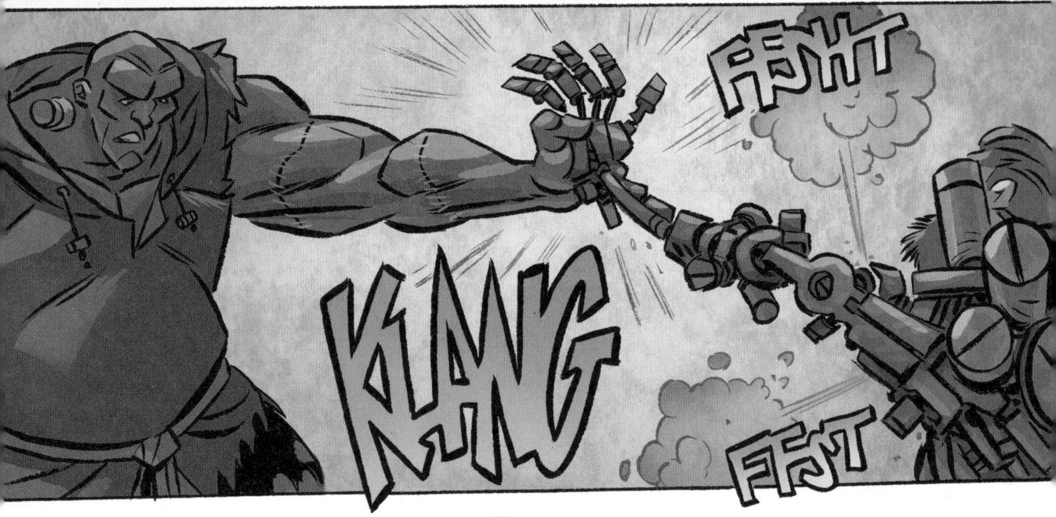
FFSHT
KLANG
FFST

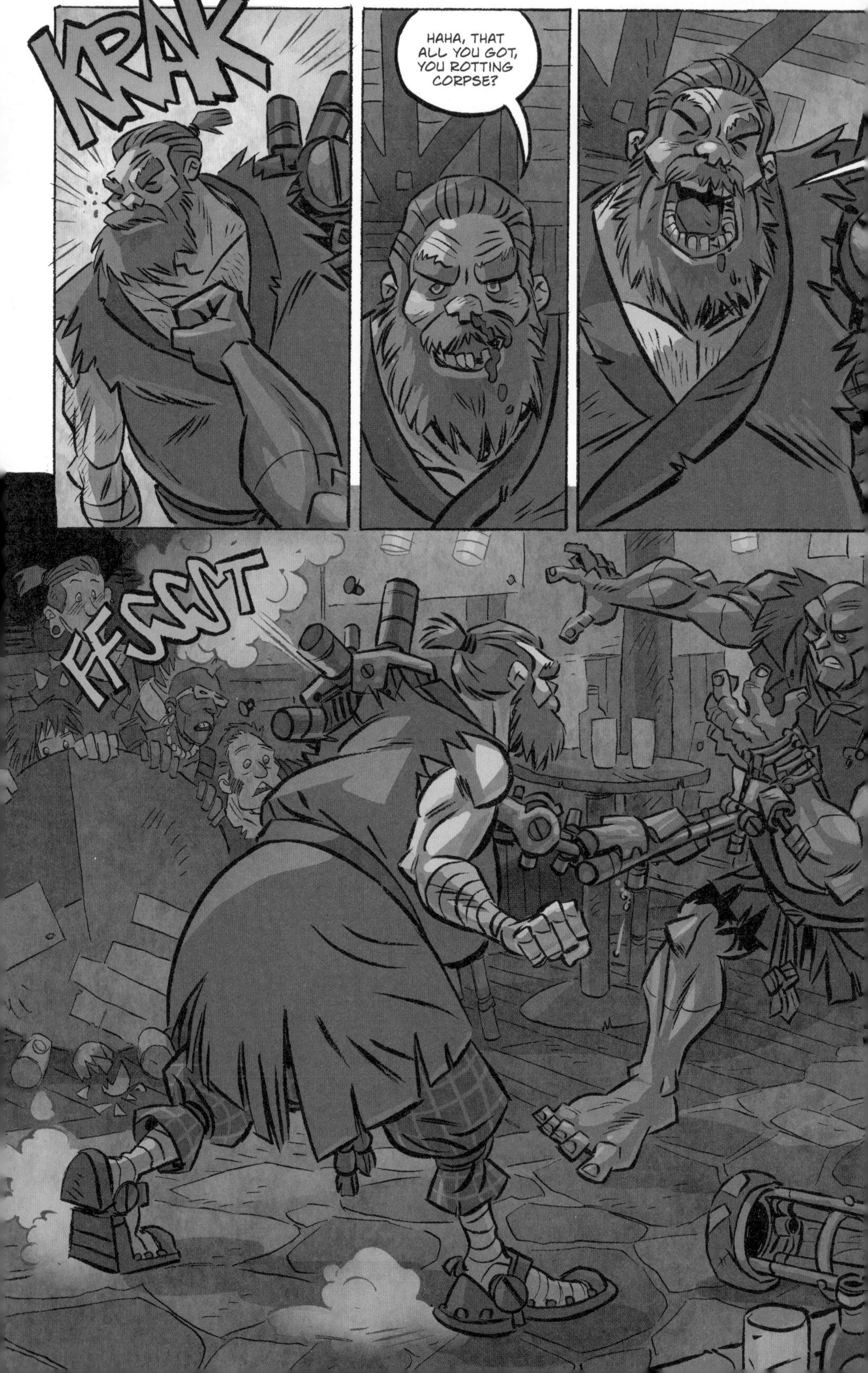
KRAK
HAHA, THAT ALL YOU GOT, YOU ROTTING CORPSE?
FFSSST

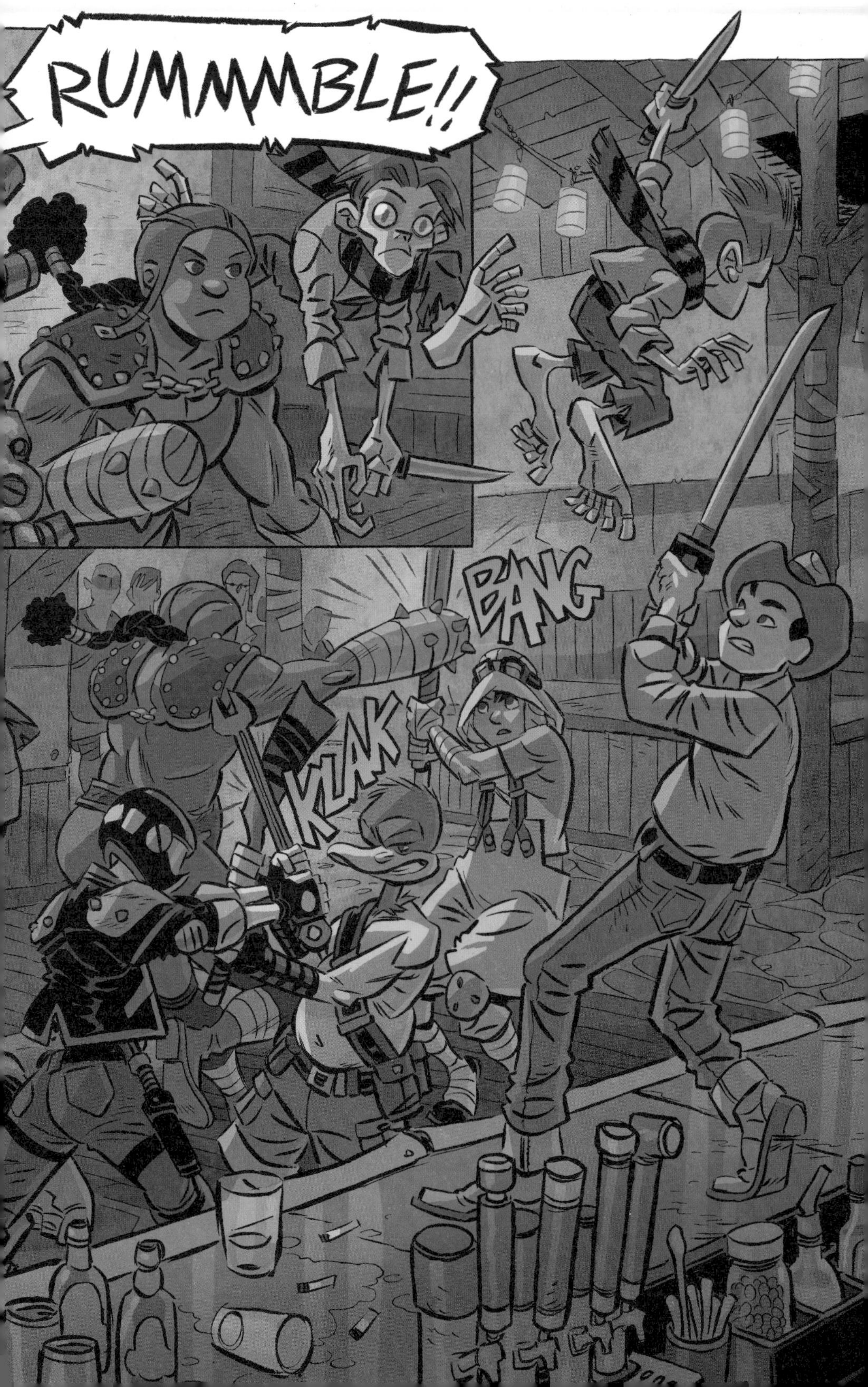
RUMMMBLE!!
BANG
KLAK

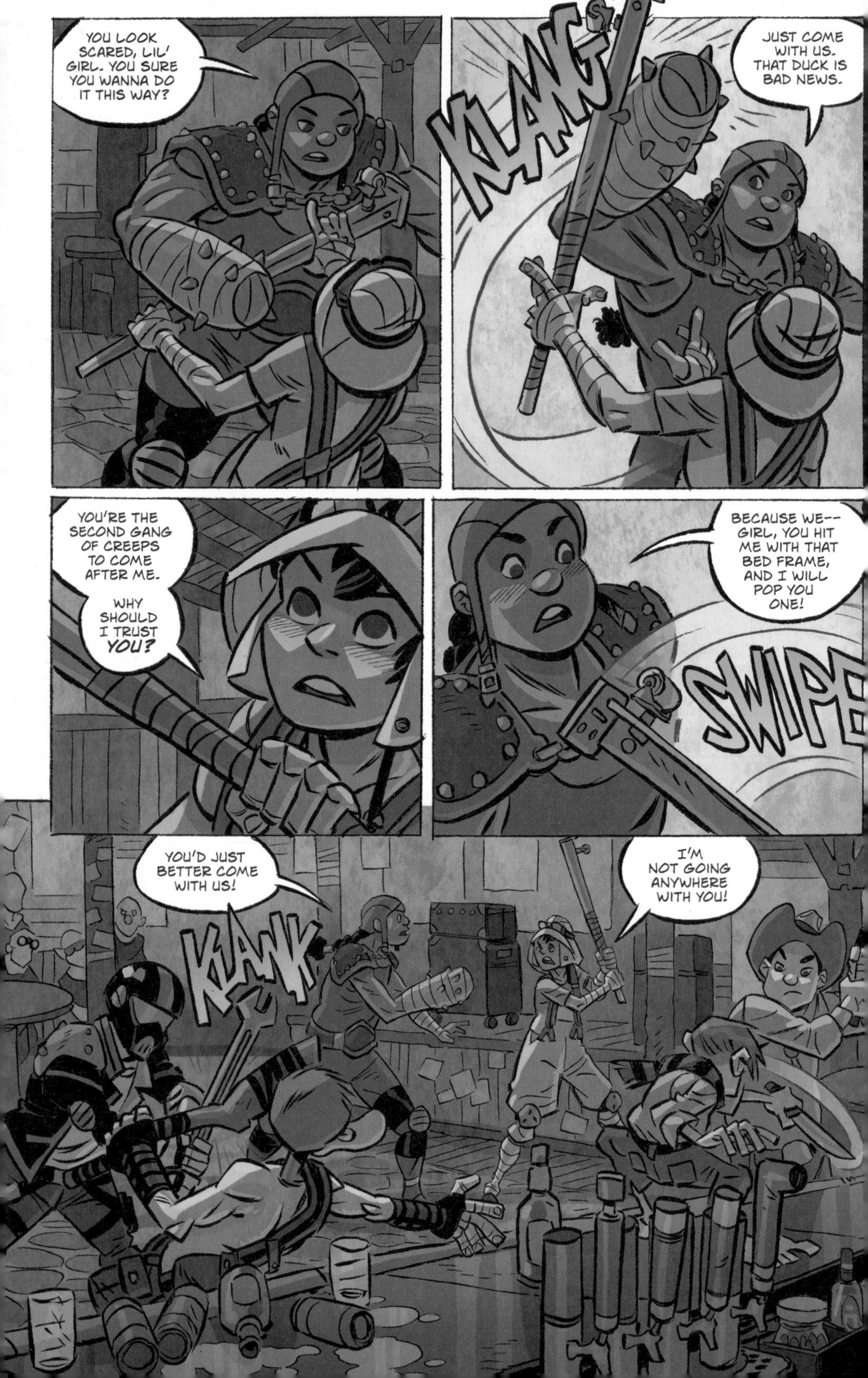
YOU LOOK SCARED, LIL' GIRL. YOU SURE YOU WANNA DO IT THIS WAY?
KLANG!
JUST COME WITH US. THAT DUCK IS BAD NEWS.
YOU'RE THE SECOND GANG OF CREEPS TO COME AFTER ME.
WHY SHOULD I TRUST *YOU?*
BECAUSE WE-- GIRL, YOU HIT ME WITH THAT BED FRAME, AND I WILL POP YOU ONE!
SWIPE
YOU'D JUST BETTER COME WITH US!
KLANK
I'M NOT GOING ANYWHERE WITH YOU!

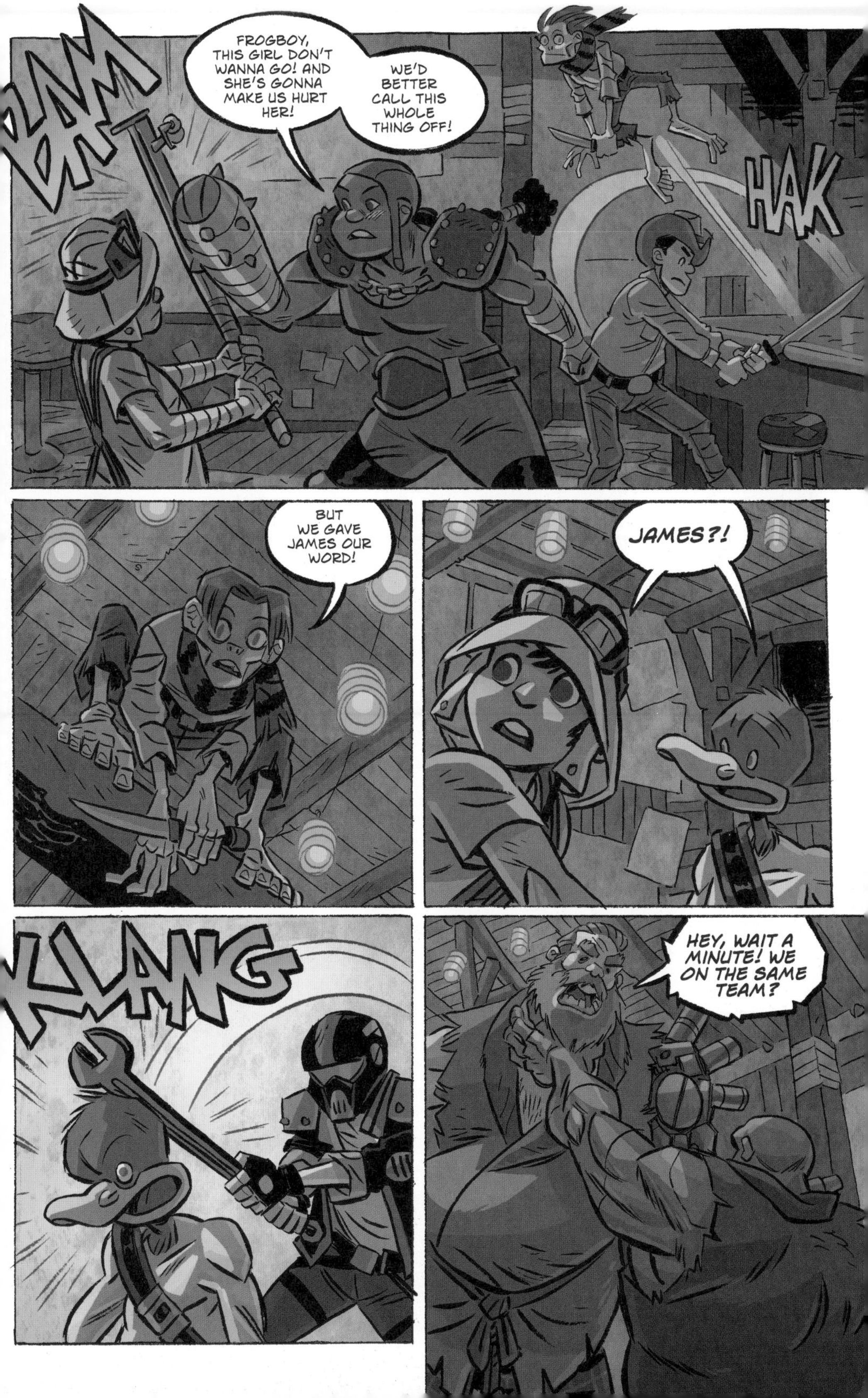
BAM
FROGBOY, THIS GIRL DON'T WANNA GO! AND SHE'S GONNA MAKE US HURT HER!
WE'D BETTER CALL THIS WHOLE THING OFF!
HAK
BUT WE GAVE JAMES OUR WORD!
JAMES?!
KLANG
HEY, WAIT A MINUTE! WE ON THE SAME TEAM?

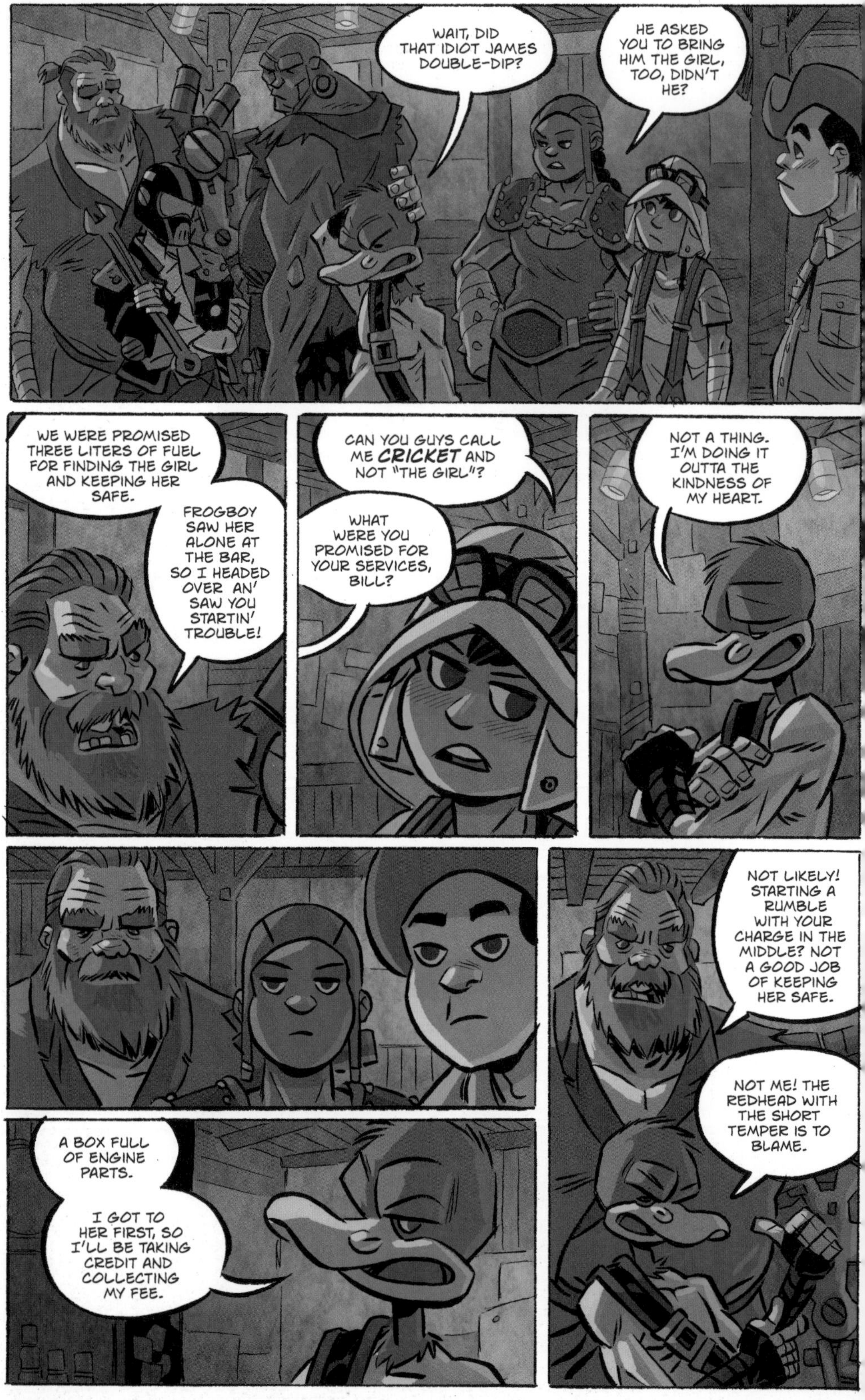
WAIT, DID THAT IDIOT JAMES DOUBLE-DIP?
HE ASKED YOU TO BRING HIM THE GIRL, TOO, DIDN'T HE?
WE WERE PROMISED THREE LITERS OF FUEL FOR FINDING THE GIRL AND KEEPING HER SAFE.
FROGBOY SAW HER ALONE AT THE BAR, SO I HEADED OVER AN' SAW YOU STARTIN' TROUBLE!
CAN YOU GUYS CALL ME CRICKET AND NOT "THE GIRL"?
WHAT WERE YOU PROMISED FOR YOUR SERVICES, BILL?
NOT A THING. I'M DOING IT OUTTA THE KINDNESS OF MY HEART.
NOT LIKELY! STARTING A RUMBLE WITH YOUR CHARGE IN THE MIDDLE? NOT A GOOD JOB OF KEEPING HER SAFE.
A BOX FULL OF ENGINE PARTS.
I GOT TO HER FIRST, SO I'LL BE TAKING CREDIT AND COLLECTING MY FEE.
NOT ME! THE REDHEAD WITH THE SHORT TEMPER IS TO BLAME.

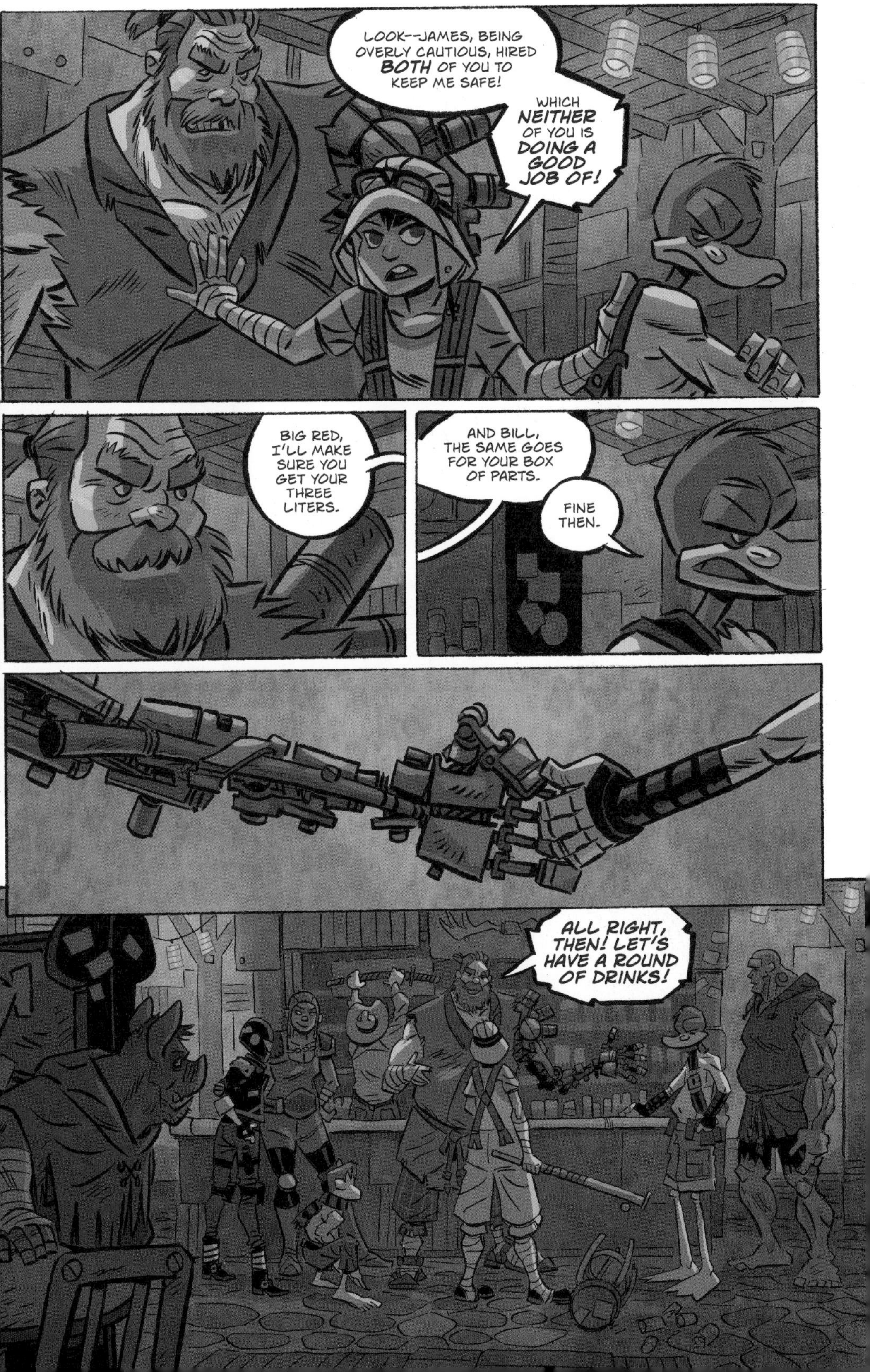
LOOK--JAMES, BEING OVERLY CAUTIOUS, HIRED BOTH OF YOU TO KEEP ME SAFE!
WHICH NEITHER OF YOU IS DOING A GOOD JOB OF!
BIG RED, I'LL MAKE SURE YOU GET YOUR THREE LITERS.
AND BILL, THE SAME GOES FOR YOUR BOX OF PARTS.
FINE THEN.
ALL RIGHT, THEN! LET'S HAVE A ROUND OF DRINKS!

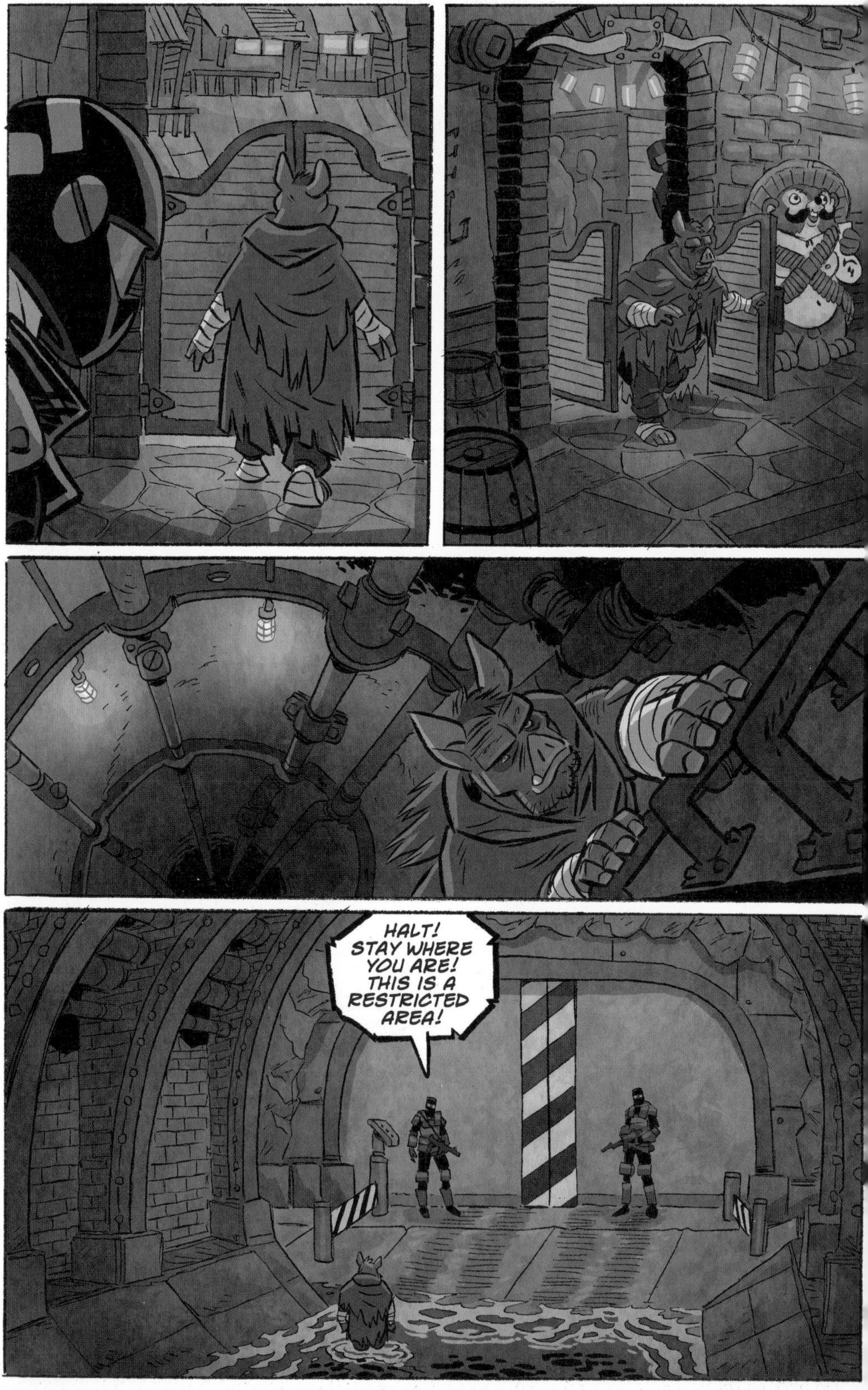
HALT! STAY WHERE YOU ARE! THIS IS A RESTRICTED AREA!

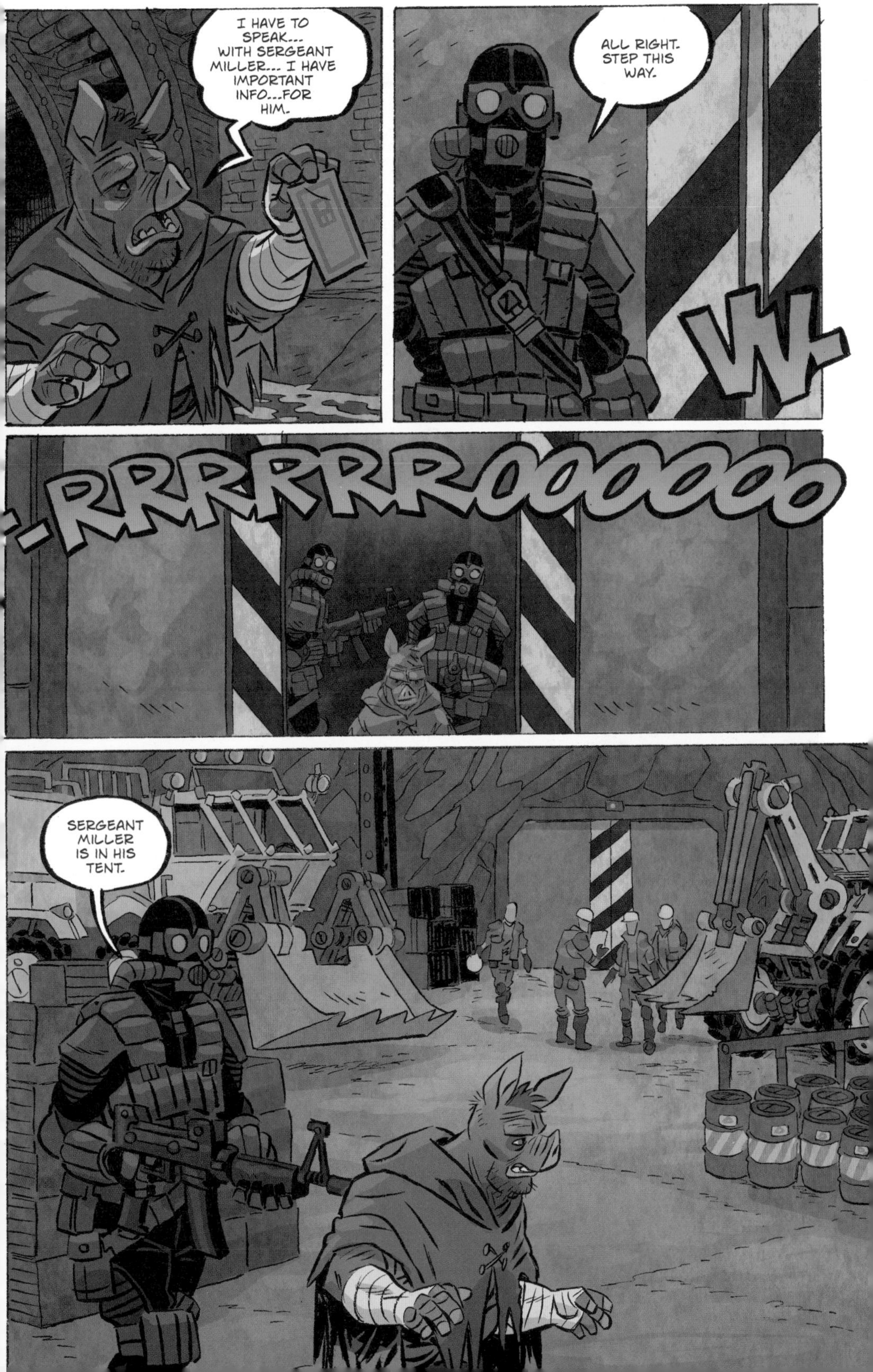
I HAVE TO SPEAK... WITH SERGEANT MILLER... I HAVE IMPORTANT INFO...FOR HIM.
ALL RIGHT. STEP THIS WAY.
VW-
-RRRRRROOOOOO
SERGEANT MILLER IS IN HIS TENT.

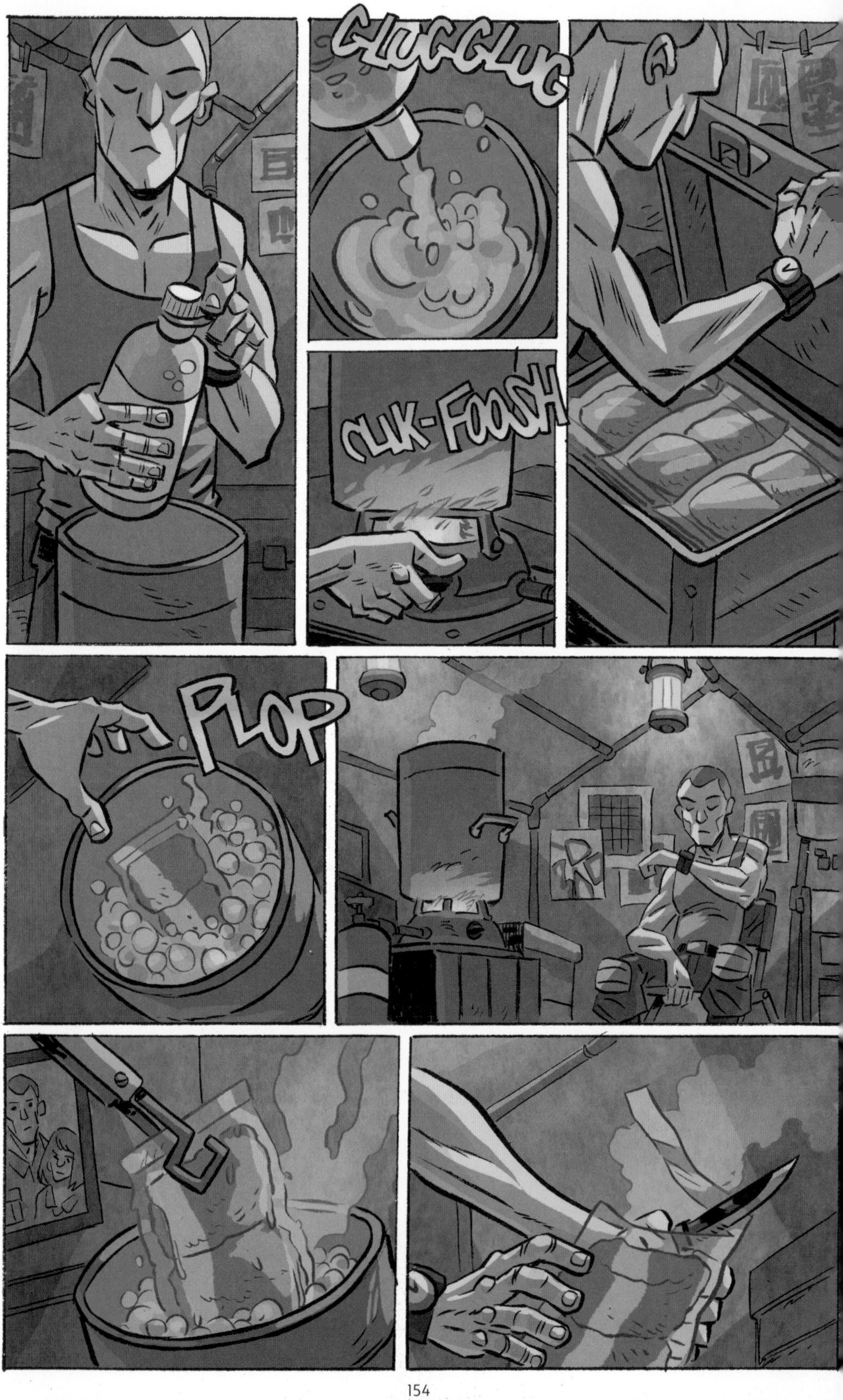
GLUGGLUG
CLIK-FOOSH
PLOP

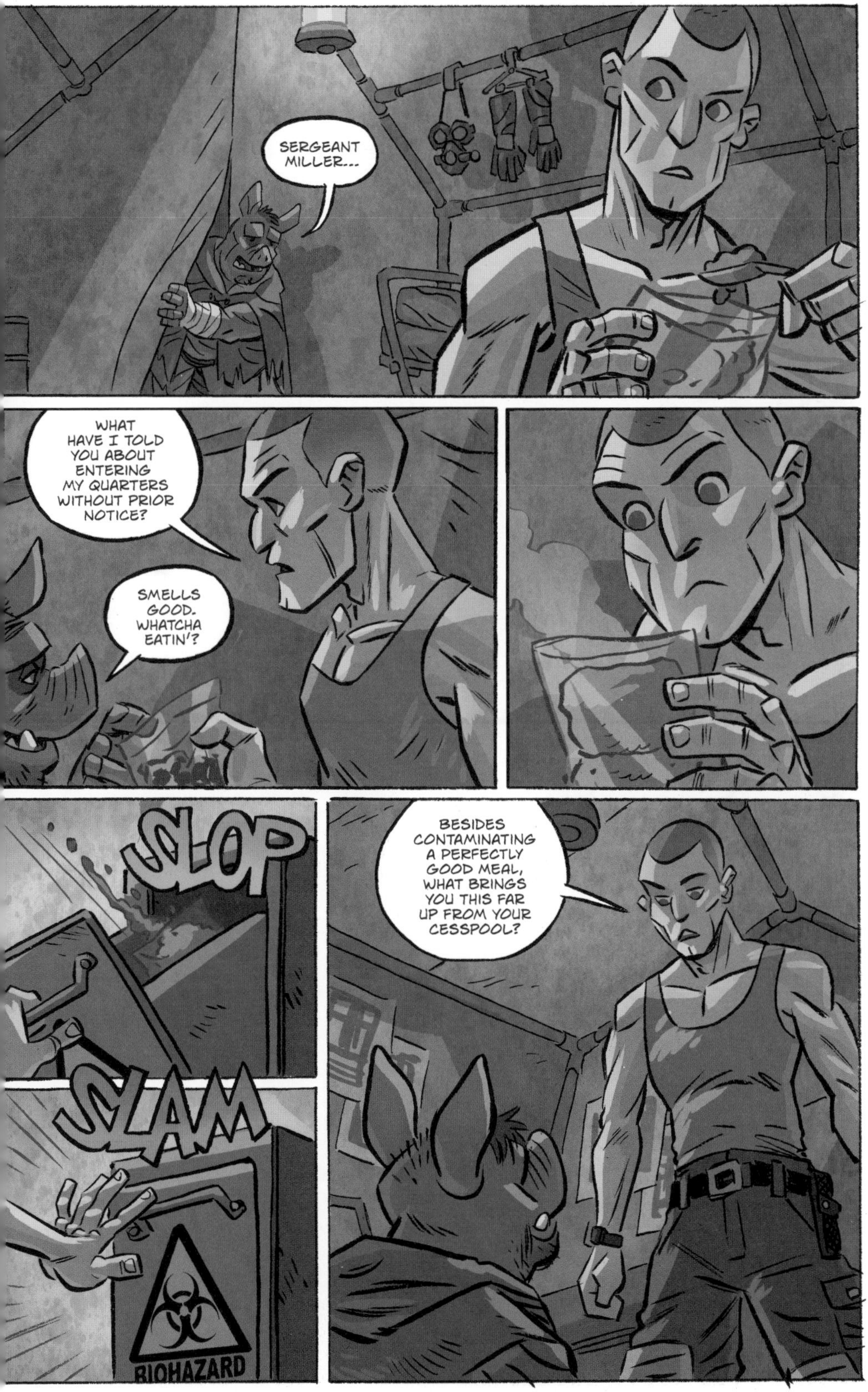
SERGEANT MILLER...
WHAT HAVE I TOLD YOU ABOUT ENTERING MY QUARTERS WITHOUT PRIOR NOTICE?
SMELLS GOOD. WHATCHA EATIN'?
SLOP
SLAM
BIOHAZARD
BESIDES CONTAMINATING A PERFECTLY GOOD MEAL, WHAT BRINGS YOU THIS FAR UP FROM YOUR CESSPOOL?

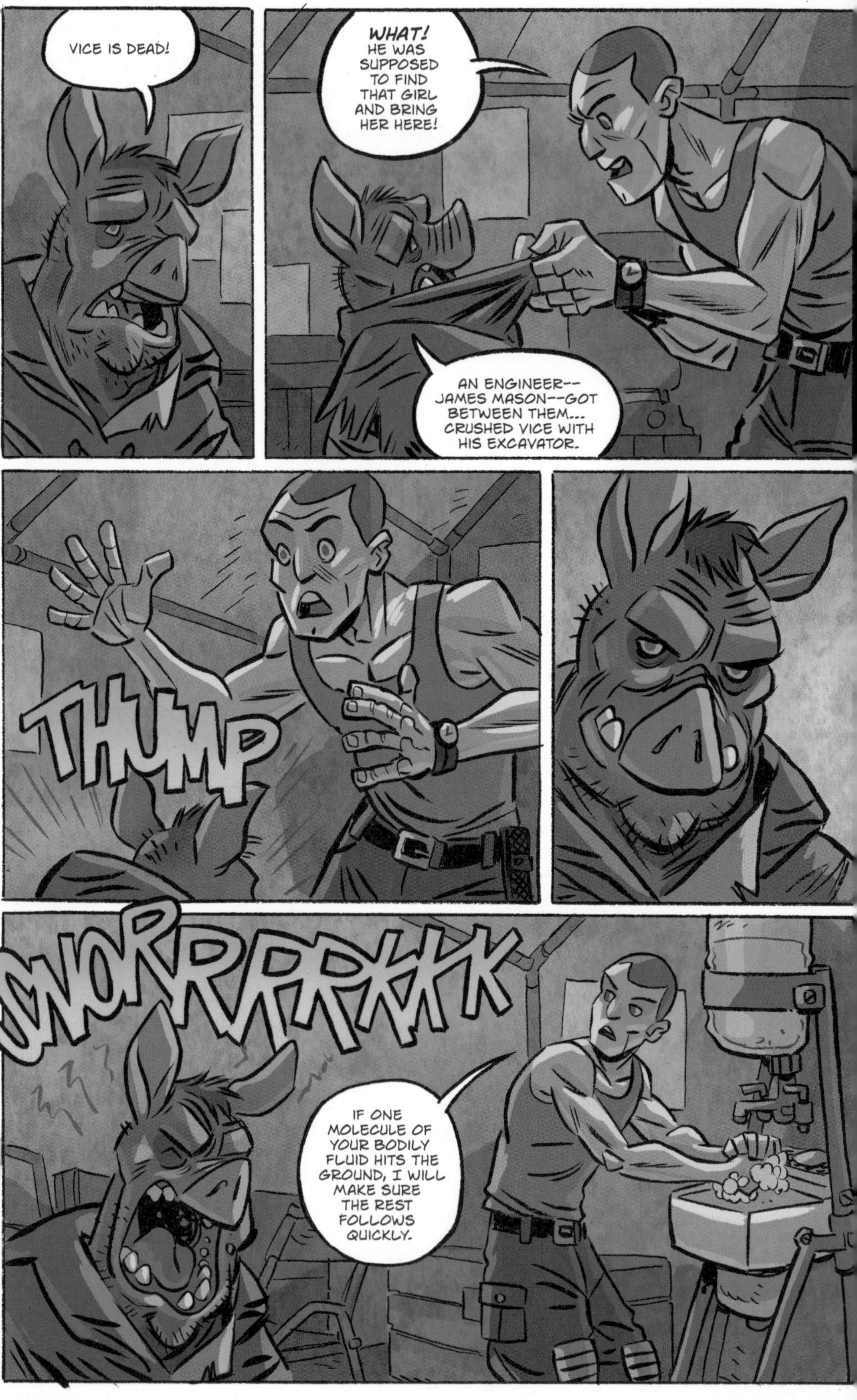
VICE IS DEAD!
WHAT! HE WAS SUPPOSED TO FIND THAT GIRL AND BRING HER HERE!
AN ENGINEER-- JAMES MASON--GOT BETWEEN THEM... CRUSHED VICE WITH HIS EXCAVATOR.
THUMP
SNORRRRKKK
IF ONE MOLECULE OF YOUR BODILY FLUID HITS THE GROUND, I WILL MAKE SURE THE REST FOLLOWS QUICKLY.

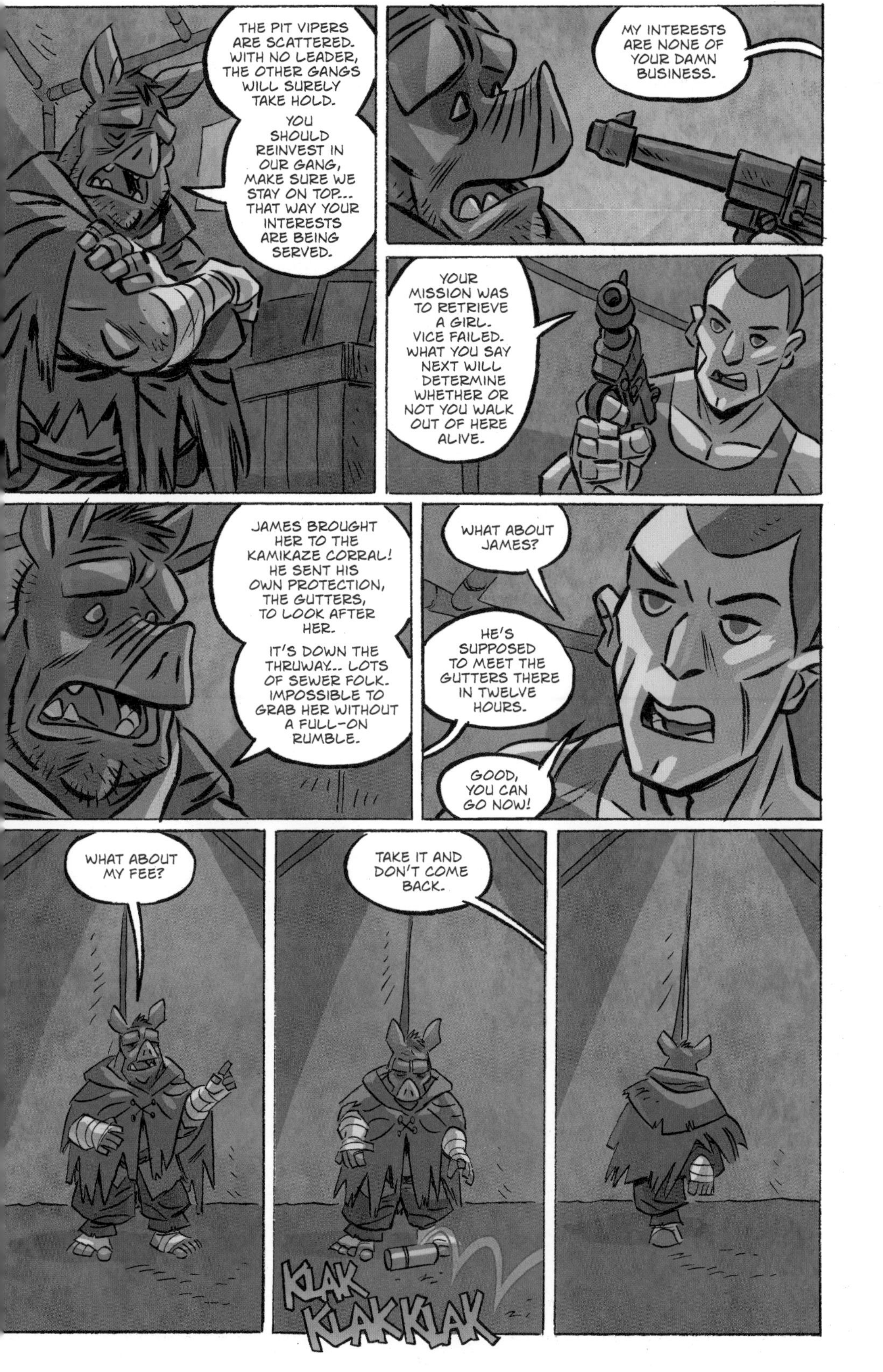
THE PIT VIPERS ARE SCATTERED. WITH NO LEADER, THE OTHER GANGS WILL SURELY TAKE HOLD.
YOU SHOULD REINVEST IN OUR GANG, MAKE SURE WE STAY ON TOP... THAT WAY YOUR INTERESTS ARE BEING SERVED.
MY INTERESTS ARE NONE OF YOUR DAMN BUSINESS.
YOUR MISSION WAS TO RETRIEVE A GIRL. VICE FAILED. WHAT YOU SAY NEXT WILL DETERMINE WHETHER OR NOT YOU WALK OUT OF HERE ALIVE.
JAMES BROUGHT HER TO THE KAMIKAZE CORRAL! HE SENT HIS OWN PROTECTION, THE GUTTERS, TO LOOK AFTER HER.
IT'S DOWN THE THRUWAY... LOTS OF SEWER FOLK. IMPOSSIBLE TO GRAB HER WITHOUT A FULL-ON RUMBLE.
WHAT ABOUT JAMES?
HE'S SUPPOSED TO MEET THE GUTTERS THERE IN TWELVE HOURS.
GOOD, YOU CAN GO NOW!
WHAT ABOUT MY FEE?
TAKE IT AND DON'T COME BACK.
KLAK KLAK KLAK

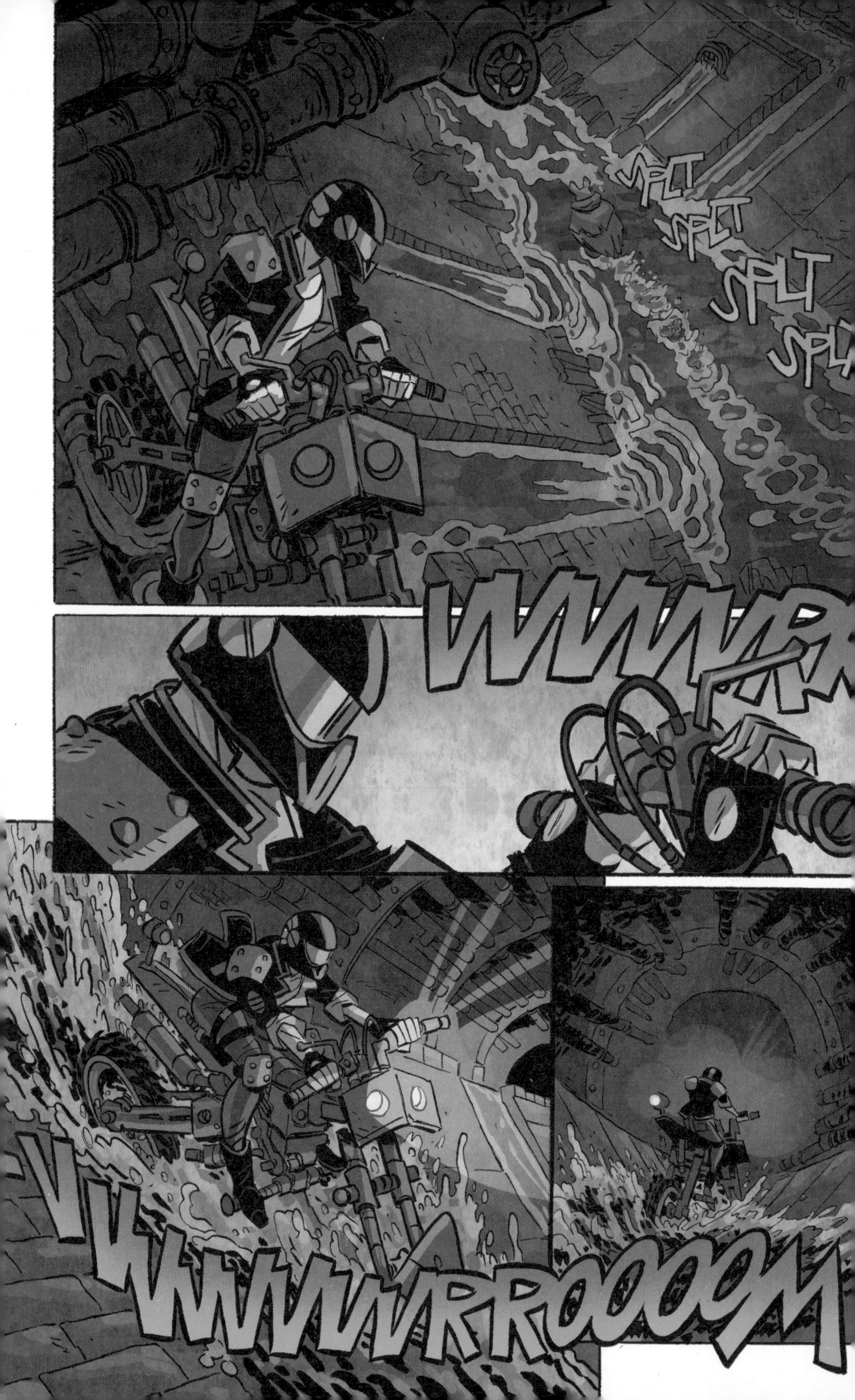
SPLT
SPLT
SPLT
SPLA
VVVVVR
VVVVVVVRROOOOM

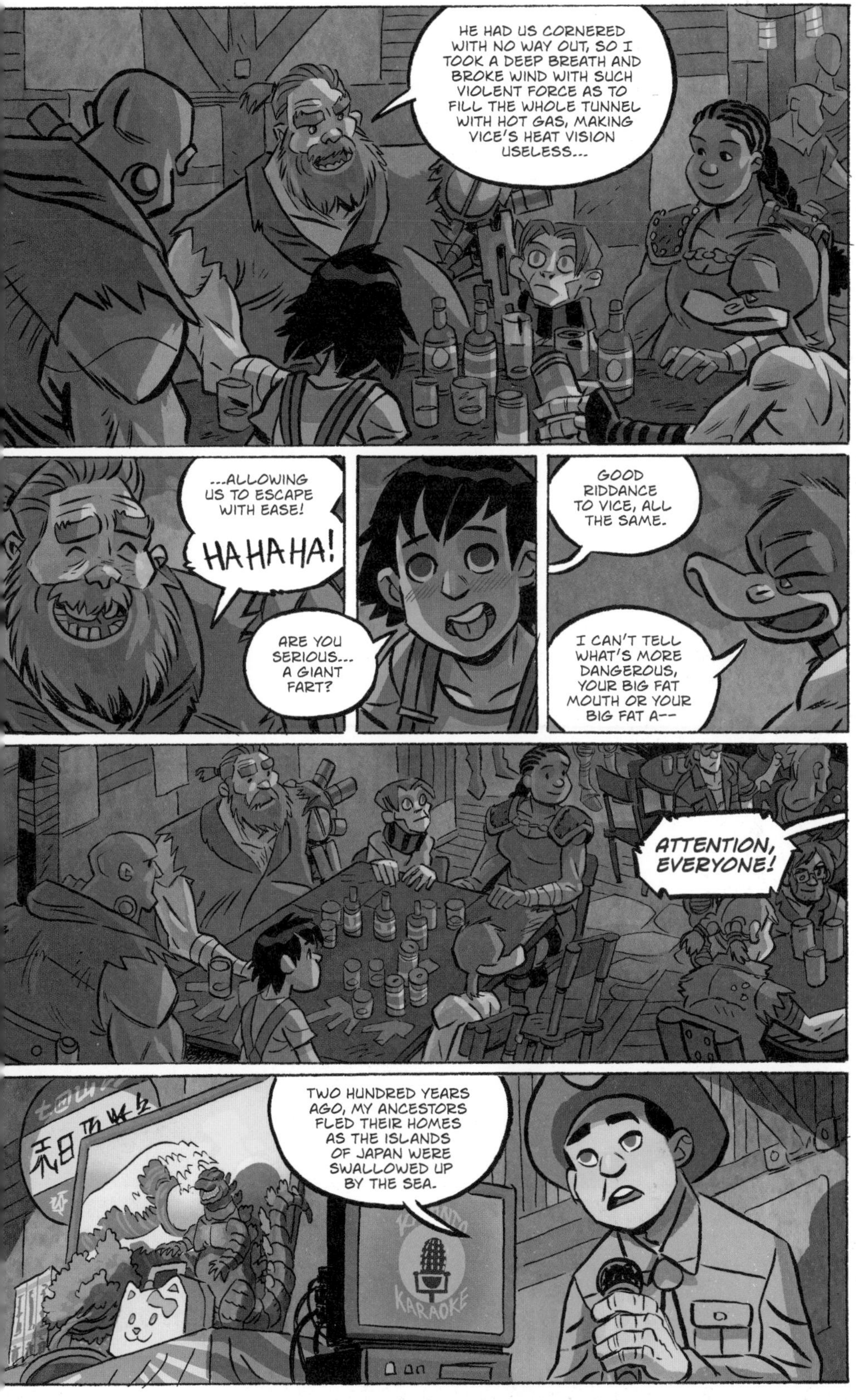
HE HAD US CORNERED WITH NO WAY OUT, SO I TOOK A DEEP BREATH AND BROKE WIND WITH SUCH VIOLENT FORCE AS TO FILL THE WHOLE TUNNEL WITH HOT GAS, MAKING VICE'S HEAT VISION USELESS...
...ALLOWING US TO ESCAPE WITH EASE!
HAHAHA!
ARE YOU SERIOUS... A GIANT FART?
GOOD RIDDANCE TO VICE, ALL THE SAME.
I CAN'T TELL WHAT'S MORE DANGEROUS, YOUR BIG FAT MOUTH OR YOUR BIG FAT A--
ATTENTION, EVERYONE!
TWO HUNDRED YEARS AGO, MY ANCESTORS FLED THEIR HOMES AS THE ISLANDS OF JAPAN WERE SWALLOWED UP BY THE SEA.
KARAOKE

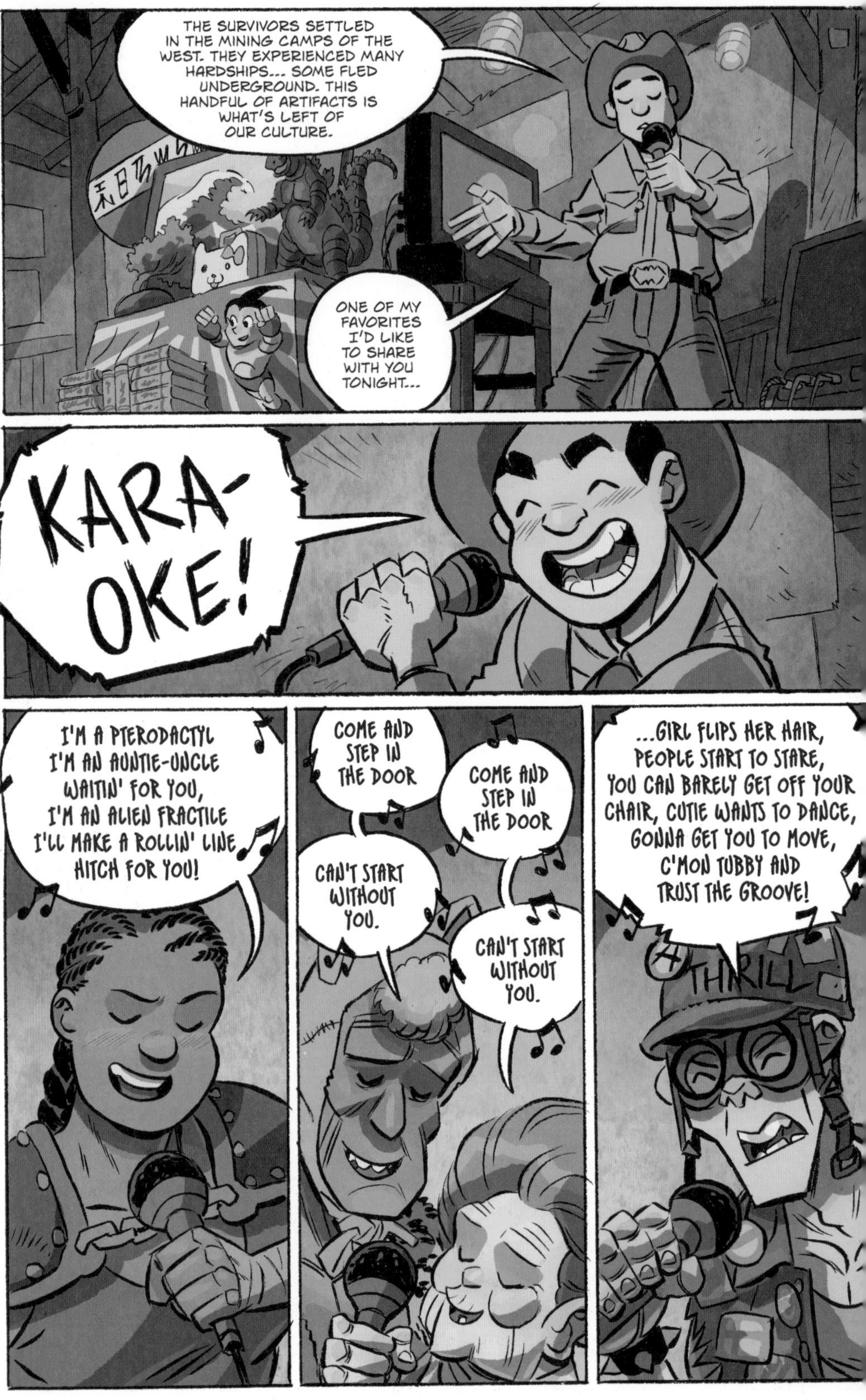
THE SURVIVORS SETTLED IN THE MINING CAMPS OF THE WEST. THEY EXPERIENCED MANY HARDSHIPS... SOME FLED UNDERGROUND. THIS HANDFUL OF ARTIFACTS IS WHAT'S LEFT OF OUR CULTURE.
ONE OF MY FAVORITES I'D LIKE TO SHARE WITH YOU TONIGHT...
KARA-OKE!
I'M A PTERODACTYL I'M AN AUNTIE-UNCLE WAITIN' FOR YOU, I'M AN ALIEN FRACTILE I'LL MAKE A ROLLIN' LINE HITCH FOR YOU!
COME AND STEP IN THE DOOR
COME AND STEP IN THE DOOR
CAN'T START WITHOUT YOU.
CAN'T START WITHOUT YOU.
...GIRL FLIPS HER HAIR, PEOPLE START TO STARE, YOU CAN BARELY GET OFF YOUR CHAIR, CUTIE WANTS TO DANCE, GONNA GET YOU TO MOVE, C'MON TUBBY AND TRUST THE GROOVE!
THRILL

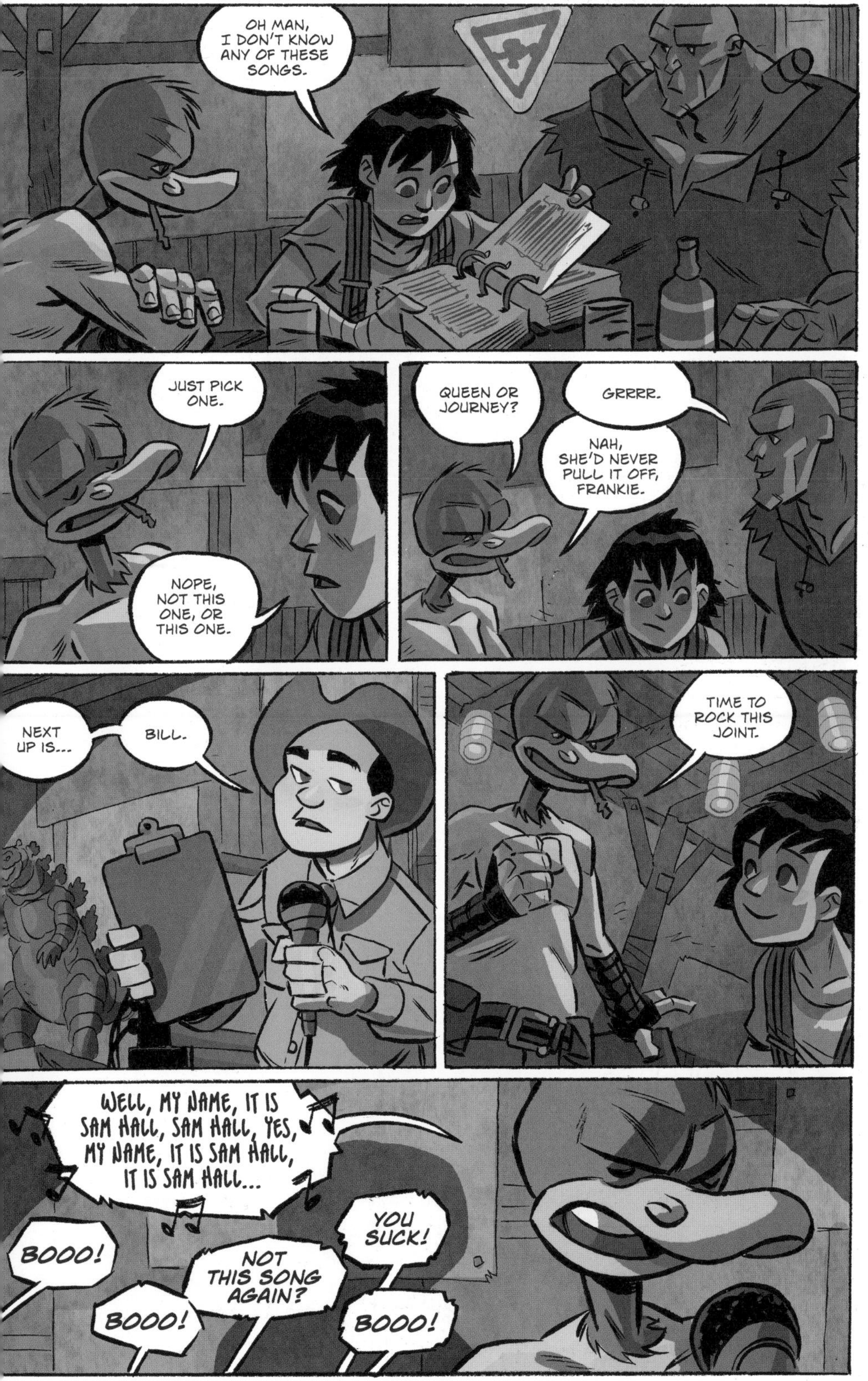
OH MAN, I DON'T KNOW ANY OF THESE SONGS.
JUST PICK ONE.
NOPE, NOT THIS ONE, OR THIS ONE.
QUEEN OR JOURNEY?
GRRRR.
NAH, SHE'D NEVER PULL IT OFF, FRANKIE.
NEXT UP IS...
BILL.
TIME TO ROCK THIS JOINT.
WELL, MY NAME, IT IS SAM HALL, SAM HALL, YES, MY NAME, IT IS SAM HALL, IT IS SAM HALL...
YOU SUCK!
BOOO!
NOT THIS SONG AGAIN?
BOOO!
BOOO!

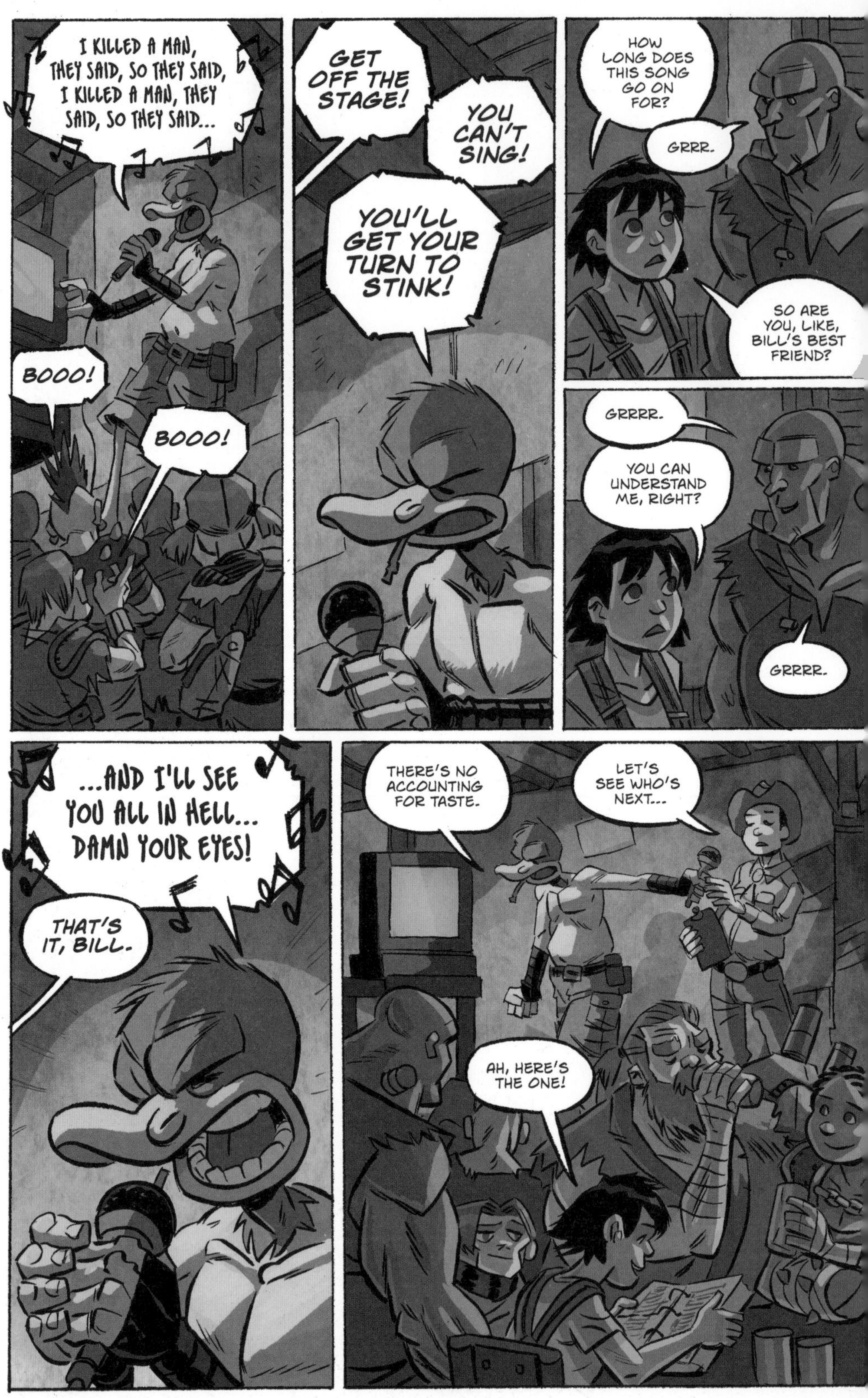
I KILLED A MAN, THEY SAID, SO THEY SAID, I KILLED A MAN, THEY SAID, SO THEY SAID...
BOOO!
BOOO!
GET OFF THE STAGE!
YOU CAN'T SING!
YOU'LL GET YOUR TURN TO STINK!
HOW LONG DOES THIS SONG GO ON FOR?
GRRR.
SO ARE YOU, LIKE, BILL'S BEST FRIEND?
GRRRR.
YOU CAN UNDERSTAND ME, RIGHT?
GRRRR.
...AND I'LL SEE YOU ALL IN HELL... DAMN YOUR EYES!
THAT'S IT, BILL.
THERE'S NO ACCOUNTING FOR TASTE.
LET'S SEE WHO'S NEXT...
AH, HERE'S THE ONE!

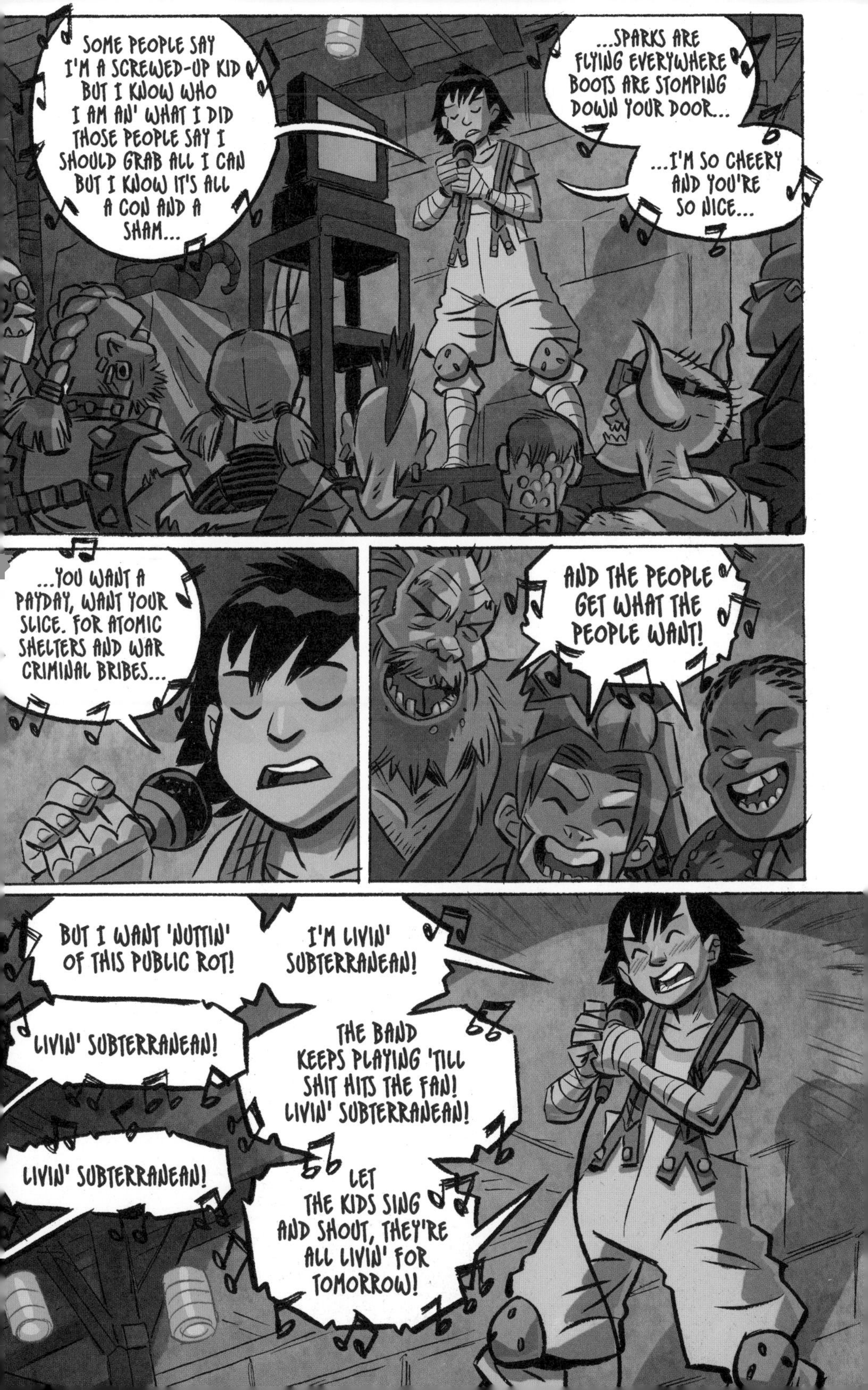
SOME PEOPLE SAY I'M A SCREWED-UP KID BUT I KNOW WHO I AM AN' WHAT I DID THOSE PEOPLE SAY I SHOULD GRAB ALL I CAN BUT I KNOW IT'S ALL A CON AND A SHAM...
...SPARKS ARE FLYING EVERYWHERE BOOTS ARE STOMPING DOWN YOUR DOOR...
...I'M SO CHEERY AND YOU'RE SO NICE...
...YOU WANT A PAYDAY, WANT YOUR SLICE. FOR ATOMIC SHELTERS AND WAR CRIMINAL BRIBES...
AND THE PEOPLE GET WHAT THE PEOPLE WANT!
BUT I WANT 'NUTTIN' OF THIS PUBLIC ROT!
I'M LIVIN' SUBTERRANEAN!
LIVIN' SUBTERRANEAN!
THE BAND KEEPS PLAYING 'TILL SHIT HITS THE FAN! LIVIN' SUBTERRANEAN!
LIVIN' SUBTERRANEAN!
LET THE KIDS SING AND SHOUT, THEY'RE ALL LIVIN' FOR TOMORROW!

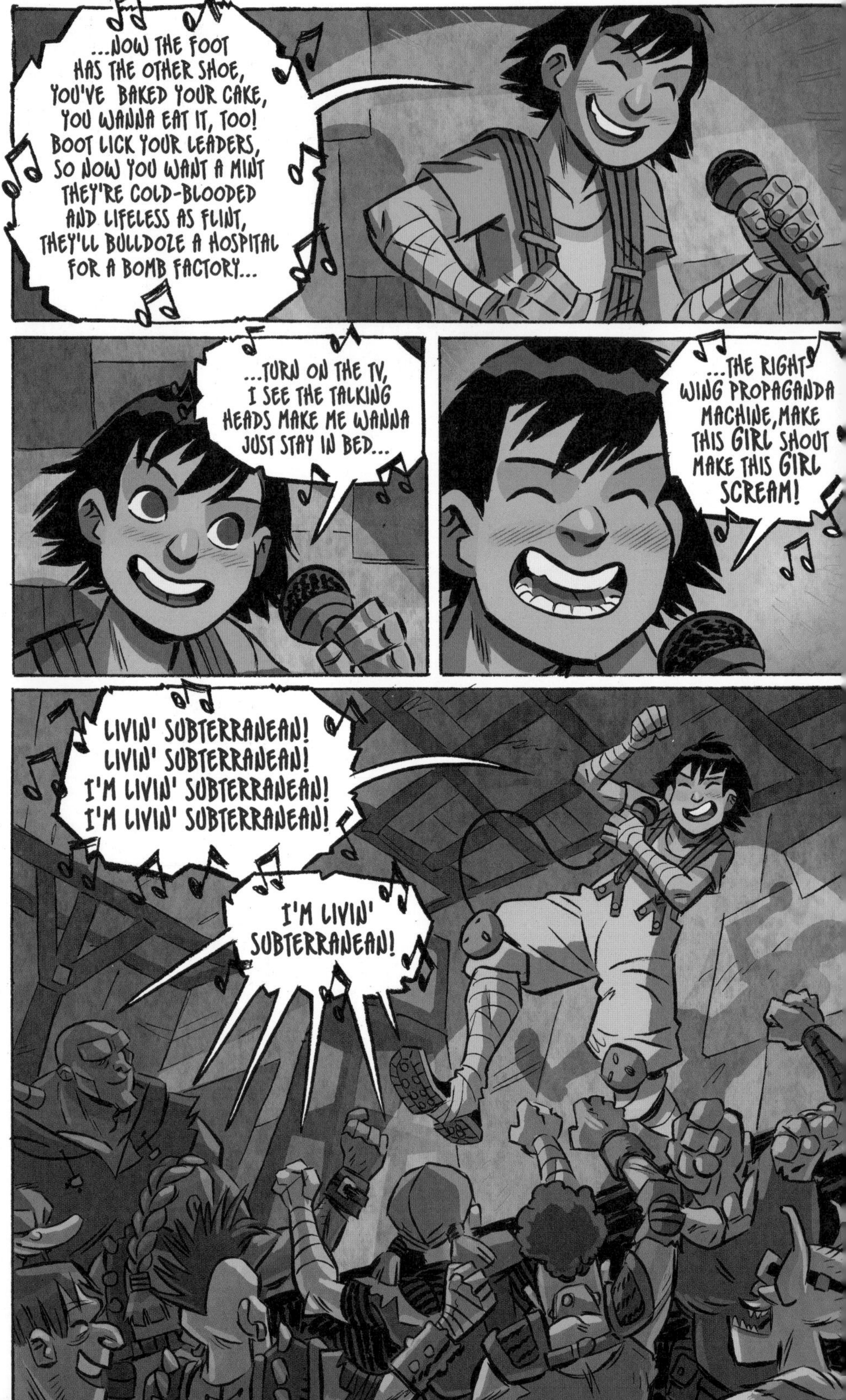
...NOW THE FOOT HAS THE OTHER SHOE, YOU'VE BAKED YOUR CAKE, YOU WANNA EAT IT, TOO! BOOT LICK YOUR LEADERS, SO NOW YOU WANT A MINT THEY'RE COLD-BLOODED AND LIFELESS AS FLINT, THEY'LL BULLDOZE A HOSPITAL FOR A BOMB FACTORY...
...TURN ON THE TV, I SEE THE TALKING HEADS MAKE ME WANNA JUST STAY IN BED...
...THE RIGHT-WING PROPAGANDA MACHINE, MAKE THIS GIRL SHOUT MAKE THIS GIRL SCREAM!
LIVIN' SUBTERRANEAN! LIVIN' SUBTERRANEAN! I'M LIVIN' SUBTERRANEAN! I'M LIVIN' SUBTERRANEAN!
I'M LIVIN' SUBTERRANEAN!

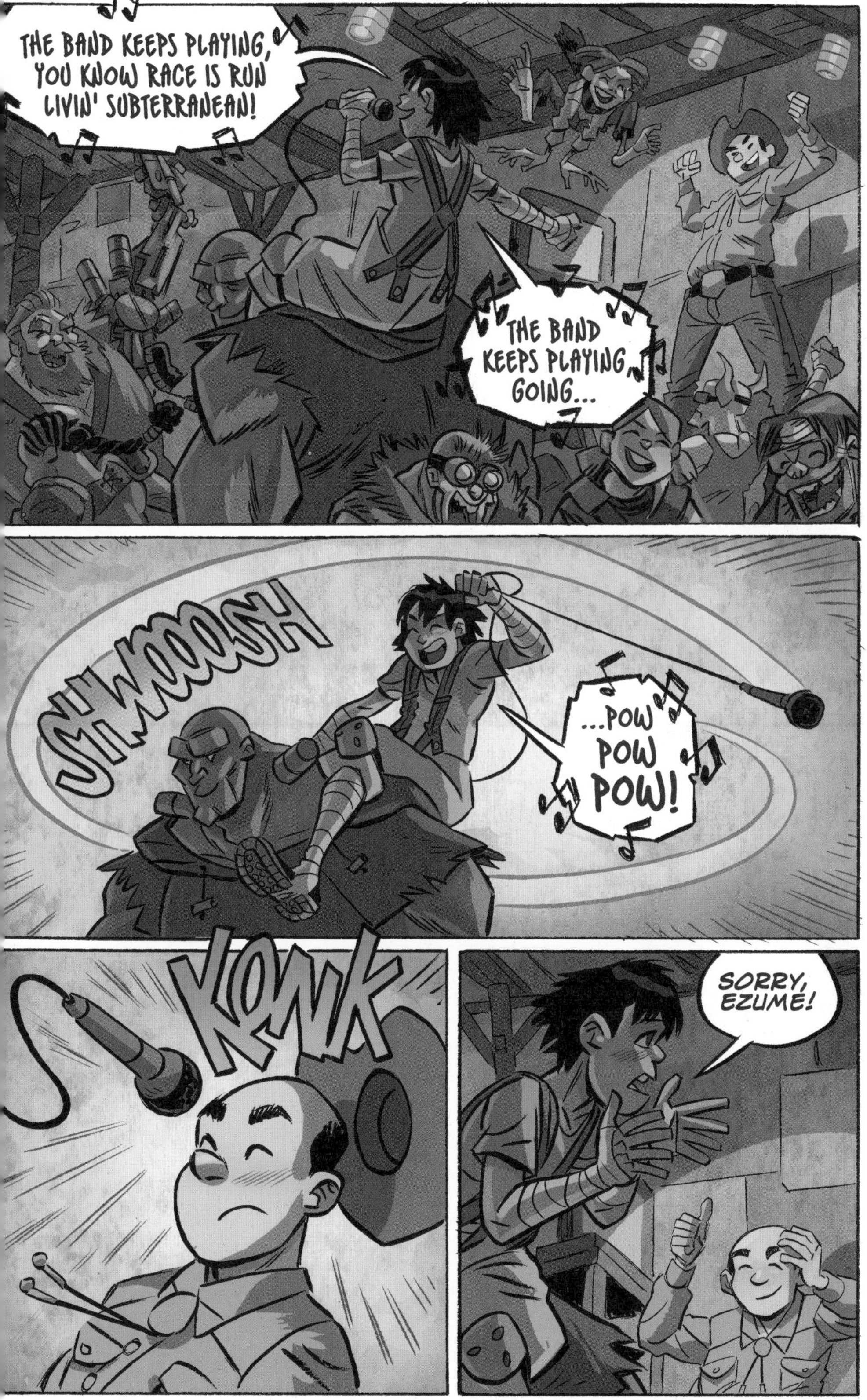
THE BAND KEEPS PLAYING, YOU KNOW RACE IS RUN LIVIN' SUBTERRANEAN!
THE BAND KEEPS PLAYING, GOING...
SHWOOOSH
...POW POW POW!
KONK
SORRY, EZUME!

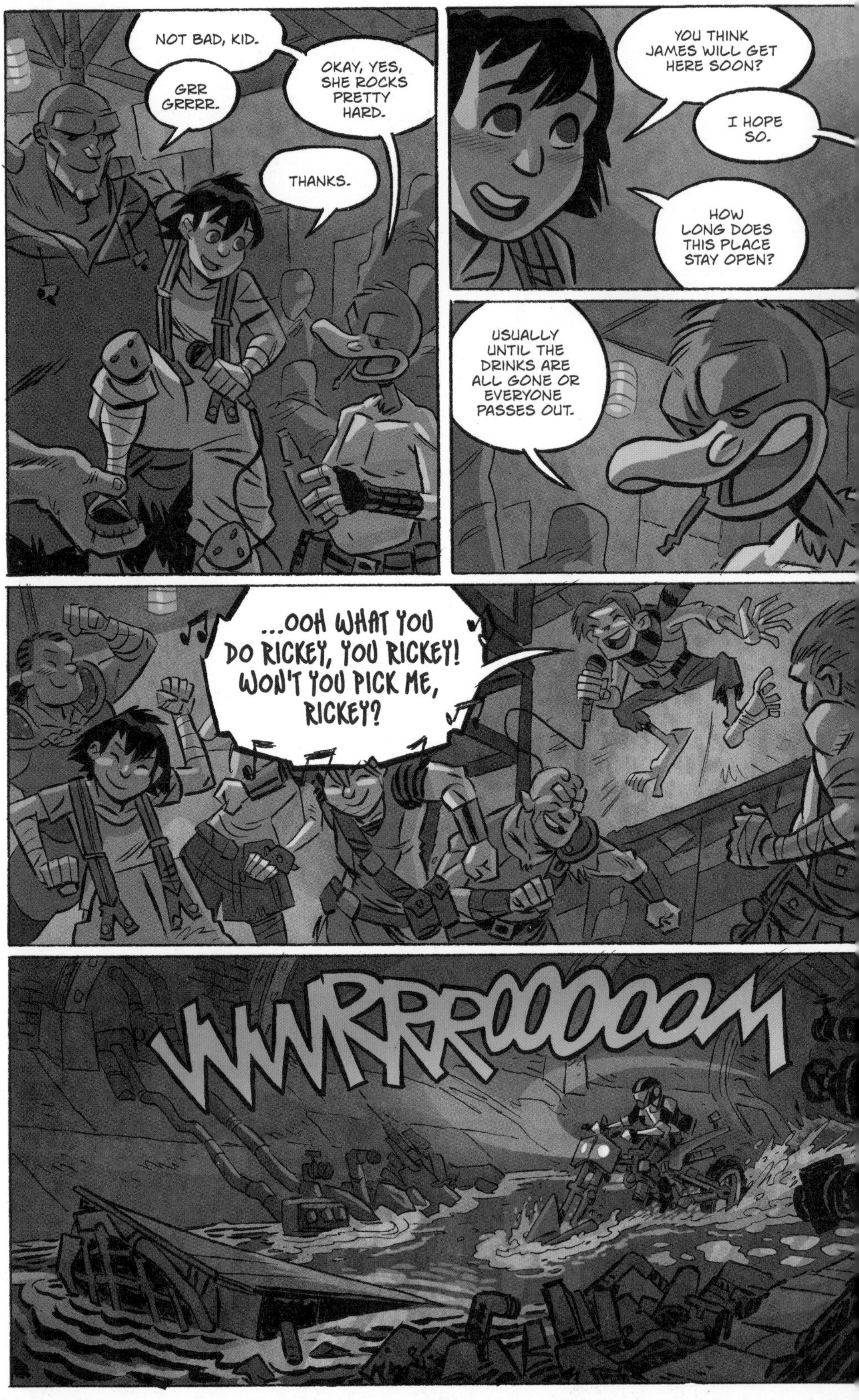
NOT BAD, KID.
GRR GRRRR.
OKAY, YES, SHE ROCKS PRETTY HARD.
THANKS.
YOU THINK JAMES WILL GET HERE SOON?
I HOPE SO.
HOW LONG DOES THIS PLACE STAY OPEN?
USUALLY UNTIL THE DRINKS ARE ALL GONE OR EVERYONE PASSES OUT.
...OOH WHAT YOU DO RICKEY, YOU RICKEY! WON'T YOU PICK ME, RICKEY?
WWRRROOOOOOM

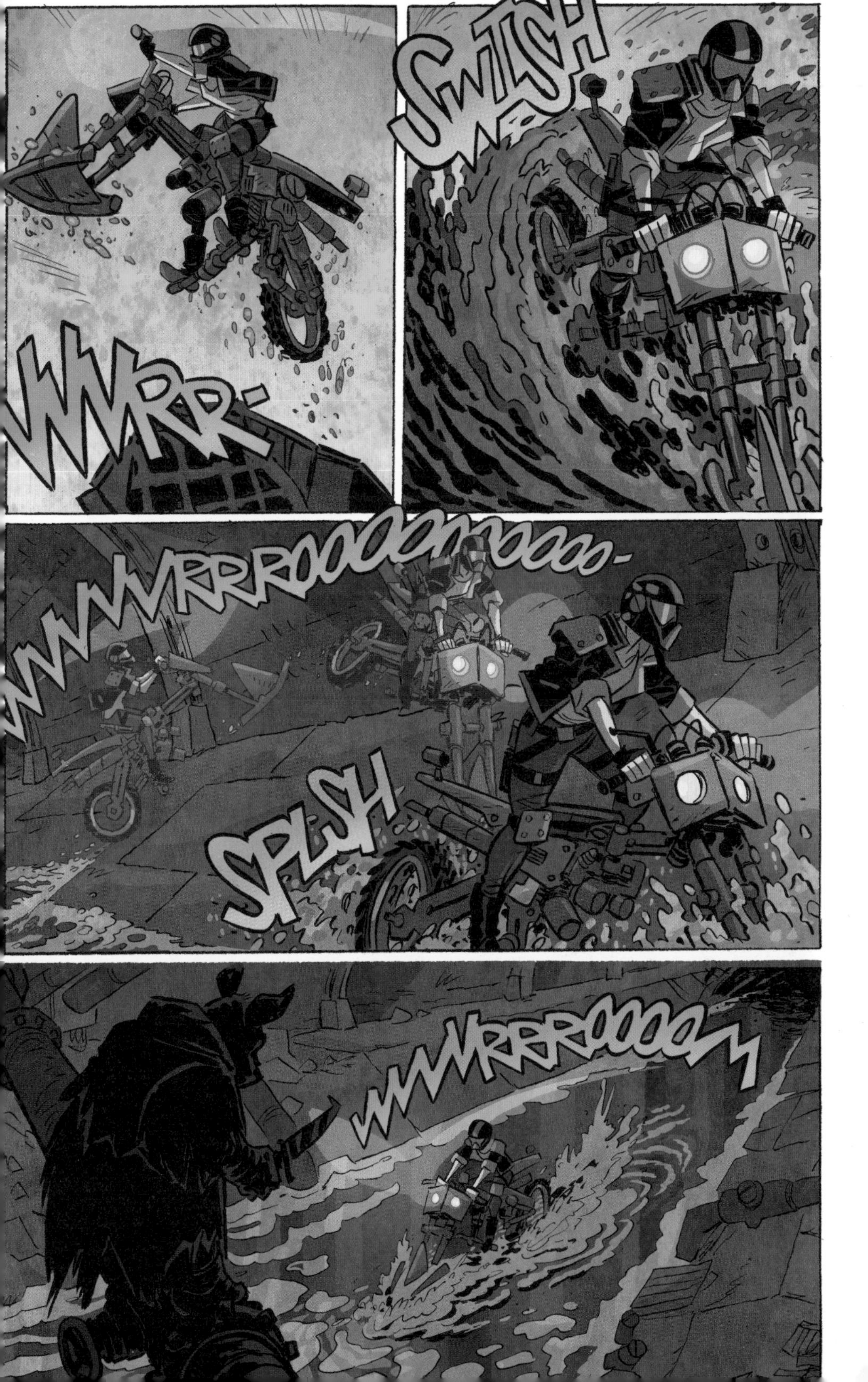
WWRR-
SWISH
WWWRRROOOOOOoooooo-
SPLISH
WWRRROOOO

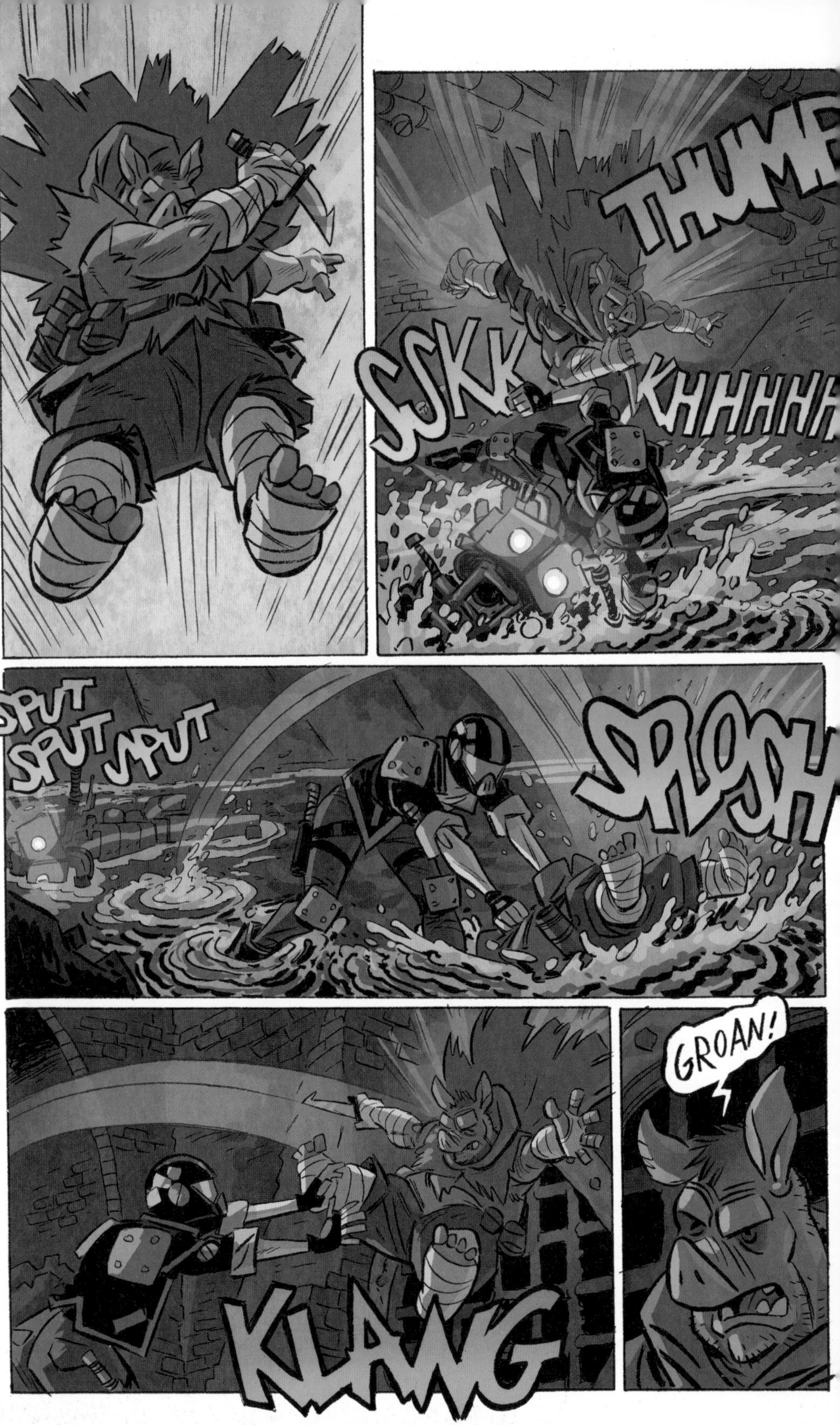
THUMP
SSKK
KHHHHH
SPUT
SPUT
SPUT
SPLOOSH
KLANG
GROAN!

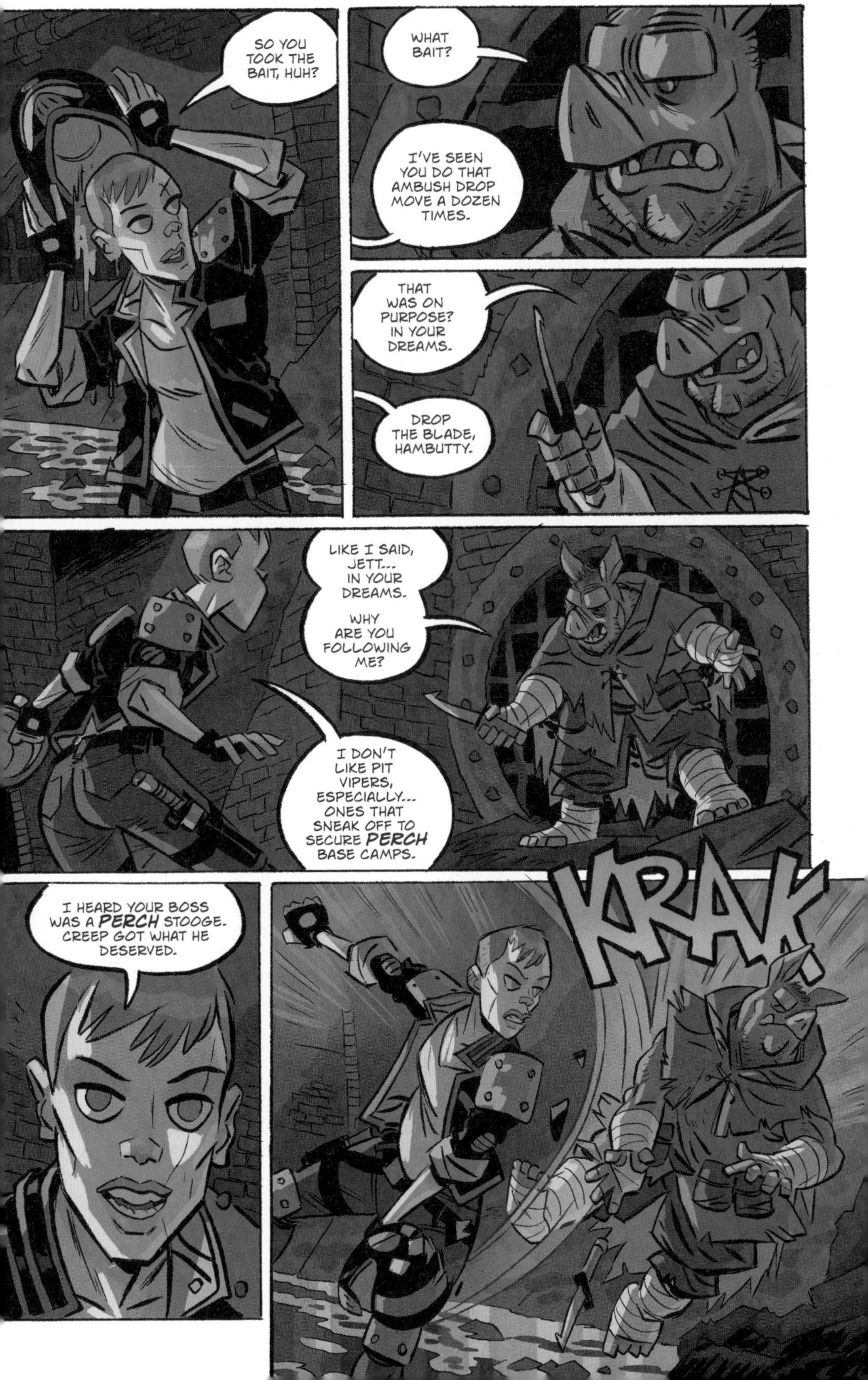
SO YOU TOOK THE BAIT, HUH?
WHAT BAIT?
I'VE SEEN YOU DO THAT AMBUSH DROP MOVE A DOZEN TIMES.
THAT WAS ON PURPOSE? IN YOUR DREAMS.
DROP THE BLADE, HAMBUTTY.
LIKE I SAID, JETT... IN YOUR DREAMS.
WHY ARE YOU FOLLOWING ME?
I DON'T LIKE PIT VIPERS, ESPECIALLY... ONES THAT SNEAK OFF TO SECURE PERCH BASE CAMPS.
I HEARD YOUR BOSS WAS A PERCH STOOGE. CREEP GOT WHAT HE DESERVED.
KRAK

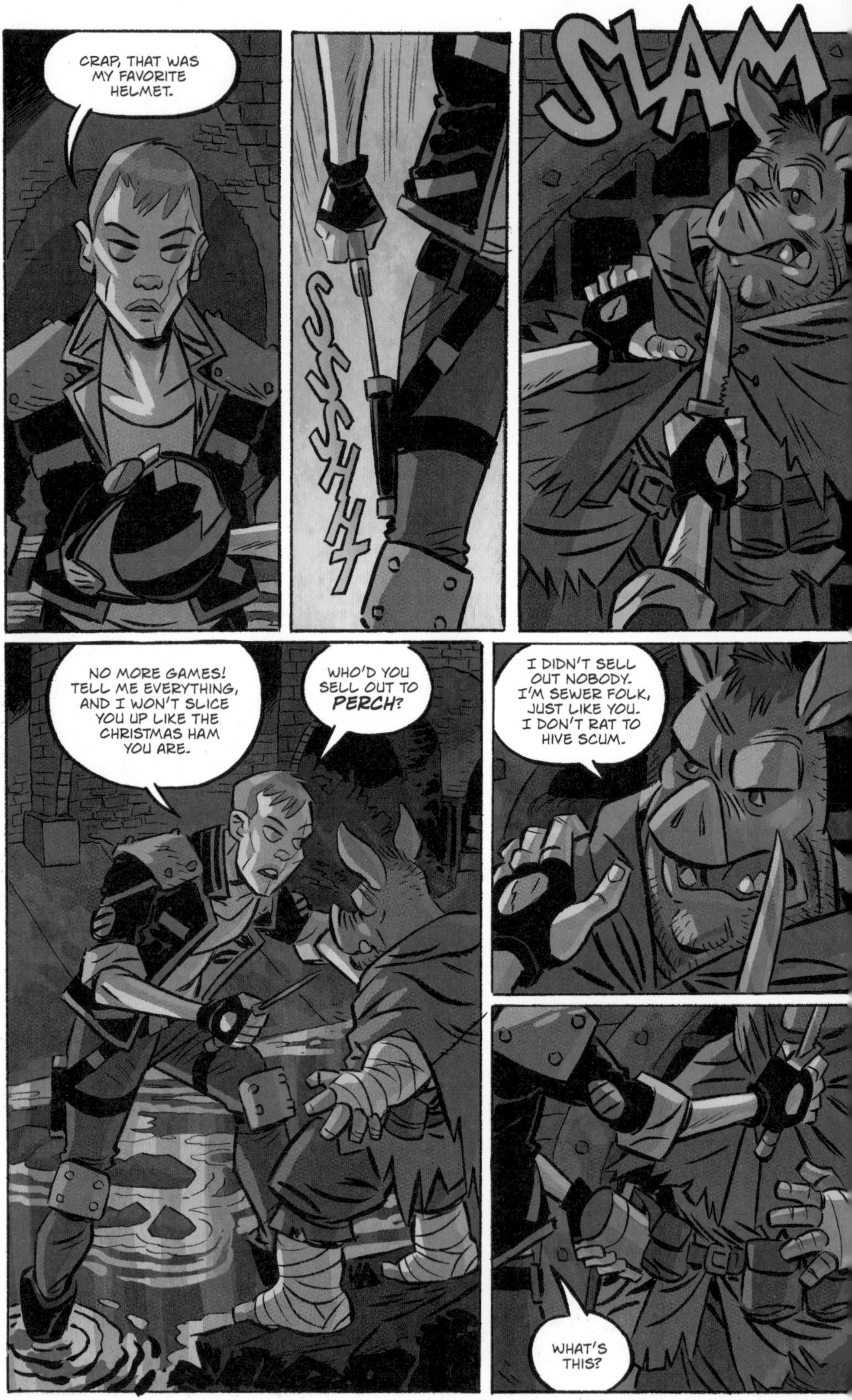
CRAP, THAT WAS MY FAVORITE HELMET.
SSSHHHT
SLAM
NO MORE GAMES! TELL ME EVERYTHING, AND I WON'T SLICE YOU UP LIKE THE CHRISTMAS HAM YOU ARE.
WHO'D YOU SELL OUT TO PERCH?
I DIDN'T SELL OUT NOBODY. I'M SEWER FOLK, JUST LIKE YOU. I DON'T RAT TO HIVE SCUM.
WHAT'S THIS?

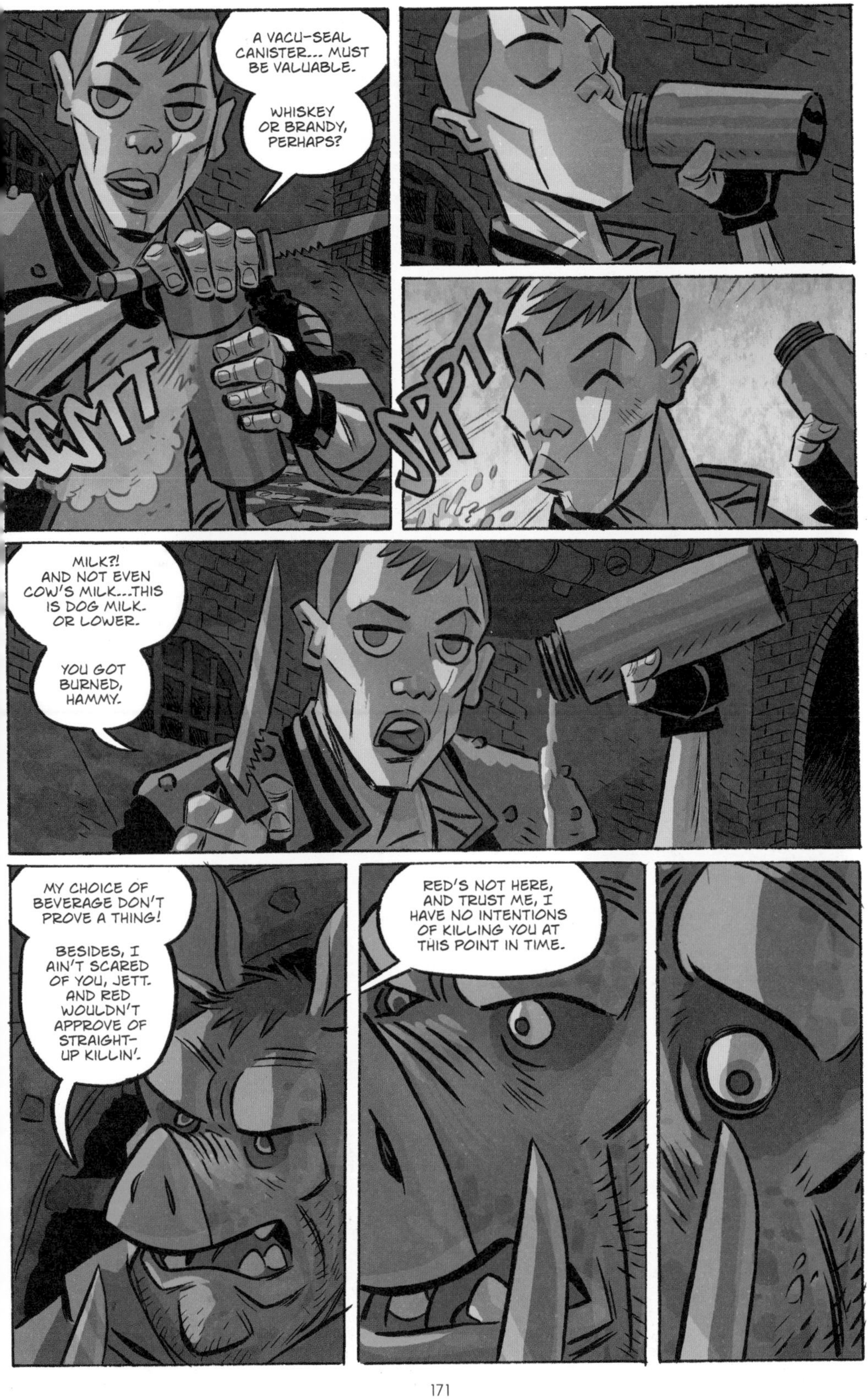

A VACU-SEAL CANISTER... MUST BE VALUABLE.
WHISKEY OR BRANDY, PERHAPS?
SSSTT
SPPT
MILK?! AND NOT EVEN COW'S MILK...THIS IS DOG MILK. OR LOWER.
YOU GOT BURNED, HAMMY.
MY CHOICE OF BEVERAGE DON'T PROVE A THING!
BESIDES, I AIN'T SCARED OF YOU, JETT. AND RED WOULDN'T APPROVE OF STRAIGHT-UP KILLIN'.
RED'S NOT HERE, AND TRUST ME, I HAVE NO INTENTIONS OF KILLING YOU AT THIS POINT IN TIME.

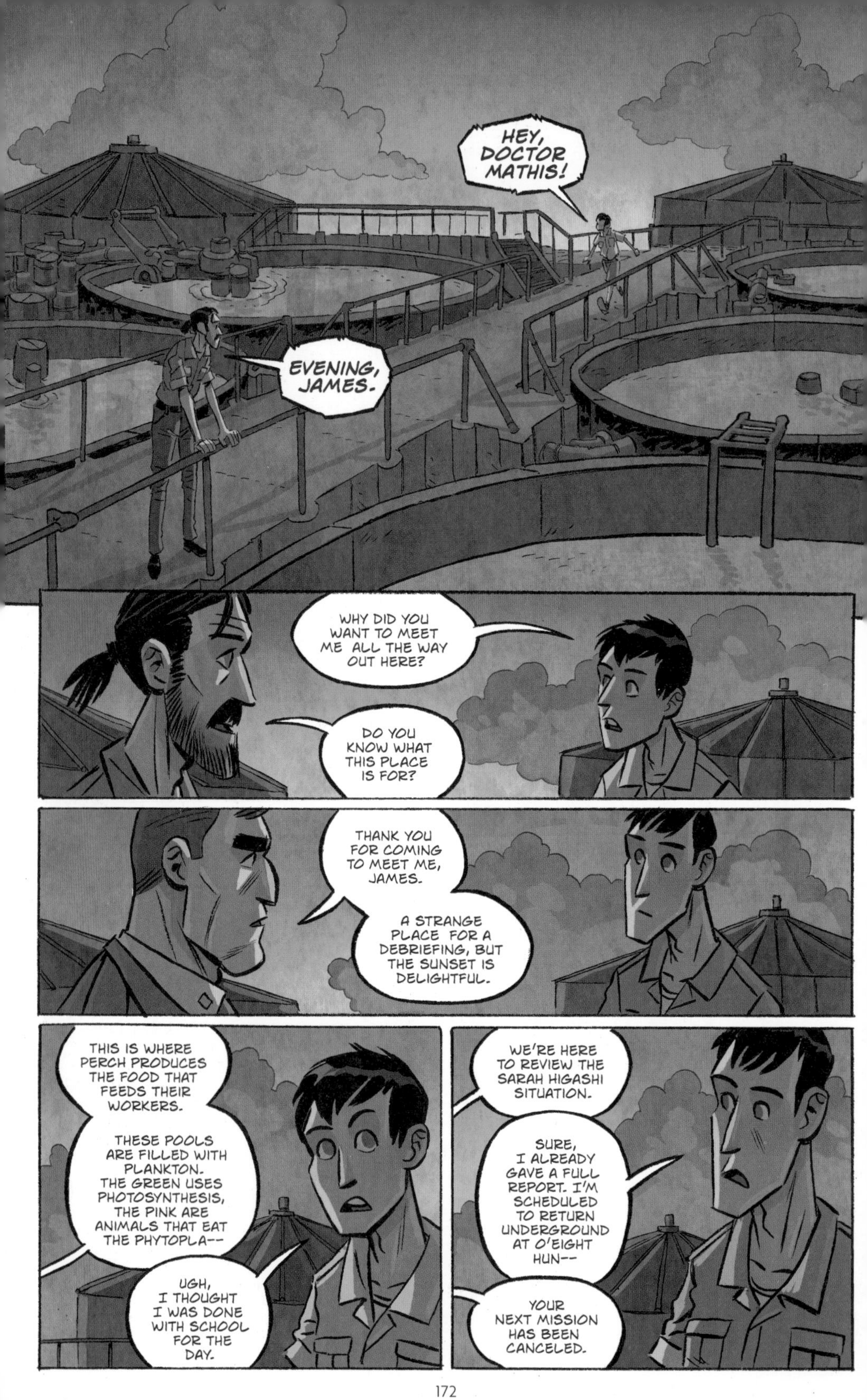
HEY, DOCTOR MATHIS!
EVENING, JAMES.
WHY DID YOU WANT TO MEET ME ALL THE WAY OUT HERE?
DO YOU KNOW WHAT THIS PLACE IS FOR?
THANK YOU FOR COMING TO MEET ME, JAMES.
A STRANGE PLACE FOR A DEBRIEFING, BUT THE SUNSET IS DELIGHTFUL.
THIS IS WHERE PERCH PRODUCES THE FOOD THAT FEEDS THEIR WORKERS.
THESE POOLS ARE FILLED WITH PLANKTON. THE GREEN USES PHOTOSYNTHESIS, THE PINK ARE ANIMALS THAT EAT THE PHYTOPLA--
UGH, I THOUGHT I WAS DONE WITH SCHOOL FOR THE DAY.
WE'RE HERE TO REVIEW THE SARAH HIGASHI SITUATION.
SURE, I ALREADY GAVE A FULL REPORT. I'M SCHEDULED TO RETURN UNDERGROUND AT O'EIGHT HUN--
YOUR NEXT MISSION HAS BEEN CANCELED.

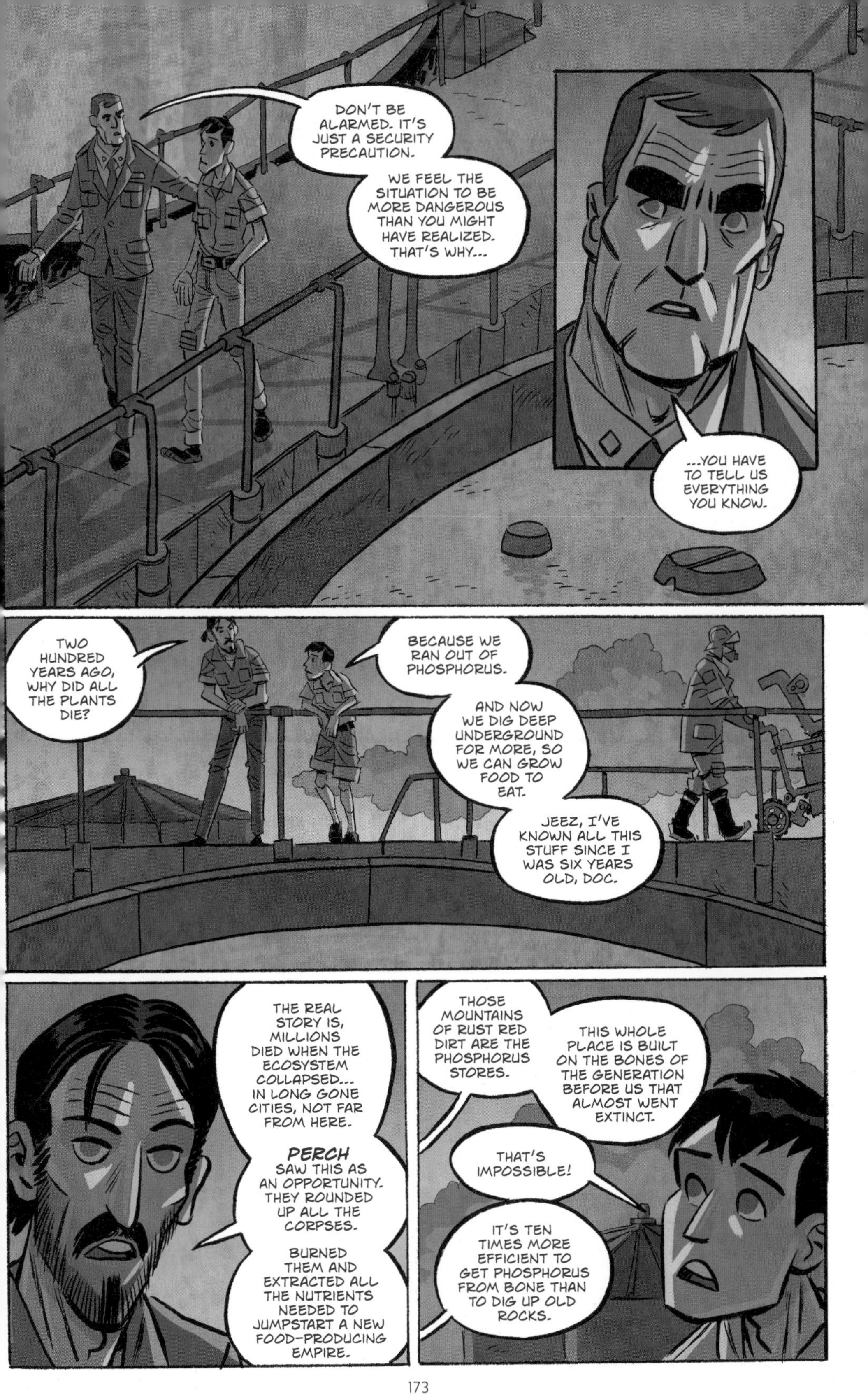
DON'T BE ALARMED. IT'S JUST A SECURITY PRECAUTION.
WE FEEL THE SITUATION TO BE MORE DANGEROUS THAN YOU MIGHT HAVE REALIZED. THAT'S WHY...
...YOU HAVE TO TELL US EVERYTHING YOU KNOW.
TWO HUNDRED YEARS AGO, WHY DID ALL THE PLANTS DIE?
BECAUSE WE RAN OUT OF PHOSPHORUS.
AND NOW WE DIG DEEP UNDERGROUND FOR MORE, SO WE CAN GROW FOOD TO EAT.
JEEZ, I'VE KNOWN ALL THIS STUFF SINCE I WAS SIX YEARS OLD, DOC.
THE REAL STORY IS, MILLIONS DIED WHEN THE ECOSYSTEM COLLAPSED... IN LONG GONE CITIES, NOT FAR FROM HERE.
PERCH SAW THIS AS AN OPPORTUNITY. THEY ROUNDED UP ALL THE CORPSES.
BURNED THEM AND EXTRACTED ALL THE NUTRIENTS NEEDED TO JUMPSTART A NEW FOOD-PRODUCING EMPIRE.
THOSE MOUNTAINS OF RUST RED DIRT ARE THE PHOSPHORUS STORES.
THIS WHOLE PLACE IS BUILT ON THE BONES OF THE GENERATION BEFORE US THAT ALMOST WENT EXTINCT.
THAT'S IMPOSSIBLE!
IT'S TEN TIMES MORE EFFICIENT TO GET PHOSPHORUS FROM BONE THAN TO DIG UP OLD ROCKS.

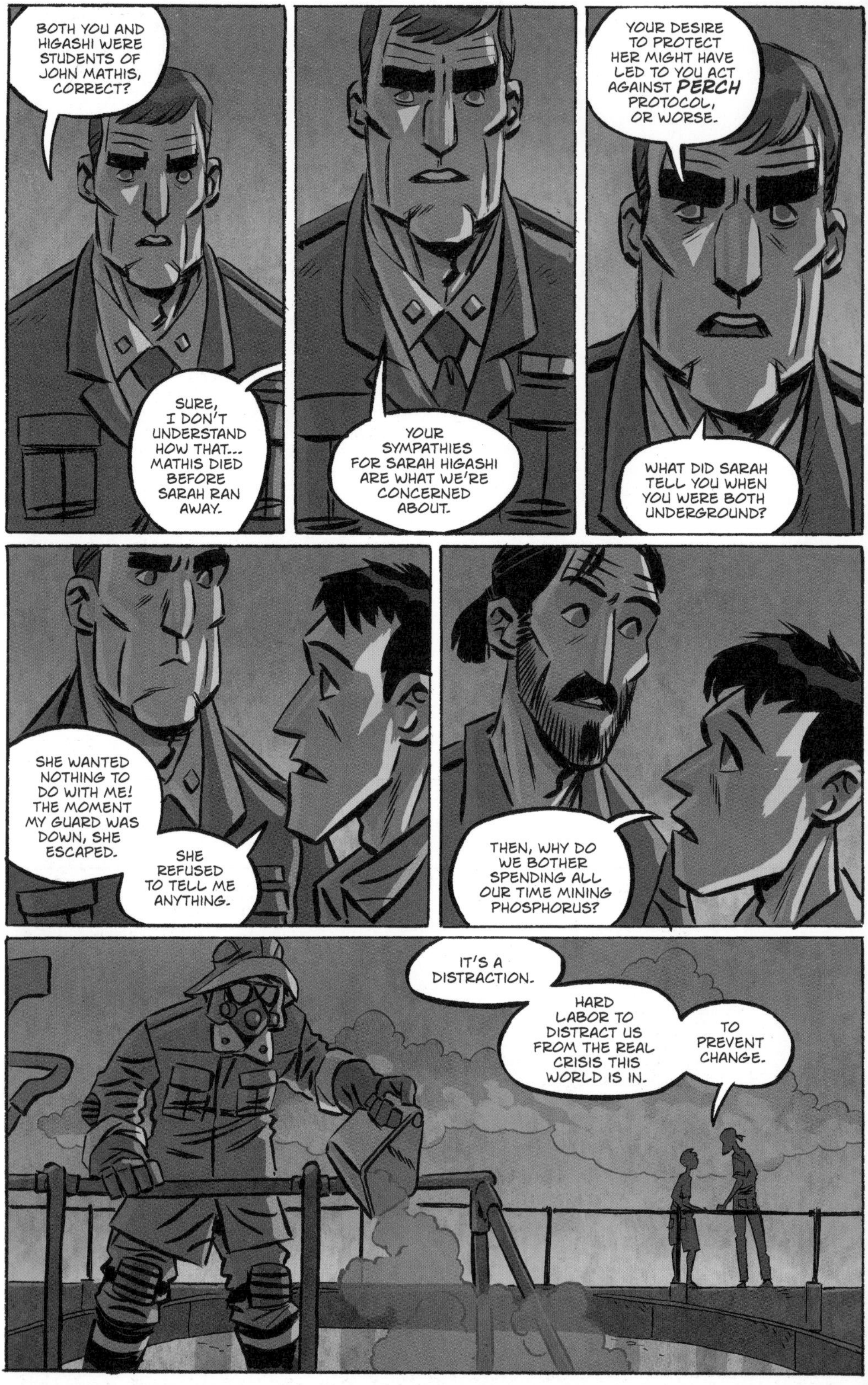
BOTH YOU AND HIGASHI WERE STUDENTS OF JOHN MATHIS, CORRECT?
SURE, I DON'T UNDERSTAND HOW THAT... MATHIS DIED BEFORE SARAH RAN AWAY.
YOUR SYMPATHIES FOR SARAH HIGASHI ARE WHAT WE'RE CONCERNED ABOUT.
YOUR DESIRE TO PROTECT HER MIGHT HAVE LED TO YOU ACT AGAINST PERCH PROTOCOL, OR WORSE.
WHAT DID SARAH TELL YOU WHEN YOU WERE BOTH UNDERGROUND?
SHE WANTED NOTHING TO DO WITH ME! THE MOMENT MY GUARD WAS DOWN, SHE ESCAPED.
SHE REFUSED TO TELL ME ANYTHING.
THEN, WHY DO WE BOTHER SPENDING ALL OUR TIME MINING PHOSPHORUS?
IT'S A DISTRACTION.
HARD LABOR TO DISTRACT US FROM THE REAL CRISIS THIS WORLD IS IN.
TO PREVENT CHANGE.

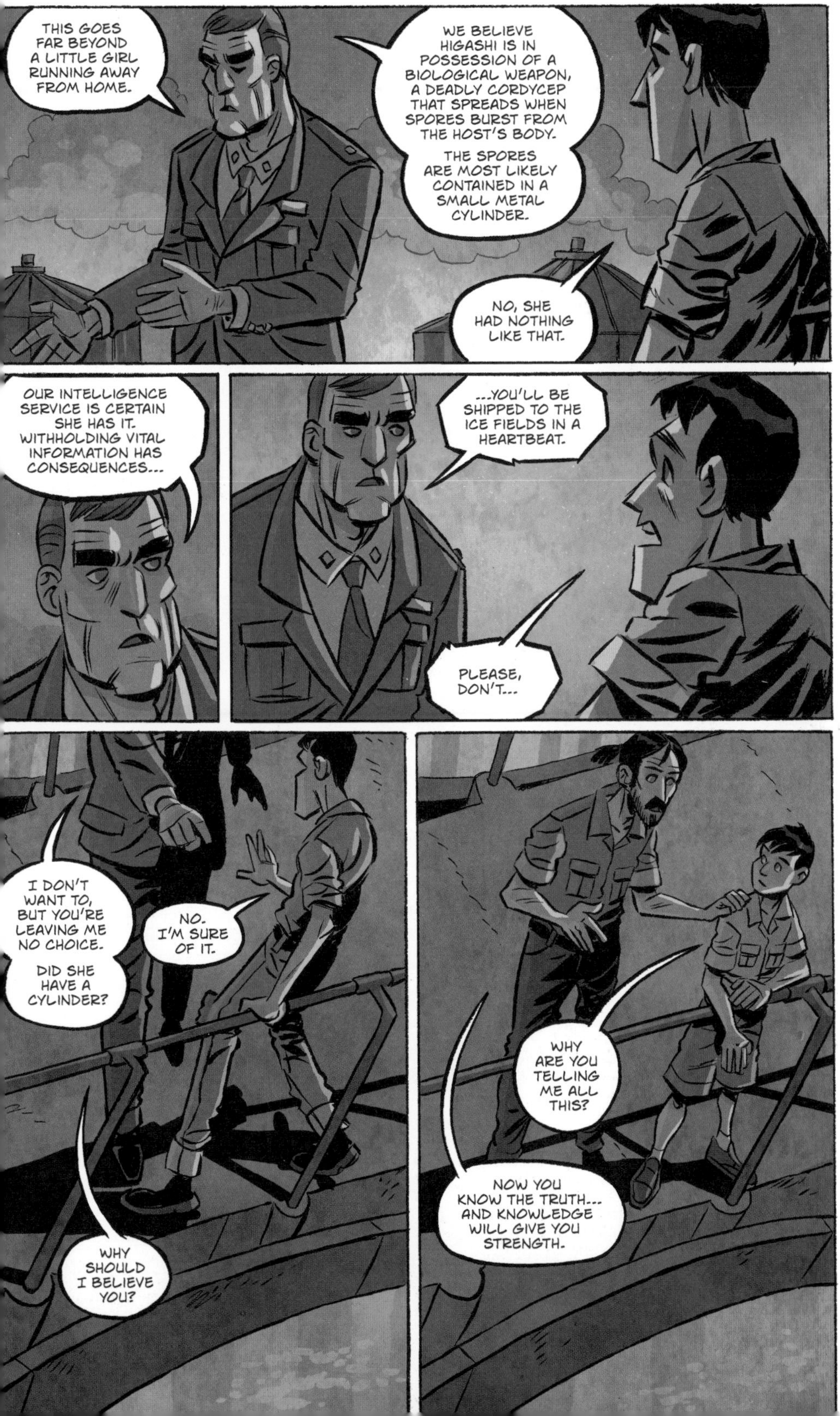
THIS GOES FAR BEYOND A LITTLE GIRL RUNNING AWAY FROM HOME.
WE BELIEVE HIGASHI IS IN POSSESSION OF A BIOLOGICAL WEAPON, A DEADLY CORDYCEP THAT SPREADS WHEN SPORES BURST FROM THE HOST'S BODY.
THE SPORES ARE MOST LIKELY CONTAINED IN A SMALL METAL CYLINDER.
NO, SHE HAD NOTHING LIKE THAT.
OUR INTELLIGENCE SERVICE IS CERTAIN SHE HAS IT. WITHHOLDING VITAL INFORMATION HAS CONSEQUENCES...
...YOU'LL BE SHIPPED TO THE ICE FIELDS IN A HEARTBEAT.
PLEASE, DON'T...
I DON'T WANT TO, BUT YOU'RE LEAVING ME NO CHOICE.
DID SHE HAVE A CYLINDER?
NO. I'M SURE OF IT.
WHY SHOULD I BELIEVE YOU?
WHY ARE YOU TELLING ME ALL THIS?
NOW YOU KNOW THE TRUTH... AND KNOWLEDGE WILL GIVE YOU STRENGTH.

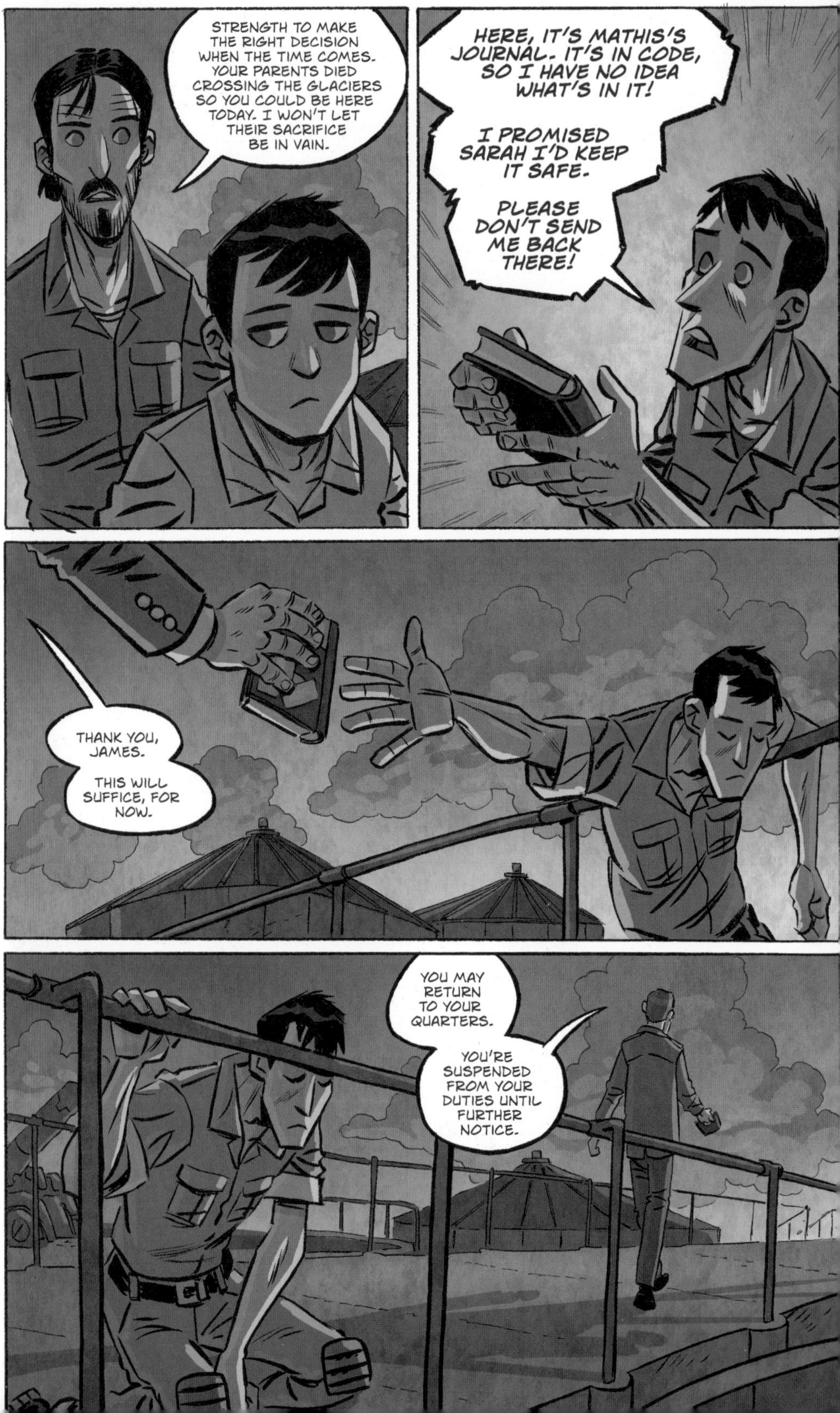
STRENGTH TO MAKE THE RIGHT DECISION WHEN THE TIME COMES. YOUR PARENTS DIED CROSSING THE GLACIERS SO YOU COULD BE HERE TODAY. I WON'T LET THEIR SACRIFICE BE IN VAIN.
HERE, IT'S MATHIS'S JOURNAL. IT'S IN CODE, SO I HAVE NO IDEA WHAT'S IN IT!
I PROMISED SARAH I'D KEEP IT SAFE.
PLEASE DON'T SEND ME BACK THERE!
THANK YOU, JAMES.
THIS WILL SUFFICE, FOR NOW.
YOU MAY RETURN TO YOUR QUARTERS.
YOU'RE SUSPENDED FROM YOUR DUTIES UNTIL FURTHER NOTICE.

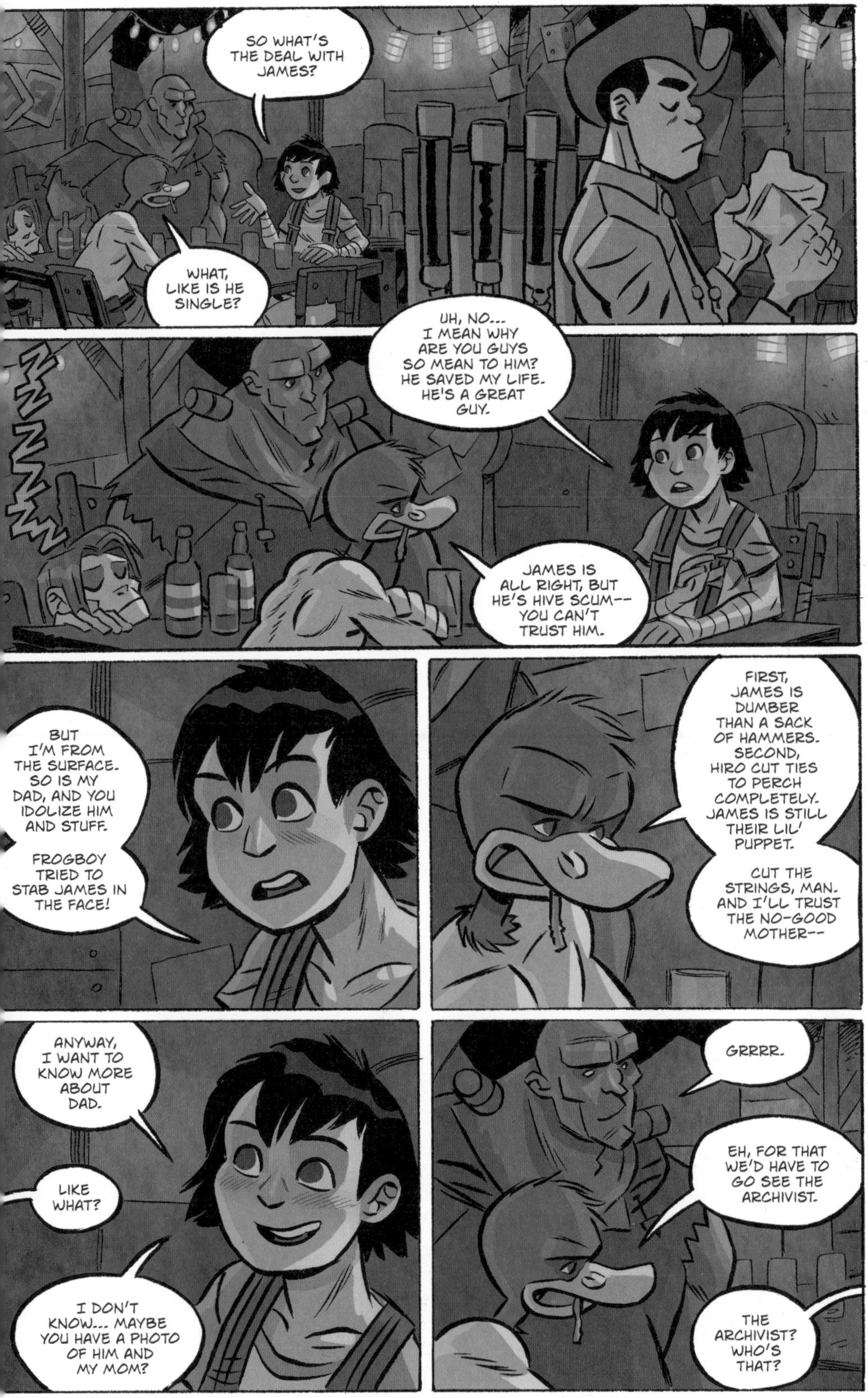
SO WHAT'S THE DEAL WITH JAMES?
WHAT, LIKE IS HE SINGLE?
UH, NO... I MEAN WHY ARE YOU GUYS SO MEAN TO HIM? HE SAVED MY LIFE. HE'S A GREAT GUY.
ZZZZZZ
JAMES IS ALL RIGHT, BUT HE'S HIVE SCUM-- YOU CAN'T TRUST HIM.
BUT I'M FROM THE SURFACE. SO IS MY DAD, AND YOU IDOLIZE HIM AND STUFF.
FROGBOY TRIED TO STAB JAMES IN THE FACE!
FIRST, JAMES IS DUMBER THAN A SACK OF HAMMERS. SECOND, HIRO CUT TIES TO PERCH COMPLETELY. JAMES IS STILL THEIR LIL' PUPPET.
CUT THE STRINGS, MAN. AND I'LL TRUST THE NO-GOOD MOTHER--
ANYWAY, I WANT TO KNOW MORE ABOUT DAD.
LIKE WHAT?
I DON'T KNOW... MAYBE YOU HAVE A PHOTO OF HIM AND MY MOM?
GRRRR.
EH, FOR THAT WE'D HAVE TO GO SEE THE ARCHIVIST.
THE ARCHIVIST? WHO'S THAT?

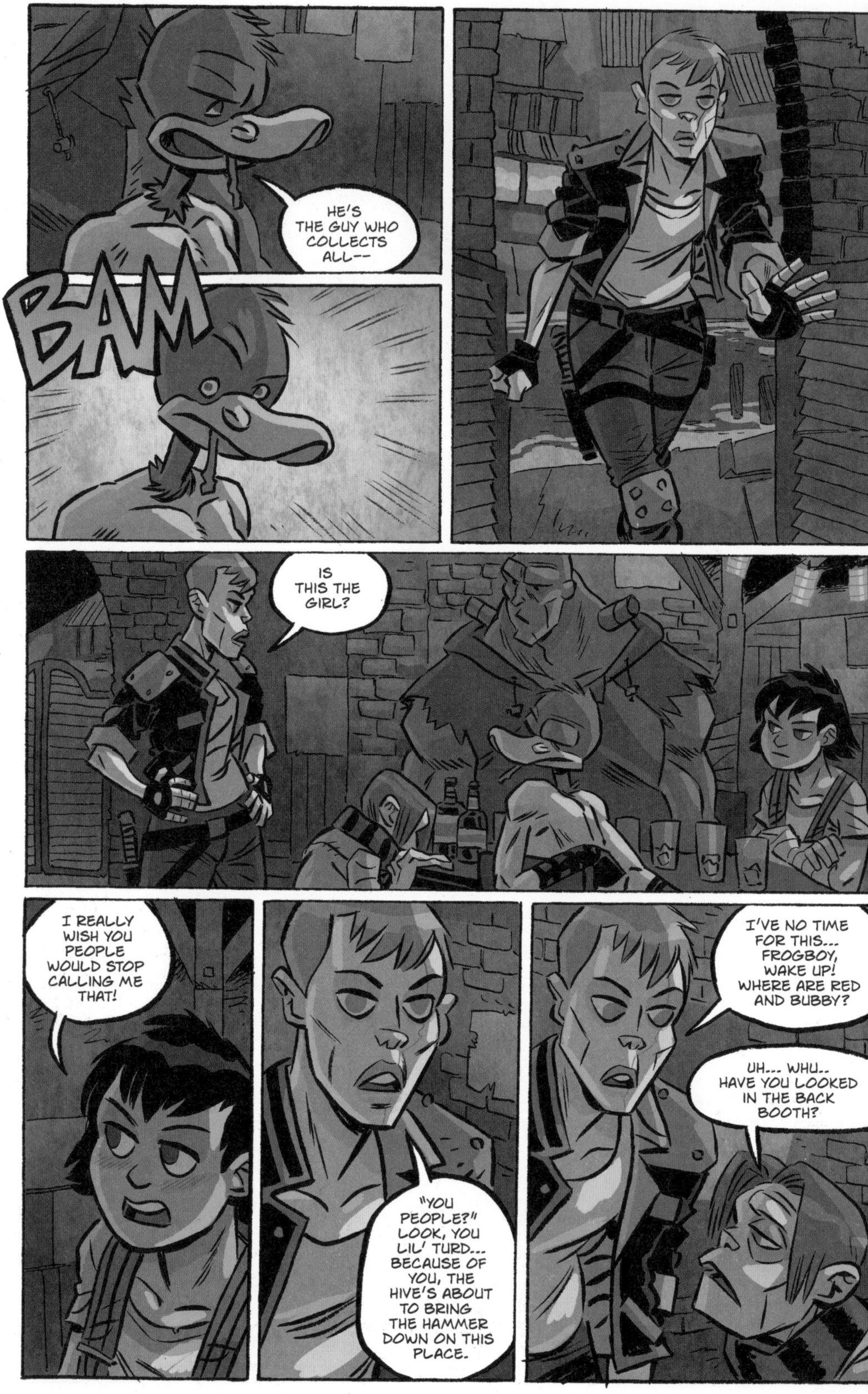
HE'S THE GUY WHO COLLECTS ALL--
BAM
IS THIS THE GIRL?
I REALLY WISH YOU PEOPLE WOULD STOP CALLING ME THAT!
"YOU PEOPLE?" LOOK, YOU LIL' TURD... BECAUSE OF YOU, THE HIVE'S ABOUT TO BRING THE HAMMER DOWN ON THIS PLACE.
I'VE NO TIME FOR THIS... FROGBOY, WAKE UP! WHERE ARE RED AND BUBBY?
UH... WHU.. HAVE YOU LOOKED IN THE BACK BOOTH?

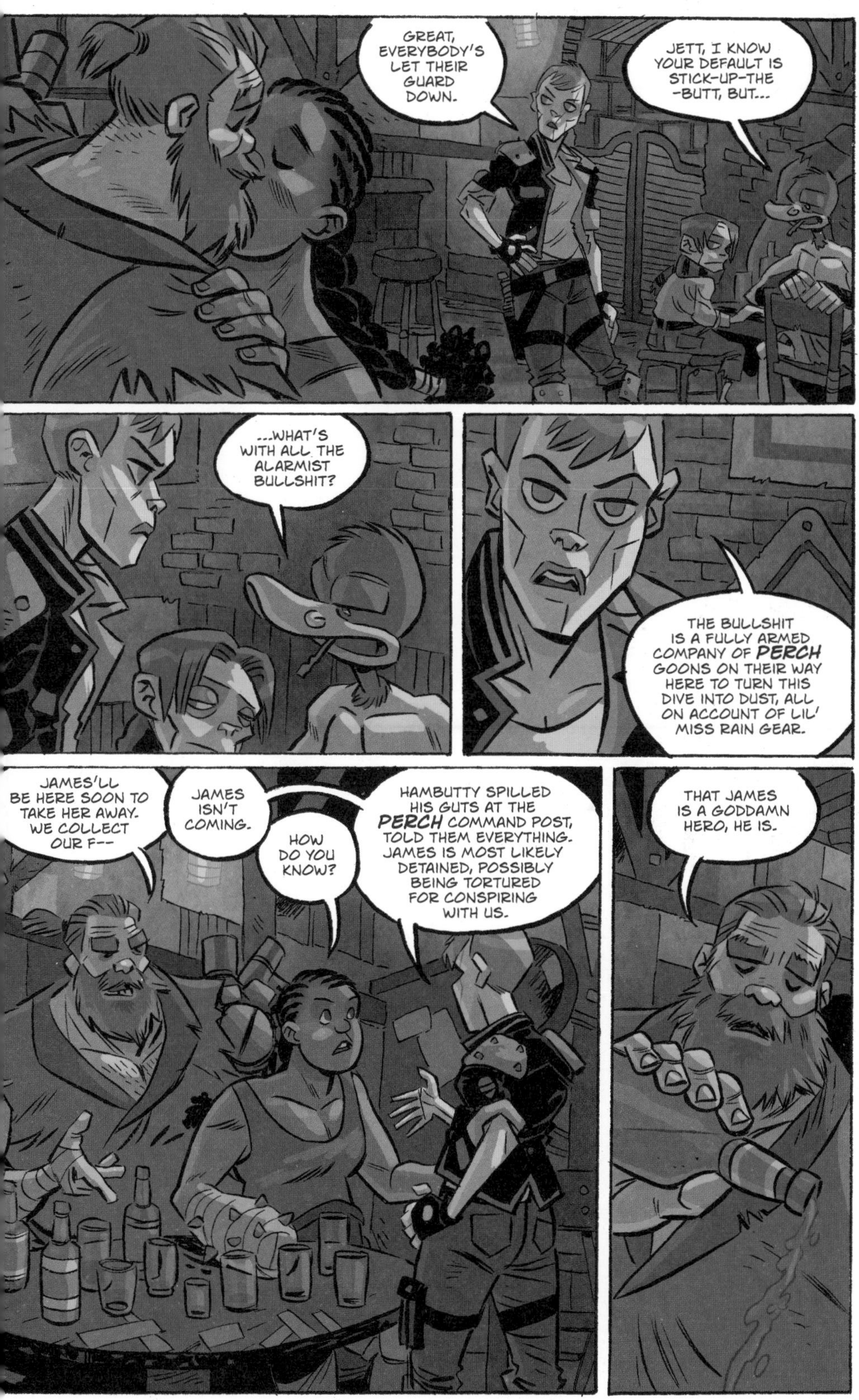
GREAT, EVERYBODY'S LET THEIR GUARD DOWN.
JETT, I KNOW YOUR DEFAULT IS STICK-UP-THE-BUTT, BUT...
...WHAT'S WITH ALL THE ALARMIST BULLSHIT?
THE BULLSHIT IS A FULLY ARMED COMPANY OF PERCH GOONS ON THEIR WAY HERE TO TURN THIS DIVE INTO DUST, ALL ON ACCOUNT OF LIL' MISS RAIN GEAR.
JAMES'LL BE HERE SOON TO TAKE HER AWAY. WE COLLECT OUR F--
JAMES ISN'T COMING.
HOW DO YOU KNOW?
HAMBUTTY SPILLED HIS GUTS AT THE PERCH COMMAND POST, TOLD THEM EVERYTHING. JAMES IS MOST LIKELY DETAINED, POSSIBLY BEING TORTURED FOR CONSPIRING WITH US.
THAT JAMES IS A GODDAMN HERO, HE IS.

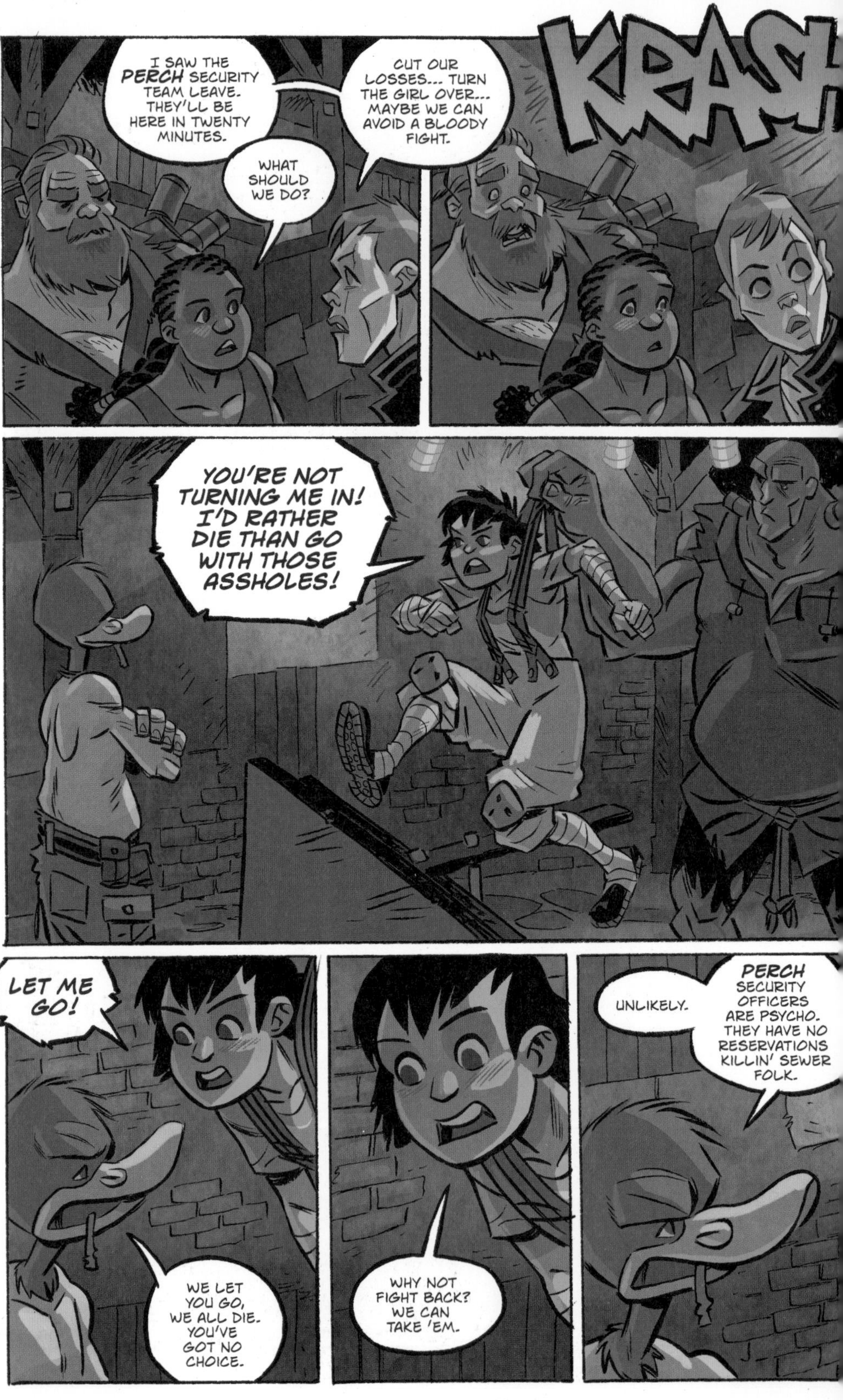
I SAW THE PERCH SECURITY TEAM LEAVE. THEY'LL BE HERE IN TWENTY MINUTES.
WHAT SHOULD WE DO?
CUT OUR LOSSES... TURN THE GIRL OVER... MAYBE WE CAN AVOID A BLOODY FIGHT.
KRASH
YOU'RE NOT TURNING ME IN! I'D RATHER DIE THAN GO WITH THOSE ASSHOLES!
LET ME GO!
WE LET YOU GO, WE ALL DIE. YOU'VE GOT NO CHOICE.
WHY NOT FIGHT BACK? WE CAN TAKE 'EM.
UNLIKELY.
PERCH SECURITY OFFICERS ARE PSYCHO. THEY HAVE NO RESERVATIONS KILLIN' SEWER FOLK.

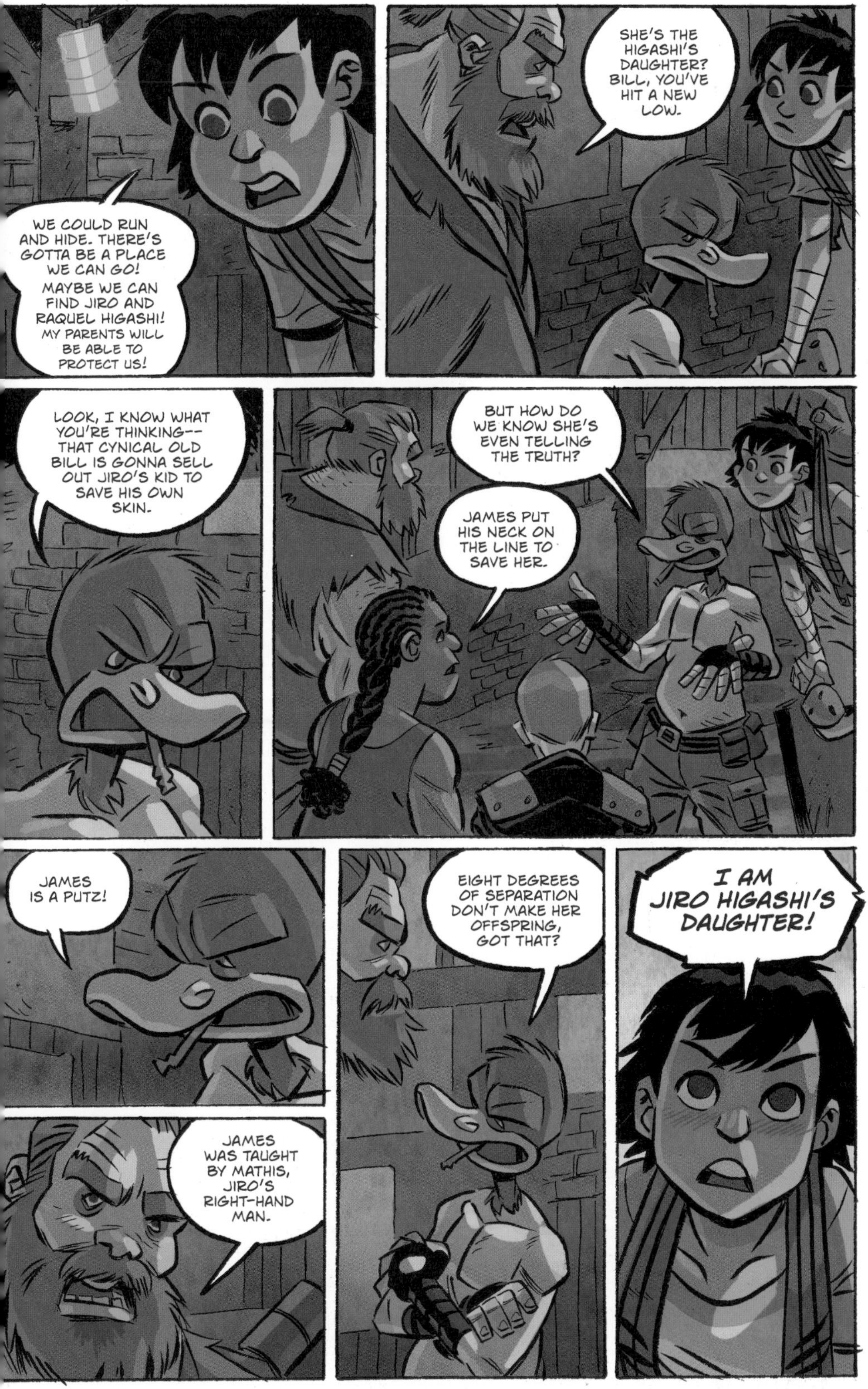

WE COULD RUN AND HIDE. THERE'S GOTTA BE A PLACE WE CAN GO!
MAYBE WE CAN FIND JIRO AND RAQUEL HIGASHI! MY PARENTS WILL BE ABLE TO PROTECT US!
SHE'S THE HIGASHI'S DAUGHTER? BILL, YOU'VE HIT A NEW LOW.
LOOK, I KNOW WHAT YOU'RE THINKING-- THAT CYNICAL OLD BILL IS GONNA SELL OUT JIRO'S KID TO SAVE HIS OWN SKIN.
BUT HOW DO WE KNOW SHE'S EVEN TELLING THE TRUTH?
JAMES PUT HIS NECK ON THE LINE TO SAVE HER.
JAMES IS A PUTZ!
JAMES WAS TAUGHT BY MATHIS, JIRO'S RIGHT-HAND MAN.
EIGHT DEGREES OF SEPARATION DON'T MAKE HER OFFSPRING, GOT THAT?
I AM JIRO HIGASHI'S DAUGHTER!

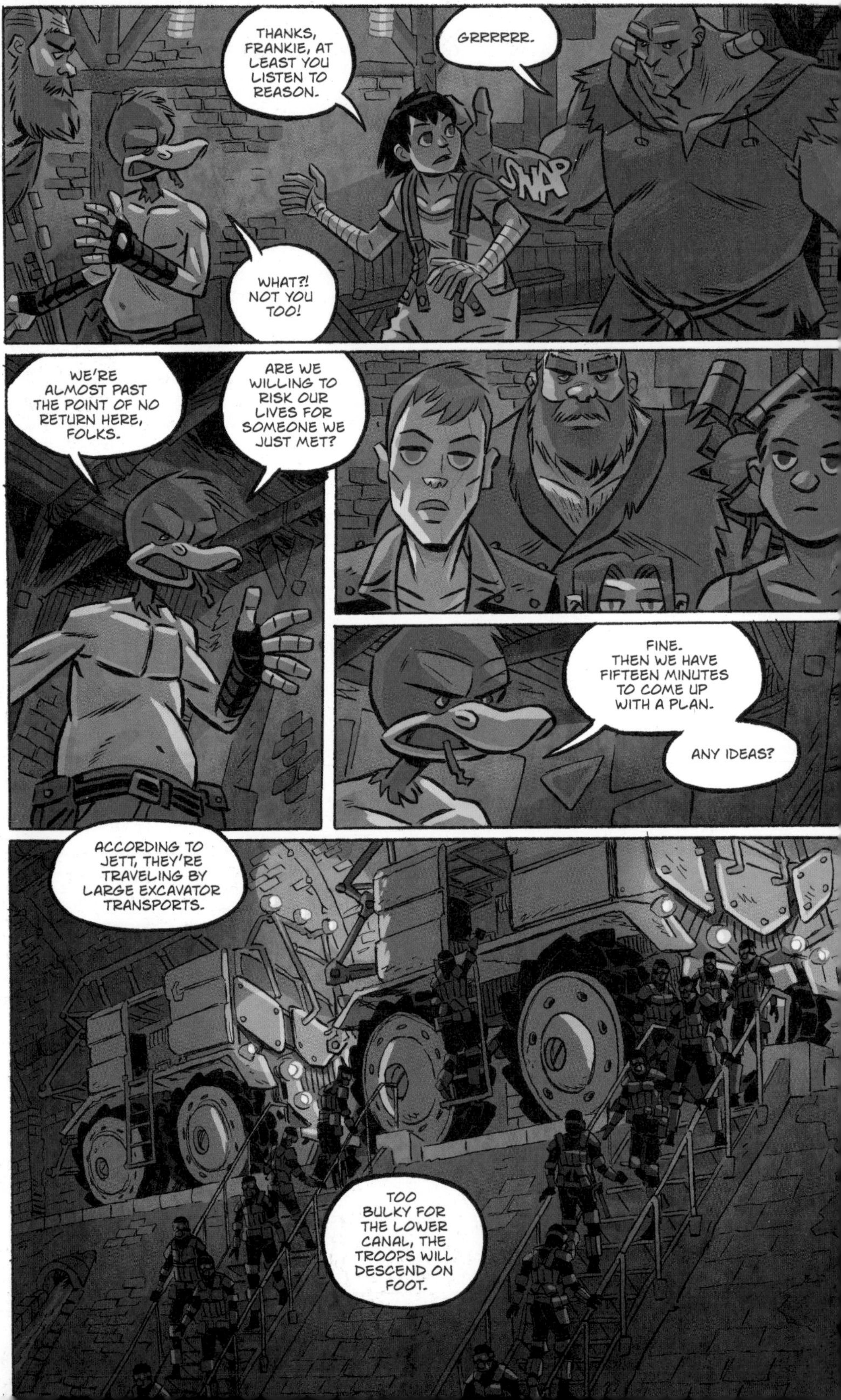
THANKS, FRANKIE, AT LEAST YOU LISTEN TO REASON.
GRRRRRR.
SNAP
WHAT?! NOT YOU TOO!
WE'RE ALMOST PAST THE POINT OF NO RETURN HERE, FOLKS.
ARE WE WILLING TO RISK OUR LIVES FOR SOMEONE WE JUST MET?
FINE. THEN WE HAVE FIFTEEN MINUTES TO COME UP WITH A PLAN.
ANY IDEAS?
ACCORDING TO JETT, THEY'RE TRAVELING BY LARGE EXCAVATOR TRANSPORTS.
TOO BULKY FOR THE LOWER CANAL, THE TROOPS WILL DESCEND ON FOOT.

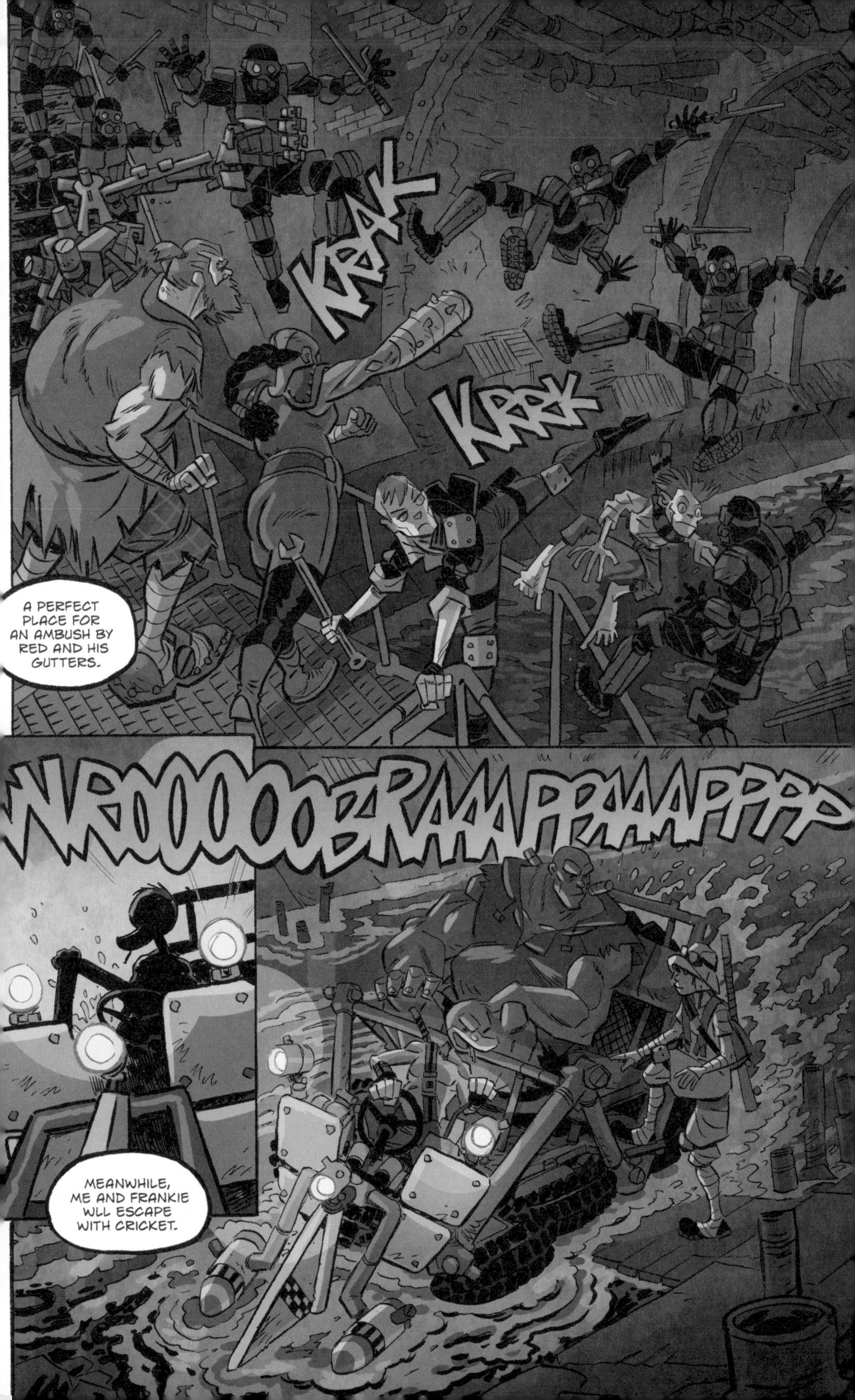
KRAK
KRRK
A PERFECT PLACE FOR AN AMBUSH BY RED AND HIS GUTTERS.
WROOOOOBRAAAPPRAAAPPPP
MEANWHILE, ME AND FRANKIE WLL ESCAPE WITH CRICKET.

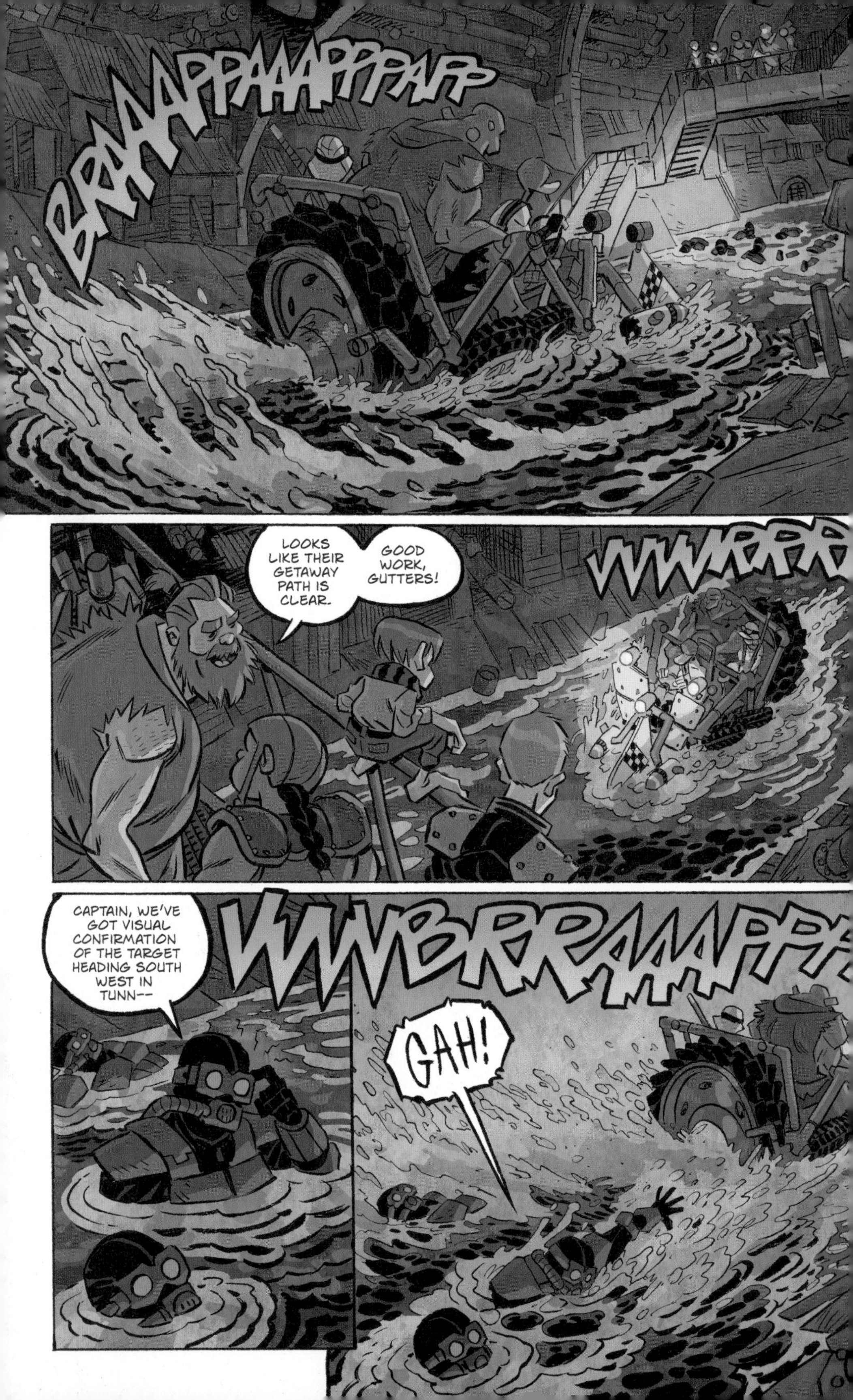
BRAAAPPAAAAPPPAPP
LOOKS LIKE THEIR GETAWAY PATH IS CLEAR.
GOOD WORK, GUTTERS!
WWAPPP
CAPTAIN, WE'VE GOT VISUAL CONFIRMATION OF THE TARGET HEADING SOUTH WEST IN TUNN--
WWBRRAAAPPP
GAH!

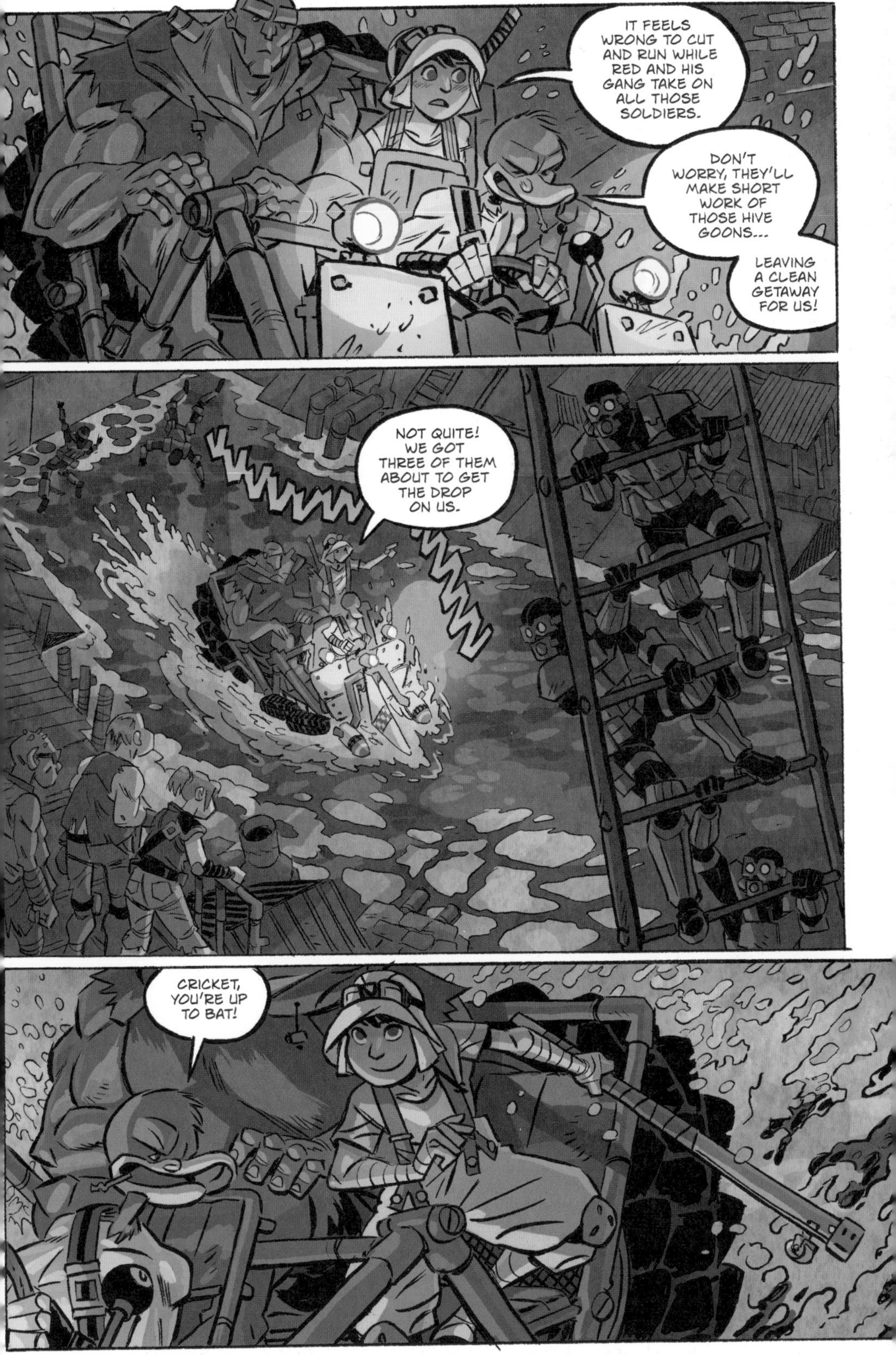
IT FEELS WRONG TO CUT AND RUN WHILE RED AND HIS GANG TAKE ON ALL THOSE SOLDIERS.
DON'T WORRY, THEY'LL MAKE SHORT WORK OF THOSE HIVE GOONS...
LEAVING A CLEAN GETAWAY FOR US!
NOT QUITE! WE GOT THREE OF THEM ABOUT TO GET THE DROP ON US.
CRICKET, YOU'RE UP TO BAT!

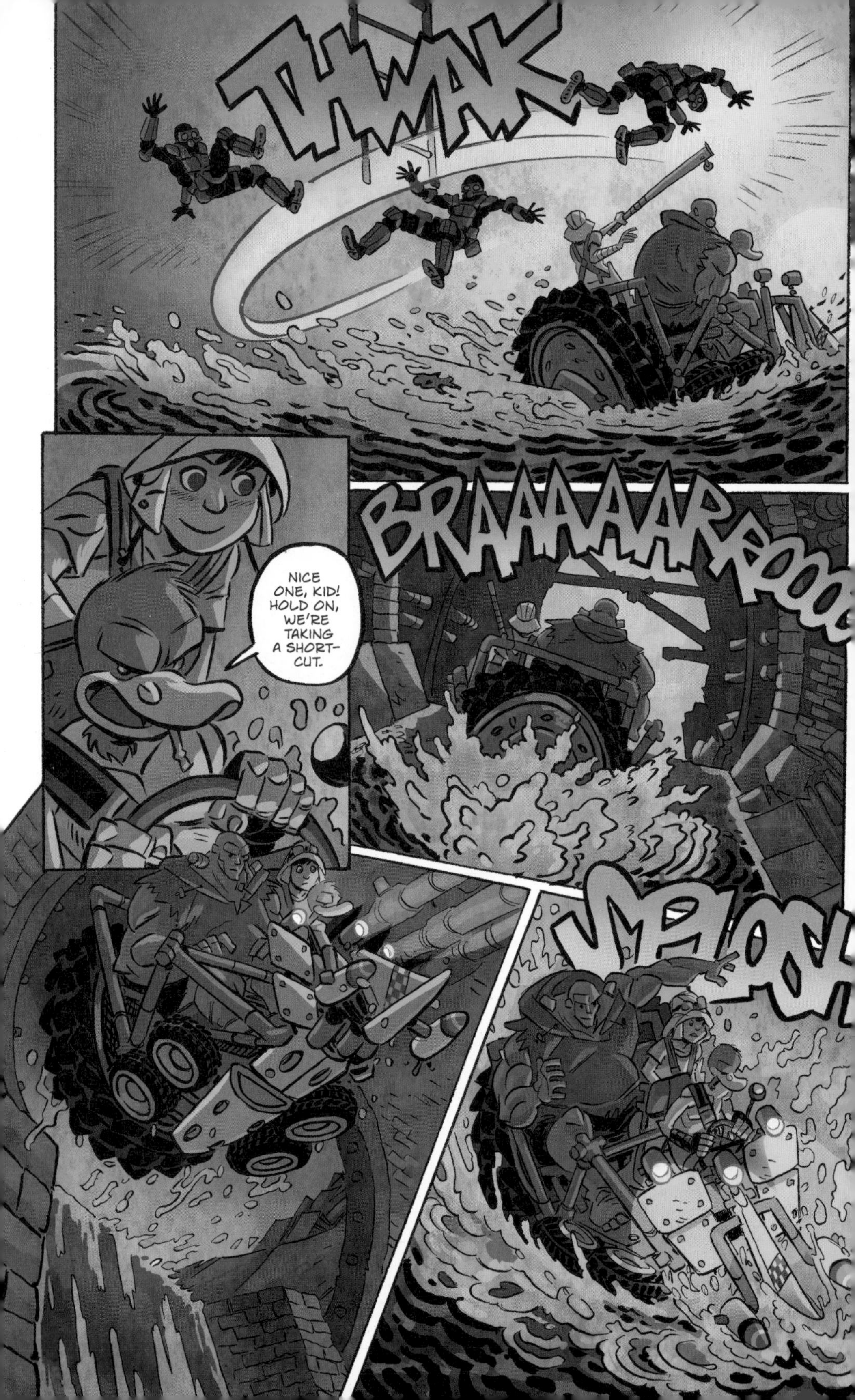
THWAK
NICE ONE, KID! HOLD ON, WE'RE TAKING A SHORT-CUT.
BRAAAAAR

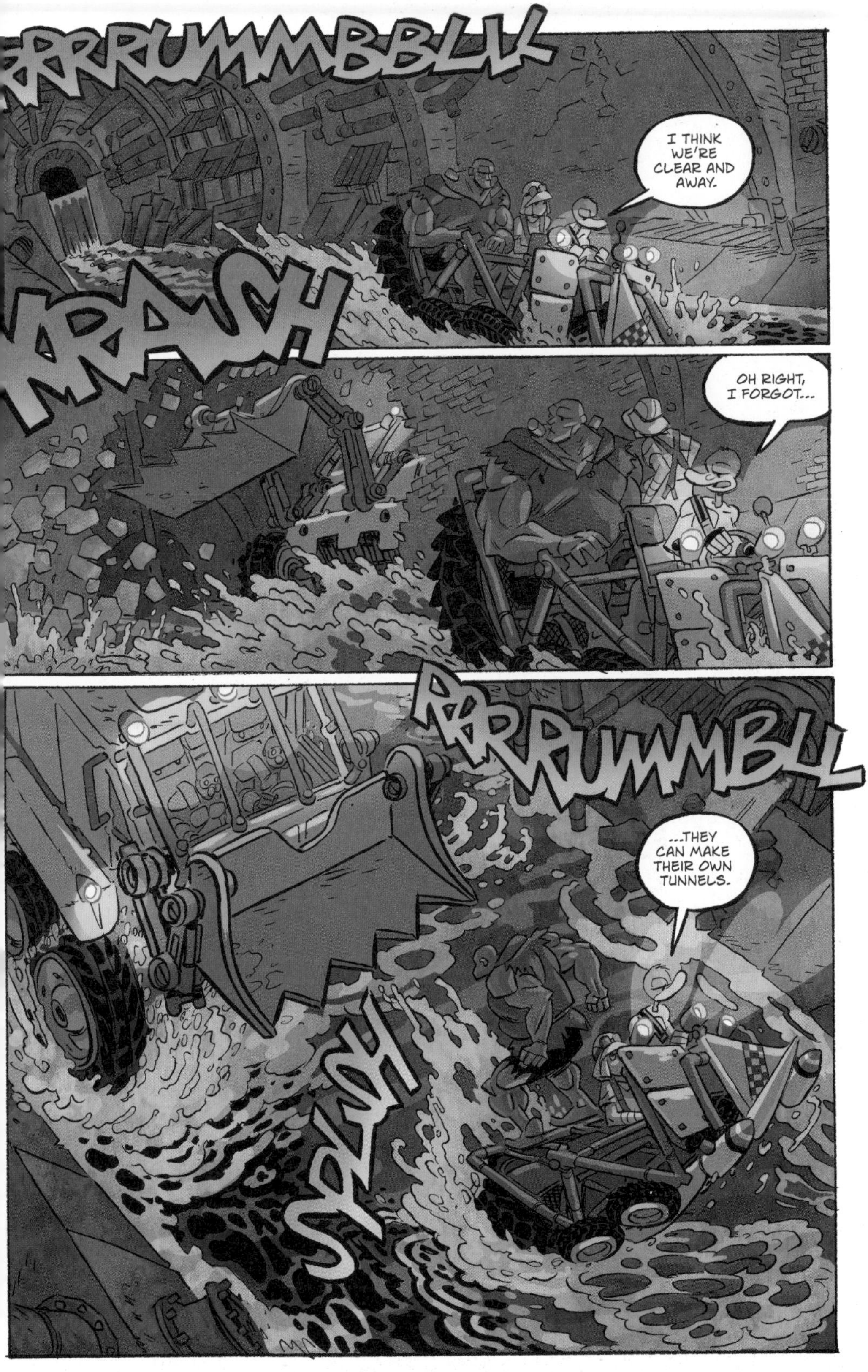
RRRUMMBBLLL
I THINK WE'RE CLEAR AND AWAY.
KRASH
OH RIGHT, I FORGOT...
RRRUMMBLL
...THEY CAN MAKE THEIR OWN TUNNELS.
SPLASH

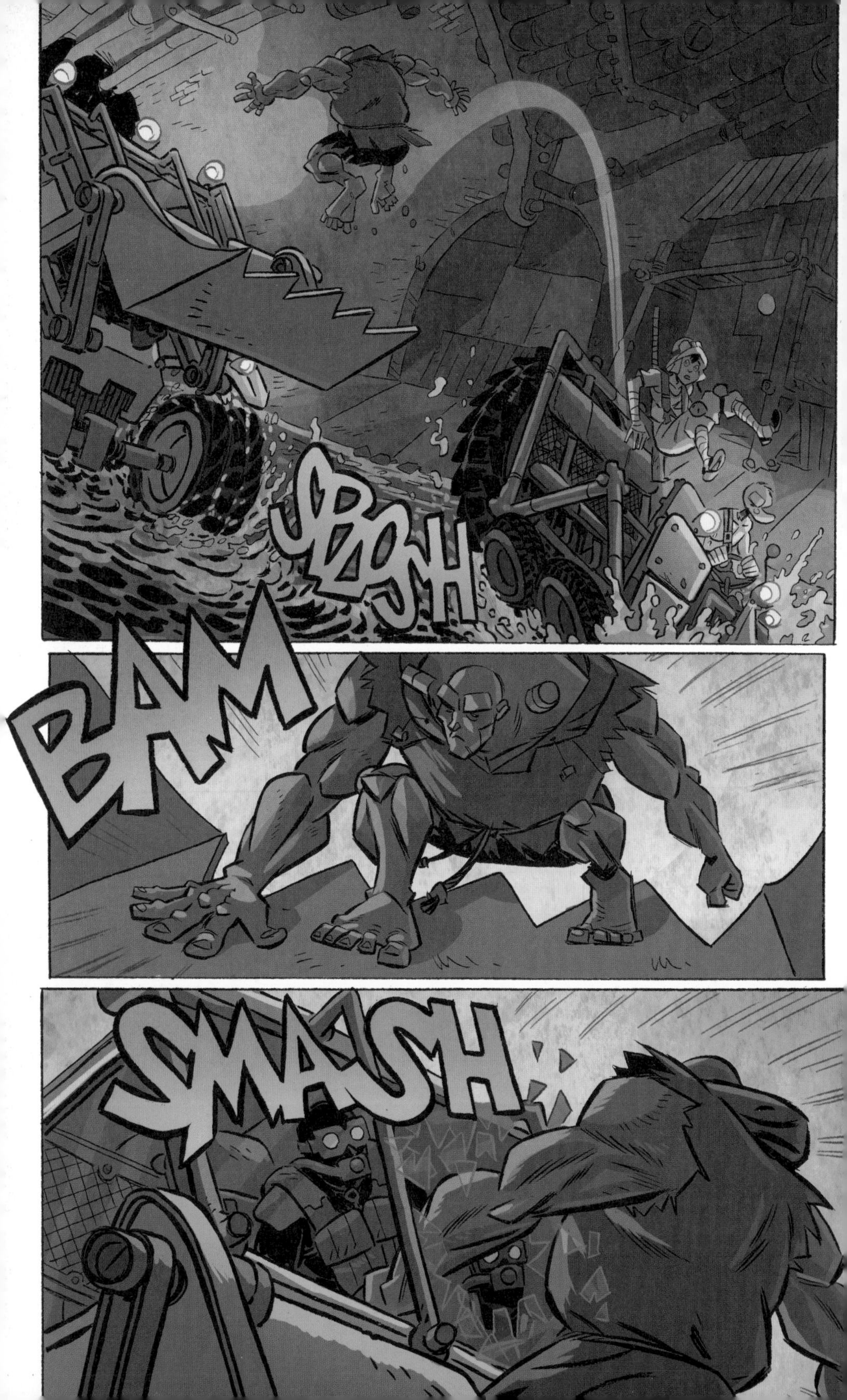
SPLOOSH
BAM
SMASH

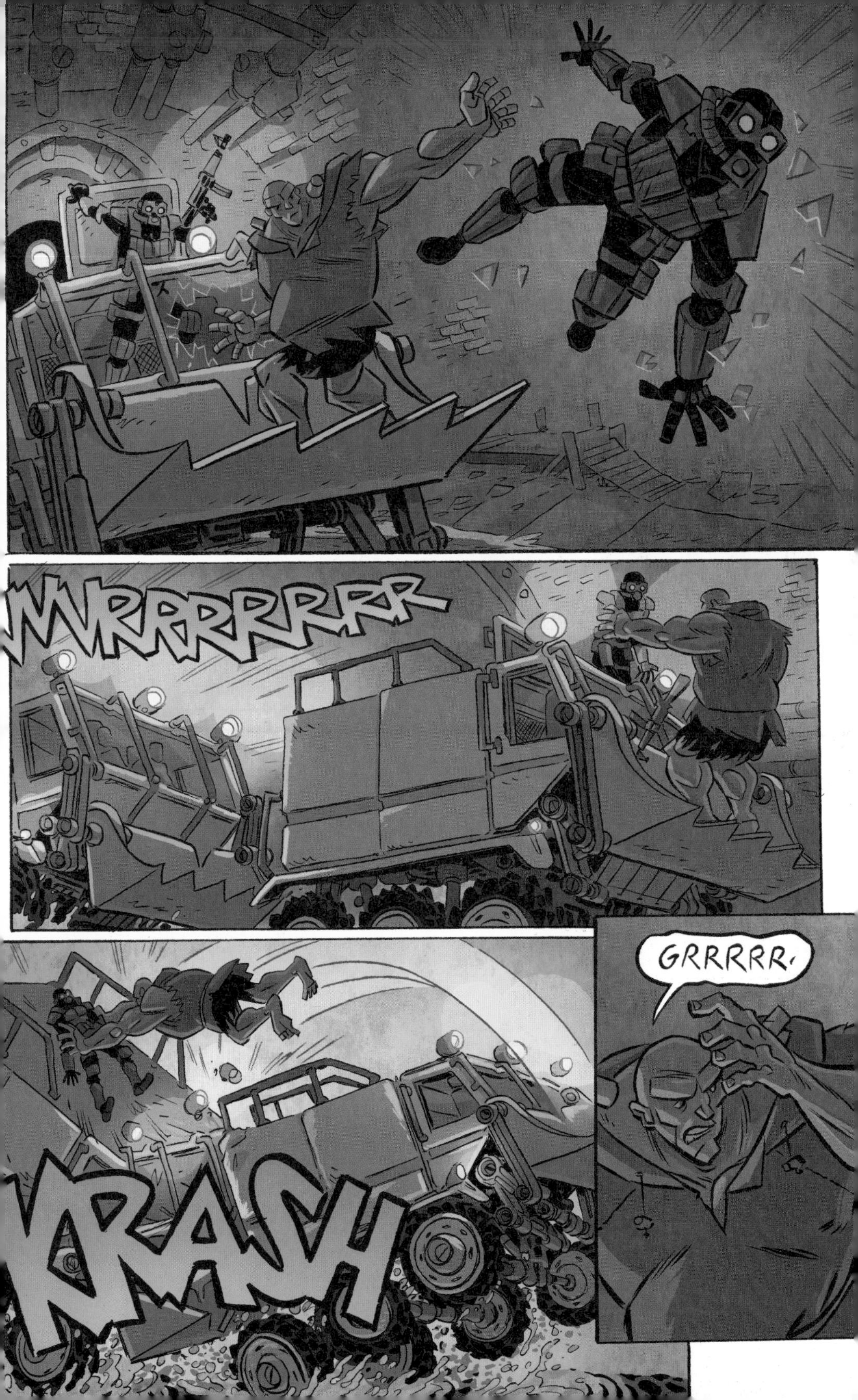
WRRRRRRR
KRASH
GRRRRR.

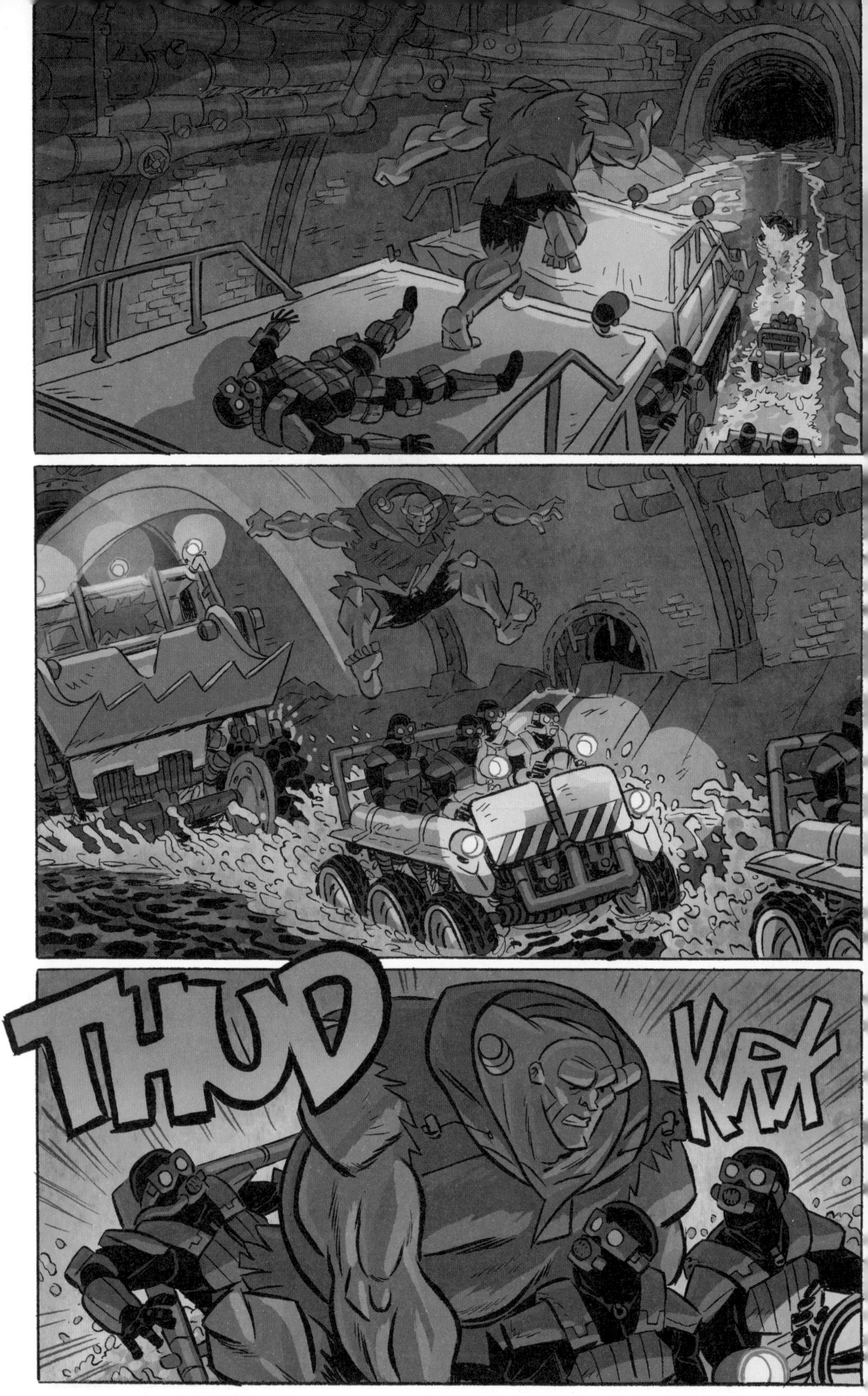
THUD
KRAK

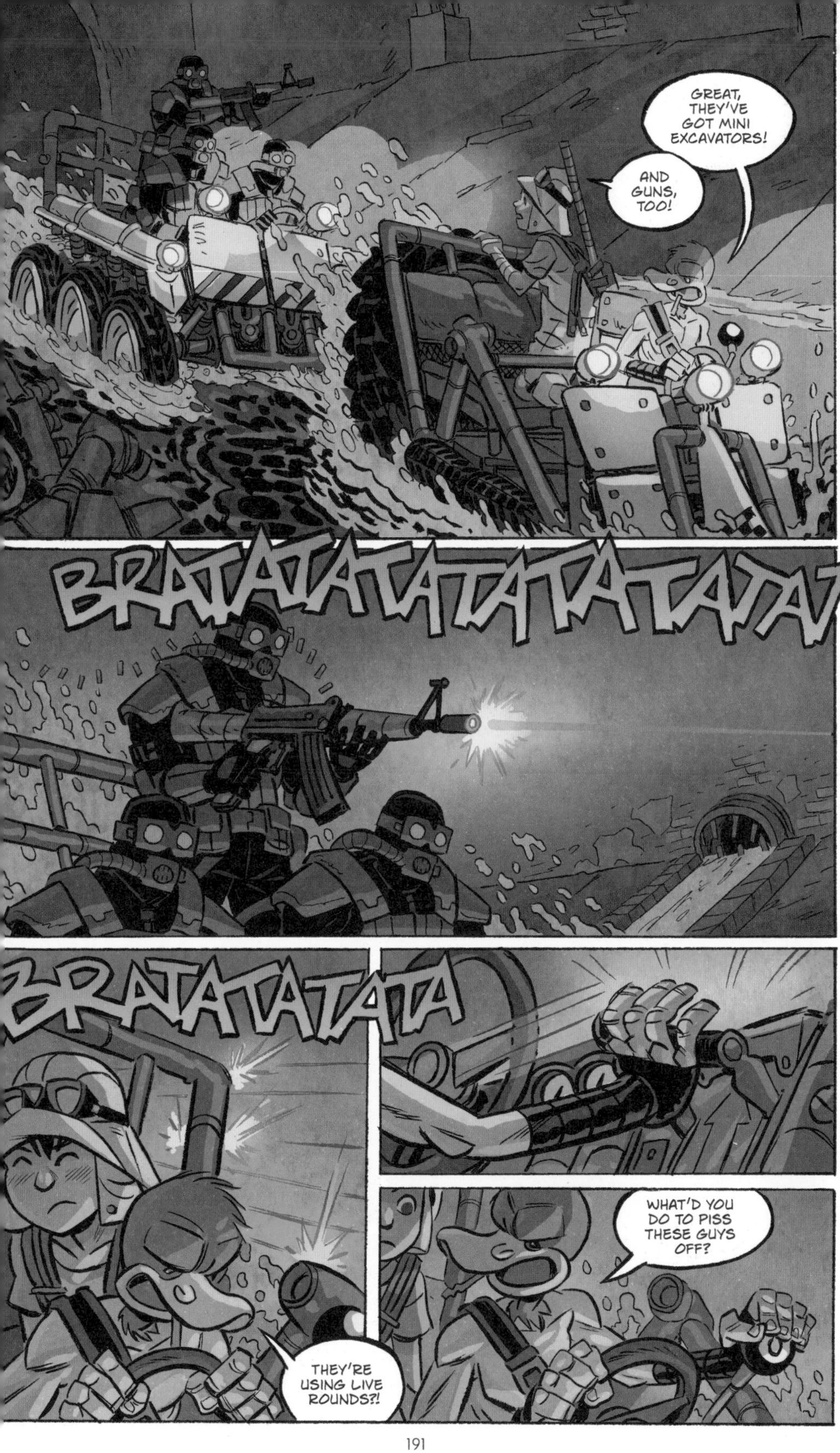
GREAT, THEY'VE GOT MINI EXCAVATORS!
AND GUNS, TOO!
BRATATATATATATATAT-
BRATATATATA
THEY'RE USING LIVE ROUNDS?!
WHAT'D YOU DO TO PISS THESE GUYS OFF?

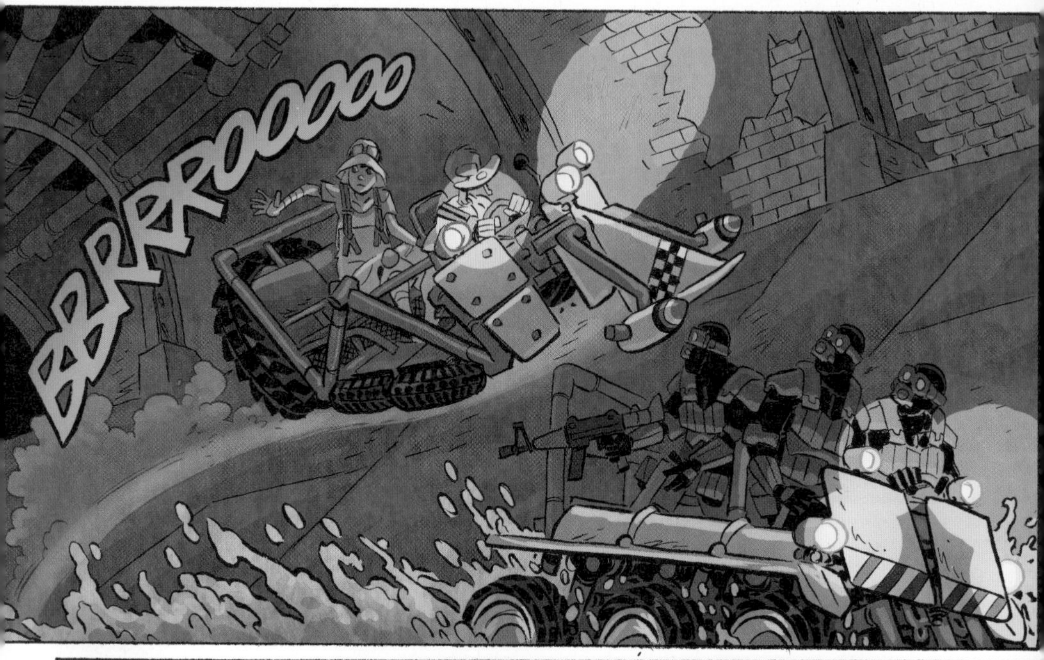
BRRRROOOOOO

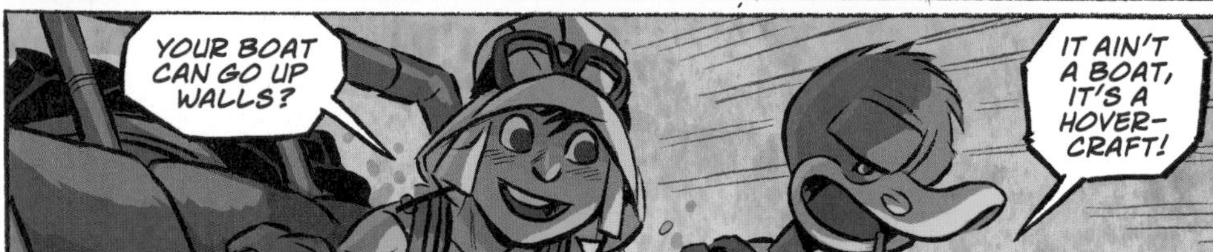
YOUR BOAT CAN GO UP WALLS?
IT AIN'T A BOAT, IT'S A HOVER-CRAFT!

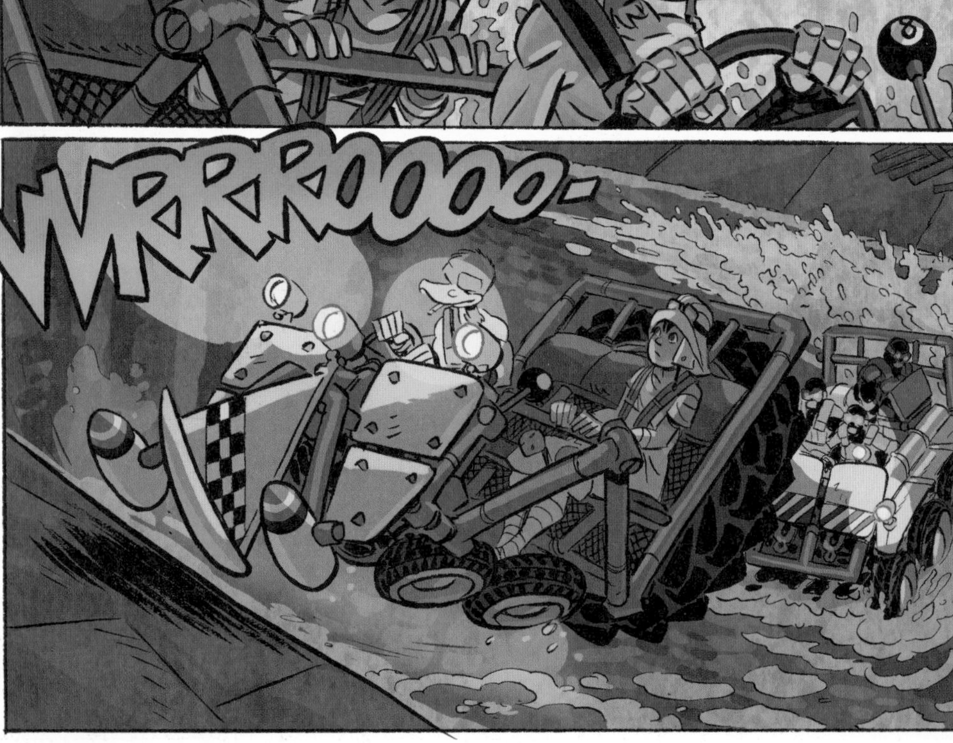
VVRRROOOO-

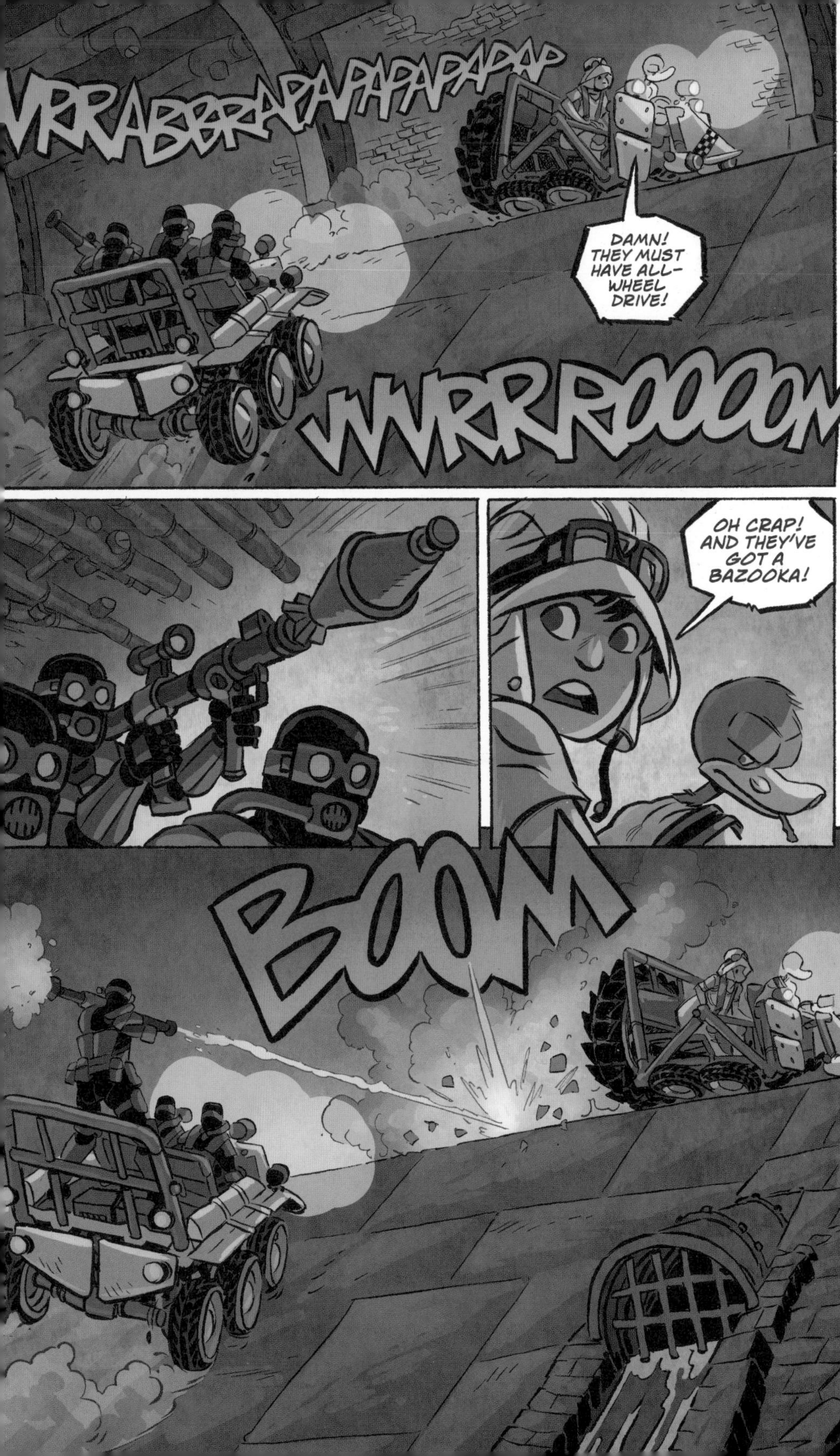
VRRABBRAPAPAPAPAPAP
DAMN! THEY MUST HAVE ALL-WHEEL DRIVE!
VVRRROOOOOM
OH CRAP! AND THEY'VE GOT A BAZOOKA!
BOOM

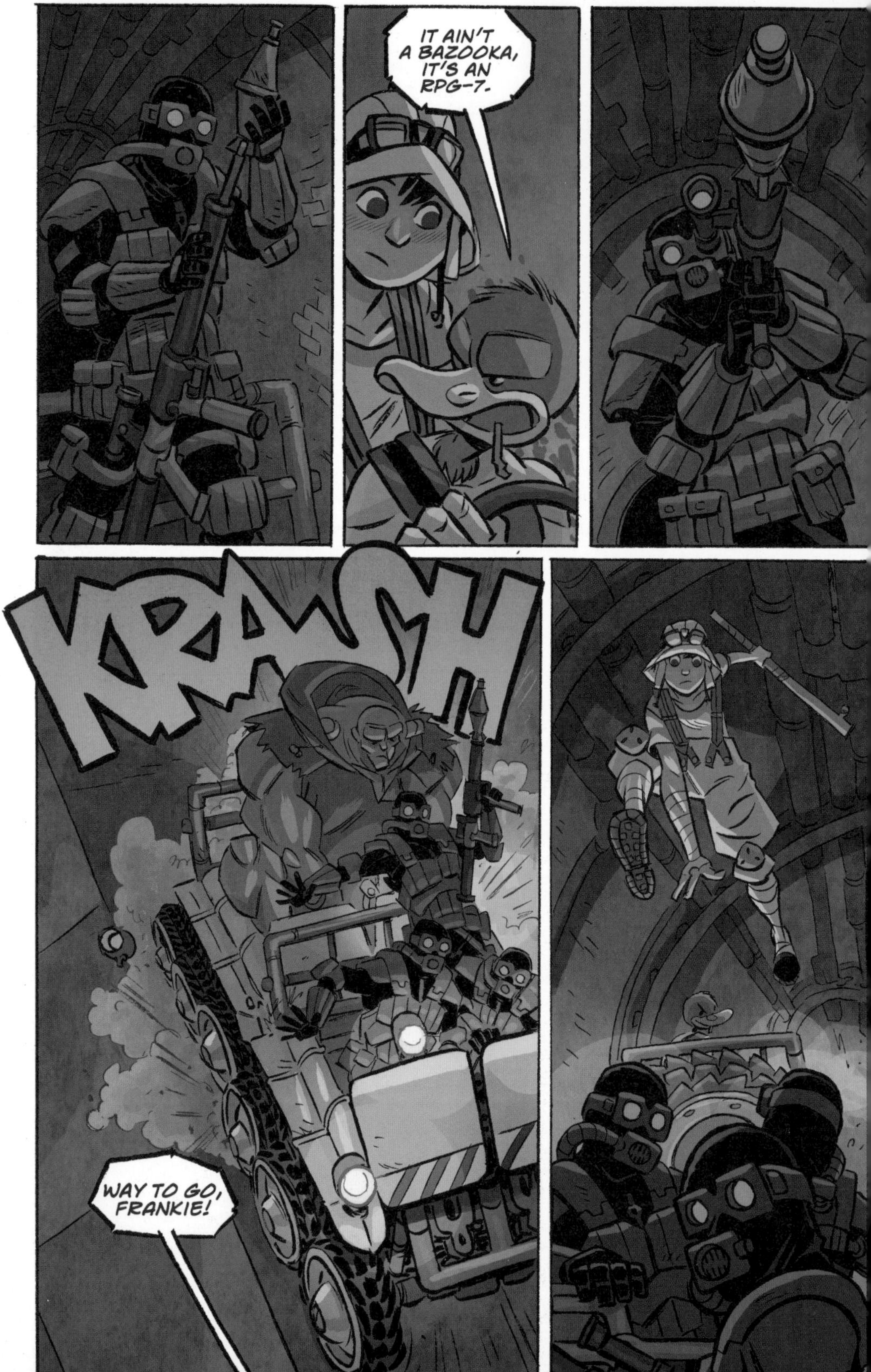
IT AIN'T A BAZOOKA, IT'S AN RPG-7.
KRASH
WAY TO GO, FRANKIE!

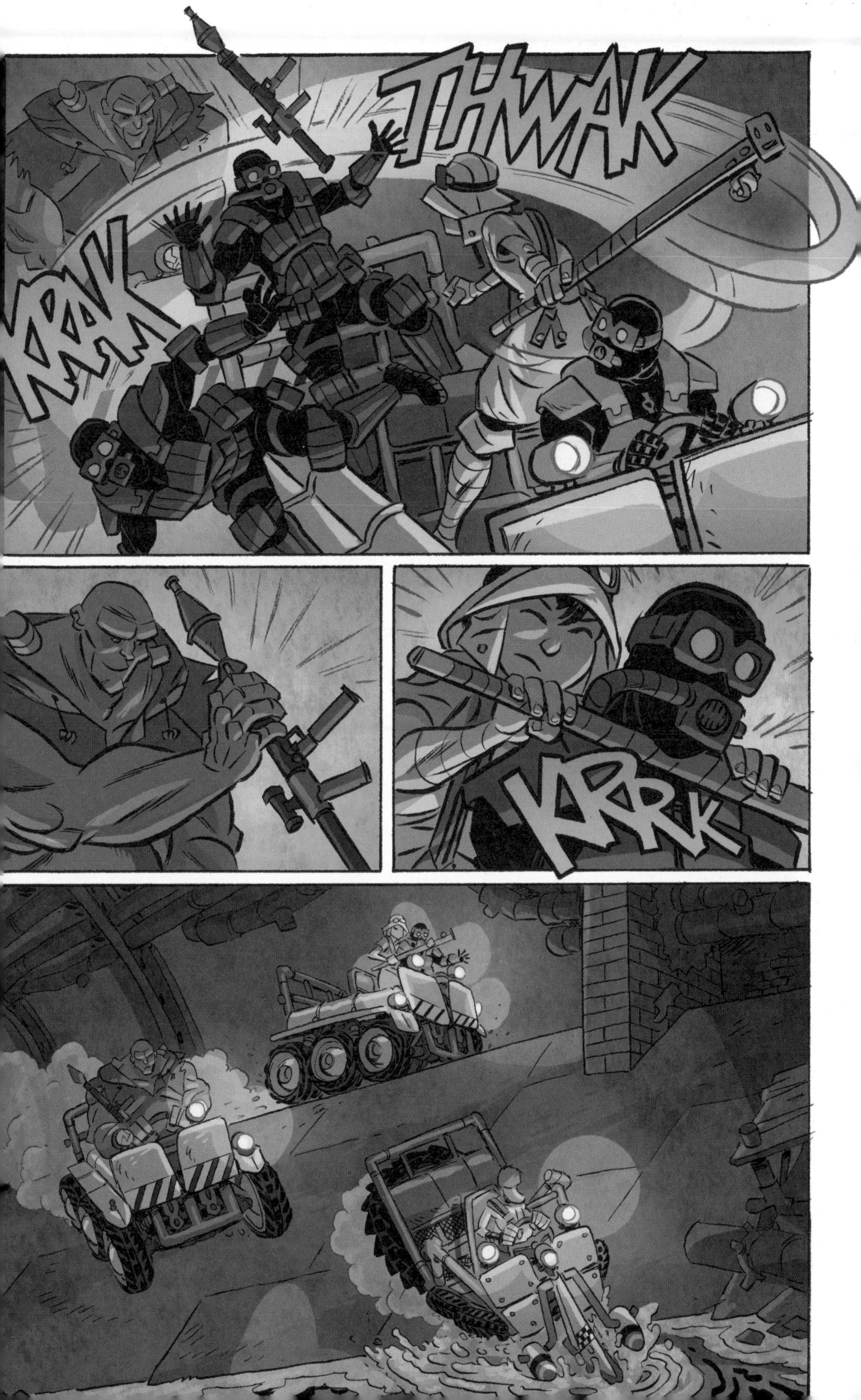
THWAK
KRAK
KRRK

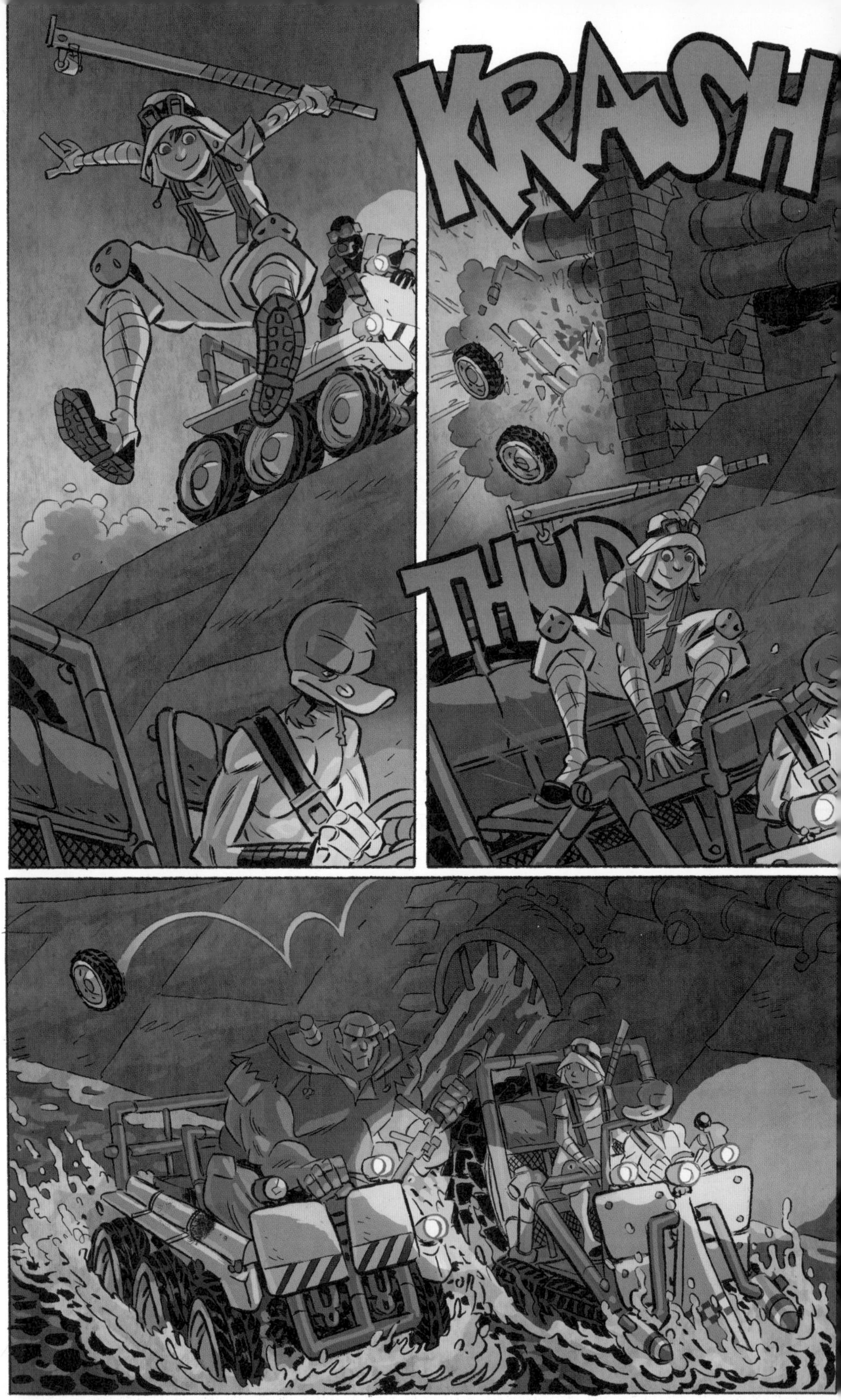
KRASH
THUD

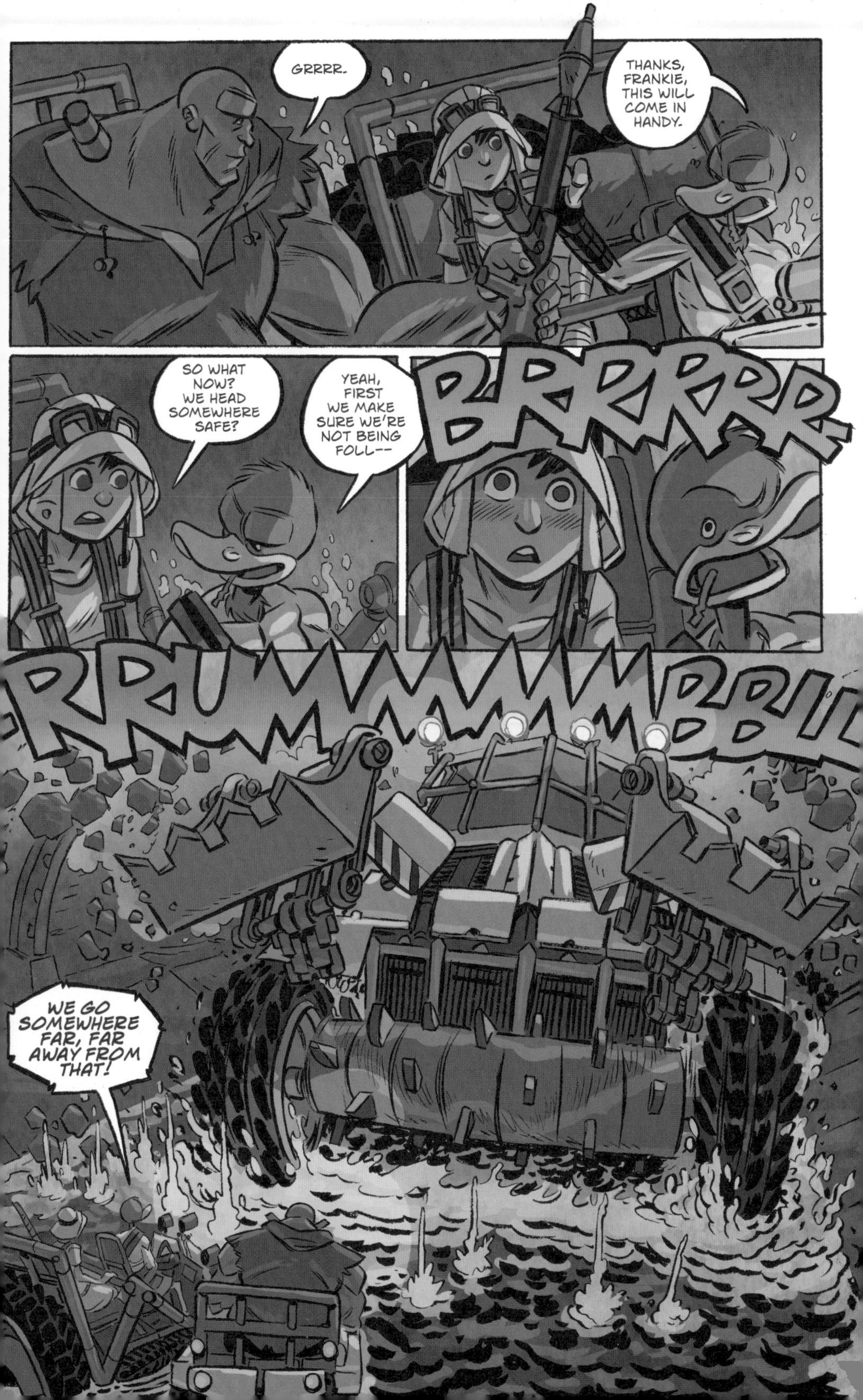
GRRRR.
THANKS, FRANKIE, THIS WILL COME IN HANDY.
SO WHAT NOW? WE HEAD SOMEWHERE SAFE?
YEAH, FIRST WE MAKE SURE WE'RE NOT BEING FOLL--
BRRRRR
RRUMMMMBBLL
WE GO SOMEWHERE FAR, FAR AWAY FROM THAT!

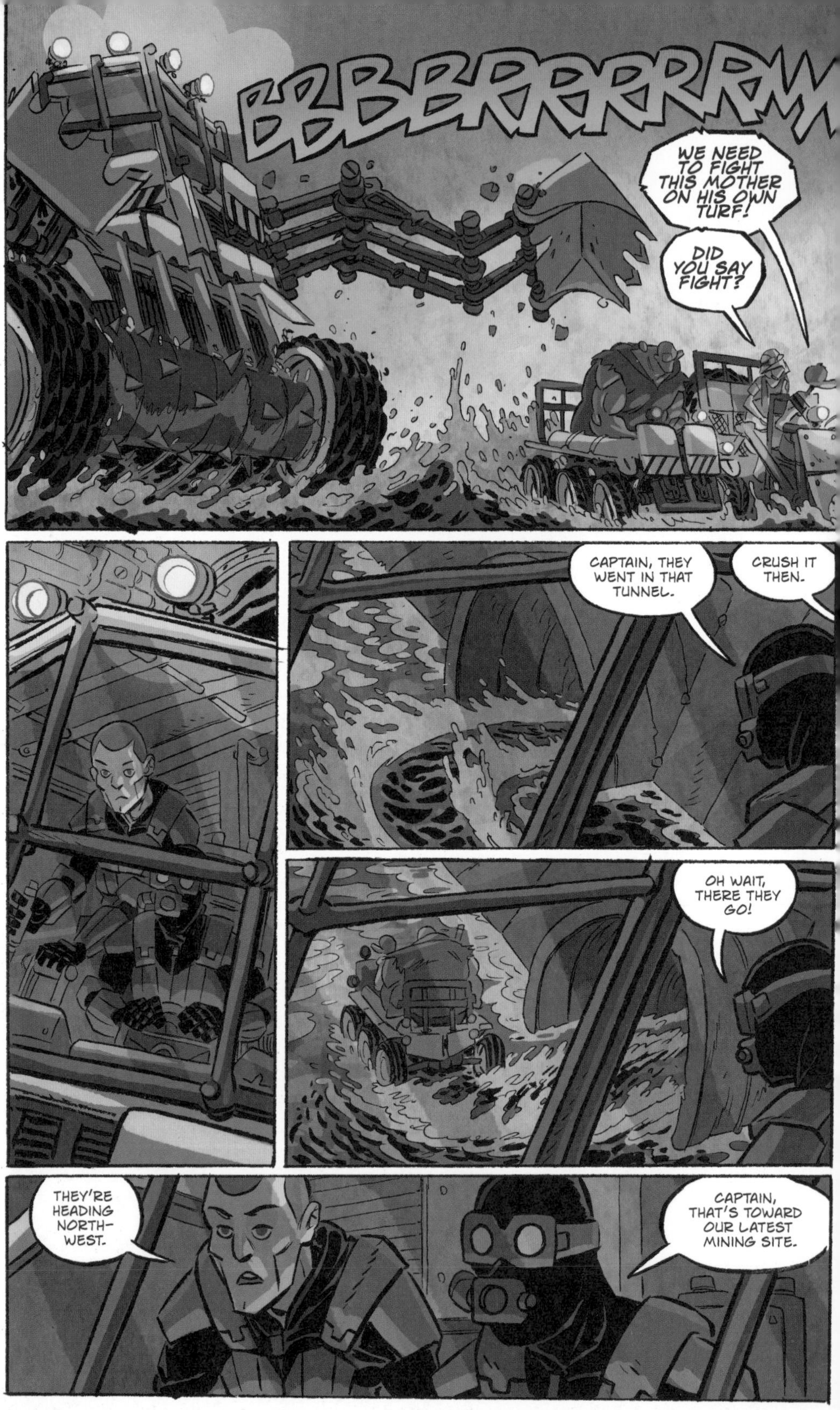
BBBBRRRRRRRW
WE NEED TO FIGHT THIS MOTHER ON HIS OWN TURF!
DID YOU SAY FIGHT?
CAPTAIN, THEY WENT IN THAT TUNNEL.
CRUSH IT THEN.
OH WAIT, THERE THEY GO!
THEY'RE HEADING NORTH-WEST.
CAPTAIN, THAT'S TOWARD OUR LATEST MINING SITE.

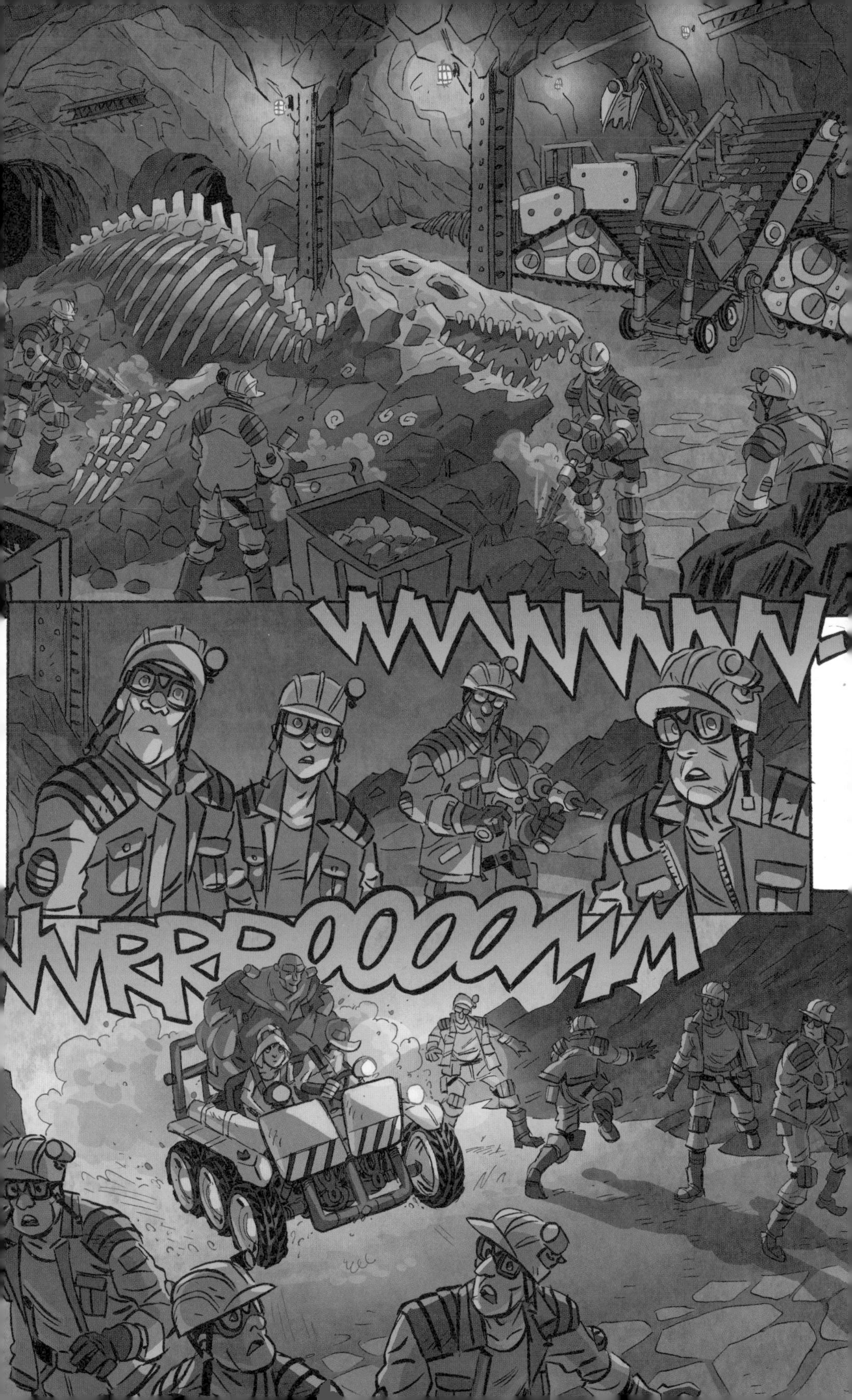
VVVAAVVVVAAAV-
WRRROOOOOMM

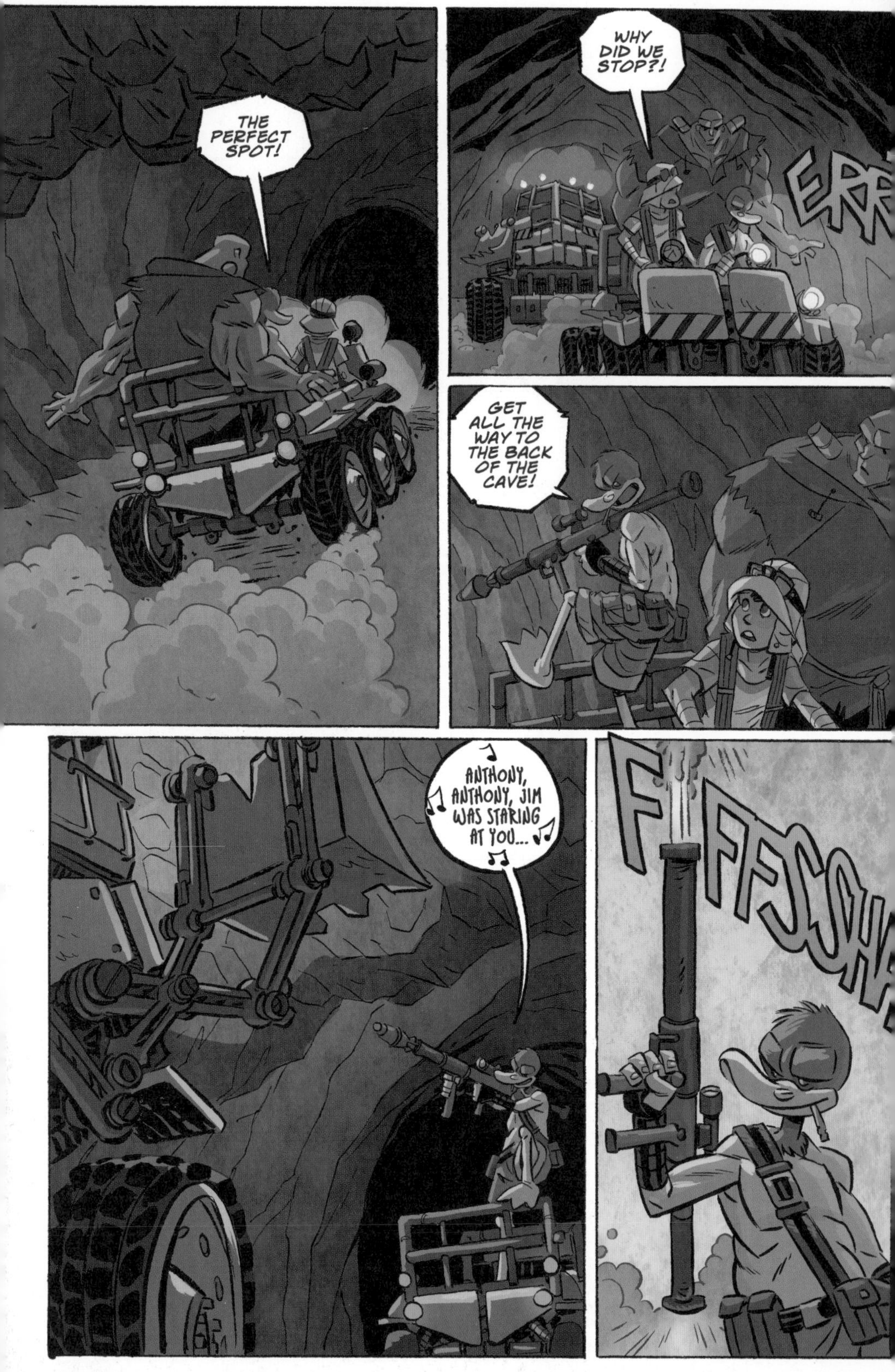
THE PERFECT SPOT!
WHY DID WE STOP?!
ERR
GET ALL THE WAY TO THE BACK OF THE CAVE!
ANTHONY, ANTHONY, JIM WAS STARING AT YOU...
FFFSCHH

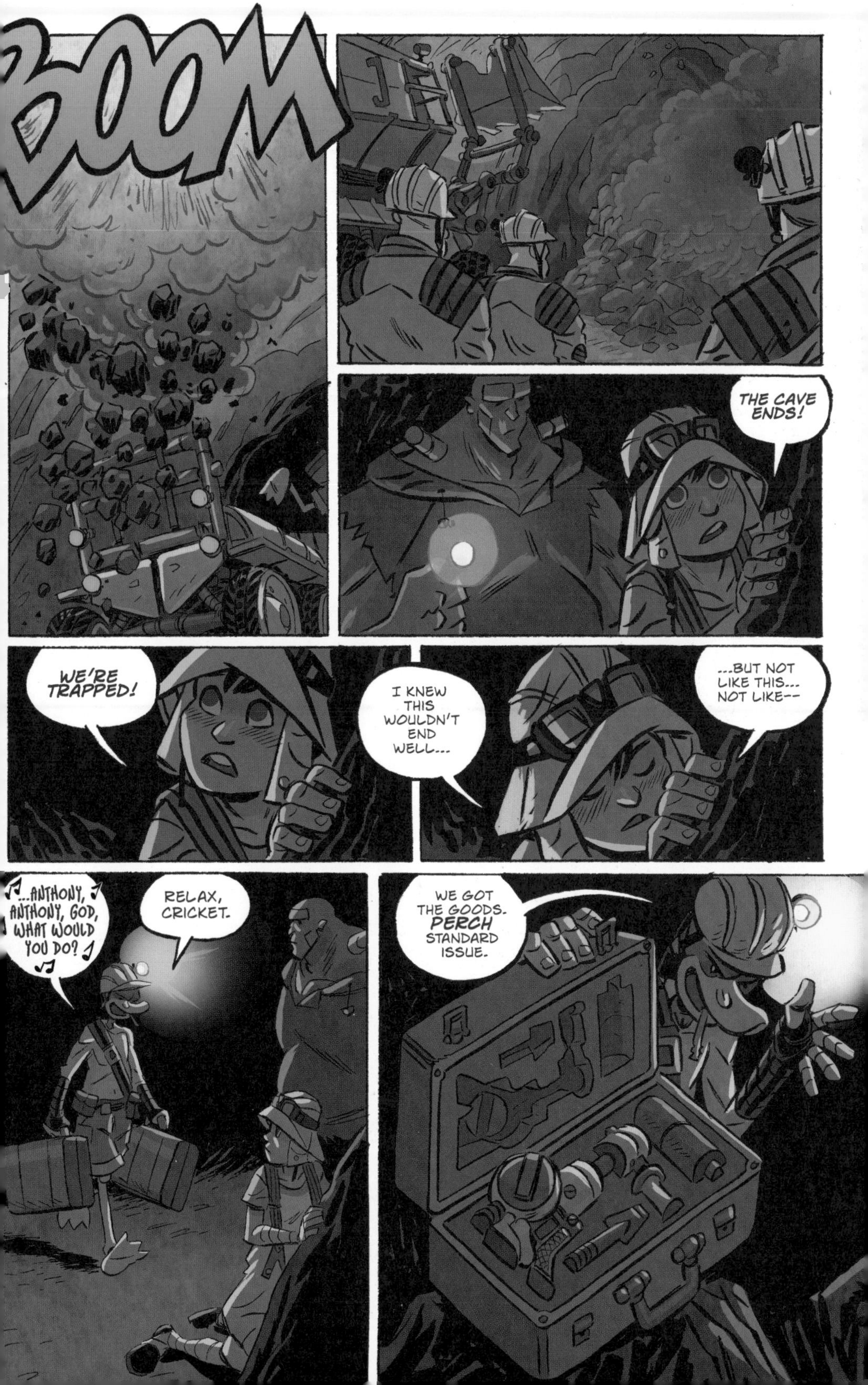
BOOM
THE CAVE ENDS!
WE'RE TRAPPED!
I KNEW THIS WOULDN'T END WELL...
...BUT NOT LIKE THIS... NOT LIKE--
♪...ANTHONY, ANTHONY, GOD, WHAT WOULD YOU DO? ♪
RELAX, CRICKET.
WE GOT THE GOODS. PERCH STANDARD ISSUE.

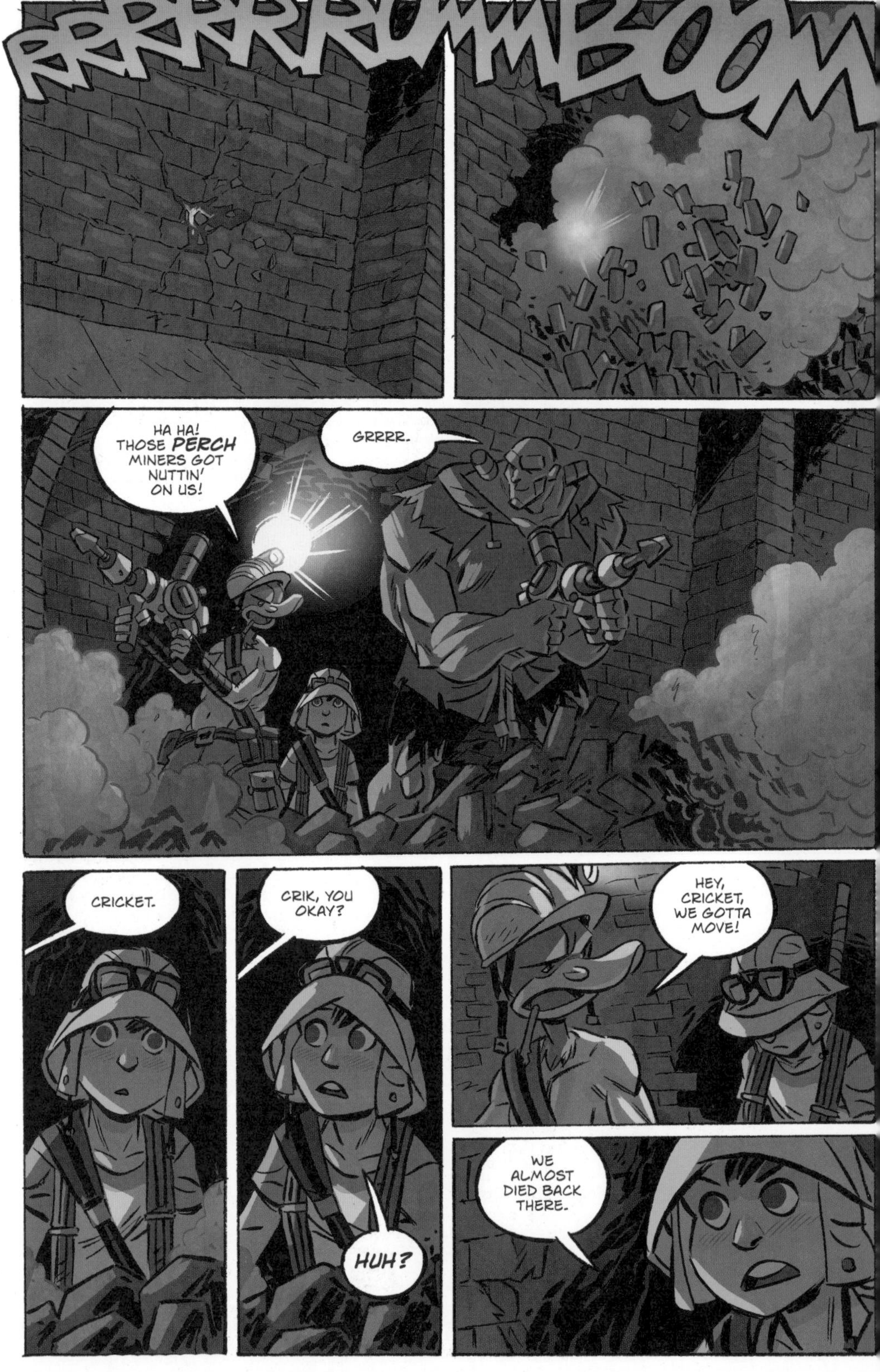
RRRRRRUMMBOOM
HA HA! THOSE PERCH MINERS GOT NUTTIN' ON US!
GRRRR.
CRICKET.
CRIK, YOU OKAY?
HUH?
HEY, CRICKET, WE GOTTA MOVE!
WE ALMOST DIED BACK THERE.

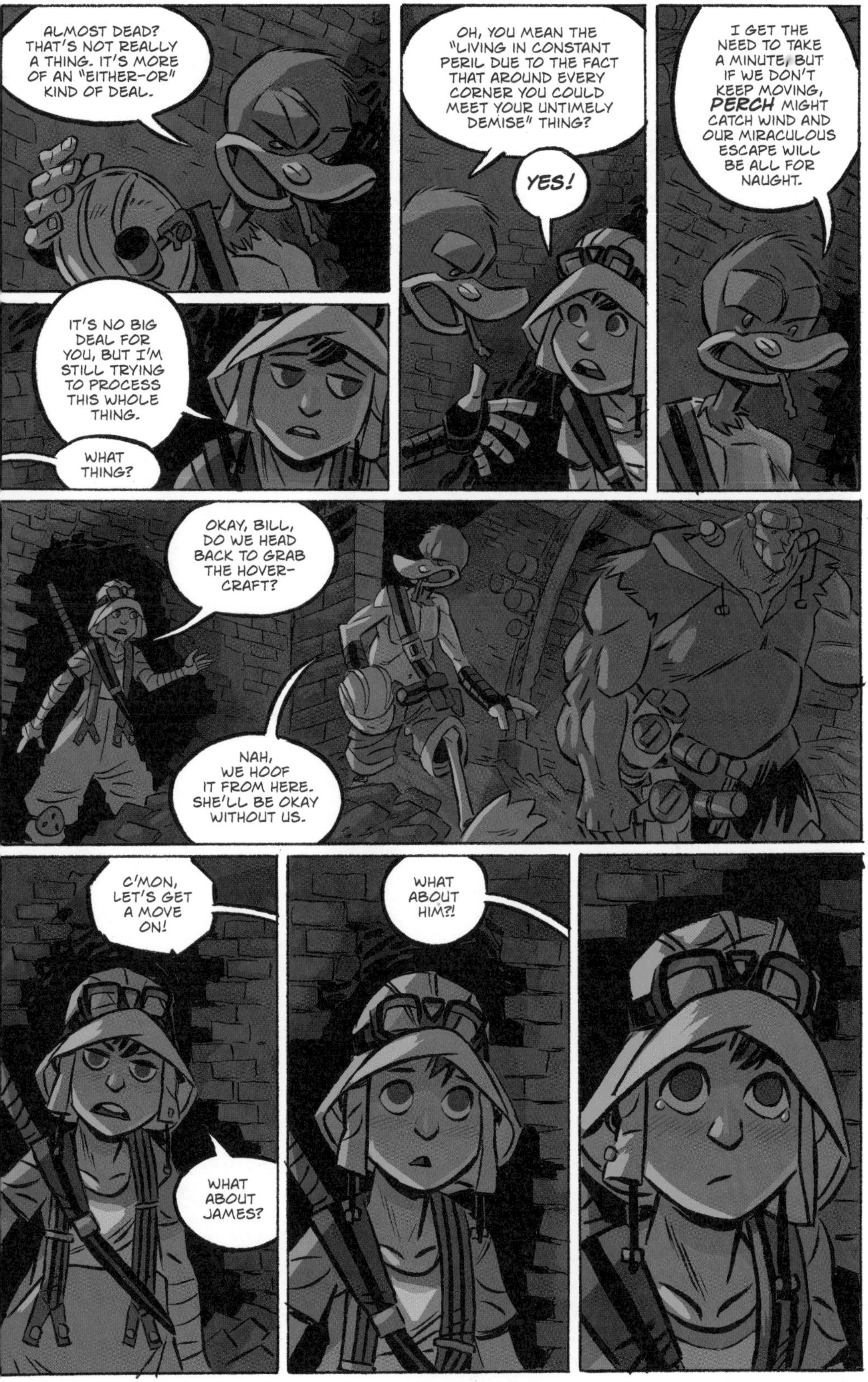
ALMOST DEAD? THAT'S NOT REALLY A THING. IT'S MORE OF AN "EITHER-OR" KIND OF DEAL.
IT'S NO BIG DEAL FOR YOU, BUT I'M STILL TRYING TO PROCESS THIS WHOLE THING.
WHAT THING?
OH, YOU MEAN THE "LIVING IN CONSTANT PERIL DUE TO THE FACT THAT AROUND EVERY CORNER YOU COULD MEET YOUR UNTIMELY DEMISE" THING?
YES!
I GET THE NEED TO TAKE A MINUTE, BUT IF WE DON'T KEEP MOVING, PERCH MIGHT CATCH WIND AND OUR MIRACULOUS ESCAPE WILL BE ALL FOR NAUGHT.
OKAY, BILL, DO WE HEAD BACK TO GRAB THE HOVER-CRAFT?
NAH, WE HOOF IT FROM HERE. SHE'LL BE OKAY WITHOUT US.
C'MON, LET'S GET A MOVE ON!
WHAT ABOUT JAMES?
WHAT ABOUT HIM?!

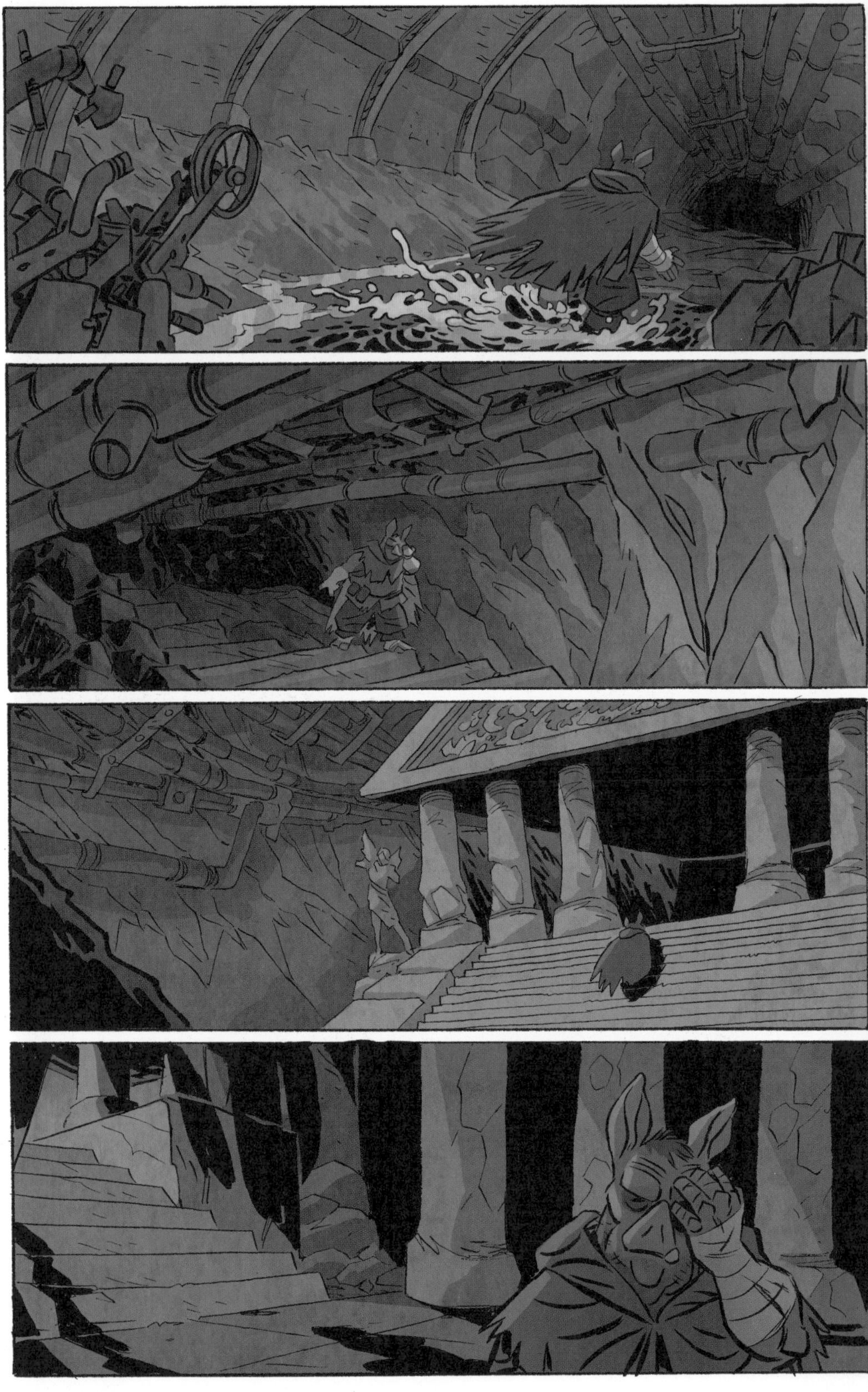

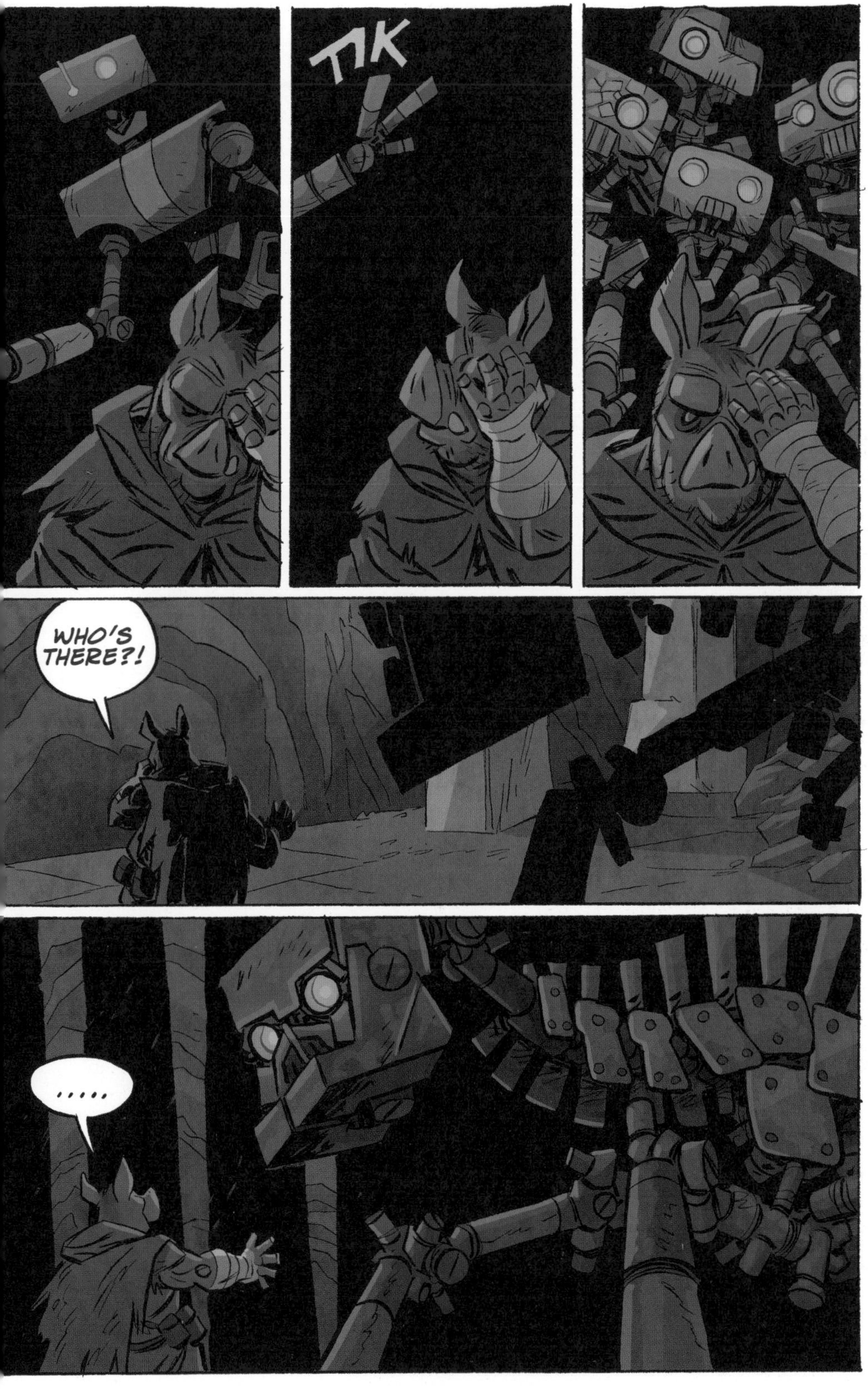
TIK
WHO'S THERE?!
.....

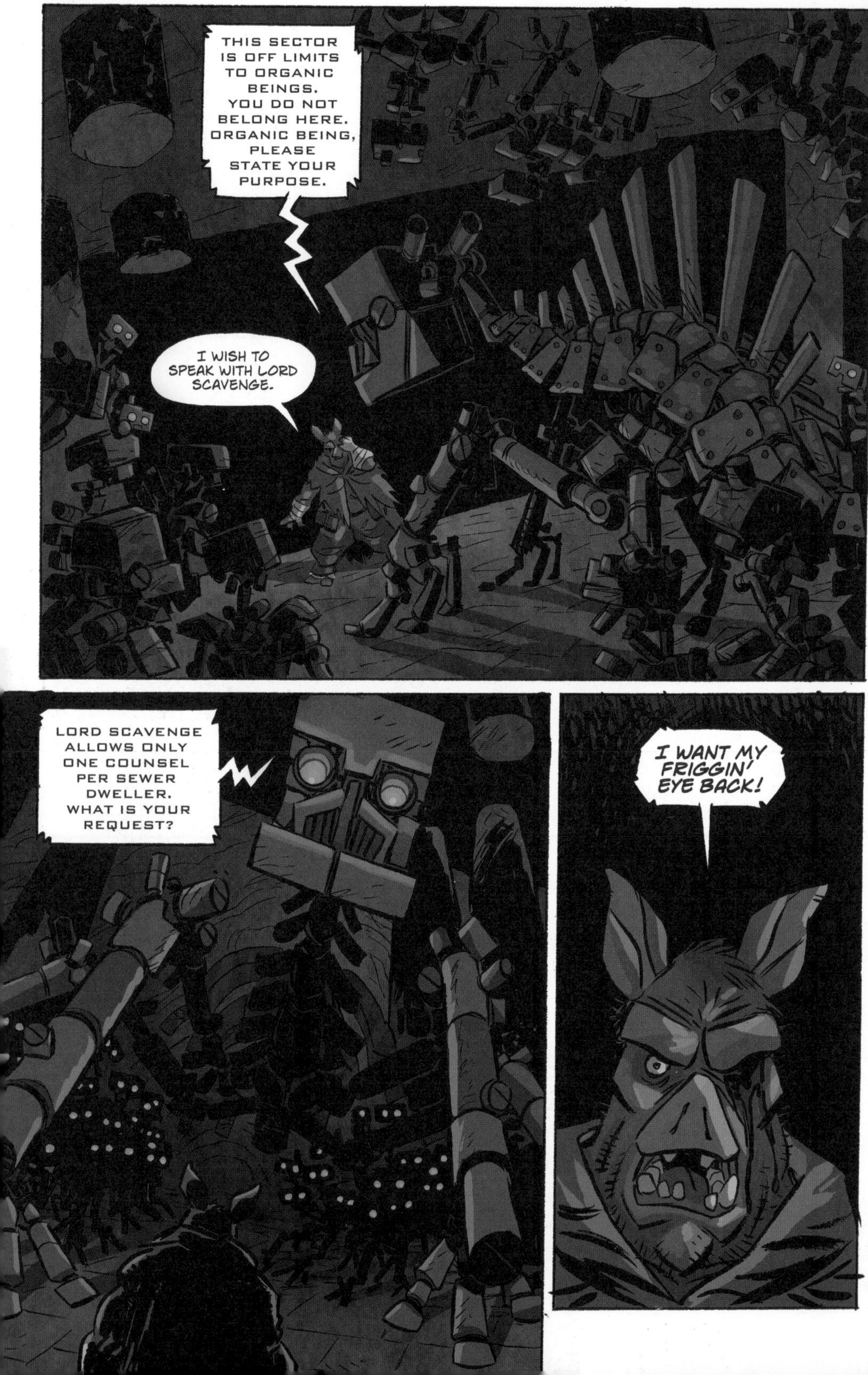
THIS SECTOR IS OFF LIMITS TO ORGANIC BEINGS. YOU DO NOT BELONG HERE. ORGANIC BEING, PLEASE STATE YOUR PURPOSE.
I WISH TO SPEAK WITH LORD SCAVENGE.
LORD SCAVENGE ALLOWS ONLY ONE COUNSEL PER SEWER DWELLER. WHAT IS YOUR REQUEST?
I WANT MY FRIGGIN' EYE BACK!

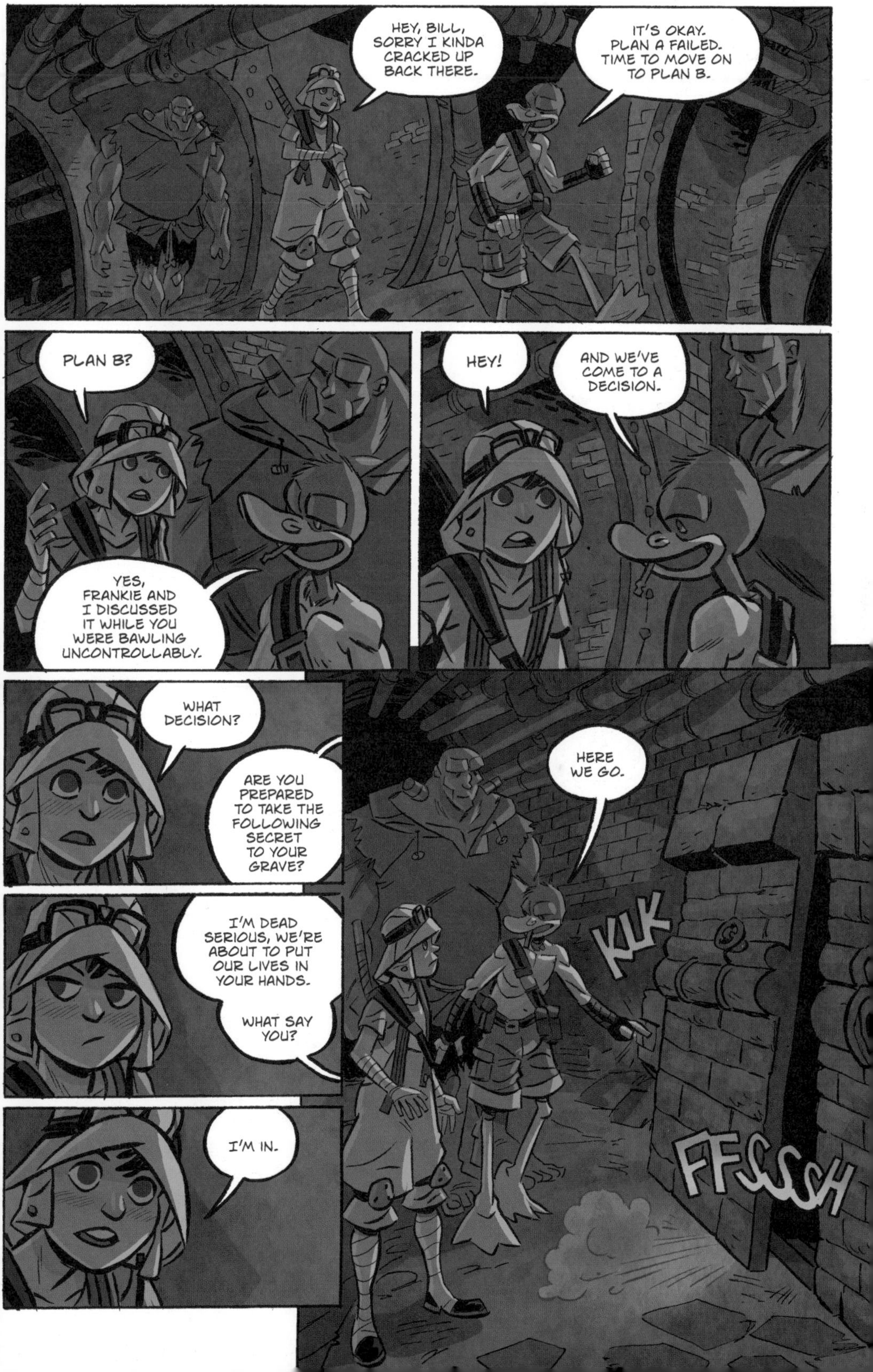
HEY, BILL, SORRY I KINDA CRACKED UP BACK THERE.
IT'S OKAY. PLAN A FAILED. TIME TO MOVE ON TO PLAN B.
PLAN B?
YES, FRANKIE AND I DISCUSSED IT WHILE YOU WERE BAWLING UNCONTROLLABLY.
HEY!
AND WE'VE COME TO A DECISION.
WHAT DECISION?
ARE YOU PREPARED TO TAKE THE FOLLOWING SECRET TO YOUR GRAVE?
I'M DEAD SERIOUS, WE'RE ABOUT TO PUT OUR LIVES IN YOUR HANDS.
WHAT SAY YOU?
I'M IN.
HERE WE GO.
KLIK
FFSSSCH

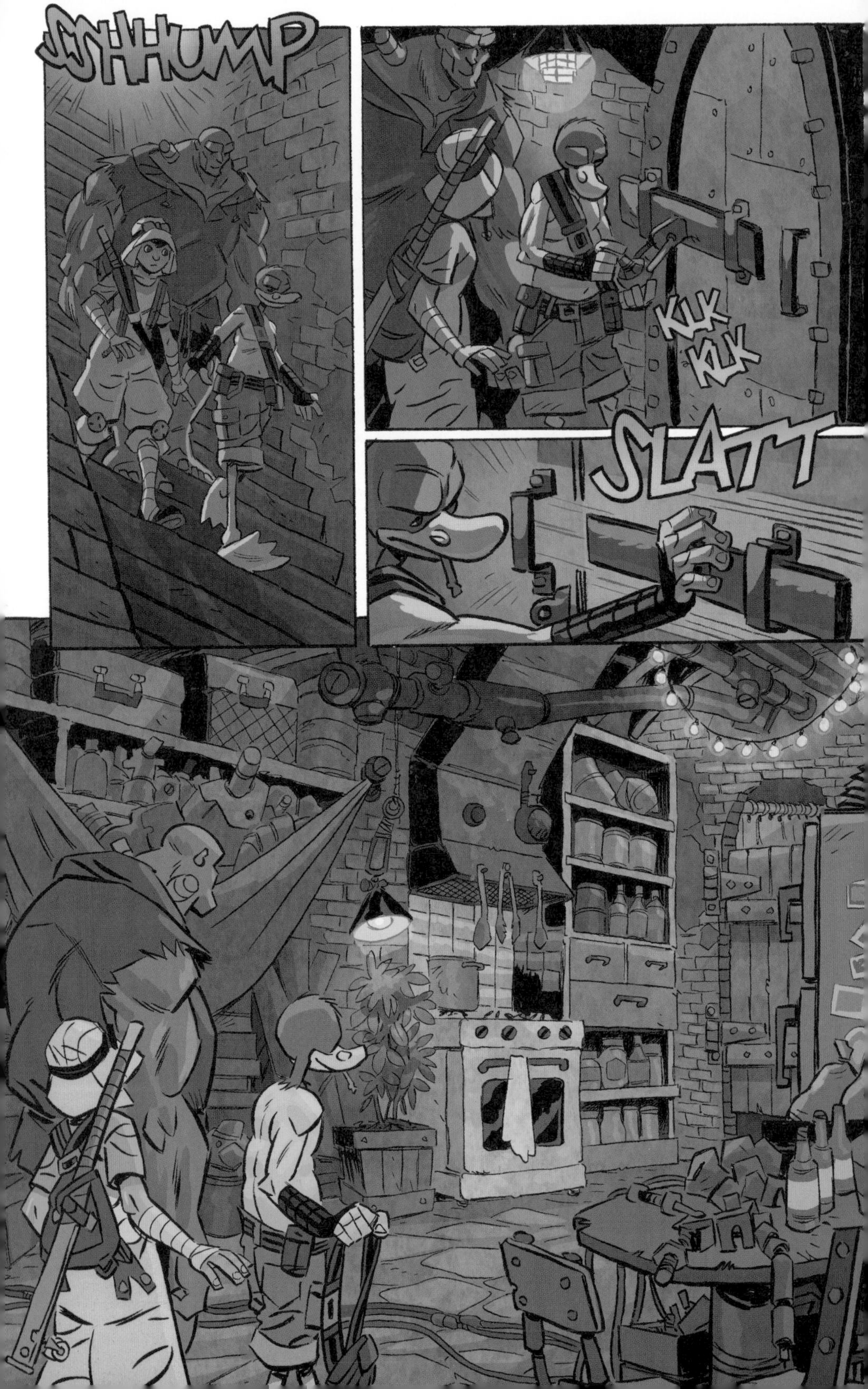
SSHHUMP
KLUK
KLUK
SLATT

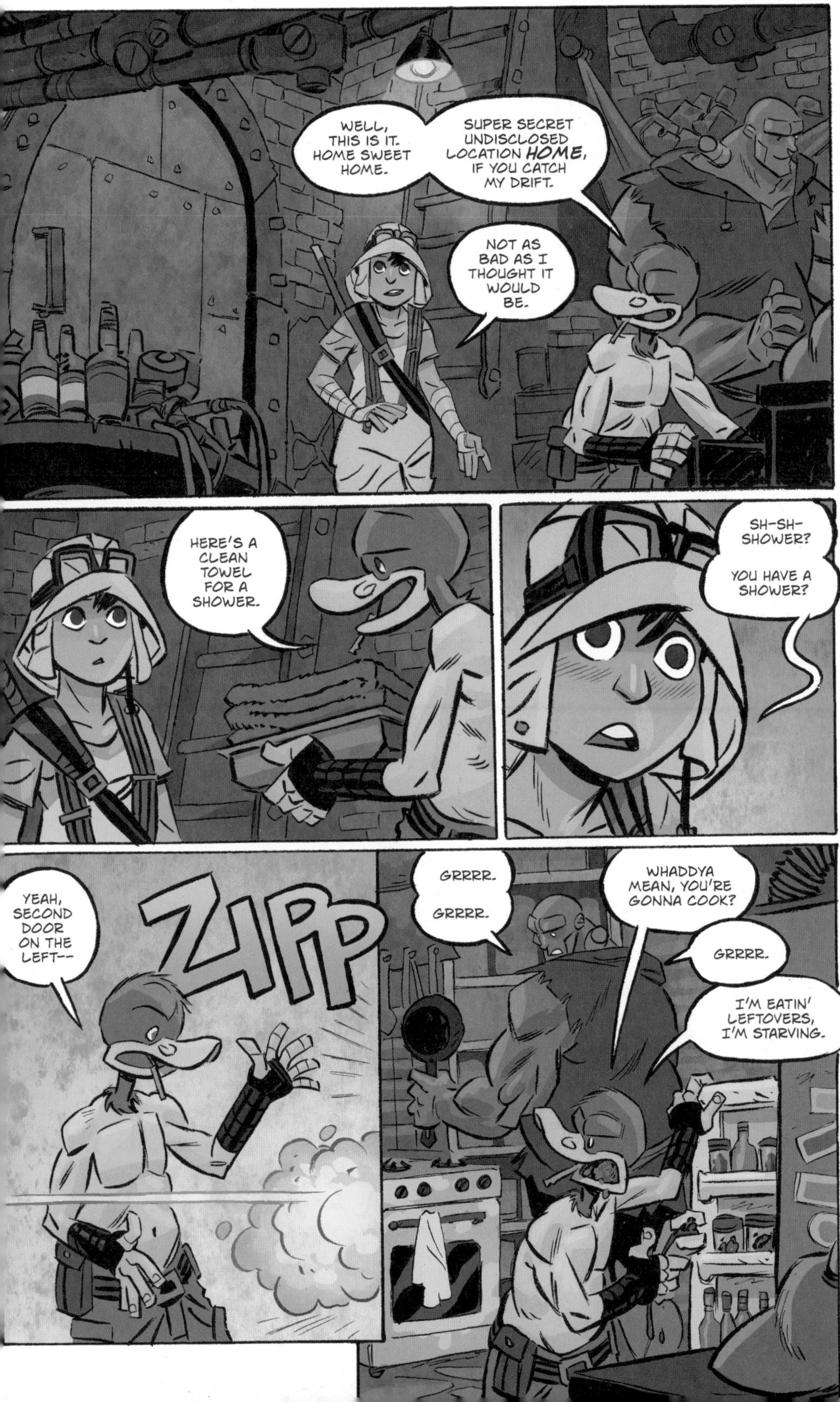
WELL, THIS IS IT. HOME SWEET HOME.
SUPER SECRET UNDISCLOSED LOCATION HOME, IF YOU CATCH MY DRIFT.
NOT AS BAD AS I THOUGHT IT WOULD BE.
HERE'S A CLEAN TOWEL FOR A SHOWER.
SH-SH-SHOWER?
YOU HAVE A SHOWER?
YEAH, SECOND DOOR ON THE LEFT--
ZIPP
GRRRR.
GRRRR.
WHADDYA MEAN, YOU'RE GONNA COOK?
GRRRR.
I'M EATIN' LEFTOVERS, I'M STARVING.

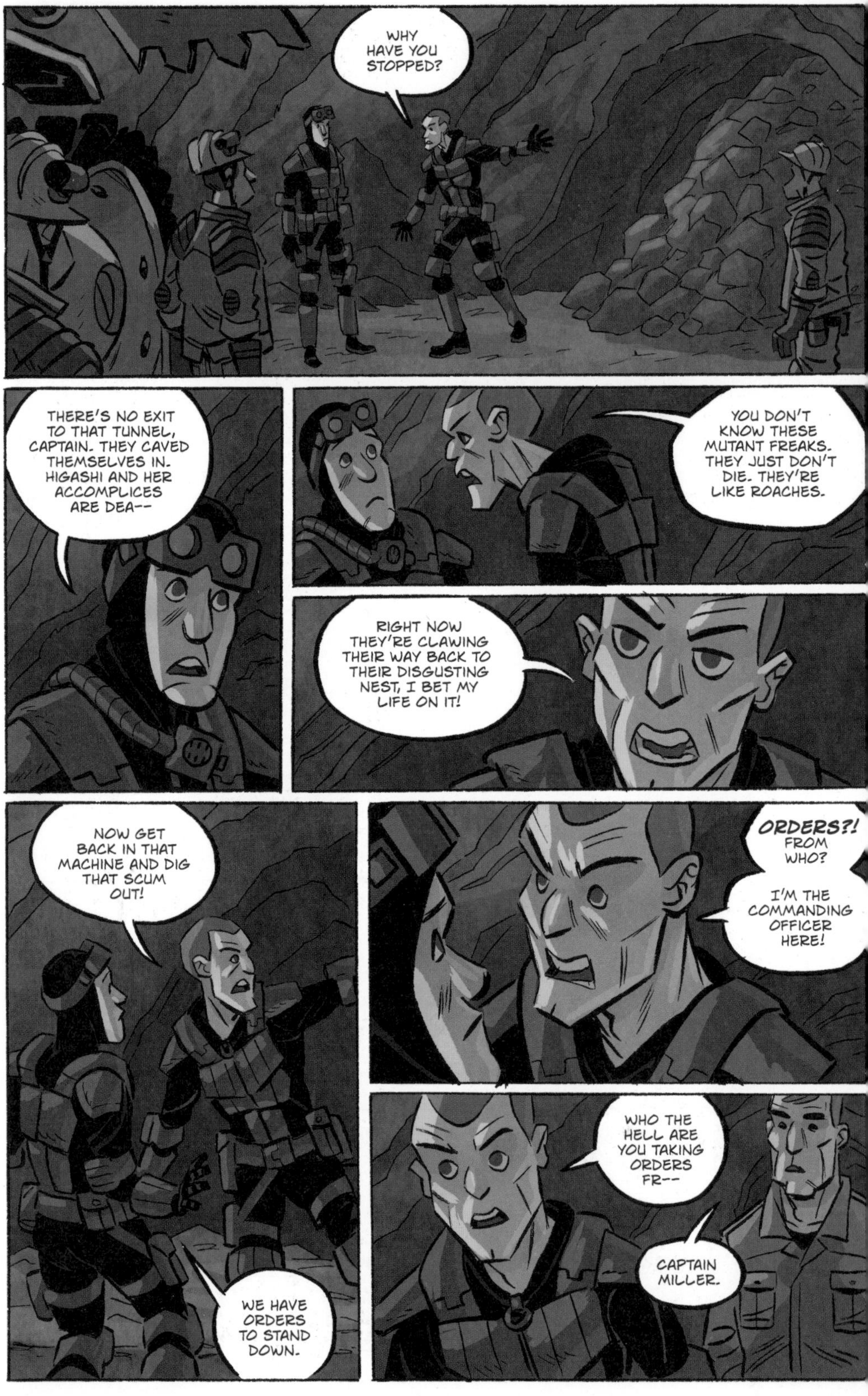

WHY HAVE YOU STOPPED?
THERE'S NO EXIT TO THAT TUNNEL, CAPTAIN. THEY CAVED THEMSELVES IN. HIGASHI AND HER ACCOMPLICES ARE DEA--
YOU DON'T KNOW THESE MUTANT FREAKS. THEY JUST DON'T DIE. THEY'RE LIKE ROACHES.
RIGHT NOW THEY'RE CLAWING THEIR WAY BACK TO THEIR DISGUSTING NEST, I BET MY LIFE ON IT!
NOW GET BACK IN THAT MACHINE AND DIG THAT SCUM OUT!
WE HAVE ORDERS TO STAND DOWN.
ORDERS?! FROM WHO?
I'M THE COMMANDING OFFICER HERE!
WHO THE HELL ARE YOU TAKING ORDERS FR--
CAPTAIN MILLER.

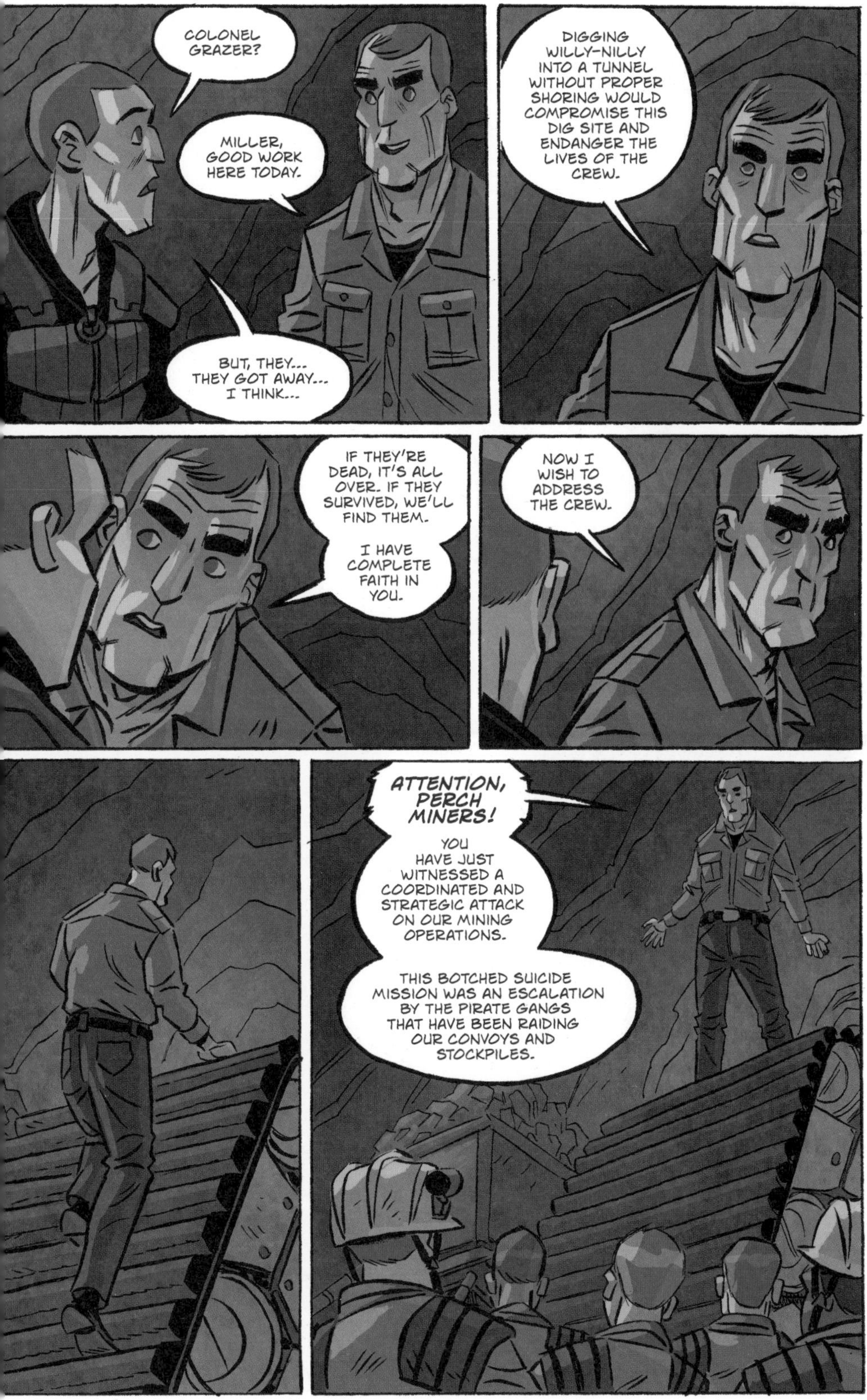
COLONEL GRAZER?
MILLER, GOOD WORK HERE TODAY.
BUT, THEY... THEY GOT AWAY... I THINK...
DIGGING WILLY-NILLY INTO A TUNNEL WITHOUT PROPER SHORING WOULD COMPROMISE THIS DIG SITE AND ENDANGER THE LIVES OF THE CREW.
IF THEY'RE DEAD, IT'S ALL OVER. IF THEY SURVIVED, WE'LL FIND THEM.
I HAVE COMPLETE FAITH IN YOU.
NOW I WISH TO ADDRESS THE CREW.
ATTENTION, PERCH MINERS!
YOU HAVE JUST WITNESSED A COORDINATED AND STRATEGIC ATTACK ON OUR MINING OPERATIONS.
THIS BOTCHED SUICIDE MISSION WAS AN ESCALATION BY THE PIRATE GANGS THAT HAVE BEEN RAIDING OUR CONVOYS AND STOCKPILES.

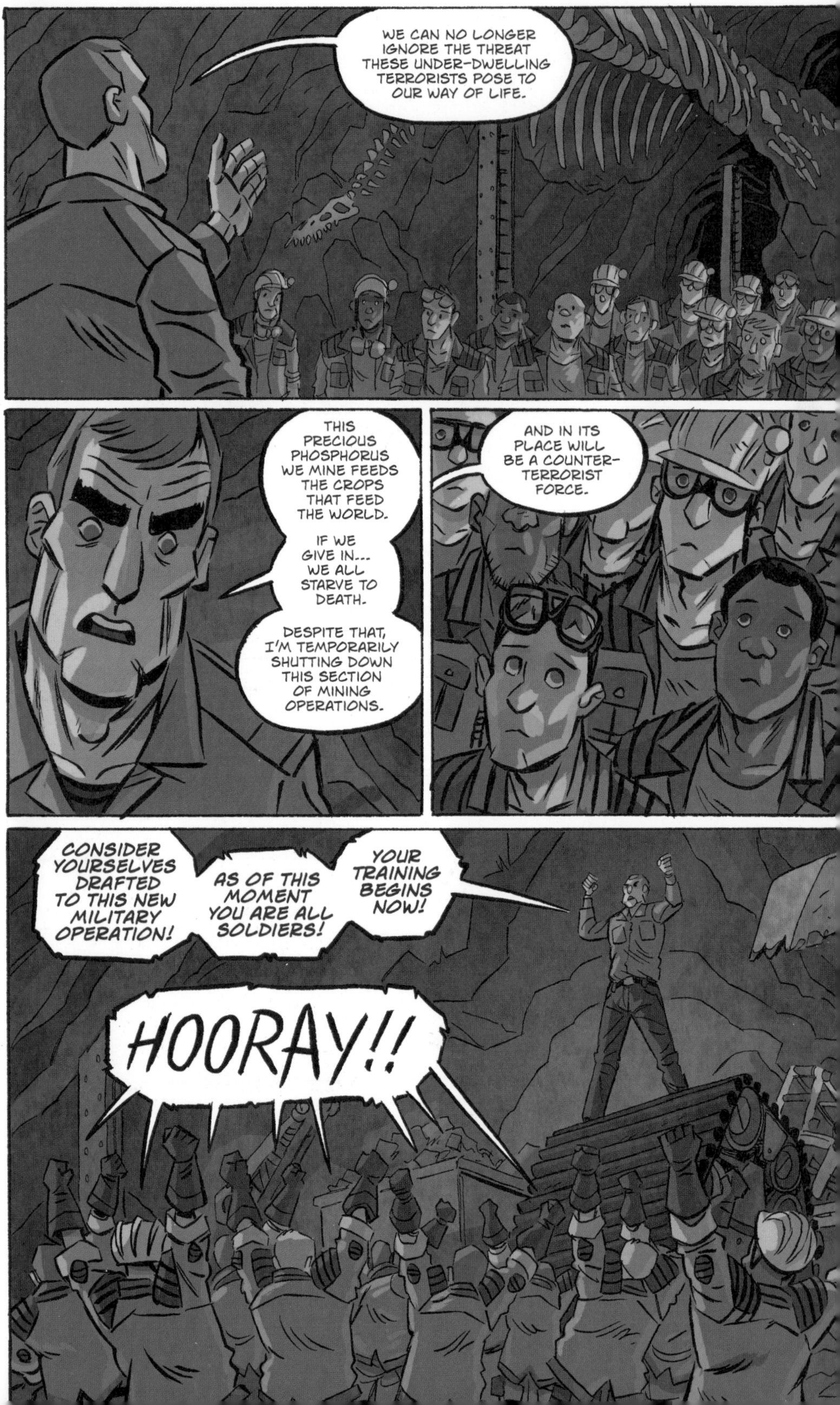

WE CAN NO LONGER IGNORE THE THREAT THESE UNDER-DWELLING TERRORISTS POSE TO OUR WAY OF LIFE.
THIS PRECIOUS PHOSPHORUS WE MINE FEEDS THE CROPS THAT FEED THE WORLD.
IF WE GIVE IN... WE ALL STARVE TO DEATH.
DESPITE THAT, I'M TEMPORARILY SHUTTING DOWN THIS SECTION OF MINING OPERATIONS.
AND IN ITS PLACE WILL BE A COUNTER-TERRORIST FORCE.
CONSIDER YOURSELVES DRAFTED TO THIS NEW MILITARY OPERATION!
AS OF THIS MOMENT YOU ARE ALL SOLDIERS!
YOUR TRAINING BEGINS NOW!
HOORAY!!

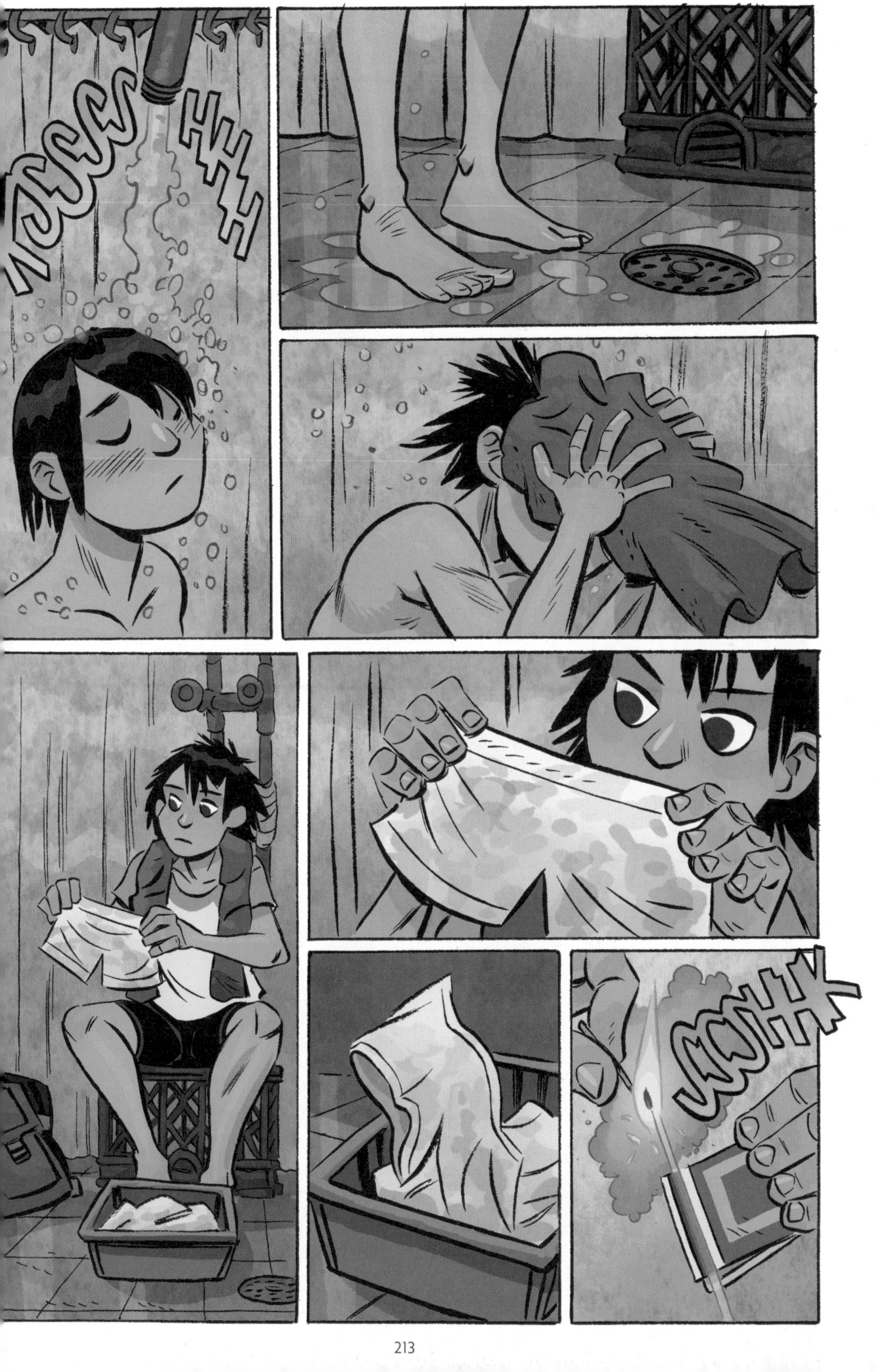

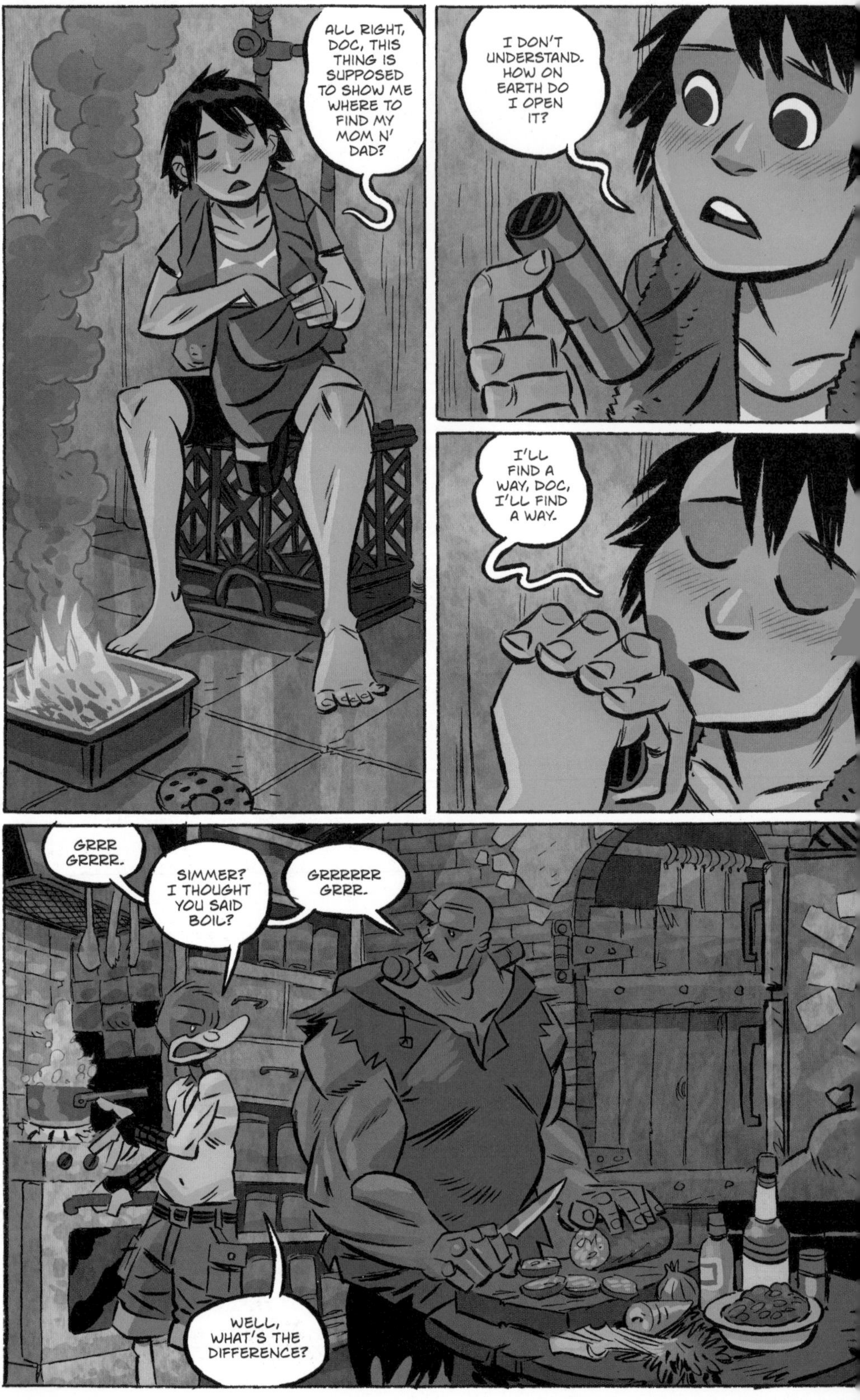
ALL RIGHT, DOC, THIS THING IS SUPPOSED TO SHOW ME WHERE TO FIND MY MOM N' DAD?
I DON'T UNDERSTAND. HOW ON EARTH DO I OPEN IT?
I'LL FIND A WAY, DOC, I'LL FIND A WAY.
GRRR GRRRR.
SIMMER? I THOUGHT YOU SAID BOIL?
GRRRRRR GRRR.
WELL, WHAT'S THE DIFFERENCE?

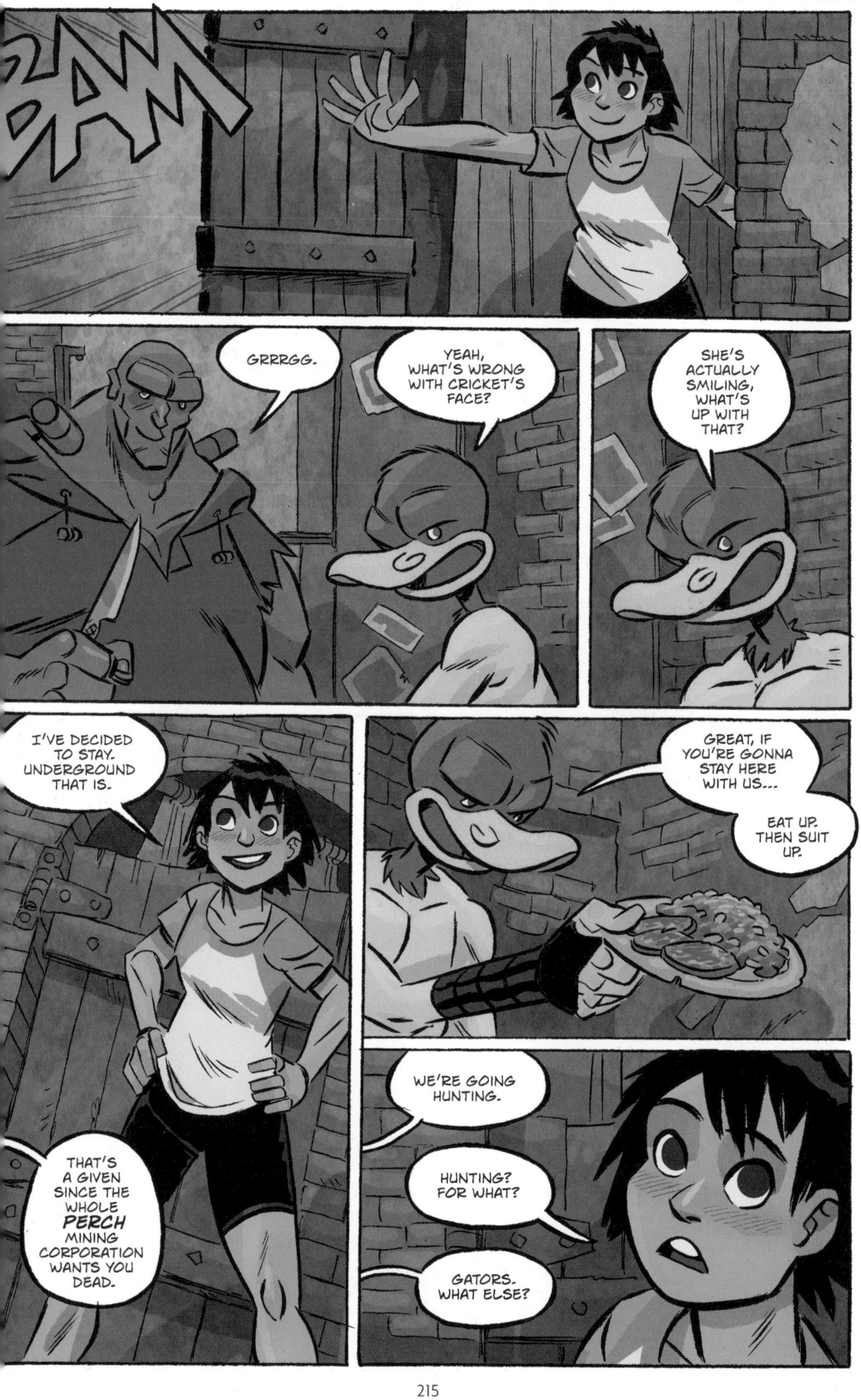
BAM
GRRRGG.
YEAH, WHAT'S WRONG WITH CRICKET'S FACE?
SHE'S ACTUALLY SMILING, WHAT'S UP WITH THAT?
I'VE DECIDED TO STAY. UNDERGROUND THAT IS.
THAT'S A GIVEN SINCE THE WHOLE PERCH MINING CORPORATION WANTS YOU DEAD.
GREAT, IF YOU'RE GONNA STAY HERE WITH US...
EAT UP. THEN SUIT UP.
WE'RE GOING HUNTING.
HUNTING? FOR WHAT?
GATORS. WHAT ELSE?

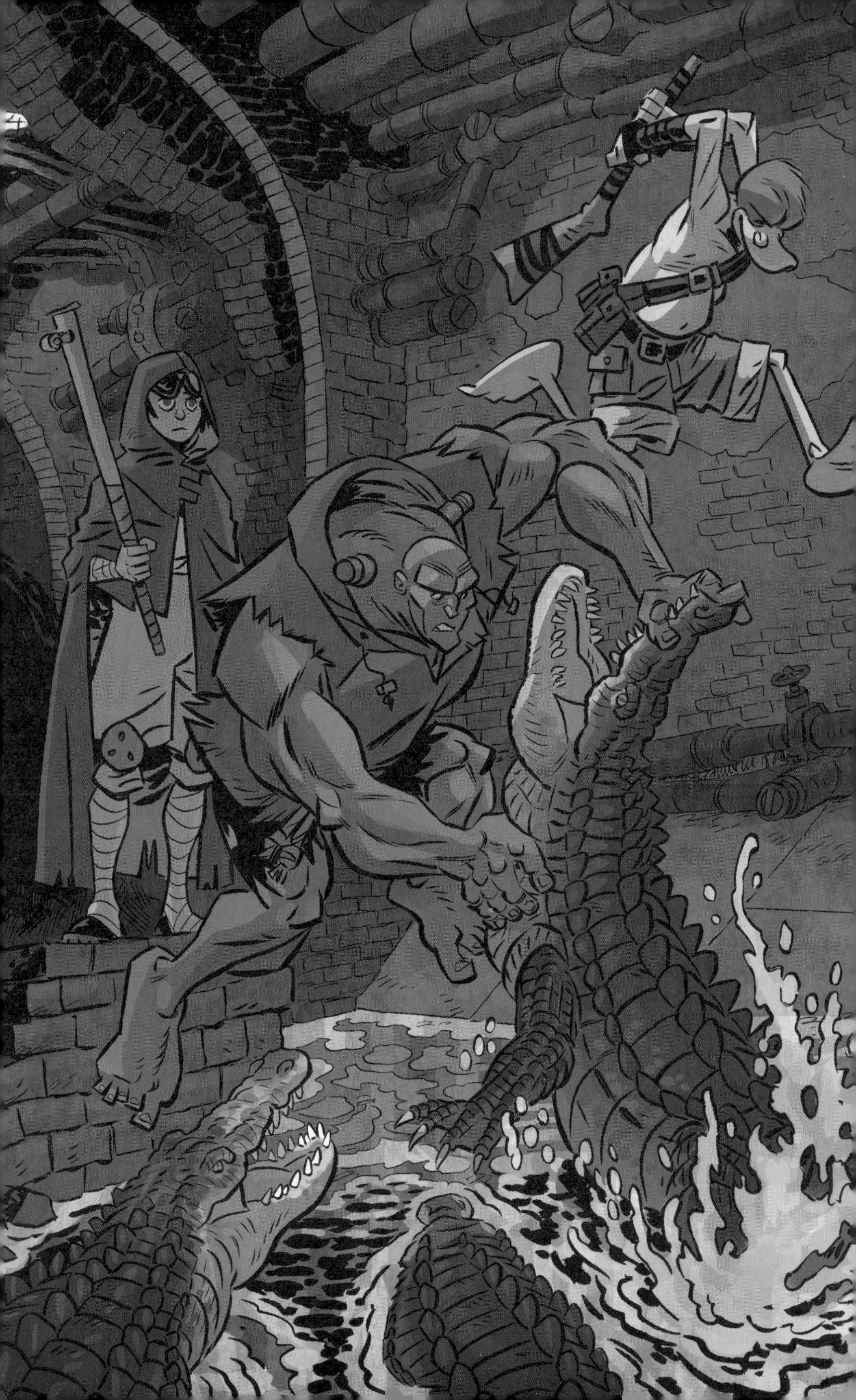

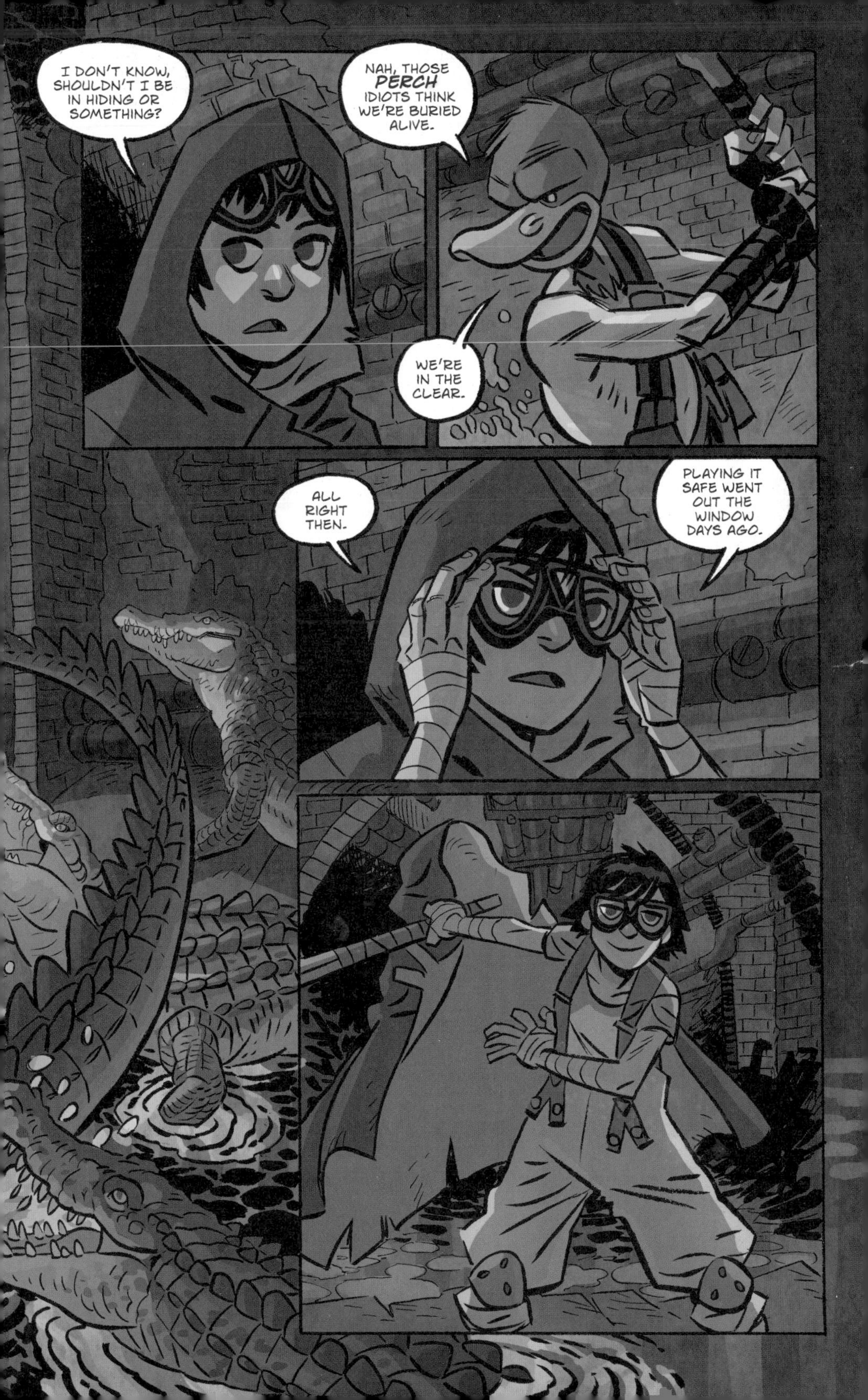
I DON'T KNOW, SHOULDN'T I BE IN HIDING OR SOMETHING?
NAH, THOSE PERCH IDIOTS THINK WE'RE BURIED ALIVE.
WE'RE IN THE CLEAR.
ALL RIGHT THEN.
PLAYING IT SAFE WENT OUT THE WINDOW DAYS AGO.

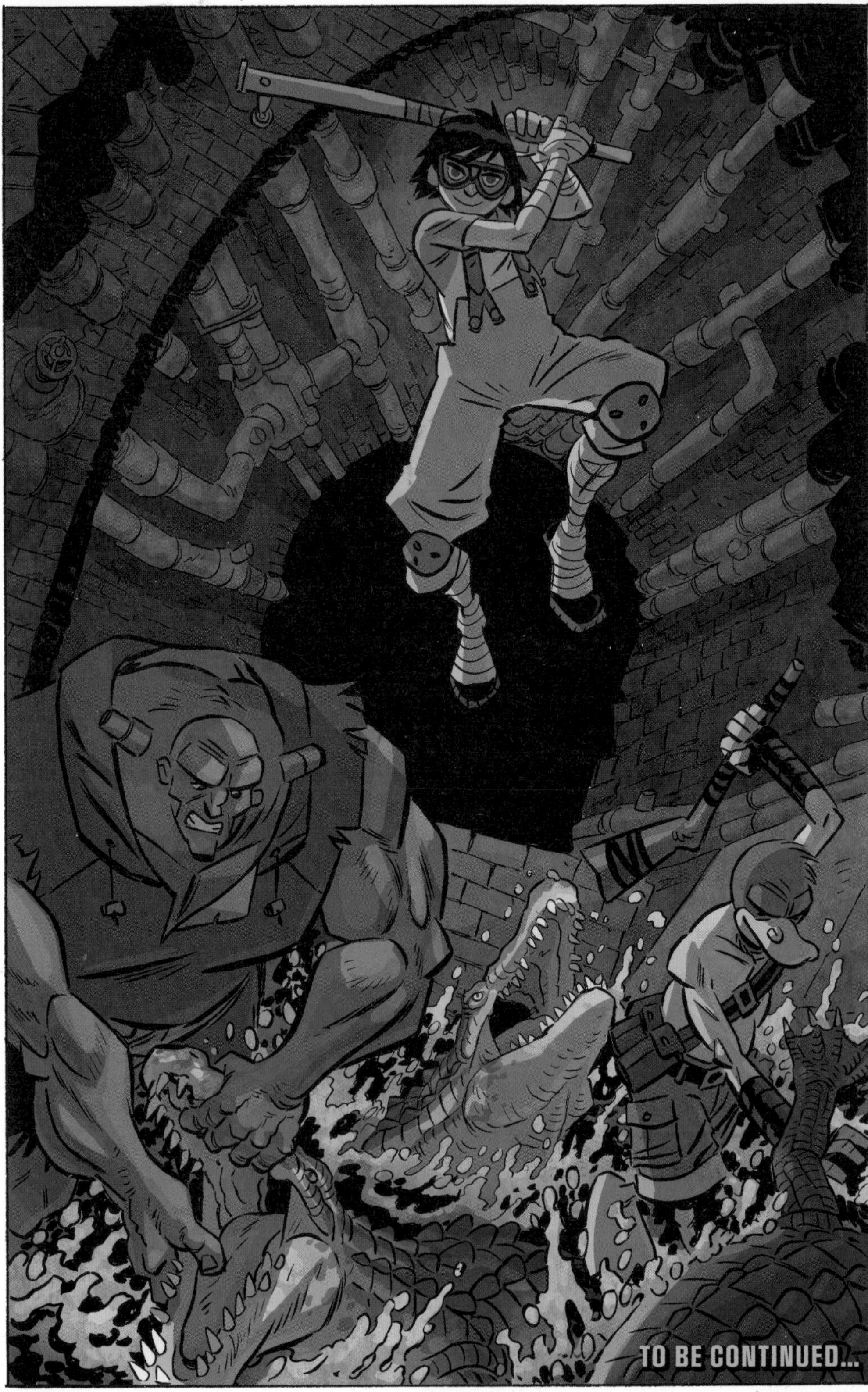
TO BE CONTINUED...